D1520824

The Man from Pontiac and the Martian Cover-Up

FREDERICK JENNY

PAGE PUBLISHING, INC.
Conneaut Lake, PA

First originally published by Page Publishing 2021

ISBN 978-1-6624-1197-7 (pbk)
ISBN 978-1-6624-5361-8 (hc)
ISBN 978-1-6624-1198-4 (digital)

Printed in the United States of America

Acknowledgment

To my family and friends, thank you for encouraging me to always follow my dreams. The publication of this book is all thanks to your love and support. To Katherine Adams and her assistance of bringing my characters to life through her encouragement and knowledge. In loving memory of Marilyn Brockopp.

ONE

Test Subject 191

Five years before document release

The center of the room was filled with bright piercing lights, leaving the perimeter dark and cold. In the middle of the lit area was an oversize metal operating table. Gray quartz flooring stretched to white soundproof walls. Three micro high-definition cameras were pointed at the operating table to document what was to transpire. A woman with shoulder-length brunette hair tied in a bun stood next to a small rolling table. A plethora of operating tools was arranged neatly on the tabletop.

The woman wore an off-white hazmat suit that covered her sun-kissed South American skin. A helmet with an independent oxygen source covered her head. The helmet was clear enough to allow a person to see into it.

Standing next to her was a man who wore the same suit with the exception of the headgear. The man took heavy pulls from a cigar he held in his right hand. He blew the smoke at where he thought one of the cameras was.

"Those are going to kill you one day," the woman snapped with a Spanish accent.

"They help me relax. Get off my ass." He spoke with a thick Austrian accent. "Prissy bitch," he muttered under his breath.

"Excuse me?"

"Nothing. Is the chairman here yet?" He moved his hand around his black-and-peppered-gray goatee.

A third voice boomed through the room. "Put out the cigar, you moron, before I shove it down your throat!"

The voice was raucous and penetrating. It sent chills down the spines of the two. Shaken, they looked up at a set of windows placed fourteen feet up and against a far, darkened wall in the room. Behind the glass was a dark observation room that usually was lit up. The only object the two could make out was the silhouette of a man with no discernible features.

"Uh, yes, sir. Sorry, Mr. Chairman," the man stuttered before dropping the cigar on the floor and extinguishing it with his work boot.

"You're both aware this is a very important moment for this company. Don't muck it up. This is the first test subject to make it here, I don't want it to spoil before its secrets are revealed," the dark figure said through a microphone. The chairman's teeth glistened off the floodlights surrounding the table as he spoke.

"Sir, I worked very hard to get Test Subject 191 here. As you know, this is the first time we have attempted cryogenics. So far, it has saved the subject. We won't lose this one like the last ones," the woman replied.

"Your overconfidence will be your downfall. Nevertheless, I would expect nothing less from employees than full commitment." Silence filled the room for a brief moment before a digital communications link located on the medical instruments table came to life.

"Test Subject 191 defrosting complete. Subject should remain immobile for testing. We'll bring it to Laboratory Four."

"Copy that, proceed as planned. Out," the man spoke into the radio. He quickly placed the helmet to his hazmat suit over his head. "Safety first." He smirked at the woman, who rolled her eyes.

"You're a child." The woman turned her head away from the man. She glanced at her helmet's heads-up display. There were many little blocks that had symbols on them. The one she was looking at had a mouth with sound waves emitting from it. The square compressed showing the helmet's retinal scanner had sensed her gaze. This activated the transmitter in her helmet. "Send in the surgical team. Test Subject 191 is en route to Laboratory Four."

Once again, silence hung in the room. A few minutes later, there was an abrupt, loud bang as the swinging double doors were shoved open, causing the man and woman to jump. An oversize floating gurney was rushed in with a white sheet over a sprawling figure.

A breathing tube was visible under the sheet near the front of the creature. Its entire body seemed to rise and fall; its respiration was rapid and shallow. Following the gurney was a contingent of men and women in hazmat suits.

"Get the subject on the table, stat. We need it alive to do the analysis. If it dies, we lose any chance of learning its secrets," the woman barked angrily at the medics. She stole a few nervous glances up at the chairman, who stood like a statue in a graveyard.

"I don't want a pile of dust to clean up like the last, 190," the man grumbled. A couple of medics lifted Test Subject 191 onto the metal table. They secured its body with three thick metal latches.

"Activate the cameras," the man said to a surgeon standing next to him.

"Cameras? I don't see any," the surgeon said.

"They're AIBM Miros. You can't see them with your naked eye, idiot. I'll do it myself!" The man looked at a block in his heads-up display that had a camera on it. When it turned blue instead of the usual red, he nodded at the woman. She returned the nod and looked up at the chairman for validation.

"Proceed," the chairman grunted gutturally as he adjusted his footing.

Everyone looked back at Test Subject 191. The woman looked anxiously at the man. She exhaled, watching as a surgeon grabbed a scalpel. "You aren't getting soft, are you?" the original man asked, seeing his partner's anxious look. He looked over the tools and grabbed a handheld pen.

"I'm not getting soft." She shot back before she saw what he was grabbing. "You're sick. That tool's meant to be a last resort."

"It was your idea to operate on the test subject while it was still alive. Plus, you asked me to help."

"Don't patronize me. There's nothing left after they die. I need this information. We can't disappoint the chairman."

"You try too hard. You know that man doesn't give a rat's ass about any of us. All he cares about is his company."

"Check yourself, idiot. He could be listening to our conversation." Above, the chairman stood in the window staring at the scene below. A surgeon grabbed the veil that had covered the test subject and threw it to the floor.

"Oh my god, w-what is that thing?" a new nurse asked, seeing the test subject for the first time.

"Ugly fucker, isn't it?" the man asked the nurse, who looked pale.

"Enough chitchat! Administer the nanobots," the woman ordered. The new nurse composed herself and grabbed a vial with light green liquid. Her hand was shaking as she stuck it into the flesh of the creature.

There was no reaction from the red-tinted monster as the self-plunging needle drained into its body. "This is the moment of truth," the woman said. Thirty seconds later, the green liquid oozed out of the creature's body and onto the floor. "Mierda! I thought the advanced bots had a chance against its immune system."

"Time for plan B," the man said as he pressed a button on his pen and a short dark blue laser extended from the tip.

"Fine, do what you want, just get results."

"You heard the lady, let's get it done!"

The mass of medical staff moved in on the behemoth. As the surgeons began to cut into the creature, it remained silent. The silence was soon punctuated by drilling sounds like dental tools as the man put down his laser scalpel and picked up a circular saw. Occasionally, the double doors swung open and shut to allow additional personnel to enter the lab throughout the procedure.

These additional personnel were expert surgeons who assisted in specific operations on Test Subject 191. There was a lot of activity around the test subject, teams were cutting into parts of the body. A group even removed one of its black eyes.

Scribes ran around the table, documenting every moment. Each scribe had a pair of glasses with a tiny camera on the side that recorded what they were seeing. A microphone implant in their tooth recorded what the scribe was saying, transmitting it to the company cloud for analysis.

There was one scribe per surgeon and about seven total surgeons cutting into Test Subject 191. They searched every inch of the test subject to collect information.

The woman walked around the seven teams with her own scribe. She would point at things, and the scribe that followed her would blink, recording a still photograph with his glasses. All this information would be available for her report. In the observation room, the chairman watched, patiently waiting as fleshy spatter hit the floor.

"It appears that the test subject is all flesh, as if it is made up of just one cell type," the woman said as she inspected the flesh on the ground. It moved as if it was trying to get back to the creature.

Soon the creature's body began to gelatinize, indicating the subject was beginning to thaw. "Get the electric test going! Everyone clear!" the woman barked in her Spanish accent. A team with a power cell arrived and hooked it up to Test Subject 191. Once ready, the woman gave the order, and the creature was shocked repeatedly.

Now thawed, the creature let out a bloodcurdling scream every time it was shocked.

The chairman grinned while Test Subject 191 was electrically shocked. The power increased until the creature stopped screaming and went limp. Another lighter shock was given, waking the test subject up.

The creature cried out in agony as it tried to move its body. The electrified restraints held the creature in place as it tried to escape, but it was too weak to corral its cells to morph around the restraints. The chairman waited calmly, never breaking his stare at the table until Test Subject 191 stopped making noise.

"It's happening," the woman muttered to herself. Instantly, the test subject stiffened before its body began to turn to a red powder. It coated everything, the floor, surgical table, and the surrounding personnel.

"Damn it, we need to find a way to know when they're going to pop," the woman grumbled.

There was a slight pause after the creature turned into dust. "Subject deceased at 2151, March 20, 2085," a male surgeon said, checking a digital clock in his helmet's heads-up display.

As quickly as they arrived, the surgeons filed out of the room, leaving just the two original occupants. "Well? Did we find what we were looking for?" the chairman's voice boomed after a moment of silence, his voice reverberating through the lab.

"The test was inconclusive, sir, but we believe we understand why they were able to hide from humanity for so long. I cannot know how much we learned until I've had time to look over the surgeon's reports," the woman said, brushing dust off her hazmat suit.

"Very good! I look forward to your future work. I foresee great things happening for you two," the man said before he turned to leave the observation room.

"I expect a full report on my desk first thing in the morning. That report will directly affect my decision to whether this science experiment of yours will continue." He placed his microphone earpiece on a small wooden table in the room and walked out the door.

The woman felt both a sense of pride and fear. She feared her own shortcomings might be the cause of her program's failure. Her counterpart had already removed his helmet and was lighting up a new cigar.

He sat down in a chair located in a corner of the room and crossed his legs. "Really? Back to smoking?"

"Of course, we have to celebrate your future promotion. The chairman obviously likes you," he said, sucking in a big puff before blowing it above his head.

"I won't put the cart before the horse, you incautious brute. Who do you think you are taking off your helmet in this hazardous area? Are you trying to die a slow and painful death?"

"The danger was over when the creature bit the dust."

"Start compiling the reports. I'll be there after I get some samples of the remains."

"Fine, but you owe me. I didn't sign up for this shit when I landed on Mars," the man grumbled as he got up with his cigar still in his mouth.

Wordlessly, she followed him to the doors. Standing in the doorway to the lab, she watched him enter the decontamination room. Hastily, she returned to the operating table and grabbed a few small test tubes. Bending over, the woman collected deposits of the dust in the test tubes. She walked toward the decontamination room; her mind flooded with thoughts of the trail she was blazing.

This new frontier, which humanity was slowly discovering, was hers for the taking. She was a survivor. She had lived through the bombing of Libertador Building in 2063. She moved to the North American Union as a refugee and used her coding and hacking skills to break into NASA's secret flies. She then sold that information to AMSPACE. The information gave her an insight into what was truly hidden on Mars. In her mind, she was on the path to become the head of her company and would replace the man who stood above her and become chairwoman.

Her mind raced at what opportunities the specimen they just brutalized could bring to advance humanity. New medicines? Regrowing lost limbs? The possibilities were endless, and she was the one who could take advantage of it all. She held the key to unlocking all these opportunities. Her determination and global events had brought her to where she was today.

TWO

The North American Union

Fifty-nine years before document release

In January 2031, NASA Commander Ben Lewis stepped onto the surface of Mars. NASA's *Preparation* rover broadcasted the world-altering event live. Launched in 2026, *Preparation*'s endeavor was to seek out Martian areas suitable for the manned Martian landings. The crew's tour lasted for two weeks, which yielded more information than the past rover missions—*Spirit, Opportunity*, and *Curiosity*.

A NASA communications satellite network was set up prior to the mission, allowing nearly instantaneous communication between Earth and Mars. The establishment of this vital link enabled live feeds from every astronaut on the surface of Mars to be shared with enthusiasts on Earth. People were enthralled viewing the daily life of a Martian astronaut. Close to the end of the mission, all of the astronaut's feeds were cut for an entire day. During the downtime, NASA claimed solar winds were interfering with the satellite network resulting in the outage. NASA's excuse for feed loss fueled conspiracy theories of a cover-up. Few people believed the conspiracy theorists and the claims were dismissed.

The return of the multinational crew ignited a strong sense of patriotism and nationalism among citizens of each participating country. These nationalistic feelings were the strongest in the United States of America. Americans were feeling the same nationalistic pride they'd felt when the Soviet Union fell. Expansionism gripped the minds of American citizens. Instead of wanting more territory on Earth, Americans looked to the stars and the colonization of the heavenly bodies above.

Citizens demanded increased federal funding to NASA and more space missions. Beginning just after the return of the Mars mission crew, the economy had slowed down significantly. Since the post-2008 boom, the economy had risen and fallen and now was ripe for failure.

The seeds of this economic collapse were sown years before. No regulations were added after the Great Recession of 2008, causing an expanding housing bubble and another serious mortgage loan crisis to occur. Over the previous few years, the largest supplier of farming drones, John Deere, gradually raised their prices. These massive vehicles resembling tractors were fully automated and would allow for easy cultivation of crops. They increased yields by 150 percent, making them a necessity for any farmer. A profit was impossible without several drones working the land. After the price hike, most farmers were forced to take large loans from banks.

The housing market had been in an upward trend with no signs of stopping. With the inflated housing prices, homeowners needed to take out large loans as well. The banks took more risks with their loans, secure in the knowledge the government would just bail them out again. This went on for years before everything came to a head.

As 2031 went on, the Federal Reserve chairman decided it was time to take money out of circulation, causing the dollar to increase in value due to deflation. As the value of the dollar increased, banks allowed few refinancing options to keep profits high. Loan defaults began to rise, causing the banks' plan to backfire.

When Wells Fargo closed its doors after their stock price fell to a dollar in one day, it created a panic on Wall Street. The panic caused the market to crash, which, in turn, created a nationwide panic, resulting in Americans rushing to the banks to withdraw their life savings. Banks did not have enough cash to cover such big withdrawals, so they began to close by the dozens.

The similarities to the Great Depression and the Great Recession were so apparent the media began calling the economic collapse of 2031 the Second Great Depression. Congress was called back from their summer recess to pass a bank relief stimulus package. With all the banks collapsing, there was not enough federal money to fund the FDIC. A $900 billion stimulus package was passed in both the House and Senate within two days.

Congressional leadership rushed the bill to the White House, where it was placed on President Adams's desk. Without any hesitation, the president quickly signed the document, making it the largest bank bailout in history. Even with the hasty response, investors all over the world continued to bet against the dollar and the US economy. The dollar's value continued its downward spiral, casting doubt on its ability to remain a global currency. Faced with poll numbers lower than Jimmy Carter during the Iranian hostage crisis and a reelection in 2032; President Adams needed a solution to save the United States' economic dominance.

The county's salvation came to fruition during the North American Leaders' Summit in January 2032. With the American economy in trouble, the Canadian and Mexican economies also suffered. Over the course of the summit, the three leaders drafted a treaty that would establish the North American Union based on the concept of the European Union. But the North American Union would go further than the European Union and establish a common government superseding each individual country's government. The North American government would be modeled after the United States, with an executive, legislative, and judicial branch.

The legislative branch would be comprised of elected officials from the three countries. Country governments would now function like state governments. A joint, unbiased military would be provided by the three countries and commanded by the North American Union legislative body. By not giving the prime minister complete power, it avoided giving one country the ability to influence the military.

The United States dollar would be the primary form of currency for the Union, as it would promote stability. All other details would be agreed upon after treaty ratification.

With the treaty completed, President Adams returned to Washington, DC, and gave a primetime speech presenting the unification to the American people. Before the speech concluded, news outlets began to spin stories. The inflammatory headlines posted all over the internet said the following:

ADAMS: THE ANTI-AMERICAN PRESIDENT

President Adams sat behind his desk Monday night presenting a treaty with Mexico and Canada to unite all of North America under one flag. Before his broadcast concluded, outrage filled the air. Americans have taken to the streets in opposition to the president's obvious anti-American views. Hundreds in California are calling for his resignation to avoid another CALEXIT on the ballot. New agencies speculate if the treaty fails in the Senate, the House will move forward with letters of impeachment.

TRAITOR-IN-CHIEF

If this were 1776, his fellow countrymen would execute President Adams for treason. You never heard George Washington asking to unite with the British. Why now do we have a president who wants to join forces with a socialist country and one that can't get its drug cartels under control? Many Americans are assembling on the Texas-Mexico frontier, telling border crossers to "go back where they came from." These are insane times, and only time will tell if this was a wise move or not.

AMERICA LOST

The founding fathers are rolling over in their graves after the president's speech earlier tonight. A united North America? That sounds like something those socialist Europeans would want. This is the United States of America; we are not like our northern or southern neighbors, so don't lump us together.

AMERICAN DREAM DEAD?

*How can there truly be an American dream if everyone in North America is a part of the same government? With two additional countries combined with the United States, there will be so many more people fighting for a smaller job market. If you want to save your American dream, then you should tell your senator to reject President Adams's **American Dream-Killing Treaty**.*

The media continued to spew anti-Adams propaganda as the Senate vote approached. Unknown to news outlets, the American people had different thoughts on unification. The majority of Americans saw the treaty as an opportunity to expand the influence of America. Many wanted to fulfill their expansionistic agenda; if they couldn't go to the stars, Earth was a great second prize.

In addition, it was America's way back to becoming the world's strongest economy after the Chinese surpassed them years earlier. As time progressed, the American people's support for the North American Union grew so strong that the old and biased politicians of the Senate could not vote against the treaty. The senators realized if they killed Adams's treaty then their reelection was in jeopardy.

After much debate, on February 16, 2033, the United States ratified the unification treaty, joining Mexico and Canada in the North American Union. The value of the dollar rose, and the stock market surged. The three countries and their leaders began the long task of identifying and solving the logistics the treaty left out.

The first order of business was the placement of the Union's capital. The three counties agreed that separating country governments from the Union's central government was necessary to avoid any political bias.

Therefore, Washington, DC, Ottawa, and Mexico City were eliminated as North American Union capital candidates. Citizens across the United States lobbied for the capital to be placed within their borders. Agreeing with his citizens, President Adams suggested St. Louis, because of its geographic location as a central city of the North American continent with easy access to infrastructure.

Not wanting to risk the Americans pulling out, the other leaders agreed, and St. Louis was established as the capital of the North American Union. With its new status, the city rebranded itself the Gateway to North America.

Two democratically held elections established the legislating bodies. The house was selected based on the population of the countries. The representatives came from different regions drawn up by the three leaders. The United States sent 435 members, electing to use the same number set in the Apportionment Act of 1911. They expected the other countries to calculate fair representation to match their population.

The Canadian prime minister redrew the country's federal electoral districts to create the 51 North American Union electoral districts for their representatives. Finally, Mexico utilized their Chamber of Deputies population map, redrawing it for their North American Union electoral districts. They were given 173 representatives based on their population. As time went forward, the census, taken every decade, would trigger a redrawing of all the population maps across all three countries.

The Senate gave each country five senators. In the United States, each North American senator was assigned to a specific region: Northeast, Northwest, Southeast, Southwest, and Midwest. Inside of those states, the governors had sections of their offices that coordinated with the office of the North American senator.

Canada and Mexico followed in similar form; they spread their senators through their country and hired staff. After the legislative body was established, an election was held for the office of prime minister of the North American Union. The election was structured like a presidential election in the United States. In a landslide result, President Adams was elected to be the first prime minister of the North American Union. He was to oversee the audacious task of integrating the three countries into one Union.

THREE

Diplomatic Disaster

Twenty-eight years after the creation of the North American Union, in the year 2061, the country was suffering from many outside difficulties. South Americans were illegally crossing the southern Mexican border with Guatemala and Belize. Economic competition from the European Union and the East Asian Trade Block was hurting the economy.

Economists and politicians suggested uniting with Central and South America to create a united American front. Their vision was to solidify the country's dominance on the world stage. Through the democratic process, people across the North American Union lobbied representatives to initiate negotiations with the South and Central American countries.

On Monday, March 14, 2061, the prime minister of the North American Union, Luis Nunez, flew to Rio de Janeiro. His goal was to lead negotiations to peacefully unite the North American Union with the countries of Central and South America.

Prime Minister Nunez entered the former consulate general of the United States of America in Rio de Janeiro, now the North American Union Consulate. It was an imposing building with many windows, a barbed-wire fence that stretched fifteen feet into the air, with a few armed guards surrounding the embassy.

Prime Minister Nunez entered the office of the ambassador, Donald West from Ottawa. The office was small yet seemed to suit an ambassador. His desk stood in the middle of the room. It was made of dark wood and had a small North American Union flag on it. The flag had horizontal green, blue, and red sections with a white circle in the center. Inside that circle were three gold stars symbolizing the three member countries.

Two chairs faced the desk, and bookshelves surrounded the room. Don liked history, and it showed; in addition to books on his shelves, there were historical artifacts. The ambassador sat behind the desk in a large red swivel chair. Donald stood up and saluted Luis.

"I might still be your boss, but this isn't the United Forces anymore. No need for a salute." Luis returned the ambassador's salute.

"I'm aware, sir, force of habit." Donald gestured for the prime minister to take a seat.

Donald had done most of the legwork to lay the foundation for the talks. They would take place in the large conference room on the second floor of the embassy.

"Don, you have no idea what this means to the Union. You've done a great service. Soon we'll have the largest economic block and nation in the world. Those commies back east won't know what hit 'em."

"Like how they didn't see us coming on the beaches of Taiwan after they tried to overthrow it?"

"Exactly, an outstanding campaign. Heavy losses, but we stuck it to the commies. Can you inform me of the plans for the talks? The suits on United Air Force One don't seem to make things as clear cut." Luis changed the subject.

"The leaders of all Pan-American countries will be arriving today. Tonight, there will be a dinner, and you'll have to do the grip and grin. Tomorrow, the real work begins; we'll see how much we need to give to unite our southern neighbors." Don laced his fingers before placing them on his desk.

"I think I would rather be back in basic than about to try to get the Pan-American counties to join us under one flag." Luis stood up.

"You'll be able to knock them dead, and you'll go down in history, sir." Don also stood up.

"I appreciate the enthusiasm, my friend. We shall see what history makes of this moment."

"Let me walk you to your car, sir." Don walked out with the prime minister.

The rest of the day was filled with a public relations tour as the prime minister went on goodwill missions in the city to gain the love of the people. That night, the prime minister shook hands in front of the press with the other Pan-American leaders and dignified guests. After an evening of interacting with the other leaders, he went to Ambassador West's residence for the night.

The next morning, Luis rode in his armored limo to the North American Union embassy, where all the other leaders were assembled. Luis entered the second-floor conference room to silence.

He stood in the front of the room and addressed the other leaders. "Dignified guests, welcome to the 2061 meeting of the Pan-American nations. I hope we can have a productive meeting full of good negotiations and positive results." The room remained silent. "This is going to be harder than I thought," Luis said to himself as he took his seat at the head of the oak table.

After the awkward silence, negotiations were off to a rocky start. Negotiations were aggressive from some countries, while others were more than willing to unify. The talks went on for days, eventually smoothing out with countries getting what they wanted in order to join. It finally appeared all countries were ready to reach an agreement, and Luis felt relieved. Unbeknownst to him, behind the facade of shaking hands and smiles, an opposition had formed.

The Brazilians, Argentinians, Cubans, and Venezuelans thought submitting to the northerner's imperialistic ambitions was not in their best interests. The four leaders hatched a plan to feed information on the location of the head of the North American Union to the Red Hand.

The Red Hand was a terrorist organization with an anti-Union stance. Based in the northern regions of Mexico, the Red Hand would constantly raid surrounding cities. They believed the North

American Union was a cancer that needed to be irradiated. They had a very high-profile weapons supplier who used them to target specific entities.

The opposition gave the terrorists information on the location and security of the negotiations. Supplied with weapons and given permission to proceed from their high-profile contact, they planed the assault on the embassy. Because the Red Hand wanting to make a statement, the terrorists happily agreed to do the bidding of the opposition and end the "tyranny" of the North American Union.

Per the plan outlined by the four counties, the attack would occur a few hours after the delegations refused the terms of unification. The leaders would be strategically placed away from the embassy on humanitarian missions. The day of the attack came on Friday, March 18, 2061.

The delegations of Brazil, Argentina, Cuba, and Venezuela stood up and left the conference room. They descended the stairs, leaving Prime Minister Nunez and Don West stunned.

"How could this happen?" the president of Panama asked.

"Please remain calm, Mr. President. We'll continue with our agreement as planned," Don said.

"Yes, let's get this agreement in writing, and I'm sure we will be able to resolve the loss of Cuba, Brazil, Venezuela, and Argentina diplomatically," Nunez said calmly, carefully concealing his anger.

"No problem, Mr. Prime Minister, we're all friends here," the Chilean president said, trying to reduce the tension in the room.

"Thank you, Valentina," Nunez said gratefully.

Downstairs, the delegates from the opposition countries walked out the door to a waiting bus. As they climbed into the waiting vehicle, there was a commotion at the guard shack.

"Pare! Halt!" a guard yelled at a quickly approaching white GMC work van. It was charging the gate and gatehouse that guarded the embassy. The guards raised their guns and opened fire. Even with the bullets peppering the van, it plowed into the barriers and disintegrated itself, sending pieces flying all over the parking lot. After regaining their composure from the adrenaline rush, the guards lowered their weapons.

"Radio to the embassy! Tell them we had an attempted incursion," one of the soldiers ordered. But before he could reach for his radio, a gray van appeared and revved its engine. On the hood of the vehicle was large, haphazardly drawn red hand. It charged for the embassy gate, which had been cleared of obstacles from the last van.

Without even asking the van to stop, the soldiers at the gate began to shoot. The bullets ricocheted off the van, which continued to charge the gate like an angry bull.

"Take cover!" a soldier yelled, dropping his weapon before hitting the deck. The van ran through the gate and plowed into the idling bus that held the delegations of the opposition, knocking the bus into the glass doorway of the embassy.

There was a brief pause as the guards picked themselves up. They raised their weapons at the van and slowly approached. They were yelling for whoever was inside the vehicle to get out with their hands up.

Just as the lead guard grabbed hold of the mangled driver's side door, an intense fiery explosion erupted from the van. The main entrance to the embassy, along with the front quarter of the building, was incinerated, causing a partial collapse of the embassy's structure.

Upstairs in the conference room, chaos ensued. People began panicking as the walls shook.

"Everyone, stay calm." Don tried to calm the panicking leaders. Before anyone calmed down, the door to the conference room burst open, and a group of men wearing suits entered. They were holding submachine guns and pistols. The group of men quickly grabbed Prime Minister Nunez.

"Sir, we have to get you out of here. There's been an attack," one of the secret service agents explained as they dragged him from the room.

"Where are we going, what about the others?" Nunez asked as they pulled him toward the back stairs.

"We're only focused on you, sir. We have to get you out of here. The limo will be in the back, and we'll get you out of here. Then we will save the others."

Out front, a blue twelve-passenger van drove through the unguarded gate. Eleven men exited in full tactical gear with a red handprint on the helmets. In their hands were fully automatic AM-55s.

"The supplier wants the prime minister dead. Kill anyone who gets in your way!" One of the men ordered in Spanish as he started to spray his weapon around. The assailants nodded before they rushed the burning building.

"We've got shots fired, sir," an agent told the lead agent as the group reached the stairs. They ran down and exited through the back door. Outside the rear of the building, a single sniper waited on an adjacent structure's fire escape just above the rear exit to the embassy.

The prime minister was led out the back door with the agents all around him. The limo was not there yet. Now trapped on all sides, they remained outside. Luis was panting and tried to control the adrenaline rushing through his body.

"Sir, keep down!" an agent said before a loud single shot crackled through the air. The bullet sailed from the sniper's rifle toward the group of men in suits. The bullet struck the prime minister in the chest.

Nunez didn't even scream as the bullet pierced his heart. One second, he was there; the next, darkness overcame him as his body went limp. The secret service instinctively returned fire, killing the sniper as he attempted to run away. The sniper's lifeless body fell from the structure before it smacked into the concrete sidewalk.

One of the agents held Nunez's body, as the limo pulled up. The agent quickly gave the body to the agent in the back seat.

"He's been shot! Go!" The agent slammed the door before they returned to the embassy to evacuate the others. The limo rushed to the airport, where doctors were waiting on United Air Force One's medical bay. The secret service could not establish who was friend or foe, so a Brazilian hospital was out of the question. The doctors pronounced Luis Nunez dead on arrival.

Don and the North American delegation escaped with a few Pan-American leaders, and the secret service agents after dodging the Red Hand assailants.

There was no news from the deputy prime minister, who was in the favela of Rio and could not be reached. She was presumed dead. Immediately following the news of the Nunez assassination, the NSA began searching for answers. Within a few hours of scanning, they hit the mother lode. They retrieved phone calls and internet logs from the Cuban, Brazilian, Argentinian, and Venezuelan leaders. They spoke about how they had been double-crossed by the Red Hand.

The NSA relayed the intelligence to the Office of the Legislative Speaker. He was the acting prime minister in the absence of the deputy prime minister. The speaker was in a bunker hidden under the old courthouse, now expanded to be the Union Legislation Building in St. Louis. He ordered Congress be gathered in a joint session and told the NSA to leak their information to the press, in an effort to anger the citizens and agitate them to war.

A day later, the prime minister was dead, and Deputy Prime Minister Florence Roy was located and sworn in as the new head of the North American Union. The leak worked as the speaker planned—citizens of the Union wanted vengeance.

In the joint session, Congress unanimously declared war on the four countries and their allies. The invasions of the four countries began on March 19, 2061. This started the Amero Wars, a group of wars that lasted for six years. When it ended, a new country named the American Union was born.

After a long bloody war, the government needed a way to unite the people of the newly formed mega country. With a better economic engine, they looked to the stars once again. Their coffers were too low after funding the war, so they created a competition for companies to put another human on Mars. The companies had to demonstrate a workable strategy of how they would get there and broadcast it back to Earth. The contract stated that the company had to put a person on Mars before 2080. If successful, it would receive exclusive rights to Martian exploration until 2092.

The American Military Space Producing Assets with Creative Engineering, or AMSPACE, won the competition. On July 20, 2079, the citizens of the American Union and the world watched as an AMSPACE lander descended. Their eyes remained wide as Dave Hughes stepped out of the lander onto the Martian surface.

As Dave walked around on Mars, a low-level manager in the space program by the name of Camilla hacked some secret NASA archives that would change the company's motivations to stay on Mars. This single event kicked off the start of the private sector's dominance of Mars and space exploration and directly affected the course of human history.

FOUR

Eleven Years Later

A piercing alarm sounded inside a bedroom, jarring Julius Stetson from his deep slumber. Clothes were strewn all over the beige shag carpet that covered the bedroom floor. A wooden dresser overflowing with clothes sat on the opposite side of the room. "It is Monday, October 9, 2090, Master Stetson, time for you to go to work." The round digital alarm clock on a nightstand spoke with a British accent. Julius rolled his eyes and groggily reached out from under the covers to wave his fingers over the snooze sensor. He closed his eyes for a few more moments of sleep.

The door to Julius's room was opened. An older teen girl spoke. "Julius? You should wake up before you miss your bus."

"Arggghhh."

"Bubby, come on."

Julius threw the covers off the bed. "Fine, thanks, Alicia. Mom would have let me keep sleeping. But I'm not happy about being up."

"I have your back, Bubby, none of us want to be up," Alicia said, leaving the door to Julius's room ajar.

Barely awake, Julius walked out of his room and across the hall to the bathroom he shared with Alicia and his younger brother Antonio. When his feet hit the cold tile floor, he cringed, cursing under his breath. The floor felt like ice on Lake Superior in January.

"Why do Mondays suck?" Julius pondered aloud, turning on the shower to warm up the water.

He pivoted to the mirror and saw his reflection. Julius was twenty-four years old. His short black hair was a mess from the night's sleep. It was so messy it almost hid his blond highlights. His tanned Mexican skin glowed in the bathroom light as did his eyes, which shone like emeralds.

He broke his gaze at the mirror and began brushing his teeth. He took his time cleaning his teeth to allow the shower enough time to warm up. He wished his parents would buy a better water heater, but they always said if it wasn't broken, they wouldn't fix it. After a few minutes of brushing and flossing his teeth, the water was warm enough for Julius to take a decent shower.

He stepped out of the shower into the steam-filled bathroom and aggressively dried himself with a towel. Julius dressed himself quickly, in his company's uniform: a gray zip-up jumpsuit with the company logo over his heart. The logo was a red oval with the Earth in the lower right-hand corner. The globe was angled so only North America was showing. White lettering that spelled out "AMSPACE" stretched across the center. Julius glanced at the mirror again, and he saw that he looked more awake. Dressed, Julius walked out of the bathroom and bedroom.

Julius turned right and walked down the hallway entering the kitchen. His mom, Marie, was hunched over an older gas stove. He hugged her. "Morning, Mom."

He broke the hug and went to prepare his lunch. Marie was cooking breakfast for Alicia and Julius's fifteen-year-old, Antonio. Marie was from Minneapolis, and his father, Carlos, hailed from Mexico City. When the two got married, they decided their kids would take Marie's last name—Stetson—to make integration easier for their children since they would be living in a northern state.

They met when Marie was studying at the Universidad de las Américas Puebla during her junior year. Carlos was studying for his MBA. They went on a date and were married soon after. After they graduated, they moved to Pontiac in 2062 because the company Carlos worked for, WeedLink, moved from Mexico City to Pontiac,

Michigan, to remain protected from the war south of the border. Pontiac, Michigan, was chosen for the new HQ, having become a reborn manufacturing hub.

Marie went on to get her law degree from the University of Michigan. After completing law school, she, along with some of her friends, started a nonprofit that helped refugees from the Amero wars find a new home.

"Mom? Is breakfast ready?" Julius asked.

"No, you can have an apple, they're at the table." His mom pointed her spatula at the table where Antonio and Alicia were sitting. Julius looked over and saw a bowl of fruit in the center of the table.

"Okay, thanks. I'll get it after I finish making my lunch." He finished up packing a brown paper bag, then walked toward the door.

"I think you're forgetting something big, bro. Catch!" Antonio said, grabbing a red apple and tossing it in the air. Instinctively, Julius caught it.

"Thanks, little bro."

"Have a good day at work, Bubby," Alicia said as he walked out the door.

"You, too, little sis, and thanks again for waking me up this morning." He didn't hear a response as the door closed behind him.

Julius rushed down the cracked brick that made up the front walk of his house. As he reached the end, he pushed the cold metal gate of the chain-link fence open.

When he was a few steps down the sidewalk, the gate slammed closed. This sent a wave of vibration through the fence, rattling each link. At a full sprint, Julius dodged multiple potholes in the worn sidewalk's concrete. To make it to work, Julius needed to reach the bus stop at the end of his street.

I'm going to be late! With my luck, the bus already left, Julius thought gloomily. The bus arrived at the bus stop at same time Julius arrived. He was as out of breath as a marathon runner who sprinted the last mile.

The bus had the late-twentieth-century box-shape style with green and yellow stripes painted down the side. Large yellow-green letters on the top spelled out HYDROGEN-POWERED and DRIVERLESS.

A Greater Detroit Department of Transportation logo was featured on the nose of the vehicle.

Guess it's my lucky day, Julius thought to himself as he entered the metal rectangle through the front sliding doors. Located on the interior of the bus was a tap-on/tap-off scanner to pay the bus fee. Julius scanned his company ID since AMSPACE covered public transportation to the factory.

The interior of the bus mirrored the bland interior of a school bus. The drab green plastic seats were lined two by two. A yellow grab rail reached from the front of the bus all the way back with straps for standing passengers to hold.

Typical, I have to stand, Julius thought, seeing the bus was full, as usual. "Can't I sit for once?" he muttered to himself.

Julius gripped one of the cold rails as the bus pulled out of the station heading south. He took a deep breath and a bit down on his apple while he surveyed the people in the bus. Most of the riders were wearing the same gray AMSPACE jumpsuits. The bus traveled ten miles, making the occasional stop to pick up more passengers, filling the bus like a can of sardines. The large volume of passengers forced Julius to shuffle further to the back of the bus where he was squashed against the rear seats.

As the final stop approached, Julius fell into a deep thought about what the impending day would bring. After mentally reviewing his routine of setting up his machine on the factory floor, he lapsed into deeper thoughts. The one that was nagging him today was why he didn't go to college straight out of high school. Instead he had jumped at an opportunity to assist in the AMSPACE Mars Program. He was already taking steps to solve this problem; his nightly college classes would start next semester.

The bus stopping and the robotic female voice announcing they were at the end of the line interrupted his thoughts. People shifted around gathering their belongings before they vacated the bus. Julius disembarked, following the other riders. Immediately after he exited the bus, the bus turned around and exited the station.

The crowd of workers slowly walked through the iron gates of the AMSPACE Rocket Development and Production Facility. The factory was originally built to produce second-generation hover-copters for the North American Union at the height of the Amero Wars. It was converted to a rocket and space shuttle factory to fuel AMSPACE's expanding reach into space post-war.

Back in 2079, the facility was critical in helping AMSPACE achieve the American Union's contract to land a man on Mars. Julius walked to a row of dark-tinted glass doors located on the side of the main box-shaped building. The austere workers' entrance was located a distance away from the extravagantly designed guest entrance meant for tours and VIPs.

The doors opened up to a large room with standard drywall and a cheap-looking red-tiled floor. The walls and ceiling were painted with intricate murals of the stars and the planets. Just past the glass doors was a large entrance hall. It was filled with many hovering robots that provided multiple layers to scan for any security anomalies. The world changed after the Amero Wars; domestic terrorist attacks increased thanks to the Red Hand. In addition, spies from the East Asia Trading Block were very bold in their attempts to steal the American Union's technology.

Julius did not pay attention to the security checkpoint; he instead looked up at the Mars mural. He saw the familiar scenes of astronauts wearing AMSPACE space suits holding mining tools with machines in the background.

Looking up at the mural, Julius was taken back to the first time he saw it. He had been standing in the same room, staring up at it. He was overwhelmed with anxiety. He had just graduated high school and acquired a job at the local rocket development factory. Looking at the mural calmed his nerves because he knew this job would one day get him on that red planet.

Still firmly rooted in this memory, Julius looked down from the mural and saw there was a forty-something man standing at the entrance to the security checkpoint waving him over. As he approached the man, he saw he was on the shorter side with olive skin, green eyes, and black hair.

"Do I know you, sir?"

"Not yet, but you will. Name's Vinnie Messina. I'm going to show you the ropes." The man had a slight Chicago accent.

"Glad to meet you, I'm Julius Stetson, sir," he said, extending his hand.

"No problem, and please don't call me sir."

"You got it." The two walked through the security bots together.

Coming out of his memory, Julius looked back up at the mural.

"One day, I am going to step foot on Mars." He spoke under his breath as he stood there, staring. He imagined what it would be like to put a foot down in the Martian dirt as Dave Hughes and his crew had done eleven years prior. He imagined the freedom of being on a new planet with none of the earthly expectations holding him back. As he stood lost in thought, he closed his eyes, envisioning what it would be like.

Suddenly, he felt two strong hands forcefully grab him from the back. Snapped away from his inner thoughts, Julius went into fight or flight mode. He felt a rush of adrenaline, as his body commanded him to fight.

He clenched his hand into a fist and was ready to turn and slug the guy who grabbed him. But a familiar voice spoke.

"Oi, Julius, are you dreaming of going to space again?" The voice had a chipper tone with a slight Scottish accent.

Julius knew exactly whom the voice belonged to. He whirled around and saw a six-foot-seven man with a big red bushy beard. The man smiled, revealing big yellow-tinted teeth.

"Damn it, John! You startled me." Julius pushed the other man's large hands away.

"I can't have you daydreaming about Mars again." John slapped him on the back.

"You know, this has been my dream. I told you that in high school when you moved here."

"Yeah, I remember, Julius, but it's time to get your head out of the stars for the day." John shoved Julius toward the beginning of the security area. "Got to get some money in your pocket."

The two friends walked through the hall, passing the hovering security drones.

"You know what grinds my gears, Julius? They inspect us to make sure we are being good employees. All we are to them is assets. We're cheaper than that robot over there."

"You aren't wrong, but at least they employ us. We have to pay the bills somehow. Hey, where's Misty?"

"I guess so. Not much more for me to do here other than work in a factory. She wanted to get in early. They had a presentation on the next-generation AM Drive engine."

"About time they decided to come out with a new Antimatter Drive. We need to get more of them on the rockets. The nuclear propulsion engines don't provide nearly enough thrust."

"Dude, that's way over my head."

"Fair enough, but it's pretty interesting stuff."

The two made their way through a long hallway with green doors on each side. Red LED displays were placed on each door identified the assigned employee group. The hallway had the same drywall and red tiles as the entryway, but it had holographic moving banners of praise for the facility projecting from the ceiling.

"Are you jealous of Vinnie?"

"Not going to lie, I am a little envious of my mentor. But I'm also happy for him. He mentored me for my first two years. You know he earned his spot on the rocket. Division policy states people can only go to Mars one of two ways. They either have a skill that the colony needs, or they win by lottery. He won the lottery two weeks ago, so he deserves to go." Julius had a hint of melancholy in his voice.

"Don't let that get you down. You will get there one day." John slapped his friend on the back.

"Thanks, John." The duo turned right and entered one of the green doors with a red sign that said "Steelers and Drivers." The locker room had wood benches and hunter-green mini lockers lining the walls.

It was not a very large area, as it was meant for the select employees who worked on the front end of the production line. Steelers and drivers were a minority in the factory. They molded the steel frames for the rocket and shuttle frames. Julius placed his lunch, phone, and wallet on his locker's top shelf.

He grabbed his white hard hat that displayed the AMSPACE logo and placed it on his head. After he closed the door, he waited to hear the lock automatically engage. Julius stared at the front of the locker, which sported a blue LED display with his name and a fingerprint reader about waist height.

"John, are you ready to go?" Julius turned to his friend across the room.

"Ready to go! You'll get there, Julius. They don't realize it yet, but you will be more valuable to them on Mars than here." The two walked together through the door opposite the one they entered.

"Thank you, it means a lot," Julius responded.

After passing through the threshold, they found themselves on the factory floor. The floor was made of concrete with brightly colored safety lines zigzagging across it. Large machines lined the length of the windowless factory as far as the eye could see. Julius and John separated with a head nod. Julius walked to the mold presses, and John made his way to the loading dock. John operated an industrial forklift that removed steel rolls from rail cars before he brought them to the first machine.

On his way to his machine, Julius walked by the one Vinnie and his new partner, Nancy Campbell, were working.

"Hey, Julius. Beautiful day for manufacturing spacecraft."

"Two more days for you, Vinnie!" Julius walked up to the short Italian man. They shook hands briefly before Vinnie spoke.

"Might be two more days, but I want to make sure Nancy knows all there is to know about this machine."

"She's in good hands."

"You better get to work, Julius. I didn't train you to have you get written up for being late."

"You haven't steered me wrong. Be safe, Vinnie." Julius walked off.

He strolled to the press he operated with his coworker and John's wife, Misty.

"Cutting it close there, Julius. Were you chatting with my husband again?"

Misty was five feet, two inches tall with shoulder-length black hair that she tied up in a bun under her hard hat. She had green-brown eyes and liked to pile on the makeup. Because of all the makeup she wore, some of the older workers called her Show Girl.

Julius and Misty had a strange history. She was a year younger than him. They went to the same high school and were friends until his junior year. Julius asked her to prom and they went, but it didn't go as well as they both expected. Misty wanted their relationship to be more and Julius didn't, so they remained friends. The next year John moved to Pontiac and went to school. During Julius's senior year, Misty and John began to date and, a few years later, ended up getting married.

"Yeah, I did, but I also ran into Vinnie."

"That's nice, everyone likes Vinnie. Good soul, that man. I hope he does well on Mars. He needed to zoozh his life up."

"What does *zoozh* mean?"

"It means to spice up. Haven't you heard what all the people in Hollywood say?"

"No, I don't pay attention to that crap."

"What do you mean Vinnie needed to spice his life up?"

"It's just I think the factory life is boring and—" Misty stopped talking briefly as a security drone flew over, quickly scanning them to make sure they were doing their job. Once it left, she continued speaking. "I hate those things, so nosy. Anyway, it's just so boring. I just think a great guy like Vinnie deserves to do something more interesting with his life."

As Misty spoke, Julius walked around the machine. It was a gigantic half circle press designed to mold superheated steel squares into a portion of the second stage of a deep-space rocket.

"I can see that, but I think he is content with his life the way it is. He does have a wife and a kid. Can't say his life is that bad."

"Yeah, I guess you're right, but still, I think this job is kind of boring.

"I mean, I'd rather be on Mars too." Julius inspected the press, making sure there were no obvious faults. If he was to miss just one defect in the machine, a rocket could fail during a launch.

"Looks like we're good to go. Did you do the detailed prework inspection?"

"Yes, Julius. I did the inspection."

"Awesome, thank you." Julius walked to his control box.

Julius's station monitored the process that brought the super-heated steel section from the oven. Misty operated the press itself with a lever to lower the press and singular button to stop it in an emergency. Julius stood at his position for about fifteen seconds before he heard the sound of a machine powering up. He thought nothing of it; sometimes people like to test the machines before the scheduled start time.

He remained unconcerned for another few seconds before a male's bloodcurdling scream echoed through the relatively silent factory.

"Oh God! Someone help!" A woman's frantic voice called from a few machines away. Julius and Misty hurriedly deactivated their machine before they ran in the direction of the troubled cry for help.

Julius and Misty sprinted along the line of machines. They were green and rusty machines that looked like they belonged in a museum rather than on a factory floor. The company favored human labor over the more expensive artificially intelligent assembly line.

Not knowing where the cry for help came from, Julius and Misty judged that the machine with the group of people around it was their destination. Julius felt his heart sink when he saw the machine was the same one where he'd been earlier. It was Vinnie's station. The group had formed a semicircle around the steel cutting machine.

"Julius, that's Vinnie."

Julius said nothing back to Misty as he looked at the scene.

The high high-tension cutter was raised and covered with a thin layer of blood and tissue. Below it, inside the cutting area, was the lower part of a man's body. It was cut just above the waist, allowing the spinal column to be visible through the ragged flesh. Julius forced back his body's overwhelming instinct to vomit.

He could not help looking at the severed body. Facedown in front of the machine and surrounded by a pool of his own blood and entrails was the upper half of his mentor, Vinnie. His body twitched as it tried to move away from the machine. Nancy was in a small group next to the machine with people trying to comfort her.

Julius could hear her talking, "I...I didn't know he was in there when I started the machine up. I had to run the test, but he was doing the visual inspection, and I chopped him in half. I killed him!" Her panic escalated as Vinnie continued to bleed out. Julius was frozen in shock as he looked down at his dying mentor.

"Where is the medical bot?" A blond-haired man yelled as he knelt beside the hemorrhaging man. The man hastily removed his own jumpsuit to try to clot the bleeding in a futile attempt to buy time for the medical bot to arrive. A woman with short red hair crouched by Vinnie's head, she held his hand and muttered something like a prayer.

Vinnie gasped for air straining for his last breath like a fish out of water. Julius watched as the light drained from Vinnie's eyes, and his body became still. The medical bot arrived thirty seconds after Vinnie had passed. The redhead and the man stood up, faces colorless.

The group stood traumatized at the scene they'd just witnessed. They were so distracted by the horror, no one noticed a man calmly approaching. He towered over the other average-sized men. He had a cleanly shaven head, scars riddled his face, and round glasses rested on the bridge of his nose.

Julius and Misty turned to look at the man. They realized he was the president of the facility, Gerald McGinnus. He wore a dark-gray suit, a navy-blue dress shirt, red tie, and a black pair of Kingsman dress shoes.

"Ladies and gentlemen, please return to your workstations. Those of you who witnessed the machine activate, please remain here. Human resources will interview you and write an incident report. I've requested they give you the rest of the day off. The factory will remain operational; we have quotas to meet. Expect more information at the end of the day. Thank you all for your cooperation." His toneless voice sent chills up Julius's spine.

"You can't just sweep this under the rug," someone in the crowd yelled.

"There will be an investigation, but until then, we have work to do, so everyone back to work. We can't fall behind." Gerald's voice held a hint of annoyance and anger. The crowd silently dissipated and returned to their workstations.

Julius and Misty returned to their machine and worked the shift in relative silence. As they worked, Julius felt numb, staring blankly at the large superheated sheets of steel that rolled by. He thought back to an incident when Julius first started working at the factory. Julius almost died in a forklift incident. A driver lost control of the lift, and it barreled toward him. Vinnie had tackled Julius, knocking him out of the way before the vehicle smashed into a wall. Julius kicked himself for not returning the favor. Julius was brought back to reality when a tone sounded over the loudspeaker, followed by an announcement.

"Attention, all employees. This is your plant president, Gerald McGinnus. An incident occurred on the factory floor today. Vincenzo Messina, an employee for twenty-two years, was involved in a fatal accident. As a result, the Martian colony is without a vital miner. We must act quickly. Per company policy, his spot will be picked by a lottery via robot tomorrow after the shift concludes. All who wish to be entered in the drawing must place their fingerprint on a scanner at security when they exit today. Thank you all for your hard work."

No one Julius interacted with knew where Gerald's office was, and those who did would not disclose what they knew. There were rumors, but all of them were unconfirmed. After the announcement concluded, everyone began to file to the exits.

Julius walked with Misty silently to the locker room. John had already gathered his things to leave. He put his things down on a bench and approached Misty.

"Angel, I heard what happened! Are you okay?" John embraced Misty.

"It was awful," Misty sobbed. Mascara ran down her cheek. John looked away from Misty to Julius. "You okay?"

"Would you be?"

"I'm sorry. Why don't you both gather your things?"

"Okay, hun." Misty walked to her locker. They both quickly gathered their belongings from their lockers and exited with John.

"You going to enter the drawing?" John whispered to Julius quietly as they walked through the hallway. Julius did not reply. He debated whether it was morally right for him to enter, given his mentor just lost his life. They approached the exit. Robots were lined up on the left-hand side of the open security area. They had their hands out displaying thumb scanners embedded in their palms.

"Julius?" John repeated.

"I don't know, John. It feels wrong. Vinnie just died, who am I to take advantage of that?" Julius stopped in his tracks. His friends turned around and looked at him.

"Look, it hurts all of us that Vinnie isn't around anymore. You don't need to feel guilty. Vinnie wanted you to fulfill your dreams. This is your chance, why not take it?" Misty smiled through her pain. Julius looked at his friends and cracked a smile.

"Someone is going to win. You might as well try, or you'll regret it," John said.

"Well, I might as well try, for Vinnie. Even though I probably will lose." Julius shrugged and walked up to a robot. Julius placed his thumb on the fingerprint reader. The robot was an older model; it was brown and had a more of a boxy stick-figure shape. It also had tracks like a tank that it used to move around.

"Julius Stetson, your name has been submitted for the drawing occurring at 1715 tomorrow. Thank you," the robot said in a choppy computerized voice.

Julius turned away from the robot and met back up with Misty and John near the doors.

"I'm in," Julius calmly said to his two friends.

"Now you have a chance to go," John said, holding the door open for Misty and Julius to exit the factory. Inside his head, Julius felt cautious excitement. He was a pessimistic optimist when it came to winning competitions. The three exited the factory and walked into the crisp fall evening. They felt chilled as the cool Michigan wind blew across their bodies. The sudden artic kiss caused the hairs on their bodies to stand at attention with goose bumps popping up on their skin.

Julius looked out at the trees surrounding the factory's brick courtyard. The leaves were a mix of bright oranges, reds, and yellows. The trees looked like one of the impressionist artists had a hand in mixing the colors. The three walked with the majority of the first-shift workers to the bus stop.

Julius looked around at the people at the station; there was a black cloud hanging over all the people there. The bus that Julius, Misty, and John rode arrived, and many people boarded the bus. The palpably sad mood removed anyone's desire to make conversation. The bus arrived at Julius's stop. He nodded to his two friends, exited the bus, and walked back to his house. He stopped outside the fence and looked in.

The house was a one-story ranch house that had peeling beige paint and a few windows. A waist-high chain-link fence encircled both the front and backyard. Julius walked through the fence's gate onto the run-down, moss-covered red brick sidewalk that led to the front door. The front grass needed some major TLC, but Julius's father didn't believe in yard work after the start of October. This left the house's curb appeal with something to be desired. On either side of the brick stairs were large plots of dirt filled with the remains of withered summer flowers.

Julius strolled up the stairs and into the front hall, where he removed his boots. He placed them next to the shoes of the other members of his family.

"Julius?" his mom's voice emanated from the family room to Julius's left.

"Yeah, Mom, it's me." Julius entered the family room.

The room had two tan couches that faced each other and a mahogany coffee table in the middle. A small fireplace sat opposite from where Julius was standing. A small flat-screen television hung above it. Marie was sitting on the couch with a book. The muted television was on and was tuned to the American Union News. Captions scrolled across the bottom of the screen as the news anchor's mouth moved soundlessly.

Today, terrorists attacked a police station in Porto Alegre. The Red Hand has claimed responsibility for the attack. The prime minister has declared martial law in the state of Rio Grande Do Sul, Brazil. The goal of the martial law is to learn where the terrorist organization is getting their weapons and stop additional attacks. The chairman of AMSPACE promised to assist the government by any means necessary. As many citizens know, twenty-five years ago, the Red Hand terrorists were responsible for—

Julius's mom turned off the television.

"The press is so depressing these days. It's all negative. They only care about death and turmoil. Where is the happy news?"

"Mom, something happened today at work." Julius's face and tone portrayed the pain of the day's fatal tragedy. His mom's expression changed immediately to concern.

"What happened?"

"There was an accident, and Vinnie died," Julius said, sitting down, fighting back tears.

"I am so sorry. Tell me what happened."

"He was cut in half. I don't want to go into it, Mom." His mom moved to sit by her son, putting her arm around him.

"Thanks, Mom."

"Tell me about Vinnie, what was your favorite memory of him?"

"Mom, how is that supposed to help?"

"Julius, I know it will help. Trust me."

"Okay, Mom." Julius began to reflect upon the life of his friend.

"I remember when I was twenty-one, Vinnie took me out for my first beer since Dad was in California. We were sitting together drinking, and I told him about my dream of being an astronaut. He encouraged me to follow my dreams. He told me no one is going to just hand them to me. I had to go take them for myself. That was my favorite memory."

"That's a great story, Julius. It's a wonderful memory that you can tuck away in your heart. Remember Vinnie that way, not the way you saw him today."

Julius let his mom's words sink in. He felt happy reliving that moment with Vinnie. "You know, Mom, that really helped."

"I'm glad. Remember to take all of those happy memories and keep them with you. That's how someone stays with you forever."

She paused, waiting to see if Julius was ready to move on the conversation.

"Your father called."

"What did Dad say?"

"He won't be back from Bogotá until Saturday. Business is hard. He is trying to get the marijuana farmers' union agree to new terms for his distribution company." Marie stood up and walked to the kitchen.

"Well, they sent in the best negotiator in the company, then." Julius followed her into the kitchen. His siblings were sitting at the table, doing their homework.

"Mom, Vinnie was going to Mars training in two days. The company still needs someone to go, so they initiated a rushed lottery. After debating what to do, I threw my name in the hat." He was a little afraid of his mother's reaction.

"You did?" Marie said, surprised. He was glad to see she did not seem upset.

"I did, it's a long shot, and I don't think I'll win, but it's worth a shot."

"Julius, I love you. I just want you to be safe. I would never keep you from following your dreams." She began to chop vegetables and place them in a waiting pan.

"Thank you. Also, miners get paid well."

"Money isn't everything, honey. You don't have to legitimize your career with money."

"Julius? You're going to be an astronaut? I bet pigs will fly before that happens," Antonio joked, looking up from his computerized paper. Schools no longer used paper made from trees. Computers had become so small and so cheap they were easily mass-produced to replace paper. They had become commonplace in the world, including in schools.

"No, Ant, but if I win, I have a chance to be an astronaut." Julius ignored his younger brother's jab.

"Mom, can I help you with dinner?"

"Yes, that would be great."

"You got it. Let me change out of this stuffy jumpsuit." Julius went to his room to change. He came back to help his mom in preparing meat loaf. After preparing and serving dinner, Julius realized he was completely exhausted. He'd had enough for today.

Julius bid his family goodnight, then went down the hall to his room. He lay down in his bed and closed his eyes. His mind was replayed his friend's ghastly death, and his thoughts wandered to what life on Mars would be like. This was his chance to finally go. He was filled with excitement and anxiety. He relaxed and was soon fast asleep.

FIVE

The Lottery

The next morning, Julius was once again jolted awake by his alarm. He took his shower, dressed for work in his jumpsuit, and went to the kitchen. "Good morning, Julius. Your lunch is over there. Good luck at work today." Julius's mom greeted him.

Julius hugged her and waved to his siblings, who were eating at the table. He put on his steel-toed boots in the front hall and exited the house. He walked down the sidewalk and arrived at the bus stop a little earlier than the day before. The stop was empty, so he sat down on the bench while he waited for the bus.

As the bus's arrival time drew closer, other riders began to fill the stop. Eventually, the bus lumbered up, and Julius boarded the vehicle. He rode it to work as he had the day before.

If my life was a movie, the audience would have already walked out of the theater, Julius thought to himself as the bus drove along its route. The bus arrived at the AMSPACE station, and Julius stepped off with the others. He walked across the courtyard and entered the facility through the black-tinted glass doors.

Julius followed his daily ritual, looking up at the Mars mural. As he started at the red planet, he realized that today felt different. Today could be the last day he gazed upon that mural.

He felt his heart racing and heard blood pumping through his ears. He felt excited and happy as he walked through the security area. He strolled down the hallway before entering the locker room. Julius saw John was on his way out the door but waved at his friend before he entered the factory floor. Julius also saw Misty, who decided to wait for him.

"Didn't want to walk out with your husband?"

"Nah, I spend enough time with him. He needs a break to remember how much he loves me."

Julius laughed as he placed his belongings in the locker. "You two have an interesting relationship."

"What's that supposed to mean?"

"Nothing, it's just fun to watch you two sometimes. I'm glad I get to be a part of your lives."

"Careful, Julius, you're starting to get sentimental. You're feeling the loss of Vinnie, aren't you?" Misty and Julius walked out of the locker room and down the row of machines.

"Yeah, you could say that." They walked past Vinnie's station; the floor was still stained with the blood from yesterday's accident. Julius felt a wave of horror ripple through him.

"Hey!" Julius turned his attention to Misty. "Don't think about it. It happened and it sucked, but you can't dwell on it. You have to move on."

Julius let Misty's words sink in for a moment before he responded. "You're right, I'm glad I have good friends to help me through this."

"That's what John and I are for! Now let's get this machine ready to go." Misty began the daily maintenance check. She made sure the machine would not activate while Julius climbed inside.

This was the same procedure that killed Vinnie the day before. Julius felt another shiver snake its way up his spine as he got into the machine. He thought back to Vinnie's gruesome death, and his insides quaked at the memory. One wrong press of a button and Julius could share the same fate as his mentor.

Feeling both tense and agitated, Julius hurriedly exited the machine, his body shaking slightly. "Hey, I said don't think about it. Get in, check, and get out."

"Okay, okay, it's not easy." Julius tried to shake off the pit in his stomach.

He worked the first half of the day in silence and had lunch at his break with Misty and John.

"You still seem upset after yesterday," John commented.

"He is John, I've talked to him about it. We're working through it, right, Julius?"

"Yeah sure, Misty," Julius mumbled as he took a bite of his turkey sandwich.

"Look Julius John and I just want to help."

"I appreciate both of you, but I don't want to talk about it right now. Can I please just stew for a moment. Everyone grieves in different ways. I'll be fine."

They finished up their lunch in silence before returning to the line. Julius and Misty worked in silence until their shift was over. The clock struck 1700, and Julius shut the machine down. Just after the machine's hum ceased, a tone sounded throughout the factory floor.

Gerald's voice came over the loudspeaker. "All interested employees, report to the loading dock for the drawing of the Mars lottery."

Julius and Misty joined a large crowd in the factory loading dock. "Oi, Julius, Misty, over here." They looked to see John waving from a spot near the center of the crowd. Julius and Misty elbowed their way through the compact crowd to get to John.

The loading dock was a large open area with an overhead crane. The rail cars were unloaded near an airplane hangar-sized door to the right. A line of interior windows resided above the crowd against the wall. Aluminum blinds blocked any visual inside of what transpired behind the glass. It was speculated that beyond the windows was an office, but no one knew for sure. Located in the middle of the windows was a small balcony with a large rusty metal door.

Julius, Misty, and John stared up at the balcony and the row of windows. "So that's Gerald's office?" Julius asked John. He realized he had never taken notice of its presence before.

"Rumor is that's where old Frankenstein resides."

"Frankenstein?" Misty looked over at John with a disapproving glare.

"Yeah, have you seen Gerald's face? He looks like Frankenstein's monster."

"You're so insensitive. That man fought in the war."

"What happened to give him that face? I thought he lost a fight with a cougar or something."

"No. Ugh, sometimes I cannot believe I married you."

"Okay, you two, that's enough. I want to hear the story," Julius said, becoming irritated.

"You're right, Julius. Sorry, John, you know I love you. Sometimes you do get on my nerves though."

"I know, but it keeps our marriage interesting. Can you tell us the story?"

"Yeah, let me set the scene. Back in 2062, the Brazilians launched a blitz on the town of Santa Rita in Eastern Colombia. Gerald was stationed there and survived brutal hand-to-hand combat. He was weaponless, and his opponent had a knife. That's how he got the scars. He's a hero and should be treated as such."

"Wow, now I feel like an asshole," John said.

Without warning, a loud lock click was heard above as a lock turned. Everyone's attention shifted to the balcony. Once all eyes were there, the rusty door squeaked open. It sounded like it had not been opened in years.

A hush fell over the loading dock as Gerald walked through the threshold and onto the small balcony. His dress shoes clicked like ticks on an old grandfather clock. A circular-shaped robot floated to the right of Gerald's head. Julius noted the robot was significantly more advanced than the old clunkers that roamed the factory.

Julius estimated it had a diameter similar to a regulation FIFA football. The bot's color was also unorthodox; it had a white base coat with red "AMSPACE" letters around the top. Blue circles of various sizes were sprinkled all around, making him think it was a football.

An odd robot for randomly selecting a person, Julius thought to himself.

"Ladies and gentlemen," Gerald addressed the crowd, before pausing for dramatic effect. "This robot will be randomly selecting one of your names to go to Mars training. In order to begin the selection, I would like you all to welcome the president of AMSPACE's Mars Division, Camilla González."

A round of excited applause erupted from the crowd as a middle-aged Latina woman walked out from the dimly lit room onto the balcony, standing to the right of Gerald, so the robot was between them. She had brown eyes, short black hair with gray strands peppered throughout. Julius guessed her age to be around fifty years old. "So that's the big boss?" John asked. No one replied. Instead, Julius and Misty kept their intent focus on the action above.

"Good evening, ladies and gentlemen. This evening, I have the pleasure of selecting one of you to join my team to further human-space exploration. As few of you may know, I was once an office worker. Through hard work and research into Mars, and a lucky break, I was given an opportunity. I helped the chairman build the Mars exploration section of this great company with Dave Hughes." Camilla paused and surveyed the crowd.

"Now, one of you will join my sector of the cooperation and continue my mission. Once your name is called, please join Gerald and I in his office promptly to discuss the next steps in the process."

Julius saw Gerald shoot Camilla a bored look. He was already tired of listening to her talk.

Camilla put on her teardrop-shaped glasses that tapered to a point on the outside of the frames. "Without further ado, bot, please select a name." Camilla turned her head toward the floating sphere.

"Selecting," the robot said before Camilla's eyes looked around her glasses as if she was reading something on the lens.

"Will a Miss Nancy Campbell please join Gerald and me in the office?"

Loud applause filled the factory floor. Julius clapped for a moment, then felt an overwhelming sense of defeat. That was his chance, and it was given to someone else. The woman responsible for his mentor's death got the position.

He was filled with anger and sadness. It was a cruel mockery of Vinnie's death that she was selected. He looked at his friends, who had turned around to see how he was taking the depressing news.

"Well, I tried, fucking told you I wouldn't win." Julius pushed his way through the clapping crowd until he was outside it. Misty and John followed and tried to comfort their friend.

"It's okay. It just wasn't your time." John tried his best to be reassuring.

"But that woman killed Vinnie, and she is getting rewarded?" Julius shot back at John.

"That isn't fair to say that. You saw Nancy yesterday. She was distraught. Be happy for her and be ready next time," Misty said, giving him a hug. Her gesture did little to placate Julius.

"Ladies and gentlemen, we appreciate your attendance and attention," Gerald said, smiling dispassionately at the crowd. The crowd couldn't tell, but Gerald's smile looked forced and painful for him.

Before the group of employees dispersed, someone yelled, "Hey, didn't she quit this morning?"

"Yeah, she couldn't handle the guilt of killing Vinnie!" another person corroborated the story.

"Are you trying to short us, Gerry!" a woman yelled up at the man. The crowd began murmuring and getting rowdy.

Seeing the crowd starting to get upset, Gerald addressed the group in a flustered tone. It seemed like he was trying to hold back his anger.

"Ladies and gentlemen, please remain calm. It seems there's been a mistake with the drawing. I wasn't aware Ms. Campbell quit this morning. Let me speak with Miss González."

Gerald turned to Camilla and started speaking in a hushed tone. Gerald's face twisted into a scowl before he faced the crowd.

"Everyone, I apologize for the mistake. Miss González has decided that since the winner has left the company, her victory is null and void. We'll draw another name."

Julius felt his spirits lift slightly, but he continued to frown, knowing deep down he still had no chance.

"Bot, please redraw a name," Camilla said, clearly annoyed.

"Selecting," the flying robotic sphere repeated. A second later, Camilla looked as if she was reading something on her smart glasses. She then paused for dramatic effect.

"Out with it, lady!" A person in the crowd yelled.

Gerald shot a scowl that would frighten a scarecrow in the general direction of the voice. Camilla cleared her throat and tonelessly said two words. "Julius Stetson."

There was no thunderous applause like before, just a few polite claps. The crowd had lost interest and was moving toward the exits. Having announced the name, Camilla, Gerald, and the robot retreated into the office without another word shutting the door behind them with a rusty creaking clunk.

Shocked, Misty and John turned to look at their friend. Julius stared up at the balcony with his mouth agape. Inside, his brain screamed that his body should move and get up there, but his body did not respond. The anger he once felt had melted away and was replaced with pure joy. His heart leaped around in his chest. He had won.

"Julius, you have to get up there!" John grabbed his friend by the shoulders and tried to shake Julius back to reality.

"That's not going to work." Misty took Julius's hand, leading him through the dispersing crowd of disappointed people. As they walked, Julius received pats on the back and wishes of good luck.

Julius finally snapped out of his daze when he and Misty reached a door below and to the right of the balcony. Misty opened the door and pulled Julius in, John followed, pushing Julius. Inside the door was a flight of grated metal stairs. The three rushed up the flight of stairs and arrived on the second floor. A hallway lined the length of the factory to their right. Further down the hallway were two large oak doors with brass handles.

"Knock on the door. We'll wait for you in the locker room," Misty said, turning to walk back down the stairs.

John made a finger gun and winked. "You got this, mate!"

Then he followed Misty. As he watched them leave, Julius took a deep breath and approached the doors. He raised his fist and knocked on the hardwood door, producing an echo that reverberated down the long hallway, escalating Julius's shot nerves.

Gerald opened the door, smiling and gesturing for Julius to enter the room. Julius passed through the door's wooden frame into Gerald's office. Looking around, Julius saw the space fell short of his expectations. The carpet was a gray mesh weave typical of an early-twenty-first-century office building.

Julius turned to look at the view out the window to his left. He was once again underwhelmed as the grand view he envisioned was just the company rail yard.

Julius made a 180-degree turn to face the right side of the room. He saw a beige wall, lined with cheap-looking medium-density fiberboard shelves filled with war books. Julius's eyes were drawn to the North American Union flag hanging next to a Marine uniform.

Various military medals, including a Purple Heart, were placed in the space below the flag. Julius connected the dots and realized Misty's story about Gerald was true or at least partially true.

"Hello, Mr. Stetson." Camilla's voice caught Julius off guard; his head snapped forward. She was sitting behind Gerald's walnut desk in his tall leather desk chair. Her hands were folded neatly on top of the desk in an annoyed, impatient pose.

"Hello, ma'am." Julius felt the butterflies in his stomach as he stared into Camilla's brown eyes.

"Mr. Stetson, please sit down." Camilla gestured to a chair in front of the desk. "Congratulations on your promotion to Martian miner. Are you still interested?"

Julius said he was, without any hesitation.

"Good. Gerald, where is the television?"

"Directly above you." Gerald pointed upward to a piece of glass above the windows.

"Good, call Dave Hughes."

"Sure, we can do that," Gerald said, pressing a button that lowered the glass pane down. Julius noticed Gerald was not happy about being bossed around by Camilla. It was understandable, but Julius found it strange. Someone subservient was acting in this manner.

Gerald turned on the glass pane by simply looking at it.

Dave Hughes? I can't believe I get to talk to the first man to step on Mars in the name of AMSPACE, Julius thought to himself as questions flew through his head. *Dave Hughes still works for AMSPACE? What does he do for the company? How did Gerald turn on the TV?*

"Can I ask a few questions?" Julius asked.

"Quickly," Camilla snapped.

Julius was getting the sense that Camilla did not like this part of her job. She was pretty crabby for someone who was meant to make him feel welcome.

"I'll make it quick, ma'am. What does Dave Hughes do for the company, and how did Mr. McGinnus turn on the TV without a remote?"

"I have a bionic eye, lost my real one in the war," Gerald said solemnly. Julius was shocked and felt guilty for asking.

"I see, thank you for your service."

"Don't thank me, I lived. Thank the men who died." Gerald had a somber tone to his voice that hid a hit of anger.

Julius didn't know how to reply to Gerald, so he waited for his second question to be answered. Gerald started a video conference. The screen said, "Starting a Call with Dave Hughes, Head of Martian Operations."

"That title will answer your first question," Camilla said as a man sitting at a desk smoking a cigar appeared on the television screen. He was wearing business casual clothing and was balding in the center of his head. He was a muscular man who looked like he could punch a someone's lights out if cornered.

"Smoking again, Dave? You know that will kill you."

"Camilla, you're my boss, not my mother. You've been nagging me for years, and it still hasn't killed me. I assume this call wasn't to nag me about my smoking." Dave had a gravelly low smoker's voice and an Austrian accent that caught Julius off guard.

"No, it wasn't. Meet your newest recruit, Julius Stetson," Gerald said, looking at Julius.

"It is an honor to meet you, sir, I watched you land on—"

"That's great, I don't have time for pleasantries. I'll meet you when you arrive here. It is my job to inspect every recruit before they join us here on Mars. You have a lot to learn before we bring you here. At least you aren't scrawny or fat. I'm sure our trainer Martin will handle you well."

Julius was devastated at Dave's apparent disinterest in him. This was not how Julius thought the first conversation with his childhood hero would go. This was the man who had inspired Julius's dream, and he was completely impersonal.

"Look, Mr. Hughes—" Julius started to say before he was cut off once more.

"Again, I don't have time for stories, Julius. Now I'm going to continue. You will train at a test facility in the New Mexican desert outside of Roswell. After your trainer gives you the thumbs up and I give you a pass, you'll travel to Mars."

Julius was fuming. He was shocked and upset that his childhood idol clearly viewed him as a waste of time. "I need to get back to work. We've got a category two terrastorm approaching the camps. Welcome aboard, Julius." The TV went black.

Camilla looked at Gerald as she stood up behind the desk. "Please arrange his travel with his trainer. I must return to Chicago. I have a meeting with the company presidents and the chairman. Julius, it was a pleasure meeting you." Camilla extended her hand.

Julius stood up and shook the woman's hand firmly, showing his resolve was not broken despite the disappointment this meeting had been.

"I am sure we'll meet again soon."

She broke the handshake and walked to the doors. She left, allowing the door to close with a thud. Gerald walked over to his desk and sat down in his chair. He adjusted it for his height. His facial expression changed, now looking more relaxed.

He pressed a red button under his desk that caused two dark-tinted glass screens to rise from the desk. Julius could not see through the dark-tinted glass.

"We need to set your travel to New Mexico. The goal is to get you there as soon as possible. Camilla has been generous enough to give you the remainder of today to say your goodbyes and get your affairs in order," Gerald said as he typed on his computer.

"I'll snail-mail some documents to your company email address. You'll need to sign them to go to training."

Julius was surprised at Gerald's friendlier demeanor. He realized Camilla's presence must have caused Gerald a lot of stress.

"Thank you, sir, for all your help with this and for this opportunity." Julius held his hand out to Gerald.

"Hold on just a second. You don't need to leave so quickly. Please take a seat. I wouldn't mind getting to know you a little more. I also want to personally apologize for the clerical error we made earlier. Additionally, I want to apologize if I've come off as rude or insensitive. I have to be that way, or people will walk all over me."

"Oh, of course, sir, and no need to apologize. I'm sure your job is stressful and makes it hard to keep track of all your employees." Julius was stunned at how kind the man was being

"You have no idea how hard it is to keep track. So tell me, why do you want to go to Mars?"

"Well, sir, I've wanted to go to Mars since I was a kid. I watched Dave Hughes land on the planet, and it captured my imagination. I went through my schooling, focusing on astronomy and survival skills so I would be ready to be an astronaut. I didn't go to college so I could join this company just to have a shot."

"Must've been hard actually meeting Dave a few minutes ago. He's not the sharpest tool in the shed. I've worked with him before, and let's say there is more to be desired."

"I am not going to lie, Mr. McGinnus. That made me feel terrible. He was my idol, and I don't think he even remembers my name."

"Well, I'm sorry about that. The problem with heroes is they never live up to what you expect them to be. I looked up to someone once or twice. My father gambled and drank away all my family's money. His demons drove me to go to MIT then the Marines." Gerald trailed off as he seemed to dwell on the thought of the Marines.

"Who was the second to let you down, sir?"

"Just a few people from my military days. You aren't worried about leaving home?"

Julius, not expecting a shift in the conversation, was taken back by the man's change in the conversation but rolled with it. "It hasn't really hit me yet. I'm sure it will when I get home to my family."

"You have family, then?"

"Yes, sir, I live with my parents and two siblings."

"Great, good to have some people at home. I never had a wife or kids. The military was my life, and running this facility is my life."

"I heard you were in the military, sir. Did you fight in the Amero Wars?"

"Yes, I did. We were in a forward operating base in Santa Rita, Colombia, when the Brazilians attacked. My unit and I were caught off guard. That's why we were so easily captured. The Admirals were the second group of people to let me down. I never forgave them for that.

"As they were marching us toward the border, I was able to steal a bayonet off the end of a Brazilian gun and stuck it into the man's throat. Four other soldiers ran at me when my compatriots started to fight with the other guards. I was beaten and got caught in the knife fight, where they carved me up, as you can see. We killed the troops and began our escape back to the North American Union lines.

"As we snuck back, I got caught in a minefield with a younger man who stepped on a mine and blew himself up. I lost my arm but was saved by a medic in our group. When we made it back, I was evacuated and honorably discharged. After the war, I started working at AMSPACE."

"I'm sorry for asking, sir," Julius said, noting Gerald's discomfort. Even so, Julius felt like something was off with his story. Marines in Colombia? The Marines were used in an amphibious assault against Rio. Maybe they were just staged there. Julius shook the thought from his head as Gerald replied.

"It's all right, it made me the man I am today. But I need to finish up these travel arrangements and complete some work."

Julius stood up and extended his hand. "Thank you, sir, for all you've done for me and the conversation. Always good to get to know someone new."

"The pleasure is mine, Julius. Good luck out there. Perhaps we will meet again."

Julius shook Gerald's right hand, which felt metallic and cold as ice. Despite the discomfort, Julius held the handshake. *That must be his mechanical arm from the mine explosion.* Julius didn't ask if it was out of respect.

"I see great things in your future, Julius. Maybe you'll even meet the chairman." Gerald quickly sat back down at his computer. He did not look up as Julius walked toward the door.

Julius exited the office and closed the door behind him. A wave of relief washed over him as he proceeded down the stairs. Meeting the chairman sounded like an amazing honor. He reflected on his exchange with Gerald for a minute. He was glad to have some interaction with his mysterious boss. He walked out the door and across the empty and dark factory floor with a new purpose.

On his way to the locker room, he caught a glance at a clock. It was long past the time he normally got home.

He strolled into the locker room and walked to his locker. He removed his phone and turned it on. The phone lit up with a single message from Alicia, wondering where he was.

"Hey! There's the big winner." Julius heard John's voice behind him. He turned around and looked at his two friends sitting on the benches. He had walked right past them on his way in.

"You guys didn't have to wait." Julius grabbed the rest of his belongings.

"Sit down and tell us what happened." John gestured to an area between him and Misty.

Without hesitation, Julius sat between his two friends.

"Spill," Misty said with an excited tone of voice.

"First off, I spoke to Dave Hughes." Julius started to say before John interrupted.

"Isn't he like, your idol?"

"Was my idol. Now I think he's an asshole. Cut me off and discounted everything I said."

"He didn't make you reconsider, did he?" Misty asked.

"No. I don't need him to follow my dreams."

"Good for you, Julius. Now tell me about Gerald," John said.

"What's do you want to know?"

"What was it like being in his office? The only people who go up there are the ones who get fired, so we can never know the secrets."

"Well, Gerald's office is quite simple. He's actually a nice guy and a war vet. You were right, Misty."

"I knew it!" Misty said.

"Y'all want to come over to my place? It's late and I could use a drink," Julius asked his friends.

"Yeah, we do," John said, speaking for his wife. They both stood up with Julius, and the three walked out of the locker room.

"I wonder how my mom is going to take this news."

"I'm sure she'll support you, Julius, but I bet she won't take it well at first," Misty said. The three walked out of the facility, then through the gate before they arrived at the deserted bus station.

Due to the late hour, the buses ran less frequently, so they waited twenty minutes for the next bus. John noticed his wife's demeanor had changed. "Misty, are you okay?"

"No, I'm not okay. Our friend is going to leave us."

"It's okay, Misty, I'll email and video message you."

"You better! John and I need to live vicariously through you!"

The small group fell silent. The bus eventually came up to them and stopped. The three boarded the empty bus and took seats near the exit located in the middle. They rode to Julius's stop and disembarked, the cool fall Michigan evening chilling them as they walked down the dimly lit sidewalk.

While they walked, Julius thought about how he would break this to his family. It was not going to go well if he didn't do a good job explaining this to his mom. When they arrived at Julius's house, they walked up and entered the unlocked front door.

SIX

❧

Last Night in Pontiac

"Mom, I'm home. John and Misty are here too." Marie rounded the corner from the living room.

"You're a lot later than usual."

"I'm sorry I missed dinner, Mom. I hope you didn't wait too long for me," Julius replied.

"We didn't." Marie walked back to the kitchen. Julius and his friends followed her as she kept talking. "It was my homemade mac and cheese. Shame you missed it. There're leftovers in the fridge."

"Thanks, Mom," Julius said, barely able to hold back his excitement. "Look, Mom, something happened today at work."

"What happened?" Marie asked, her voice cautiously interested.

"I won the lottery! I'm going to Mars!" Julius looked at his mom as her expression turned into total disbelief with a hint of sadness.

"You what?"

"I won the lottery to train to become a Martian miner." Julius was grinning from ear to ear.

"Bubby, that's amazing," Alicia said from the table.

Antonio was sitting next to her. "Good for you, just don't get eaten by a Martian." Julius ignored his brother's comment and looked back at his mom. She still seemed a little shocked but shook it off before she said, "Tell me more."

"I was called up to a meeting with the head of the factory and the president of Martian operations. We discussed the logistics of astronaut training, and I spoke to Dave Hughes," he said, suddenly feeling a bit giddy.

"Wait, you talked logistics? When do you leave?" Marie asked, interrupting Julius.

"I leave tomorrow morning," Julius said. Marie's expressed a look of shock. "Are you okay, Mom?"

"I'm sorry. I-I need a moment." Marie had a few tears forming in her eyes. She walked out of the kitchen to her bedroom, where she closed the door.

"What'd I do?" Julius turned to his friends.

"Dude, you just dropped an atom bomb on your mom. She handled it well at first, but you are leaving kind of quick," John said.

"Yeah, you literally just told her you're going to go away to another planet tomorrow," Misty echoed her husband.

"Oh, crap. I guess I was so excited about getting a chance I forgot I leave tomorrow."

"It's okay, man, we're here for you. A support cast, if you will." John slapped his friend on the back.

"I have your back, too, but I'm really going to miss you. You probably should talk to Mom," Alicia said as she looked up from her computerized paper.

"Thanks, you're right, sis." Julius walked over to his mom's door and knocked on it.

"Mom, can we please talk?" Julius asked.

Marie heard her son, but she was not ready to face him. She basically raised the kids on her own. Her husband, Carlos, was always on travel. He was an amazing man and provider for the family, but it was up to Marie to raise the kids. She thought about how she had done as a parent and she wouldn't have changed anything. This conversation with Julius was going to be hard for her.

Julius heard his mom speak softly asking him to come in. He turned the handle and pushed the door open. He saw his mom sitting in her reading chair in a corner of the room with a crumpled-up tissue in her hand.

In the other hand, she held a family picture from when they visited Chicago. The trip was his graduation gift in 2084, six years prior. Julius closed the door softly standing on the opposite side of the room relative to his mom. He remained silent trying to gather his thoughts, as his mom seemed to stare out into space.

He took a deep breath, calming his mind. Then he walked to her, kneeling by her chair. He took his mom's hands, and he looked into her eyes.

"Mom, I love you so much. You mean the world to me. I'm so sorry for dropping this on you like I did. It's a little overwhelming for me too. You've always told me to follow my dreams. This is my chance to follow the dream I've had since I was a kid. Can we please have a good night? I want to spend my last night in Pontiac with my family and friends."

He smiled warmly at his mom with tears welling up in his eyes. Julius's mom cracked a small smile and stood up. Julius rose to meet her. She pulled him in, and they embraced each other.

This was the most important hug of their lives. It might be the last one they'd give each other for a while. This thought made Julius shed a tear.

"Honey, I want you to follow your dreams. I'm just being self-ish." She sniffled as she spoke.

"I need to realize that you've moved past me being the primary fixture in your life. I'm now playing a supporting role, so I'll fully support you. It's hard for this mom to watch her son leave the state, let alone travel to another planet. So please be patient with me as I deal with this," she said.

"Of course, I'll be patient with you. I'm happy I have your sup-port." After a few moments of hugging, Julius felt his mom relax. "Are you feeling better, Mom?"

"Yes, honey. I just love you so much."

"I love you too, Mom," Julius felt happy and relieved his mom wasn't that upset anymore.

"This is going to be so hard for me."

"I know, but can't we have a nice last night together, no crying?"

"That's all I want. To spend a nice night with my son. You go back out there, I need some time to get my bearings."

"Okay, Mom," Julius said, leaving her room.

He returned to see that Misty, John, Alicia, and Antonio were sitting around the table, waiting.

"Mom will be out soon. John? Misty? Want a beer?"

"Can I have one too?" Antonio asked with a straight face.

"No! John, can you get two Cokes for Alicia and the Joker?"

"Sure thing, Julius." John stood up and grabbed two Cokes from the pantry. Meanwhile, Julius grabbed three beers from the refrigerator.

John and Julius sat back down at the table. John passed the Cokes to Alicia and Antonio. At the same time, Julius passed the beers out to John and Misty.

"So how long will you be gone?" Antonio asked in a more serious tone. Julius was not used to hearing his sarcastic little brother be serious.

"I'm not really sure."

"You aren't sure? Does this mean you won't be back for my graduation in May?" Alicia sounded a little upset.

"You know I don't want to miss it! I just don't know what the rules are. It's not like I'm going to be living in Ohio. It's Mars." Julius took a sip of his beer.

"Well, if you ask me, that sucks. I'm going to miss you." Angry tears formed in Alicia's eyes.

Julius stood up and went behind his upset sister. He put his arms over the back of the chair and hugged her. "I love you so much. I'll miss you too."

As Julius hugged his younger sister, he heard the sound of a beer bottle opening. Julius looked up to see Marie standing by the fridge, dabbing her eye with a tissue.

She walked over to the group and sat in the open chair at the head of the table. Alicia had stopped crying by this point, and Julius sat back down in his chair.

"You know, man, I'm going to miss you a lot," John said.

"Hey, we're going to miss him a lot," Misty cut in.

"I know you both will miss me, but don't you dare discount how much I'll miss you. You both have had by back since high school. It'll be hard to find friends as good as you up there on Mars."

"You got that right," Misty replied.

Marie cleared her throat before lifting her bottle. "To Julius," she said, holding back tears.

"To Julius! We'll miss him!" John lifted his beer. The others around the table lifted their drinks. After they held them in the air for a brief moment, the group pushed the drinks together.

Julius was the first to remove his beer from the drink collection, followed by everyone else. They all took a sip before Julius spoke.

"Each one of you means so much to me. I wouldn't be the man I am today without you. I'm really going to miss you all." Julius was getting a little choked up.

"You're going to do amazing things up there, Julius!" Marie said.

"It's where you're meant to be, not in that rundown factory," John chimed in.

Alicia looked down at her computerized paper and noticed the time. "Julius, I'm sorry. Please don't take this the wrong way, but it's 9:30, and I have school tomorrow."

She stood up from her chair and hugged Julius. As they hugged, she whispered in his ear, "I'm happy for you, bubby." Alicia broke the hug with her brother and walked to her room.

A pit formed in Julius's stomach as he watched his sister leave; he was really going to miss her. Marie turned to her youngest, "Ant, bed for you too.

"But, Mom," he started to say before Marie shot him a look.

"Fine, but Julius better not leave without saying goodbye," he said, going to his room.

During the conversation lull, Julius took out his phone to text his dad. He drafted and sent a text:

> *Dad, I wanted to call you, but I know you are on business in Colombia. I thought I would tell you I am going to be an astronaut for AMSPACE. If you find time to call me before I ship off tomorrow, I'd like to chat. I love you.*

Julius turned his attention back to his friends and mom. He observed that everyone's beers were low, so he grabbed another round of beers from the fridge. Marie refused another beer. "It's time for me to go to bed, dear. Good night, John. Good night, Misty."

Both Marie and Julius embraced, and she started to cry softly.

"Thank you, Mom, for everything."

"You're welcome. Just come back to me."

"I will, I promise." He released her from the hug, and Marie retired to her room.

Julius turned back to his friends before his phone buzzed with a new text message. He glanced as his phone and saw it from his father. The replying message made him smile:

> *Son, I'm so proud of you! You will do amazing things. Let me know how things shape up. I will always be there for you. We will video-message you when time permits. I want to hear about the whole story, if not from you I'm sure your mother will tell me.*

The friends, now alone, talked and drank more together. At some point during the night, Julius walked to his room and fell asleep on his bed. John and Misty passed out on the family room couches. Julius felt happy. He didn't know if it was because he spent a great night with his friends or if he was drunk, but he was content.

The next morning, Julius woke up with a pounding headache.

"Damn it, I didn't drink any water," Julius grumbled as he got out of bed. He stumbled out to the kitchen, where he saw his mom. She smiled at him while making waffles. His siblings were already eating them all dressed for school. John and Misty were no longer on the couches.

"Did they leave?"

"Yes. They left to go to work, but they left you a note." Marie handed Julius a handwritten note that read,

> Julius,
>
> Misty and I are so happy to call you one of our best friends. We will miss you dearly, but we both know that this is your dream. Go fight some Martians for us and send me a rock for my collection. Misty says to meet a girl up there and don't stay away for too long. We will keep old Frankenstein company for you. Don't forget to call or write.
>
> John Michel Andersen
> *Misty Miller Andersen*

"That was a nice letter. I'm going to miss them." Suddenly, he felt overwhelmed. He worried about leaving everything and everyone he knew for a job on another planet. He felt knots forming in his stomach as he fell deeper and deeper into his thoughts.

"They'll miss you too, as will we. You have good friends. I'll keep tabs on them for you." Marie went back to mixing the waffles.

Julius did not reply to his mom feeling sick to his stomach about leaving home. He went back to his room without saying a word

"Don't forget to pack, Bubby," Alicia called after him as she poured syrup on her second waffle.

On his way back to his room, Julius snagged a glass of water and ibuprofen to help his hangover. Having returned to his room, Julius grabbed a suitcase and stared at it blankly.

"This is so stressful," Julius said to himself as he tried to take deep breaths to relax. Eventually, he was able to calm his mind and could think clearly about what he needed to pack.

He packed some underwear, shirts, pants, shorts, socks, and shoes. He then dragged his suitcase out to the kitchen. As he left his room, Julius stopped and slapped himself on the forehead.

"I almost forgot."

He scooped up his passport and AMSPACE Rocket Development Factory ID, then left his room. Entering the kitchen, Marie was putting more waffles on the table. He sat down and began to eat his breakfast with his mom and siblings.

"Oh crap, I forgot to sign my documents." Julius jumped up and rushed into his mom's room to grab the family AI-Pad. He logged into his e-mail and hastily signed the documents Gerald had sent him the night before, without reading them. He returned to the table and sat down and prepared to eat, relived he had dodged a bullet. Before he could bite into his waffle, a hard knock came at the door.

Marie huffed and walked out of the kitchen to the front hall. She opened the door to reveal a man in a charcoal gray suit, blue shirt, and aviator sunglasses. Two bald men flanked the gray-suited man. They wore black suits with similar sunglasses.

Marie's eyes were drawn to what was attached to the two men's hips. Each man had a plasma pistol. Her heart rate increased, and sweat formed on her brow. The man in the gray suit was about Julius's height or slightly shorter. His hair, a very dark brown with gray hairs peppered on it, was buzzed like a soldier's.

His face was stuck in a slight frown, and his brows were folded as though his was focused or angry. "What can I do for you, gentlemen?"

"Good morning, ma'am. I'm here to collect Julius Stetson for his training. My name is Martin Fisher. I'll be his trainer." The man extended his hand. She looked down at the hand and took it in a firm shake.

"Is Julius home?" Julius's mom turned her head and looked back to the kitchen.

Julius met her gaze. She had a longing look in her eyes, the same look all moms have when their children leave. It hit Julius like a bullet in the heart. He felt guilty for what he was about to do.

The feeling passed as Julius stood up from the table and hugged both Antonio and Alicia goodbye. He grabbed his suitcase and walked into the front hall before he stood behind his mom.

"We'll have a lot of time to talk in the car to get acquainted. I'll let you say your goodbyes." Martin turned around to walk back down the front walk.

The two men followed Martin after briefly inspecting Julius. He looked and smiled at his mom. He wrapped his arms around her, embracing her in a tight hug, the last one for a long time. The sudden embrace made his mom tear up.

"I love you, Julius, be safe." She held her oldest son tightly.

"I love you too, Mom. I'll be safe, promise."

Marie broke their hug. "Go on. Mars is calling." She gestured for him to go, her tears falling down her face.

Julius looked to his mom, "I'll call soon, Mom." He walked down the front walk toward a black four-door town car in the street.

The guards stood outside the car, one was by the driver's door and the other next to the open back door on the passenger side. The guard by the open back door gestured for Julius to enter the vehicle. He left his suitcase on the sidewalk before he entered the back of the car. Martin was already in the seat next to him. He felt nervous as he got into the car. He thought about what would happen on the long ride to New Mexico.

SEVEN

The New Mexico Research Facility

"Hello, sir, I'm Julius." Julius put his hand out to shake Martin's.

"Sir? That's a good start, kid! I'm Martin Fisher," Martin almost shouted back in a booming voice. He grasped Julius's hand and squeezed before shaking it hard. Julius felt his hand go a little numb while he looked into the dark-green eyes of the man.

If Julius wasn't anxious about the situation before he got in the car, he was now. Martin released Julius's hand as the vehicle's hood slammed shut. Julius realized this was where one of the bald men had placed his suitcase. The bodyguards took their seats in the front of the car and began driving away from his house.

Julius looked out the window. His mom, brother, and sister were waving as the car silently glided down the road. He smiled and felt his heart yearn to stay with his family just a little longer. He pushed this feeling down as the car turned off his street onto the main road.

"Dumb question, Mr. Fisher, but why did the driver place my suitcase where the electric motor and batteries go?"

"This car is fit to fly on the Skyway, so the trunk is used for the scaled-down AM-Drive propulsion engine." The car drove west through downtown Pontiac before turned south on US-24. Julius's face lit up with excitement, he was in a flying car.

The Skyway was a two-leveled intercountry highway. The first level was built like the original United States Interstate Highway System. The second level was designed for flying cars to cruise at sub supersonic speeds.

With interstates getting more crowded, the United States had begun creating small sections of Skyway in major US cities to prevent congestion. After the unification of the North American Union, it was expanded and completed before the Amero Wars. Some cities still had not built skyways on their outer belts; Detroit was one of those cities.

"You're probably interested in who I am and what I do for the company? I also think you want to know where we're going," Martin said.

"Yes, sir," Julius responded.

"We're on our way to the New Mexico Training Facility in Roswell. I'll help you learn to survive the harsh Martian environment."

The car stopped at a red light, to the right was the entrance to I-696, not Skyway capable, which would lead to I-275. The car turned right and drove up the ramp and onto the interstate.

"So, Julius, tell me a little about yourself. Why join up to be a miner?"

"Mr. Fisher, I've always wanted to be an astronaut. As a kid, I watched Dave Hughes land on Mars for AMSPACE. In the late '80s, I witnessed the next completion of the Neil Armstrong Moon Colony. I've always wanted to be in space, and this is my chance."

"Please call me Martin. Mr. Fisher was my dad. We enjoy having passionate candidates in the program, but keep it in check. There have been many avoidable deaths because people get too excited."

"I see, sir. I'll do my best." Julius glanced out the windshield, where a large green interstate sign said "I-94 Skyway Exit."

The driver removed his hands from the steering wheel, letting the AI navigate off I-275 onto the Skyway onramp. The car accelerated forward, heading straight for a large ramp like a hover-bike stunt jump.

Even though he knew it was safe, Julius gripped the seat tightly. The ramp was designed to catapult cars into the air to reach the Skyway. There was a metallic popping noise as the car's trunk unlatched, extending a small tail. The action also exposed the car's miniature AM-Drive engine used to propel the car forward.

The car's speed steadily increased; wings unfolded from the undercarriage as the car neared the end of the ramp. Time seemed to slow down as the car rocketed off the ramp. All the occupants of the vehicle felt a brief moment of weightlessness. Julius watched out the window. He felt a little fear as the car sailed through the air. A jolt snapped his head back against the headrest as the propulsion engine increased its speed. The car rose up and entered the Skyway and rapidly approached five hundred miles per hour.

Astonished at what just happened, Julius sat in his seat with his mouth agape. He used to watch cars launch onto the I-75 Skyway down the street from his house. He never imagined he would experience it firsthand.

"Pretty amazing, right?" Martin smiled as he enjoyed the look of wonder on Julius's face.

"Very amazing, I never imagined I'd take a ride on the Skyway." Julius looked down at the cars stuck in traffic below on the concrete I-94.

"Julius, I'm going to be straight with you. Since we'll be arriving in the New Mexico in three hours, I'm going to give you a tranquilizer. This way, you'll be alert when we arrive."

Martin pulled a syringe out of the seat back pocket and pulled the plastic cover off. Before Julius could even react, Martin stuck Julius in his left leg, and quickly pushed the plunger down.

"Martin, what are you doing?" Julius started to feel weak and light-headed. The liquid in his body began to affect him immediately. Darkness clouded his vision, starting from the outside and moved in. He slumped against the window in the back of the flying car as it traveled to Roswell.

While Julius and Martin traveled on the Skyway, Camilla González walked down a hallway in AMSPACE corporate headquarters. The building resided at 400 North Lake Shore Drive in Chicago, Illinois. It stood at an impressive nine hundred feet tall. Originally the site of a large residential skyscraper bombed by resistance countries during the Amero Wars, the AMSPACE Building was created to symbolize the progress that came out of the war.

The building started in a smaller base but then expanded outward as the building's height increased, like Walkie-Talkie in downtown London. The building's design was chosen to symbolize AMSPACE's passion to look toward the stars. Across the top of the building on all four sides was the company name proudly displayed for the city of Chicago in large red letters.

Camilla was on the eightieth floor and approaching two double oak doors. She opened one to reveal a large conference room. Inside the room around a large bloodwood rectangular table sat nineteen other people dressed in suits.

The room was so dim it left the perimeter of the room dark. The nineteen people sat in leather chairs. Camilla sat in one of the two free seats. The other open seat was larger and reserved for the chairman. She pivoted her chair to face the chairman's empty seat.

Camilla was relieved she didn't arrive after the chairman; he didn't like tardiness. She looked around the room; it was filled with the presidents of all the AMSPACE divisions.

As she looked around at the other presidents, a small door behind the chairman's chair opened. Everyone looked toward it and stood up; a dark figure walked out of it and toward the table.

The chairman came into the light, revealing a middle-aged man of Germanic descent. His hair was a light brown with small gray hairs sprinkled in. He stood taller than the average man and carried himself with a confidence few people do.

He stood behind his chair and flashed a wide, white smile to the room. "Good morning, everyone, thank you all for being here for our weekly company status meeting. I'm not going to waste time. I have an interview with American Union News about the future of Mars. Please take your seats."

Everyone sat down, as did the chairman. "I want to only hear about a few important business areas. Mr. Sanders, please give me a status on auto production."

A black man in a suit across from Camilla began to speak. "Markets are exploding in the East Asia Trading Block, sir. We expect a good quarter and a continuing expanding market. There is stiff competition from General Ford, but we anticipate our new AM Drive propulsion engines from our research and development department will reduce that risk."

"Good, I expect detailed reports and charts on my desk tomorrow. I want to keep tabs on that market. If our takeover of Chrysler-KIA isn't going to turn a long-term profit, we need to spin them back off."

"Understood, sir, I'll have those reports by you COB."

"Thank you. Mrs. Turner, military contracting status." The chairman turned his head to a woman three seats down from Camilla.

"We've recently won the new air carrier contract for the United Forces Navy and expect to build twenty-five carriers on that contract with the same new propulsion engines Mr. Sanders mentioned. In addition, we expect to win the contract for new communication satellites."

"That is excellent news, Mrs. Turner. I hope we're planning to build those satellites to allow company use."

"Yes, sir, we're working on the government contract to add our capabilities in and not interfere with the government side."

"Let's talk offline about how we can write that proposal."

The chairman shifted his gaze to Camilla. "Miss González, please enlighten me on the status of Mars."

Camilla cleared her throat before speaking. "Sir, we're currently tracking another shipment of assets from the Mars territory. It should arrive at our research center in British Columbia within the day. We hope that this shipment will help us understand more about what we are mining. I believe this shipment will help us increase our profits from the planet. The scientists plan on running specific tests on the shipment, I would be happy to give more information to you in a more," Camilla said, then paused, looking around the room before continuing, "secured environment, sir. Additionally, sir, we had an accident on Mars that has left us shorthanded. I would like permission to immediately send our current trainees to Mars as soon as I think they are needed."

"You have my permission to send them. Related to your work in Canada, I expect you on the next Hyperloop to Vancouver. We will speak again after the shipment arrives, then you can tell me more about your testing plans. I want a status when you arrive at our Planetary Research Facility."

The chairman looked around the room to see if there were any other people he wanted to talk to. "That's all I have, thank you all for attending the meeting. If we did not get to your business area, expect a phone call from me after my interview."

He stood up from his chair and returned to the door in the back of the room.

Camilla stood up from her chair and exited the conference room. She walked to the elevator and took it down to the twenty-fourth floor. She went to her office and gathered her belongings before taking a self-driving ULift to Union Station.

Julius jolted awake as the car stopped at an off-ramp outside of Roswell, New Mexico. It was already on the ground like a traditional car.

"Where are we?" Julius groggily asked before realizing what happened to him. "You drugged me!"

Martin sat calmly on the opposite side of the car.

"Relax, Julius. I did that so you could be focused for the training, plus I could smell the booze on your breath back in Michigan. It helped cure your hangover." Martin smirked.

"Still, I didn't want that drug, even if you cured my hangover."

"Well, kid, remember to always read contracts, because in the papers you signed this morning it stated that AMSPACE can do anything they need to make sure their miners are in top shape."

Julius was shocked that his signature allowed Martin to drug him. "This is how you get to Mars, kid, by following orders."

"Fine. Can't I at least have some warning next time?" Julius looked out the window at the desert landscape.

"Maybe. No promises. We are just a few minutes away from the perimeter of the facility," Martin said, pointing at a gray line on the horizon. Julius looked out the window as he rubbed his right forearm. It was sore. *Must've slept on it funny*, Julius thought to himself.

The car drove down a paved road toward the perimeter. As they approached, the gray line increased in size. The perimeter was an immense wall made of reinforced concrete and measured forty feet tall. The top had a perfectly circular barbed wire that ran the entire length of the wall.

The car approached a twenty-foot-tall steel grated gate that had a small guard shack next to it. Scattered around the gate were steel Czech hedgehogs, antivehicle obstacles made of carbon nanofiber angled beams. They were used to force all approaching vehicles into a single-file row. In addition, to the Czech hedgehogs, large assault robots roamed around the entrance.

The robots walked on two long legs with knee joints. The legs attached to a double-tapered, oval-shaped body. The upper part of the wide body had a large black screen with a red slit used for the targeting system. To the left and right of the body were circular pods that closed to a point at the front. Julius suspected that those were the primary weapon system. The bots were a light forest green, so they stuck out like a sore thumb in the desert landscape. This was to deter any would-be intruder.

The car maneuvered around the maze of barriers, stopping next to the guard shack. They were close enough for the driver to speak to the guard. Two of the robots stopped walking and pivoted to focus on the car. The side weapon systems opened to reveal quad plasma cannons with a laser dot sight for each independent plasma cannon. Julius tensed up and felt intimidated by the assault robots. Having seen what plasma cannons did to enemy tanks in the Amero Wars, he did not want to find out what they would do to a small town car.

The man in the driver's seat rolled down his window and waited. Julius looked at the guard shack; he saw the guard was dressed in full military tactical gear. The guard stood up from his position and walked out of his shack to the open car window. His face had three grotesque scars that extended from the top of his right temple down to the left side of his neck. Julius thought it looked like he got in a fight with a bald eagle and lost. He had a bionic eye in place of his real eye.

The guard spoke roughly. "AMSPACE New Mexico Research Facility IDs for all occupants."

The man in the passenger seat handed the man in the driver's seat three IDs.

"The robots detected four heat signatures in the car." The guard narrowed his eyebrows in suspicion. The robots also changed their stance to a staggered, aggressive position bracing themselves to fire. Julius felt sweat trickle down his neck as he saw the robots prepare to attack.

"That's the new recruit. He's here for training," the driver said.

"Carry on, but be prepared for the next guard," the man grumbled, slowly handing back the IDs. He returned to the shack and pressed a button on his desk. There was an intense sound of metal screeching as the large gate slid open.

Julius watched as the robots changed their stance and closed their weapons systems before then resumed their patrol. The car lurched forward and drove though the large open gate, which slowly closed after the car entered. He expected to see a large building on the other side of the wall, but he was disappointed to see more desert.

"What gives?" Julius asked Martin, irritated.

"We need to have space between the wall and the research facility in case an aerial incursion occurs. There needs to be room for the artificial gravity generators."

"The artificial gravity generators are located underground? Is their purpose to increase the gravitational force of the earth in a specific area and bring down an aircraft?"

"Yes, that's exactly what they are used for. It makes sure the facility is protected. It was a thrill to watch the testing of that system. If you're lucky, you'll see a carcass of an aircraft around."

Julius still had a lot of questions. "I understand this facility needs to be protected. I just want to know why you need to have it so heavily protected? Isn't it just a training facility for astronauts?"

"We take the safety and protection of our employees very seriously." Martin's voice almost sounded rehearsed. That struck Julius as odd, but he paid it no mind as his eyes were once again drawn out the window.

On the horizon was a multistory building on the top of a small hill. It was conspicuous against the barren desert horizon. As the car approached, the building grew larger, and Julius was able to make it out better. He saw the building was an off-white color and had lots of windows. It appeared have wings attached to the main building and multiple unattached buildings scattered around the campus and in the desert.

"That is quite a large facility for just training people."

"Only the best for our astronauts," Martin replied with a hint of exasperation in his voice.

Turning away from Martin, Julius observed a blue haze at the base of the hill. Initially, he thought he was seeing things, but as the car drew closer, he saw it was another perimeter fence. The fence was much different than the first one. Blue plasma beams protruded from the ground measuring ten feet tall. They were placed six inches apart to prevent anyone or anything from squeezing between them.

A metallic line ran across the bottom of the blue beams that provided their power via a subterranean wall.

"That wall looks like a series of lightsabers," Julius said softly.

"They call it the Saber Wall. It surrounds all critical buildings for the company on Earth."

"That's a perfect name," Julius remarked. He was a *Star Wars* fan and appreciated any reference to the old films.

Julius saw the car was approaching a large steel building that broke up the plasma wall. Located on the structure's roof, were shorter beams to complete the wall. Julius stared at the blue beams like a moth drawn to a flame. He realized how secure this wall was; there was no way a car could penetrate unless they got creative. The vehicle would be like cheese going through a grater.

The driver stopped the car ten feet to the right of the reinforced steel guard bunker. The door to the metal building slid open, and a woman in full tactical desert camo stepped out. She walked over to the car. This woman was more intimidating than the first guard. Her plasma pistol was clipped to her hip, and she had an assault rifle swung over her shoulder.

As she approached the car, Julius could see strands of long red hair sticking out from under her nanofiber helmet. She had green eyes that looked like they could pierce nanofiber armor. The driver rolled down Martin's window.

"Mr. Fisher, I understand you're bringing us a new recruit. Please give me his identification papers, and we'll get him an AMSPACE New Mexico Research Facility ID."

Martin looked at Julius before nodding. Julius reached into his pocket and produced his passport along with his AMSPACE Rocket Development Factory ID. He quickly handed them to Martin, who, in turn, handed them to the woman.

"Hope this is enough for you, Megan." Martin smiled at the woman.

"I'll be the judge of that, Mr. Fisher," she said dryly before she turned and returned to the bunker.

Julius sat there a little nervously for about five minutes before Megan returned. She handed Martin Julius's passport and his new ID card. He gave it to Julius.

"Thank you," he said as he inspected the new card. The front of the ID had his picture and said, "Julius Stetson: Martian Miner 7744."

"You may proceed, Mr. Fisher." She smiled quickly before looking back to give the bunker a firm nod.

The fifteen beams directly in front of the car deactivated, and the driver slowly drove over the metal speed bump. Once across, Julius looked back at the wall and saw the beams had reactivated, closing off the entrance.

The driver drove up the hill and pulled the car into a drop off roundabout by the main entrance of the building. Martin exited the car first, followed by Julius, then the two men who walked to the hood of the vehicle and retrieved Julius's suitcase.

Something caught Julius's eye. Looking to his left, he saw a beautiful black marble fountain that spelled out "AMSPACE." The water falling over the marble glistened in the hot New Mexican sun. *That looks like it belongs in a postcard*, Julius thought to himself as he stared.

"Julius, time to go." Martin gestured toward the sliding glass doors to their right.

"Yes, sorry." Julius caught up to Martin, going through the doors.

Past the doors was an elegant, grand lobby that would make King George jealous. The floor was a dark green granite that stretched into a waiting area full of empty seats. Julius thought few people had ever used the waiting area, given all the security of the complex. A receptionist sat behind a mahogany desk. Next to the desk, the same beams of plasma blocked access to the next room.

The receptionist, an older lady, about sixty-five, looked up from her computer and smiled at Julius and Martin.

"Please scan your badges, gentlemen."

Martin and Julius scanned their badges on a simple badge reader. Julius looked up and saw a more advanced flying security drone than the ones at his old factory. It seemed to be scanning them to make sure they are who their badges say they were.

"Thank you, gentlemen." The receptionist looked at the plasma beams, which deactivated. Martin walked through, followed closely by Julius. As soon as they were past the barrier, it reactivated.

"Julius, this way please," Martin said, turning to the right at the T-corner at the back of the lobby.

EIGHT

The Mainframe

Julius turned right and followed Martin up four flights of stairs to another hallway. They walked down to an office door with an LED nameplate that displayed "Martin G. Fisher" in blue letters. Below his name were the words "Training Specialist" in smaller letters.

Martin flung open the door and walked in. Julius followed and was greeted with the smell of pine, courtesy of a scented candle. Julius spotted the candle atop an early-twentieth-century drafting desk. The rest of the office was not much to look at. Behind the desk was a large brown leather couch with a small coffee table. The couch faced a massive glass window. Outside the window, Julius saw something only the great science fiction writers of old could dream up.

Beyond the window was a white room that measured five hundred feet by five hundred feet. Many different small black outlines formed hundreds of squares. At the center of each square was a black circle. The room looked so out of place, its presence puzzled Julius, and Martin knew it.

"Marvelous, isn't it?" Martin asked, sitting on the couch, holding a tablet in his hands that produced a hologram with the Apple-IBM logo.

"I'm sure I would marvel at it more if I knew what it was."

"Maybe this will help."

Martin pressed some buttons on the hologram. Julius gazed into the room as the black circles inside the squares began to glow with white light. The light radiated out of the dots sending shimmering beams down to the ground.

Beams also shot out of the floor a few feet, where they created a platform. It sparkled as it changed from a platform of white to a full-sized football field.

"That's impossible!" Julius's mouth was wide open.

"It's a computer simulation on steroids Julius, and it's entirely possible. We call it the Mainframe. It uses a massive supercomputer located underground to build the world of my choosing."

"Is it real? Or is it like one of those fake virtual reality rooms that rich people live in?" Julius's mind raced back to classic movies he'd watched as a kid like *The Matrix* and *Ready Player One*.

"The simulation is very real. It uses particles programmed by my tablet to create the physical objects. You won't be able to tell the difference between the real world and the Mainframe."

That statement scared Julius. If this machine existed, then people could become trapped in it forever. It would be a real prison, no one could know if they were in it or not.

Julius shook this thought out of his head. "Do I get to use it for training? And when do I start?"

"Yes, and you start right now." Martin swiped a bar on the hologram. A bookshelf to the right of the door they entered flipped up. The action revealed an all-white space suit with a blue outline along the panels that dotted the suit. An AMSPACE logo resided on the left panel of the chest. On its back was a pack that held the air tank, critical onboard computer, and communications equipment.

A white circular helmet rested at the foot of the suit. It was metallic like a tin can and had a large clear section to allow the user to see out.

"Grab the suit, and go down those stairs." Martin turned his hand like a door handle in the hologram.

"What stairs?" Julius looked around the room. A door to Julius's right swung open to reveal a set of stairs.

"Those stairs. Doctors will administer a physical to get your genetic makeup. We need it to be able to heal you if you get injured. I've lost too many recruits to simple things. I don't want to have to take you to the morgue."

"I don't want you to take me to the morgue either. Are you sure this is safe? I could die in there?"

"Yes, it's as safe as you make it. Be smart and stay alive. If you don't want to continue the training, we can arrange for your return to Pontiac."

"No way! I'm staying!" Julius felt a rush of confidence.

"Good! Get your ass downstairs!"

Julius left his suitcase by the window and moved quickly to the other side of the room where he gathered up the space suit. Swiftly, he walked to the open door and passed through the threshold.

The door slammed behind him and locked itself. Julius had only one choice, keep moving forward. He descended the stairs and knocked on the metal door, at the bottom. A metallic ringing sound echoed around the small staircase. After his knocking, Julius stood in silence for a few moments. Just when he was about to knock again, a loud symphony of clicking sounds emitted from the door as it unlocked itself.

The door opened to reveal a large shower room. Gray tile lined the walls and floors, and six showers were divided by stainless-steel stalls on each side. Another metallic door resided opposite the one he entered. Julius noticed that one of the shower stalls had a faded blue hospital gown hung up with a towel.

"Am I supposed to shower before this test?"

"Mr. Stetson, please place the space suit down in the shower stall adjacent to the one with the towel." A male voice said over a hidden speaker in the room.

He hurriedly put his suit down, waiting for further instructions. They came quickly.

"Mr. Stetson, please remove your clothes and shower. Once done, put on the hospital gown, grab your suit, and come to the next room."

This isn't what I pictured, Julius thought to himself as he removed his clothes, hanging them on a hanger. Behind him, the shower sprang to life.

Julius slowly approached the shower and put his foot in to check the temperature. He expected ice-cold water but was pleasantly surprised when it was actually warm. He quickly showered using the provided soaps.

This has to be to sterilize me for the medical exam, Julius thought to himself as he relaxed, letting the hot water flow over his hair.

Without warning, the water changed from warm and comfortable to ice-cold.

"Ahh!" Julius yelped, as he jumped out of the shower

"Dicks." Julius cursed under his breath as he toweled off. "I was enjoying that." He continued to complain as he put on the hospital gown. Leaving his clothes behind, Julius grabbed his suit and knocked on the far door.

It swung open, revealing a white room filled with medical equipment. *This just keeps getting better*, Julius thought to himself while he scanned the room. Most of the equipment was foreign to him. It was not the standard furnishings he saw at his general practitioner's office.

There was a more reinforced metal door across the room. In the center-left of the room was a chair that looked like a dentist's chair. Behind the chair were many men and women in different color scrubs, surgical masks, and medical caps. This sight alone gave Julius a hot flash as sweat began to form all over his body.

"Please place your space suit over there," a woman in gray scrubs and purple surgical gloves pointed to a corner of the room.

Julius nodded and set the suit down carefully before he turned around.

"Julius, take a seat in the chair," a man in teal scrubs ordered. Still nervous, Julius walked over to the chair and sat down. Once he was in the chair, everyone in the room began to move around like a bunch of angry drones. He observed them grabbing different equipment and charts.

A nurse handed a see-through tablet that looked more like a pane of glass to the man who had asked Julius to sit in the chair.

"Okay, we need to get this test going." The man looked at the nurse.

"What's happening? Can I at least get an explanation of what you all are about to do to me?" Julius's voice quavered a bit, indicating his anxiety level was rising.

"Oh, it's standard procedure, Mr. Stetson. Did Martin not inform you of the details of this medical test?" The man looked up from the tablet.

"Not in detail. He just said I needed to come down here for a body scan."

"I see. Well, we'll take your DNA first. Then we will use that chair to scan your whole body to get its composition and makeup. The body scan is for nanobots to be programmed to repair your body if you have an accident. Additionally, we'll monitor your vitals. Any potential issues that come up during your training, we'll know about it and know how to treat it. We can't let something as treatable as asthma keep you from going to the stars."

While the doctor spoke, a woman stepped up to Julius. "Please open your mouth, sir." The woman was holding a metallic Q-tip.

He complied. The nurse quickly put it in his mouth. The Q-tip opened, and a small knife took a small piece of skin from inside his mouth before it retracted, closing around the sample. The nurse took the sample to a machine on the other side of the room to log it.

Without warning, Julius felt pain in his arm. "Ow!" Julius looked to see a man in gray scrubs had stuck him in the arm with a syringe. The man drew some blood and took it over to the same machine.

"A little warning would have been appreciated."

"Sorry, Mr. Stetson, we have to make this quick," the man behind the tablet said as he kept messing with the tablet's settings. "Can we get the scanners set up please?"

The other people around the room began to grab what looked like street lamps on wheels. They had long poles with an overhanging perpendicular line. Julius determined that it was an infrared light strip. There were many of these scanners placed all around Julius, about ten in total. He was perplexed as to why they needed so many.

What are all those for? Julius thought to himself as he watched the workers adjust the scanners to their optimal positions.

"We're going to start the scan now," the doctor announced to the room. Immediately, people hurriedly backed away from Julius.

"Why are you moving away from me?"

The doctor finally realized that Julius was not comfortable in this situation. "We're moving so we don't interfere with the readings. One mistake and you could end up with an extra limb."

That statement made Julius cringe. The doctor did not have the best bedside manner. A nurse quickly walked up to Julius and threw a thin blanket over his body and handed him what looked like tanning goggles.

"What are these for?"

"They're meant to protect you from any additional radiation, but they aren't thick enough to prevent the scanners from doing their job," the nurse explained as she backed away.

Julius put on the goggles and tried to relax. The doctor pressed his finger on his tablet, and an elliptical glass wall rose from the floor, cutting Julius off from the medical staff. The wall separating him from the rest of the room intimidated him and made him wonder if this procedure was truly safe.

"Three, two, one." The doctor pressed a button, initiating the scan.

Julius could not see what occurred outside; the goggles restricted most of his vision. The scanners lit up and shot different wavelengths at his body.

Across the room, a model of Julius's body started rendering on the doctor's tablet. It appeared one layer at a time as the scanners cycled through the wavelengths.

Once the scanning concluded, the wall was lowered, and the medical staff buzzed around the room again. The blanket and goggles were removed, and the scanners were placed in a hidden closet with a vertically opening door.

"Our tests are complete, Mr. Stetson. Please proceed to the next room." The doctor turned his back toward Julius.

Dazed from the exposure, Julius looked at the two doors and could not remember which one he used before. Making up his mind, he walked toward one of the doors. As he was walking, the doctor spoke up.

"Wrong way, Mr. Stetson."

Julius stopped and looked at him with a confused look on his face.

"You entered via that door. You want to go out the other one. Over there." The doctor's voice was patronizing as he pointed at the correct door.

"Oh, right." Julius turned to head for the door the doctor indicated.

"Mr. Stetson."

"Huh?"

"Don't forget to put on the suit. We don't want you to suffocate." The doctor pointed at the suit still in the corner.

"Suffocate?" Julius questioned groggily, walking back over to the suit, his mind racing to understand. He began to wonder how he could suffocate if air was plentiful in the facility.

"Yes, suffocate. It's not my job to explain, but good luck out there!" The doctor turned his back on Julius once again.

Frustrated at the company's policy to tell him as little as possible, Julius grabbed his suit and walked back over to the opposite door.

Once at the door, Julius pushed the heavier door open. The room he entered was a tiny with almost no room for him to maneuver.

My closet's bigger than this, Julius thought as he looked around. He turned his head to the right and saw yet another thick metal door.

How many of these doors are there?

Behind him, the door he walked in closed and clicked as it locked. Next to him, was a small metal bench with compression shorts and an undershirt on top. Julius placed the suit and helmet on the bench. A pale red light bathed the room from a single bulb. Julius removed the hospital gown and put on the undergarments.

"Put the suit on, Julius," Martin's voice echoed through the small room. Julius looked at the white suit, perplexed. He had no clue how he was going to put on the suit. He inspected it and saw a button and key. The button was on the back, and the key resided in the front, a built-in lockout to prevent accidental separation.

Julius pressed the button and turned the key, and the suit released the bottom half with a click sound. As he slipped on the lower part of the suit, his body was trembling with excitement. He was putting on a space suit.

With shaking hands, he reached down and put on the top half of the suit. It was significantly heavier than the lower half. Julius held it up then shimmied it down his torso until he heard an automatic click. He grabbed at the top to try and remove it to check if it was really locked into place. Once satisfied, Julius extended his arm to grasp the final piece of equipment, the helmet.

He placed it over his head and moved it around until he heard the same click, but this time there was an additional pressurization noise.

"Okay, Martin. I have the suit on. Now what?" Julius received no response. He looked around the tiny room for some clue as to where he was. As he scanned around, he realized where he was, an air lock.

"This is insane!"

"No, it's training!" Martin's voice filled Julius's helmet, sending a chill down Julius's spine.

"Does that door lead to where I think it does? Do I want to know what waits for me in the Rendering Room?"

"You know, I like that name, Julius. We should call it the Rendering Room instead of the Mainframe. We picked the Mainframe originally because it sounded better than the technical name. Who calls something Stimulation Immersion Machine, or SIM? It will be what you expect. It's not like I'm going to drop you into an asteroid mining operation, or a black hole. I want to keep you alive, for a bit."

Julius was anxious and excited as he heard clicking emit from the door as it unlocked. The pale red light in the room flashed, signaling the obvious—the door was opening.

"Here's the deal, Julius. Your suit has an air tank. That is why the top half was heavier, meaning it will last quite a while. When you go out there, you'll be standing in the middle of a Martian moonscape. The heads-up display on your helmet will activate and show you the status of your suit. I'll explain more once you're in the Mainframe."

Julius was thrilled about what he was about to witness on the other side of the door. As it opened, a bright light blinded Julius for a few seconds. Julius lifted his arm to shield his eyes before they adjusted. He saw something that should not be possible.

On the other side of the threshold was brown soil with a slight red tint. In his general vicinity were red rocks strewn everywhere. The sky was a hazy light blue, much different than the blue sky of Michigan. It looked more like Salt Lake City during an inversion event.

"No fucking way!" Julius was unable to control his excitement. His body shook with exhilaration, like a kid meeting Mickey Mouse for the first time. He extended his leg, taking a cautious step through the doorway and onto the soil. After taking a few more cautious paces, Julius stopped and looked back at the door.

"No!" Julius gasped as he saw the door had disappeared. Instead, he gazed upon more soil and a few small mountains that dotted the horizon.

"It will mess with your head for a bit. I can assure you that this is as real as Mars. Even the air around you has the consistency of the air on Mars. The atmosphere is improving, thanks to our crack terra-forming team, but it is still hazardous."

"How can I not see you or any of the doors I saw from your office?" Julius picked up a rock and inspecting it. It was so realistic; he could not believe a machine created this.

"The simulation acts like a two-way mirror I can see into the simulation, but you cannot see out. We had to make this as real as possible. Now please walk in that direction."

"What direction?"

"Look up."

Julius looked up and saw a large arrow appeared in the sky.

"That's not realistic."

"It works, though. Just go that way, your shelter will be there."

Julius threw the rock aside and began to walk in the direction Martin pointed. Since the gravity was lower, Julius was almost bounding his way to the shelter.

After about fifteen minutes of galloping through the Martian landscape, Martin ordered Julius to stop. Julius was on cloud nine. He could not believe what he was doing.

"How is this not real?" Julius asked himself. He looked into the distance and saw a large dust cloud.

What's that? Julius thought before his question was answered. A large forklift emerged from the dust cloud. It looked like the industrial forklift John drove in the factory. There were a few differences. It had no driver and was significantly larger than the one Julius was familiar with.

"What is that thing carrying? And why didn't you just have whatever it is render in front of me?" Julius wondered aloud, seeing a strange structure on the forks.

"It's your shelter, and we want it to be as realistic as possible. Those forklifts move shelters and other things around on Mars." Martin's voice crackled over the commlink as the industrial vehicle stopped a few feet from Julius.

The forklift lowered the shelter down to rest on the soft Martian soil. The structure was made of three bubbles. The center was larger than the two other bubbles. They were connected by tubes that were large enough for an average person to walk through.

The shelter had three doors that led to individual metal air locks to allow for multiple points of access. One resided on the central bubble, and the other two were on the smaller bubbles. The shelter's skin was white, with orange stripes and a few small windows in each section.

Julius stood about fifteen feet away from the shelter as he watched the forklift drive back the way it came before it disappeared in the distance. He started to walk toward the main door of the shelter when miniature explosions emanated from the structure's base.

Julius jumped back. On closer inspection, he observed that cables had been blasted into the Martian dirt.

"I assume that is to prevent it from flying off in a storm?"

"Yes, but the proper term is terrastorm. People are a resource. We don't want to lose them in preventable accidents."

Julius felt the same disconnection from valuing human beings that he got from Gerald the day Vinnie had died so horribly. AMSPACE didn't treat its employees well, but at least they would hire people.

"It would've been nice to have a class or briefing before this real-world testing, Martin."

"We determined that classrooms are a stupid way to learn. People don't learn much by being lectured, they learn by doing. I've found that the trial by fire style of training is much more effective for my recruits."

"Trial by fire. Got it. Not much fire happening. I'm just amazed at how real this simulation is, though. Am I supposed to just act like I'm on Mars?" Julius walked toward the main door to the shelter.

"We'll have you learn about specific survival skills and what happens on a day-to-day basis. First, why don't you get acquainted with your shelter? It's similar to the one you'll have on Mars. Also, you will find a training robot inside. Please remember the Martian SOL is forty minutes more than an Earth day, so the simulator will act as such." Martin's commlink clicked off.

"Okay, see you later, then." Julius opened the door. Once inside the air lock, Julius closed the door and looked around.

He saw a panel that displayed the current oxygen level and had two buttons, one green and one red. He pressed the green one. Julius watched the display and saw the oxygen level begin to change on the display before it glowed green.

Once the oxygen level was safe, Julius removed his suit and helmet, ditching it on the floor. He placed the helmet on top of the bench and opened the next door. It was like walking into a living room.

The room had a small sofa, coffee table, and a TV capable of receiving Earth television channels. The walls were made of a semithick wrinkled plastic. The floor was black rubber, like a workshop. Julius heard a robotic voice greet him before a familiar hovering sphere flew over from the other side of the room.

"You look a lot like that robot that selected my name yesterday."

"Yes, I am the Teaching Autonomous Mars Robot, or TAMR for short. A different version of me picked your name. I am merely a rendition of that robot," the floating sphere said with a chipper mechanical voice.

"Nice to meet you. What did you mean by one of you picked me?"

"The real TAMR robots are among many designed to assist the employees of AMSPACE. They are mainly used in asteroid mining operations since those are more dangerous. Did that answer your question, Mr. Stetson?"

"Yes, it did."

"Good. Now let us take some time to look around the shelter. Please follow me."

The robot flew into the hallway off to the right. Julius followed slowly. He entered the hallway and exited the other side; this room was significantly smaller but aesthetically looked the same. There was a bed with storage drawers under it; a nightstand with a lamp stood next to the bed.

"Cozy," he commented sarcastically at the limited space the room offered. A section of the room had a divider that hid a small toilet and sink.

"No place to shower, TAMR?"

"Not here, sir. Not enough space. The showers are in the central building, which has not been rendered yet. Now follow me back to the central part of the shelter." TAMR flew out of the room. Julius walked through the living room and went down the other hallway and into the other bedroom.

"TAMR, why do I need two bedrooms?"

"When you get to Mars, you will have a roommate. You have the potential of having one to seven roommates. Did that answer your question?"

Before Julius could answer in the affirmative, he heard light hissing noise emitting from the living room.

"What the—"

TAMR spoke urgently—a noticeable change of his voice to an ominous monotone. "Rapid decompression warning."

"What does that mean?" Julius frantically looked around; he didn't see anything that could cause the decompression of the shelter. He knew if he didn't act quickly, he could suffocate.

He continued to look around the room and noticed a bright yellow button flashing next to the hallway. There were blinking red words below the button that said "Seal Room."

Julius pressed the button, causing a door to close off the hallway. Peering through the door's small circular window, he watched the rest of the shelter implode. The furniture flew everywhere, and she shelter ripped itself apart as the oxygen escaped.

"Holy shit! I thought this was a controlled environment!" Julius's body shook. His heart rate was high as adrenaline pumped through his body. He could have died.

"That was your first test, and you lived. I guess you passed," Martin's voice transmitted through TAMR.

"You-you almost killed me!"

"Watch it, Stetson. Mars won't be forgiving. What makes you think I'll make training forgiving? Do you want to quit? We can arrange to take you out."

"No! I'm sorry, Martin. I'm just high on adrenaline. I need to go out for a walk to clear my head." Julius took deep breaths to control his racing heart.

He looked around the room for a new space suit since his old one was in the other air lock. Julius opened the door to the room's air lock expecting to see another suit. He was disappointed when there wasn't one. He closed the door to the air lock, making sure it was sealed shut.

"Hey, Martin? Can I have a new suit? I want to go for a walk."

"Look again, kid."

Julius unlocked the door, not expecting a change. Hanging on a small rod was a space suit with a helmet resting on the bench.

"This is so confusing. I'm going to go crazy in here," Julius said to himself.

He grabbed the suit and dressed himself. He was able to change faster than last time since he was familiar with the suit now. He made sure the door to the shelter was closed, as he did not want to compromise this part of the shelter. He turned around, opened the opposite door, and stepped back out into the Martian landscape.

NINE

Terrastorm

After leaving the air lock, Julius turned to his left, where he saw the remains of the main shelter and the secondary bedroom. The bubbles were deflated, having exploded. Red Martian dust was sprinkled over top of what used to be the floor. The furniture was spread around the immediate area, broken into several pieces. The air lock was still standing but was obviously unusable.

"Well, shit, I wonder how many people died during that part of the test. I'm glad I wasn't one of them."

"One hundred and twenty-one trainees have perished in depressurization scenarios. You would have made one hundred and twenty-two." TAMR spoke inside Julius's suit.

"What the—How are you talking to me? How do people not know about the high rate of casualties from this training?" Julius moved his head in his helmet, looking for the source of TAMR's voice.

"Money keeps things out of the news. Camilla likes to keep her program in full control. I am integrated into your suit to assist you in learning how it works. This will only be for training. I am not integrated into the suits on Mars yet."

Julius tried to absorb what TAMR was saying. Camilla keeping the death of hundreds of people a secret by just throwing money at it seemed very unethical. He had stopped moving, and his mind began to spin.

"Sir? Are you still there?"

"Yes, sorry, I was, uh…enjoying the view," Julius lied. "Is there anything else you can tell me about the suit?"

"Everything you need to know can be seen in the HUD."

"What's a HUD?"

"HUD is a heads-up display. It is the information highlighted on the glass of your helmet."

Julius moved his eyes around the helmet and saw the oxygen tank status that was green at 100 percent. There was a small map of his surrounding area provided by something called the Mars Positioning System, or MPS. Finally, he saw a full-body image of him showing his body's vital signs.

"Okay, this is really cool."

Julius started to wander away from the shelter. He kept walking for another thirty minutes, and when he realized he could no longer see the shelter, he stopped.

The MPS informed him he was about two and a half miles from the shelter. Julius was surprised at how far he had moved. Thanks to the lower gravity on Mars, he could walk much faster than on Earth.

Julius took a deep breath and spun around, enjoying where he was. Even if it was technically fake, Julius felt overjoyed that he was strolling around Mars.

"This is the happiest I have felt in years." Julius jumped around, taking some dirt off the ground before throwing it in the air. It was blown away, which perplexed him, since there was no wind.

Julius's bliss ended when a message abruptly appeared in front of his eyes. INCOMING TERRASTORM. SEEK SHELTER. He was perplexed by the message.

"Storm? I don't see a…storm…" Julius trailed off as he turned to his rear. Off in the distance, rising like a tsunami, was a massive dust cloud.

"Sir, you should seek shelter. That is a category two terrastorm, and it is moving fast!"

"Thank you, I can see that!" Julius turned around and ran away from the approaching dust wall.

"Why are these things so massive? I didn't think terraforming would cause this, and what does category two mean?"

"They occur when there is an imbalance in the chemicals the planetologists mix, and it's so large because—" TAMR began explaining before Julius ordered him to shut it.

Still running hard, Julius felt the wind on his back as he attempted to reach the shelter. A mix of fear and curiosity compelled Julius to look back. He regretted the decision as the dust wall was almost on top of him. Knowing his life was in imminent danger, Julius searched for somewhere to take cover from the storm. He spotted a ditch that was about ten feet deep. Julius thought this was theoretically deep enough for him to safely take cover from the storm.

"Perfect, a low-lying area to hide. These things are like twisters, right?" Julius asked himself as dove into the Martian ditch.

He hastily pushed his back up against the rocky side that faced the incoming storm. His breathing was heavy from all the sprinting. As he tried to catch his breath, dust and small rocks began to fall around him. Julius instinctively looked up and watched as the dust wall eclipsed the ditch. The light from the sun disappeared, leaving Julius in complete darkness.

"I need to see. Does this suit have lights?"

As if on cue, two LED light strips rose from his helmet and lit up. The lights were so bright, Julius could see deep into the dust cloud whizzing over his head. He noted that the wind had no clear direction; it swirled around the ditch like a tornado in the Midwest. As he looked, more rocks continued to fall around him, making him worry he could be struck compromising his suit.

"Key phrases will cause your suit to do what you ask."

"Thank you, TAMR. It would've been nice to know that before I went out."

"You did not ask, sir."

"Thank you, TAMR. I'll ask next time." Julius gritted his teeth.

"You are quite welcome, sir."

I have to get back to my shelter if I'm going to stay alive, Julius thought, as his instincts screamed at him to run. He assessed his surroundings and took deep breaths to keep calm. He knew if he made a rash decision, he could end up in the morgue.

He leaned forward, and army-crawled to the opposite side of the ditch, where he leaned on his stomach. The ditch was deep enough to protect him from the brunt of the storm but shallow enough for him to slide up and down the sides with ease.

Once again, curiosity got the better of Julius. He gradually raised his head above the plain of the ditch into the whipping winds. Immediately, Julius felt the wind pull at the seal of his helmet. He grabbed the top of the helmet and ducked back into the ditch.

"Julius! Are you insane?" Martin screamed into the commlink, causing Julius to wince at his piercing voice.

"Sir, the possibility of you surviving that storm is approximately seventy-six to one," TAMR said.

"TAMR, shut it. I don't want to know how many trainees died at this point."

Julius couldn't believe this was just a simulation. It was simply too real. He regretted coming here and leaving home. He thought of his family and that they might never see him again if he failed here. The thought caused his eyes to well with tears.

Then he snapped out of it and gave himself a pep talk. "I can't think this way. I can figure this out. If I can't leave the ditch without dying, then what can I do? If I stay in here, my suit could rip from the flying rocks."

"Look, kid, the suit has a higher chance of tearing outside the ditch. You could also be picked up and thrown by the storm and break something. If it was me, I would stay where you are and call for help," Martin offered.

"Sir, that is the best option. All you have to do is tell me, and I will transmit the signal," TAMR said.

"Why are you waiting for me? Send the distress signal," Julius ordered TAMR. A message appeared in the upper left-hand corner of his helmet. In blue text, the words "Distress Signal Transmitting" flashed across the screen. Simultaneously, the lights on the top of his helmet blinked blue. An inferred signal was emitted, to be detected from the planet's satellite system or a passing drone.

Exhausted, Julius lay down in the ditch. He listened to the storm whipping and howling around him, keenly aware his life was in danger. He felt drowsy and fought to keep his eyes open.

Julius was not aware that Martin was furious, typing and changing displays on the hologram in his office. Martin used the program to manipulate the gas inside of Julius's oxygen tank. The gas went from being oxygen to a form of sleeping gas called BZ. As Julius breathed in the gas, he started to get drowsy and slumped in the ditch. After a few minutes, Julius passed out and slid to the bottom of the ditch.

"Sir? Sir?" TAMR's frantic robotic voice rang in Julius's ears like a far-off call in a tunnel. The darkness began to clear, revealing dust covering his helmet. He groaned loudly.

"Wh-wha-what happened, TAMR?" Julius cleaned the front of his helmet with his hand.

"You passed out, sir."

Julius took a deep breath before his eyes focused on a blinking red line located in the bottom center of his helmet. It read "Oxygen 25 Percent." Julius felt a rush of adrenaline and fear. He looked up; his lights illuminated the dust still gusting above the ditch.

"TAMR, I'm low on oxygen. I can't wait for help, it's not coming." Julius was panicking.

"Sir, I can assure you that the help will come."

"TAMR, if I'm going to live, I have to go out in the storm!" Julius prepared to exit the ditch.

"But, sir, I said help is coming and—" Julius cut him off.

"No, help isn't coming. This is a simulation. If help were coming, it would be here already. Martin is testing me. If I'm to survive, I have to go now!" Julius leaned up against the side of the ditch in the direction of the shelter.

He slowly raised his hand up above the plain of the ditch, but the strength of the wind forced it down.

"Well, this is gonna suck. Here goes nothing," Julius muttered to himself before pulling himself out of the ditch. As soon as he got half of his body over the top, he was pressed against the dusty ground as though someone had pinned him. He rolled around to get the rest of his body out of the ditch.

Julius was now completely exposed to the storm. He stood up quickly but got blown forward. He threw his hands out as he lost his balance and hit the Martian ground hard. He groaned in pain as dust flew all around him.

"Julius, what the hell do you think you're doing?" Martin's surly voice crackled over the commlink.

"I'm not going to die out here. I'm low on oxygen. I have to get back." Julius attempted to reason with Martin despite the pain shooting through his body.

"You're going to kill yourself, you idiot. Don't think for a second I'll make this easier on you because you're being stupid." Martin abruptly cut off his commlink leaving Julius in silence.

"TAMR, can you enlarge the MPS map?"

"No, sir, the storm is causing satellite interference. I cannot get a connection."

"Well, can you link to the shelter to give me a correct heading?" Julius struggled to get to his knees while the wind battered him.

"Again, no, sir. The storm is too strong."

"Thanks for nothing. It's almost the twenty-second century, and the internet still sucks." Julius extended his leg to get to a lunging position. From there, he pushed himself up into a staggered standing position to prevent the wind from knocking him down again. Standing successfully was a small victory, but he didn't celebrate. He began walking in the direction he believed the shelter to be.

It took all his strength and concentration to not be knocked over by the wind again. He wandered aimlessly in the storm for a long period time, trying not to fall down when he spoke to TAMR again.

"TAMR, can you activate the lights on the shelter?"

"I will attempt to contact the shelter again and ask it to turn on the lights."

While TAMR tried to establish a link with the shelter, he took cover behind a large boulder.

This is insane, Julius thought as the dust and rock flew by him.

"Sir, I have connected to the shelter, and the lights have been turned on."

Julius stood up and looked around, hopeful he had a way out of this mess.

Off in the distance, he saw a dim light obscured by the dust. His heart leaped with excitement. The shelter was near. With new confidence, Julius began moving a bit quicker to the shelter. He felt something in the pit of his stomach, like a nervous quiver. Julius stole a glance at his oxygen meter. It displayed "OXYGEN 3 PERCENT." Julius felt his stomach drop.

"Shit!" Julius started to feel a little dizzy. He began to run in a full sprint through the storm toward the light.

He panted as he watched his oxygen level continue to drop.

"I will not die this way!" Julius saw the shelter bathed in bright light. He reached the air lock and pulled it open, now gasping for air as his oxygen level hit zero.

He shut the door behind him and pressed the exchange button. He watched the screen as the oxygen began to fill the room. Spots of darkness began dotting his eyes. Julius could not hold on to consciousness anymore. He passed out and fell forward. His body hit the floor of the air lock, completely limp. The impact broke his helmet open, and it scattered all over the air lock. One piece cut his forehead.

The air lock had filled with oxygen; the shattered helmet allowed the air into Julius's suit. A few minutes later, Julius regained consciousness and inhaled deeply. He sucked in some dust, which caused him to cough it back up before he threw up all over the floor.

Julius stood up and noticed the air lock was covered with Martian dust, shards of glass from his helmet, vomit, and blood from his cut. Defeated but relieved to be alive, Julius removed his suit and helmet. He opened the door to the shelter, where he thanked whatever power saved his life.

Julius listened to his surroundings. He could still hear the storm howling outside as ferocious as ever.

"Welcome back, sir, congratulations on not dying!" TAMR said, flying to Julius.

"TAMR, I'm not in the mood to chat," Julius said, coughing weakly. He lay down on his bed.

"Please, just let me sleep." As he lay on his bed, Julius began to think about how much his life had changed in the last two days.

He thought about his family, his friends, where he was and where he had yet to go in life. He tossed in the bed, trying to shake these thoughts, but he couldn't. Finally, after three hours of deep thought, Julius remembered a relaxation method his mom taught him when he was a kid.

He lay on his back, closed his eyes. Then as he called out specific parts of his body, he would relax them. He repeated the same words his mom taught him. "Toes to ankles, calves to knees, thighs to hips, stomach to chest."

He continued up the rest of his body. "Fingers, wrists, elbows, arms, shoulders, neck, head, and out and out and out." He repeated the same sequence over and over again until he was finally able to sleep.

TEN

❧

A Gloomy Night in British Columbia

Hundreds of miles away from New Mexico, a spacecraft began to descend through the atmosphere above the Canadian wilderness. A remote airstrip lay below the spacecraft in a part of British Columbia, just north of Vancouver. Camilla stood in the dark as rain poured, beating the tarmac. The driving rain bounced off the top of the umbrella that covered her head. A man in a soaked black suit stood next to her. He was stuck holding Camilla's umbrella that provided no protection for him.

High above them, a thunderous boom cracked through the sky, but no lightning preceded it. A bright orange light accompanied with a strange-sounding engine roar lit up the stormy night sky. As it descended, Camilla could make out the familiar shape of an AMSPACE shuttle developed at the AMSPACE Rocket Development Factory in Pontiac.

The ship looked like an eagle slowly approaching the ground for a graceful landing. It touched down on the long runway and deployed a carbon nanofiber parachute to slow the craft to a safe speed before retracting the drag.

The massive spacecraft looked like a scaled-up twentieth-century Concord. In the place of traditional jet engines were AM Drive engines. The tail of the craft boldly displayed an AMSPACE logo.

The American Union flag was also displayed midway down the starboard side of the ship. A few windows dotted on the front of the port and starboard sides of the craft. Slowly and smoothly, the ship moved to a hangar. Centered on an ominous-looking dark building, the hangar stood open to receive the craft.

The dark, windowless concrete structure stretched to the sides of the hangar. There was a significantly taller tower in the center of the building. The tower had the only windows on the building positioned near the top.

Beyond the windows, the tower extended a little further, ending in communication towers. There were no markings on the structure indicating it belonged to AMSPACE or any of its subsidiaries. A thick pine forest surrounded the complex, shrouding the dark building. In the distance, mountains stood guard as if they were guardians of the building's secret location.

Camilla walked to the hangar. The man holding her umbrella followed. The nameless aide was determined to prevent a single drop of rain from ruining Camilla's perfectly kept hair. As she entered the hangar, she was met with organized chaos. Hundreds of workers descended on the spacecraft as it rolled to a stop. The workers wore white jumpsuits with red stripes down the arms and the AMSPACE logo over their hearts. The back of the jumpsuits had an additional insignia.

The patch was the planet Mars with a white line flying out from the North Pole. The line ended with the spacecraft coming out. Under that logo, it said, "Mars Supply Shuttle Ground Crew: The Colonies' Last Chance." A white hard hat with the AMSPACE logo on the center completed their uniform.

The ground crew had metal cargo crates waiting to load the Supply Shuttle. The craft was much faster than traditional supply rockets that could take a month to complete its mission. The shuttle took a week to reach Mars and was only used for desperate supply runs.

A drone staircase rolled up to the port side where a door opened, allowing the two-person crew to step out. The captain and first mate were dressed in dark-gray space suits. These dark-gray suits were only worn by pilots and copilots. Before they disembarked the spacecraft, the captain, a woman in her midthirties, pressed a button on a small panel just inside the door. Immediately, the back hatch of the supply craft began to descend while white air vented from the pneumatics. Camilla stood at the back of the craft and observed as the back gate hit the ground with a metallic thud.

Inside the cargo hold was a group of people who wore dark red spacesuits with black tinted helmets. The helmet acted as a two-way mirror, obscuring the wearer's identity. The group walked down the ramp led by a single person who held a small tablet in their hand.

Thirteen hovering circular metallic ten-by-ten crates followed the group. The large crates were made of blackened steel with blue outlines and looked to be pressurized. They each had a small touch screen that showed the current temperature inside the box. They also had different number markings. The closest crate to Camilla displayed the number 240.

"Excuse me," Camilla said, her voice commanding and flippant. She quickly approached the person leading the procession of crates. Her face conveyed suppressed anger and determination.

"Yes, Ms. González?" The person used a robotic speech enhancer to disguise their voice.

"What makes you think it is a good idea displaying the internal temperature status of the crates?" Camilla asked through gritted teeth.

"It's not a good idea. I'm sorry, Ms. González. I'll correct the oversight." The person pressed their covered fingers on the tablet's screen.

"It's done, ma'am." The person sounded audibly nervous. All the screens on the crates went black.

"Good. Don't ever do that again. We can't let the underlings know what we're really doing at this facility." Camilla turned away from the person and walked ahead of the group. She led the procession through the hangar and past two large blast doors in the back.

Once the personnel and crates were through the large doors, a metallic creaking sound was heard. The doors slid closed, clanging when they connected, sealing off the hangar.

Once the rear doors were closed, the people dressed in white began to move around like worker ants. They loaded the colony's supplies into the back of the supply craft. Two new pilots walked through a side door in the hangar and entered the supply craft before the ground crew completed the loading. When the craft was loaded, the grounds crew had a robotic pushback tug move the ship out of the hangar.

Once outside, the doors to the hangar closed as the shuttle taxied away and prepared for takeoff. All the crew inside the hangar could hear was a sonic boom as the shuttle took off to return to Mars. They cheered and patted each other on the back before they began preparing for the next shuttle.

Inside the concrete building, Camilla walked with the crates down a massive hallway. The hallway led to a cluster of rooms in the middle of the building. She broke away from the parade of crates before they reached their destination.

She walked down a side hallway to a small conference room. She shut the door and sat in a chair. Camilla turned the chair to face the wall where a projector produced a picture of the chairman sitting behind his desk at the AMSPACE Building in Chicago. Behind him was the city of Chicago along the Chicago River.

"Did the new test subjects make it safely, Miss González?"

"Yes, sir, all thirteen subjects have been securely deposited in the lab."

"Good, I hope these tests bear more fruit. You haven't been produced good results with the test subjects in years. It's been since the one that I witnessed five years ago. What was that test subject again?"

"Test Subject 191, sir."

"Yes, that one! It's been too long since we've had a big breakthrough. I'm hoping you will have something for me as a result of these tests. If not, I might need to consider finding a new president of Martian operations."

"Sir, with all due respect, that won't be necessary. I promise this test will be the best you've seen. I'll oversee these tests personally, just as I oversaw Test Subject 191. My scientists say they've had a big breakthrough that could be tested on humans."

"Very good, you don't want to end up like the head of asteroid mining operations. He was a branch that didn't bear fruit, so we had to let him go. You know the whole Alpha Bravo incident. Instead of leaving the company in shame, he elected to oversee the first mission to Pluto."

"Very good, sir. I won't fail you. I plan on giving you a full report of the results in my written statements."

She felt a chill run down her spine. Camilla knew how unreliable experimental craft were. The chairman had just told her he sentenced a man to death. Without any further response, the chairman disconnected the call, leaving Camilla in the dark room.

Having disconnected the call, the chairman sat in his office. He used a touch pad to tint the windows obscuring the city behind him.

"Margaret!"

A screen turned on in front of him, and a blonde woman looked at him. "Yes, sir. What can I do for you?"

"Get my counsel, I want to talk to him about something."

"Right away, sir."

After a few minutes, the door to the room opened, and a short, plump man walked in. "Mr. Chairman, are we secured?"

The chairman pressed another button on the tablet making the room soundproof. "Yes, Burt, you can call me by my first name."

"Okay, Arnold, tell me what's going on."

"I'm going to be straight with you."

"As you should be, Arnold. We fought together."

"I know, Burt, I can't hide anything from you. I'm conflicted, I've been hiding for years under that alias and this chairman persona. Do you have any idea how hard it is to hide in plain sight? I just want to be who I am in public, not be the fake man you see before you. My father made me run away, and I hate him for making me join the Marines."

"It wasn't your father who made you join the Marines. You wanted that."

"To get away from his abuse."

"Yes, but that was a choice you made."

"I regret that decision."

"Because of Taiwan and the South China Sea?"

"Of course!"

"Arnold, you had your vengeance on the people who hurt you. Now you need to let go of that bitterness. It's in the past. It's over, time to move on."

The chairman slammed down his fist. "It's not over until I'm sitting in the Executive House in St. Louis! It's not over until I'm in charge of the United Forces! It's not fucking over until the last person in the United Forces comes back with a flag draped over their coffin from a botched military operation!"

The chairman paused, taking a deep breath before continuing a little more calmly.

"Burt, you were there with me; you pulled me out by my pack. My arm was missing, and I had shrapnel in my face. I was a victim, not of the enemy, but of incompetency. I get a Purple Heart while the men in charge get parades. How could you fucking say I've finished my revenge?"

"Arnold, you conducted an operation with the Red Hand that resulted in—"

"I know what I did and how it was a catastrophic failure! It galvanized the North American Union instead of weakening it!"

"I'm aware of what happened, Arnold. Why not just let it go? You're one of the richest, most well-liked men in the country. People want to see you, be with you, and—"

"No! People don't want to see Arnold. They want to see the chairman of AMSPACE. Arnold died on that fucking beach in the South China Sea."

"Arnold, this hate you have inside is going to destroy you. It almost cost you everything back during the assassination. You were lucky we were able to intercept the communications from the rebel countries and feed them to the NSA."

"Enough! I killed my senior officer. That was good enough then. It's not good enough anymore."

"Okay, Arnold, what's your next move, then?"

"Simple I use my puppet terrorists to continue to weaken the American Union. As you said, I'm very well-liked by the people, and

I'll use that to run for senator. Once in the AU Senate, I'll be easily voted in for prime minister. You know how money makes everything run in St. Louis."

"I see, sir. I'll do my best to help you with that plan. Since you brought up the Red Hand, I've brokered a new deal with them."

"Oh, really? And? Was it what we were expecting?"

"Yes, sir, they've agreed to the same terms, weapons for targets of your choosing. I still don't understand why you insist on using them. They have a high failure rate and are unreliable."

"They do, but that's what makes them the perfect partner. I don't want them to succeed. They also don't bite the hand that feeds them. Tell them the weapons will be sent from the New Mexico facility in a few weeks in the usual manner. We need them to start attacks as soon as possible to keep the government asking me for help."

"Yes, sir, anything else?"

"No, Burt. Thank you for being here for me. I need to get things together for my flight."

"You're welcome, sir. Consider my thoughts about being you again. Burt left the room, leaving the chairman alone.

Having just hung up with the chairman, Camilla sat in the chair. She noticed her heart was racing, and her hands were shaking. "Q-qué mierda," Camilla felt beads of sweat drip down her brow. She realized she was breathing hard—almost hyperventilating.

"Get it together, Camilla." She tried to control her breathing. "I didn't sign up to get shot into space with no way back." She stood up and caught her breath. "I'm going to replace that psycho." She walked to the door.

Everything she wanted was on the line, and she could be killed if she failed. It was do-or-die for Camilla, literally. She kept thinking about drifting through space all alone—the consequence of failure.

Camilla walked back down the hallway before she entered a locker room where she donned a hazmat suit. She exited the locker room and took a deep breath, preparing herself. Then she walked through a set of double doors.

Above the doors was a sign that said Laboratory 4. Her boots fell against the gray quartz floor. The lab looked the same as it did

THE MAN FROM PONTIAC AND THE MARTIAN COVER-UP

five years prior, when she watched the dissection of Test Subject 191. The room was kept at a cold temperature to preserve the test subjects. All the crates were placed in one corner of the lab surrounded by soldiers with their guns pointed at them, set to stun.

"Turn on the cameras," Camilla said to the people behind the windows in the observatory room where the chairman had once stood. All the tiny cameras activated and began recording. One of the cameras turned to focus on Camilla.

"Open crate 240 and bring out the test subject. I'm ready to start the tests." Camilla took a deep breath. The assistants opened the crate and lifted out the test subject.

"Call in the doctors and surgeons. I have deadlines to meet." As Camilla talked, the assistants strapped the covered Test Subject 240 to the table.

The double doors swung open as additional personnel entered the room to begin the experiment. The doctors prepared for the procedure and asked Camilla to stand back a little farther. She complied, then turned around just in time to see the first incision made. She felt a sense of pride rush over her as she was taken back to the first time, she was on the floor in Laboratory 4, watching Test Subject 191 get torn apart. Camilla was ready to impress the chairman once again.

ELEVEN

The Other Trainee

Julius awoke several hours after falling asleep to light streaming through the windows and walls of his shelter. "No shades on the windows?" Julius thought as he rubbed the sleep out of his eyes. "I'm going to need an eye mask when I'm actually on Mars." Julius got out of his bed and felt his stomach grumble.

"TAMR, what am I supposed to do for food?"

"I have some freeze-dried fruit until Martin completely renders the camp. After that, the simulation will take care of your food."

"Umm, okay. I'd like some food, please." TAMR flew over and opened up a compartment in his side, producing a silver package of freeze-dried fruit.

Julius ripped open the silver package, and hungrily ate the small banana and strawberry pieces. He had to use his saliva to moisten them, so they felt more natural. Once the food was finished, Julius took a look out his window.

Adjacent to his shelter sat an identical one. Julius was confused, he wondered why Martin would have rendered another shelter. He turned around and got ready for his day before he went exploring again. After he was ready, Julius proceeded to the air lock to get on his suit. The suit wasn't the way he left it the previous night. He saw the suit was hung neatly, and a new helmet sat on the floor. His vomit and the glass were no longer on the floor, but the dust remained.

"Well, this place seems to clean up well." Julius closed the door to the shelter. He grabbed the suit and prepared to venture back outside.

Julius opened the heavy outside door and walked into the Martian morning. *The new shelter was still in front of me, so it's not a figment of my imagination,* Julius thought to himself.

"Is it possible for another person to be in the simulation with me?" Julius asked, puzzled at the computing power it would take to render a world around that person too.

"Yes, sir, it is possible. In fact, they render everything around that person using a temporary rendering wall that comes down to separate the—"

"I've got it, TAMR. Thank you, it was rhetorical."

"Sorry, sir, I am not good at understanding human emotions yet. I am a young AI who has not learned enough about human behavior," TAMR explained to Julius.

"I'm sorry, TAMR. I didn't know. You'll get it eventually." Julius felt a bit guilty for snapping, even if TAMR wasn't human.

He walked toward the other shelter, curious about who was inside. After reaching it, Julius checked the air lock indicator in the upper right-hand section of the outer door. It displayed a green light meaning it was safe to open it.

Martin's digitized voice came over the commlink. "Don't think about it, Stetson. You're not to interfere with the other trainee until you're given permission by either their trainer or me. Walk behind your shelter. I will turn over command to our resident expert in Martian equipment, Demetrius Ware."

Julius didn't reply as he walked away from the other shelter. He was frustrated he could not meet the other trainee yet. His curiosity had been piqued, and now he would have to wait.

Once behind his shelter, Julius was greeted with more Martian dust and rocks. "I'm here, but there's nothing around." Julius was irritated he was taken away from something he wanted to do for seemingly no reason.

"I haven't gotten around to rendering your gear yet, Mr. Stetson."

Julius was surprised by the voice that spoke to him. It was a soft male voice with a slight brazen undertone.

"Oh, I'm sorry. Mr. Ware, I presume?" He had expected a more abrasive tone to come over the line, given his previous interactions with Martin.

"It's quite all right. Now let's get started. My name is Demetrius, but most people find it easier to call me DW. So I expect you to call me DW. I'll be teaching you how to use the equipment for the mining operations on Mars. I'll also briefly explain what happens on Mars on a day-to-day basis."

Up in an office that could view the Rendering Room, DW sat in a small recliner. He was a short black man with a military buzz cut. He was younger than Martin, at thirty-seven years old.

"Okay, so how will that work? Will you just—"

DW interrupted Julius. "Martin will render the cafeteria later, but breakfast is at 0700 sharp, lunch will be provided in a mobile shelter at your worksite, and dinner will be held at 1800 in the cafeteria."

"Okay, I understand." Julius was annoyed with DW's rude attitude.

"Now, after breakfast, you will go to either a hyper-rail."

"What exactly is a hyper-rail?"

"The hyper-rail is one of a few modes of transportation on Mars. It's closely related to the Union's high-speed rail network. The hyper-rail uses maglev technology. It has small sails on it that capture the solar wind to boost its speed."

"Solar wind? Isn't that toxic to people?"

"You don't need to worry about the solar wind effects, just like your suit and shelter, the train is protected. Can I please complete my explanation?"

"Yes, thank you for explaining that to me." Julius elected to ignore the man's tone of voice.

"Thank you! As I was saying, you'll take either the hyper-rail or a people hauler to your rally point. Once there, you'll separate into smaller groups with your core mining team. Your core mining team will be assigned when you get to Mars. Before you interrupt me again, asking what a people hauler is, let me show you."

Above, in an office, DW imported a file into the active files running in the Rendering Room. He placed the file next to Julius.

Julius stepped back as white bubbles began to appear before him. When they popped, they were replaced with pieces of a vehicle. This continued until the bubbles stopped. What remained was a large vehicle with six metallic bulky tireless wheels. Two wheels resided below the cab, and four were in the back. The cab was a pod with two seats for a driver and a passenger. Across the top was a large LED light bar to illuminate the surrounding area in the dark.

Julius walked toward the aft of the behemoth. As he walked, he saw that harnessed seats lined the side of the people hauler. He counted six as he reached the aft of the vehicle. He assumed there were more on the other side, which brought the total to twelve seats. In the rear of the vehicle, he saw the space between the two rows of seats was an open compartment with toolboxes on the sides.

"What's the purpose of the open section, DW?"

"The open area is meant to hold all the tools your team will need for a specific drilling day. Let me render the tools." Bubbles appeared in the toolboxes and in the open section as they were was filled with organized tools.

"So what type of machinery do I get to work with?"

"I was just about to get to that. You and your crew are just cutting down to the rich mineral deposits located in caves below. Once you hit the stopping point, a precision-mining team will take over the mining. They are specialized in extracting the materials."

"What exactly does the precision-mining team do?"

"That is information you don't have a need to know."

"I see," Julius said, disappointed.

"Sorry, Julius, I wouldn't know anyway. I was a miner like you will be. I never made it to precision mining because I had an accident. They couldn't fix me up, so here I am on the training side. Now let's continue. You'll sometimes use tunnel borer machines to drill. Some are attached to trucks, and others are giant drill bits. They look similar to the tunneling machines used to make the subterranean intercountry freeway under the great lakes."

"That sounds amazing. When do I get to use that machine?"

"Once you have completed your environmental training."

"Well, what else is there? Martin has already blown up my shelter, almost killed me in a storm through a lack of oxygen, and now I've talked to you. Seems like I've moved past environmental tasks."

"I have an idea to test you further. I want to see what you do when one of your comrades is in danger." DW laughed a little bit.

Julius heard a soft high-altitude explosion. He snapped his head up in the direction of the sound and saw an object on fire falling toward him. He couldn't make out what it was, but it looked like a flaming hunk of junk.

"Oh, shit!" Julius dove under the chassis of the people hauler.

He buried his helmet under his arms as a loud crash and subsequent explosion tore through the air. The explosion was so loud; it caused Julius's ears to ring. After grasping what just happened, Julius crawled out from under the people hauler and stumbled back toward the front of his shelter, dazed.

In front of him was a large crater located about twenty feet behind the other shelter. The depression was smoking, and the shelter was decompressing. Some of the shrapnel from the falling object had punctured the shelter's fragile lining.

The punctured shelter produced a small explosion as pieces of it flew everywhere.

"Y-y-you killed them." Julius's whole body shook. He felt dread and sympathy toward the unknown dead person.

"That's what you think, Julius. Better get to work." DW cut off the commlink.

Julius was momentarily confused. He snapped out of it and ran over to the damaged shelter. When he reached its remains, Julius observed the air lock was partially collapsed from a piece of metal from what Julius speculated was a satellite.

"Hello?" Julius yelled for the person while looking around the air lock.

"Sir, I can detect a distress signal from a suit. I can connect you to the other suits' comms," TAMR informed Julius.

"Do it, damn it." Julius was desperate. He had to help this person before it was too late.

"Communications link established, sir."

"Hello? Where are you?"

"In…air lock," a strained female voice responded.

"Okay, I need a knife to cut the fabric away to get to you out." A large twelve-inch blade protruded from his suit above his wrist.

"Knife deployed," TAMR said.

"I think my leg is pinned," the agonized voice said.

"Okay, let me cut away the fabric to see you." After he had cut the material, he ordered TAMR to retract the blade.

Julius peeled back the material, revealing a supporting metal cage that was partially collapsed in the back. Underneath that cage was a person in a space suit like his. She was face down on the floor, her right leg pinned under the collapsed cage.

"Is your suit compromised?" Julius asked.

"Not yet. I have a crack in my helmet from when I dove for cover." She was trying to control her voice through the pain.

"What about your right leg? Can you feel it?"

"Yes, I can feel it! And it hurts!" the woman yelled at Julius. As he looked down at the motionless woman, Julius had a flashback to Vinnie's body in the factory. He started to shake in fear and felt like he was going to throw up.

"Come on! Get me the hell out of here!"

Julius came to his senses. "I'll get you out, Miss—" Julius made an attempt to lift the frame off her leg.

"My name is not *Miss*. My name is Abigail! What makes you think you're able to get me out of here? Why don't you just call for help?"

"No need to get upset. They don't send other help in here. I'm all you have." Julius tried to think of an easier way to get her out. He remembered the tools in the back of the people hauler and took off running toward them.

"Hey, where're you going?" Abigail winced in pain as she tried to move.

"I'm going to get some tools to get you out of there. Don't move." Julius disappeared behind his shelter.

"Don't worry, I won't," Abigail said sarcastically.

Once he made it to the people hauler, Julius began searching through the toolboxes for anything that could help. He pulled open a cabinet and found a compact circular saw with a laser tip.

"This should work."

He quickly ran back to Abigail's collapsed shelter and flipped the switch to turn on the saw. There was a humming sound as the blade spun up, and a green glow formed on the tip of the blade.

Julius started to cut the metal frame to the right of Abigail's pinned leg. He didn't want to accidently compromise Abigail's suit by cutting too close. Dim sparks flew as Julius pushed the saw into the metal.

The metal buckled once Julius completed the cut, allowing Abigail to slowly crawl out from under the collapsed section. Julius placed the saw down in the Martian dust and quickly moved to the front of the air lock. He opened the door, revealing Abigail still on the floor crawling toward him.

Julius stepped into the collapsed air lock and extended his hand for Abigail to grab. She took his hand, and he pulled her up on her good leg. He slid his back under her left shoulder to prevent her from putting weight on her right leg. Julius did not have to bend down too far to get under her shoulder as she was only a few inches shorter than him.

While he helped her up, Julius looked upon Abigail for the first time. She was absolutely beautiful. He guessed she was in her late twenties or early thirties. A few blond curly hairs hung down in front of her face. They had fallen out of the ponytail that held her hair behind her ears. Her face was tan with a few freckles. He ended by looking into Abigail's bright blue eyes and saw the intense pain they held.

Julius helped her limp out of the wreckage and across to his air lock. He pulled her into the air lock and leaned her against the opposite door.

"Do not take off your helmet. I'm leaving the door open." Julius turned around and left her.

"Where're you going? You're supposed to help me!"

He chose not to respond as he returned to the collapsed air lock. Julius grabbed the saw from the dirt and used it to cut two long pieces of metal from the cage.

"TAMR, give me the knife back." The knife protruded from his wrist. He used it to cut strips of fabric from the shelter.

"Okay, retract." The knife folded back into his suit. Julius gathered up all the materials he had procured and hurried back to Abigail. He reentered the air lock, closing the door behind him.

Julius pressed the Oxygen Exchange button then dropped the materials on the dirt-covered floor next to Abigail's leg.

"What's that crap for?" Abigail asked, taking off her cracked helmet and revealing her face.

"That crap is going to be used to splint your obviously broken leg."

Abigail went silent, surprised at Julius's reaction. He knelt down next to her taking off the top half of his suit.

"I'm going to need to get the bottom of your suit off so I can splint the leg."

"You aren't a doctor, obviously. What qualifies you to help me…uh…"

"You don't know my name, it's Julius. I have training from my time at the factory. One person at each station needed to have Red Cross first aid training."

"Fine. You can help me."

Julius gently began to move the lower half of Abigail's suit down her legs. Once the suit was removed, Julius took the two metal rods and placed them on opposite sides of Abigail's injured leg. He lifted her leg, which caused Abigail to scream.

"I know it hurts, but it's okay."

"No, it's not okay. It hurts, damn it!"

"Bear with me. I'm trying to tie the rods together. I have to get the fabric under your leg, and I can't do that without lifting up your leg."

"Just be careful."

Julius nodded moved five strips of fabric under her leg. After treading the strips, he tied them together. This gradually pulled the metal rods flush with her leg. Abigail winced in pain each time Julius tied a different fabric strip.

"You know, your quality of care isn't the best."

"I wasn't trained to be gentle, just get results and save a life."

After he was done, Julius helped Abigail remove the top of her suit to make her more comfortable. He removed the bottom half of his suit before he helped Abigail to her feet. He brought her into the shelter.

"You can lie on my bed until we can figure out how to get you proper care. I'm sure our trainers are working on it."

"Thank you, Julius."

"You're welcome." Julius laid her on the bed and closed the air lock door. He returned and sat on the bed next to Abigail. He was about to speak when they heard the sound of the outside air-lock door opening. Both Abigail's and Julius's eyes met and widened.

"What was that?"

"That was the air lock opening," Julius nervously wondered what was now in the air lock.

Julius felt Abigail grab his hand and hold it tightly as the light next to the door turned from green to red.

"Who could be in the air lock?"

"TAMR, do you have a defense mode?"

"No, but here is a knife. I don't believe you will be needing it, sir." TAMR produced a small three-inch blade from the same hole that gave Julius the freeze-dried fruit earlier.

Julius took hold of the knife's hilt and held out in front of him. He positioned himself between Abigail and the door in a defensive stance. The sound of the second door unlocking sounded like an earthquake in Julius's ears. His breath became shallow, and his heart rate rose as he watched the metal door slowly open.

A figure dressed in a strange-looking suit stood past the open door. It differed compared to the space suits Abigail and Julius wore. It had a helmet that was round on the bottom but moved to a rectangular shape on the top. The glass had a larger surface area to see more compared to the traditional suits. In addition, the helmet had an orange tint and a two-way mirror, preventing Julius and Abigail from seeing inside.

Julius gripped the knife and was preparing to lunge at the intruder when the person spoke using an electronic voice dampener.

"Mr. Stetson, you did a good job thinking on your toes. You saved your teammate from a very painful death. That being said, you did make a mistake. You failed to check her suit for leaks when you recovered her. You don't take a person's word, always check. And put that knife away before you hurt yourself."

The person walked past Julius as he put the knife back in TAMR. "Miss King, I'll administer a nanobot serum that will repair your leg. Which will be restored to its preinjury state thanks to the scan of your body taken earlier. You'll be able to walk again within the hour. The bots will pass naturally."

Julius and Abigail could not tell if the person was a male or female. The person reached into a pocket and produced a small vial of light-green liquid and a syringe. They filled the syringe with the green liquid and tapped it with a finger. The figure took the needle and stuck it in Abigail's broken leg. She cried out in pain as the liquid drained into her broken appendage.

"I'm also to inform you that training will be suspended until Miss King can walk again. You're not to leave the area around." Before Julius or Abigail had a chance to say anything, the person about-faced and walked out of the shelter.

"So, Abby." Julius had started to speak before he was cut off.

"My name's not Abby. You don't see me calling you Jules, do you? Don't call me by anything except my name. It's Abigail."

"My mistake, Abigail. So tell me about yourself. Why are you going to Mars? It isn't to mine like I am? Is it?"

"You ask a lot of questions, no offense."

"You have to ask questions to get to know someone."

"I mean, I guess. I wouldn't be caught dead working in the Martian mines. I'm going to Mars to study and enhance the terraforming efforts of the Martian atmosphere. Someone has to make sure humanity has a sustainable home if those politicians can't reverse the climate change crisis. I have master's degrees in both civil and environmental engineering with concentrations in terraforming. It's safe to say that I won't be in the mines with you."

"Good for you. I'm not sure we'll be able to get your head out of the air lock since it's so big," Julius remarked dryly.

"Sorry, didn't mean to brag. I can get a little carried away."

"I can tell, but it's cool. About this terraforming, is it possible for it to create these terrastorms?"

"Yes, it's an almost direct result of the terraforming machines. They pump tons of gasses and nutrients into the air and can create some violent storms if improperly balanced with the Martian atmosphere."

"It seems my trainer was preparing me for one of your messed-up science experiments. I almost died in here last night, the storm was so intense, and I almost suffocated."

"I know how to deal with storms. I don't plan on letting myself get caught off guard."

"I would assume you would know how to deal with them. I was just warning you."

"It can't be that bad, and if it is, I would have you to rescue me." Abigail gave him a wink.

Julius laughed. "That was nothing. I didn't want you to die there."

"Well, I appreciate you not wanting me to die. Julius, tell me about you. What's your background?"

"I made it here on the company lottery. I was a factory worker in the AMSPACE Rocket Development and Production Facility."

"That's a mouthful, where is it?"

"It was a mouthful, and I'm glad I don't have to work there anymore. It's in Pontiac, Michigan. By the way, how did you know to get into the air lock and into your suit?"

"I was told by the lady who brought me from Silicon Valley that I needed to get in my suit. Once I had my suit on, I heard a roaring noise. I know now that noise came from the object that fell from the sky. After the explosion, I passed out briefly. When I woke up, I felt intense pain in my leg and you calling for me."

"This training is intense. They don't seem to be very forgiving here." Julius stood up from the bed.

"I'm starting to realize that." Abigail began moving her leg a bit.

"I wouldn't do that yet, Abigail. I don't think your leg is fully healed."

She winced in pain. Julius took her hand and held it. She squeezed his hand as she repositioned her leg. Julius felt happy holding her hand; he smiled at her when she looked up at him.

She looked away from him, feeling a little awkward. Julius saw her discomfort and let go of her hand. "I'm sorry."

"It's fine. Uh, I think I might get some rest."

"I understand, I'll go, um, put the tools back while you rest." That was the best excuse he could come up with to leave the shelter.

"No, you don't have to go."

"It's really okay." Julius was already at the door to the air lock.

"I'll come outside when I can." She smiled, but it seemed forced.

"Okay, I'll be around." Julius looked back at her and closed the door.

He put on his suit and left the building. *Well, you ruined that, why did you grab her hand?* Julius thought, beating himself up.

Julius walked around the shelter to the people hauler; he sat down in the bed of the vehicle, staring up at the pale blue sky.

TWELVE

The Joyride

Julius remained there for a long time, thinking about how he could remedy the situation with Abigail. As he thought about it, he realized he was being melodramatic. She was not mad about the handholding, but she was embarrassed that he had to save her.

All he needed to do was to let her have some fun, and the awkwardness of him rescuing her would go away. He sat up when he heard the shelter door opening.

"That's an interesting-looking machine," Abigail commented, walking up to him.

"Yeah, it's definitely different from anything I saw on Earth."

"This simulation is amazing. My suit was folded neatly on the bench when I got up to leave."

"It can really mess with your head."

"I believe it. I don't understand how people can live in these things. So want to do something since our training is suspended?"

"Yeah, I have an idea, hop in." Julius jumped out of the bed of the vehicle and climbed into the driver's seat. Abigail looked around the vehicle a little more before she joined him. The doors locked, and the cab began to pressurize, filling with oxygen.

"Clear to remove helmets," a robotic voice said.

Abigail brushed her hair out of her face after taking off her helmet and looked around the vehicle. The people hauler's interior looked very similar to a cargo carrier. It had a steering wheel, along with many gauges that displayed the status of the vehicle's critical systems. It also had numerous multicolored buttons around the dashboard.

"What are you looking for?" Julius asked as he noticed Abigail was digging through the glove compartment.

"I'm trying to find a manual to tell us what all those buttons and gauges do." Abigail gestured to the dashboard that encircled Julius and separated them. He looked around at all the buttons, wanting to discover the function each one performed. Being more of a hands-on learner, Julius thought about which one to press first.

Meanwhile, Abigail found a computerized manual in the cluttered glove compartment and electronically opened it up to the page with the dashboard diagram. It showed what each of the buttons did and what the gauges represented.

Julius had decided on a red-orange button that displayed a seat with a spring underneath it and a small triangle that pointed in Abigail's direction. He reached out to press it.

"Don't touch that one!"

Startled, Julius pulled his finger away from the button and looked over at Abigail.

"Why?"

"Because the manual says that button activates my ejection seat, and I would prefer not to be launched to my death."

"Oh shit, thanks for stopping me. How about we read the manual so we can get this thing started properly?"

"Give me a second. I'll try to figure it out." She pulled out a pair of glasses.

"You wear glasses?"

"Yes, and no, I have contacts in, but I need these for their better heads-up display. I've deactivated the correction app in them, so I'm not blind." Abigail did not break her concentration on the manual.

She pressed a small button on the right temple of her glasses, which caused the lenses to light up. The full heads-up display was activated, scanning the manual's file, creating a map on the lenses. The software then overlaid the digital map to the actual dashboard.

"Find Start button." Abigail waited for her glasses to assist her.

On her lenses, a red outline highlighted a button that resided to the right of the steering apparatus. Below the Start button was a series of smaller buttons marked Park, Drive, Reverse, and Autopilot. Abigail reached over the dividing section between the two seats and pressed the start button.

"Put your foot on the brake to tell the machine you are ready to move."

Julius pressed his right foot down on the horizontal pedal, and Abigail pressed the drive button. "You're ready to move."

"How did you know how to do that?"

"I used my glasses and heads-up display to scan to manual. The top button I pressed turned on the electric motor, the brake allowed you to change the mode of the computer, and I pressed the drive button. It's similar to an early-twenty-first-century car. Now you can use the pedals and steering apparatus to drive."

Julius smiled at her as he took his foot off the breaks. The people hauler lurched forward, heading away from Julius's shelter. They both looked out the window and saw a new shelter next to the remains of Abigail's collapsed shelter.

"Hey, looks like you don't have to stay over anymore."

"Yeah, I like having my own space," Abigail said.

"Yeah, I get that, but it's also nice to have company."

"I don't disagree, but space is space, and I enjoy having my alone time."

"True." For some reason, he couldn't explain, Julius was not happy about her not sticking around in his shelter. He was happy she was independent, but he felt himself enjoying being around her.

They drove the people hauler around for hours, trying to see the extent of the simulation. They were close to a mountain range when the commlink in Julius's helmet turned on with Martin's voice.

"Julius, I want you to stop the people hauler. Then go back to your shelter. You'll have an hour or two to return. Abigail won't be joining you. We have a different mission for her."

At the same time, Abigail heard her trainer, Becka, speak via the commlink in her helmet. "Abigail, after Julius stops the people hauler, you're going to drive to a destination and take soil samples to test the terraforming progress. Julius will be leaving you."

Julius looked at Abigail, and she nodded, "Roger, Martin." Julius brought the people hauler to a complete stop.

He looked at the button series and pressed the "Park" button before he pressed the start button to turn off the vehicle. Both trainees donned their helmets. Abigail pressed a button on the ceiling that removed the oxygen from the cab. The two opened their doors and exited the people hauler. Abigail walked over to the driver's side, where Julius was getting out.

"Have a nice walk home, Julius." Abigail winked as she got into the people hauler. Julius watched Abigail drive off into the setting sun.

He turned away and threw his hands in the air. "TAMR, where am I? How do I get back to my shelter?"

"Here is what the MPS says, sir," TAMR opened the MPS map on Julius's heads-up display. Julius could see he was about fifteen miles from his shelter.

"TAMR, is there an easier way to get back other than walking?"

"Other than walking, sir? No."

"Well, this sucks!" Julius looked at the MPS before he began to walk in the direction of his shelter. After a few minutes of walking, the commlink activated and Martin's voice came through.

"Hold up, Julius. I have a better solution."

"What, Martin?"

His trainer had left him in the barren Martian desert; Julius wasn't in the mood for games or more training.

"You can take this."

The bubbles appeared, and something began to materialize in front of Julius. As it rendered, Julius started to make out what it looked like. He easily could tell it looked similar to a speeder bike from the *Star Wars* prequels that came out ninety years ago.

The front was like a dirt bike with the handlebars that swept back like a chopper. The body was one solid metallic shape tapering off to a point, giving it a sleek look. A black seat resided in the middle of the body and could fit two people.

The paint color was red, allowing it to blend in with the Martian ground. The coolest thing about it was that it used a micro AM Drive engine to levitate off the ground. Julius approached it, put his foot on the rung before he vaulted himself onto the seat.

"TAMR, how do I drive this contraption?" Julius was puzzled as he looked down at the handlebars.

"To drive the hover bike, you first need to grab the handlebars. The one on the right that you can twist is your accelerator." Julius looked at the handlebars as TAMR highlighted the right handlebar using the helmet's HUD.

"The brake is located on the right footrest." Julius looked down at the footrest and pressed the brake to test it out.

"The start button is in the center of the handlebars, below the speed gauge and MPS display." A green button was lit up by the heads-up display in the location specified by the robot.

"To turn, simply move the handlebars left and right to maneuver the bike."

Julius reached down to press the green start button. The bike emitted a soft hum as the engine kicked on. He gripped the handlebars and turned the accelerator hard. The bike jumped forward, and Julius felt himself launched backward off the bike.

He hit the ground hard and rolled as like a person thrown from a Jet Ski. He skipped across the dirt before he came to a stop and groaned in pain. Sensing it had no rider, the bike shut down.

"Sir, I forgot to mention the bike is very sensitive. It is advised to start slow."

"Could've been a minute earlier with that suggestion, you oversized soccer ball," Julius slowly brought himself back to his feet, his body aching all over.

"Sorry, sir, I see I have hit a nerve based on your name-calling. I will work to give advice before you make a mistake."

Annoyed at himself and the robot in his suit, Julius got back on the bike. His sore body ached as he sat back down on the hover bike.

He put his hands over the handlebars again, but this time he was gentler with the accelerator. He turned his right hand slightly, and the bike gradually moved forward. Julius maneuvered at a snail's pace to get used to the feeling of the bike. After about ten minutes of learning the bike's quirks, he turned the accelerator more. Soon he was off flying through the Martian landscape at high speeds.

"Wooo! This is amazing!" Julius drove in the direction of the shelter but stopped halfway back. Since he had gotten the hang of the bike, Julius elected to turn toward a bunch of small hills.

He wanted to jump them, flying high into the air like a BMX trick artist would. He laughed and ignored TAMR's constant warnings he could hurt himself. He continued to goof off with the bike, not aware of the amount of time passing.

Julius stopped when he heard a familiar yet scary sound in the distance. It sounded like the roar of the high-speed freight train. Julius had a feeling of what the sound was as he turned around.

He was met with a thick, towering cloud of dust heading toward him. As he looked at the dust cloud, the storm warning appeared on his helmet.

"Sir, you need to take cover, this is a category four."

"I thought terrastorms were few and far between." Julius was shocked at the presence of another storm.

"They are. We just need to catch Miss King up to where you're at in training. We plan to send both of you to Mars on the same shuttle." Martin's voice was heard over Julius' commlink.

Julius turned the bike toward his shelter and hit the accelerator.

"So she's going to be out in this storm with minimal oxygen?"

"Yes. Now get in your shelter, or you can repeat the course." Martin cut off the commlink.

Julius looked behind him and saw the storm, drawing closer. Julius was starting to get worried he stayed out playing for too long. He drove right into the center of the shelters and parked the bike.

"That's going to fly away in the storm unless you tie it down."

Julius listened to what Martin said. With the information, Julius opened the half-standing air lock of Abigail's old shelter and maneuvered the bike inside.

"Not bad, kid. Few trainees think of putting the bike in there. Most put it in their air lock, which is an issue since they can't get into the shelter themselves. Others just leave it, which is a violation of company policy since bikes are so expensive." Julius smiled to himself as he entered his air lock. Right after he closed the door, the air lock rocked as the storm slammed into the shelter.

Julius braced himself and hoped the shelter would hold as he looked around for breaches. Seeing that nothing had been breached, he removed his suit and entered the shelter.

This storm's intense, Julius thought to himself as he looked at the walls of the shelter. They continued to shake from the constant assault from the storm's wind. Lying down on his bed, Julius thought of Abigail and hoped she would be safe. This storm was significantly stronger than the earlier one, and it worried him. He relaxed a little when he remembered she had the people hauler, plus she seemed like a strong, independent individual who could take care of herself.

THIRTEEN

Trapped

A few hours earlier, Abigail was driving the people hauler along the edge of a mountain range. She had parted ways with Julius and was now driving aimlessly.

"Becka, what exactly am I looking for?" Abigail asked her trainer. Abigail was annoyed with the lack of direction she received. She realized this seemed to be a common theme with this program. Outside the Rendering Room, a woman stood in the office located on the same floor as Martin's.

Becka had short brown hair that was cut into a choppy bob. Her pale-green eyes monitored what her trainee was doing. Becka wanted to get a better view of where Abigail was heading, so she walked to the other side of the window. As she walked, her robotic leg clanked against the carpeted floor.

Becka had been training planetologists for five years. Before she started working for AMSPACE, she worked for the UN on the climate change committee. After she got tired of working with apathetic people, she thought her next move should be to help shape humanity's new home, Mars. She and Martin worked very closely to make sure that everyone got effective training.

"You're looking for a group of structures. There you'll stop the people hauler. Then—"

"Why do I have to do that? I thought I was going to be taking soil samples, Becka."

"Because you need to learn about the buildings."

"What buildings?"

"The buildings you and the other planetologists will be using on a day-to-day basis. It's called the terraforming compound. We'll start there, then you'll learn to take a soil sample."

"Understood." Abigail was still annoyed to be driving without guidance.

As she drove, she thought she could make out something on the horizon. Abigail squinted her eyes before they focused on the reflective material of multiple buildings glistened in the setting Martian sunlight. The buildings had smokestacks that reached high into the air at different levels. Each one spewed different colors of smoke.

"I assume that's where I'm heading

"That's correct."

Abigail approached the facility slowly. She saw it had a prison-grade fence surrounding it. It was a carbon nanofiber-chain-lined fence with barbed wire on the top; additionally, there were a few lasers sticking out of the ground, like the saber wall.

Abigail drove up to a gate and stopped. The plasma turrets that flanked the gate activated and pointed at her. She sat there a moment and was getting impatient.

"Am I just going to sit here all day?"

"Give it a minute, the AI has to scan the vehicle to validate your identity. We can't just let anyone into a terraforming facility." A few moments later, the gate slid open and Abigail drove her vehicle through the gate. She drove the people hauler to the middle of the compound and parked. She exited the vehicle, standing in a center of the square that separated the surrounded four large buildings.

"So, TAMR, what are these buildings?"

"The few large ones in front of you are the main terraforming buildings. They hold all the machines and chemicals used to terraform the planet."

Abigail looked upon a few concrete buildings with solar panels on the roof. Each building had multiple smokestacks, the very same ones Abigail had seen from afar. She had never seen something like this in person, only pictures in her classes. Abigail felt a flush of excitement. She was ready to start getting her hands on the real-world application of terraforming.

"Miss, have I lost your attention?" TAMR realized Abigail was not following his explanation of the next building.

Abigail stopped daydreaming and came back to reality. "I, uh… yeah, sorry, TAMR. Can you explain that again?"

"Yes, the building to the left of Terraforming Engine Complex is the laboratory. It has labs and computers required to do the precise calculations needed to accurately contribute to the terraforming of the planet."

The building was sandy beige and made out of concrete like the first buildings, but it had lots of windows and seemed more welcoming.

"To the left of that is the complex's security force barracks. They are needed to make sure that no person accesses the facility without permission." Abigail looked at the smaller barracks. TAMR's voice was replaced by Becka's Canadian accent.

"Abigail, you can't do anything on the grounds of this facility, or any terraforming facility, without notifying security. If you fail to notify security, you're subject to the use of deadly force. They take security very seriously on Mars."

"I know these facilities could be used to create catastrophic storms, but who would do that?"

"The company is concerned that a group like the Red Hand or the East Asia Trading Block could infiltrate one of the colonies on the other side of the planet. They then could attack us and try to crash the American Union's economy."

"That's awful. We can't let that happen. Is there a lot of security in the colony?"

"Yes. Again, we take the safety of our personnel very seriously. AMSPACE is a pillar of the American Union's economic might, and we cannot let AMSPACE be used to bring down the country. Now I'll turn you back to TAMR to finish up your training here."

"The last building is a garage for vehicles like your people hauler."

She took a quick glance at the garage, another concrete building with windows, and a large two-layer air lock garage.

"I now have to ask you to go to the people hauler."

"Why TAMR? I haven't even looked inside the buildings. Don't I need some hands-on experience? Don't tell me I came all this way to just look at the buildings. I want to get my hands dirty."

"You'll do that later, probably on Mars itself. We need to get you caught up on environmental testing before you can do any work in the buildings," Becka interjected.

"But I've done the training. I was a survivalist and camped all the time."

"No, Abigail, this is the way it is." Becka's command made Abigail's blood boil a little. She took a breath and let herself calm down.

The deep breath did little to calm Abigail down. She decided she would ignore both Becka and TAMR. Confident in herself, Abigail began to walk toward the terraforming engine complex. Suddenly she ran into the driver's side door of the people hauler.

Becka had reoriented the simulation to put the vehicle in the woman's walking path.

"Ow. What did you do that for?" Abigail stepped back from the machine.

"I gave you an order, Abigail. You need to learn to listen and follow orders."

Abigail was fuming, but she bit her tongue and got in the vehicle.

"This place is going to de-render. Head toward the shelters on the way you'll stop and collect a soil sample."

"Okay, Becka," Abigail spoke through gritted teeth. Once the cab was filled with oxygen, she removed her helmet. She watched as the buildings around her were covered in white bubbles. When the bubbles cleared, it was like the buildings were never there. Abigail found this very disorienting but ignored the feeling of uneasiness. She pressed the drive button and drove in the direction of the shelters. She occasionally glanced at the MPS in her helmet as she traveled.

Abigail traveled for a few minutes before Becka spoke.

"Abigail, please stop to take a soil sample."

Abigail brought the people hauler to a stop.

"I'll render a predug hole. On Mars, you'll have a skilled miner with you to dig the real hole. Since we pair you with a skilled miner on Mars, there is no need for you to learn to use a drill hauler. You'll take a soil sample and place it in this box."

Abigail was startled as the white bubbles appeared on the passenger seat. When they cleared, a metallic box remained on top of the seat. The cube had one side with a touchscreen; the other five sides were metallic. The top had a hexagonal depression with more metallic material below. Abigail speculated that it was an opening of some sort in which she should place the soil.

"That's the Soil Analyzer 3000. It has a slot on the top that will open. You'll deposit the soil sample in that opening. The device will break the sample down to the molecular level and relay the data back to your terraforming team."

"Okay, I understand." Abigail put her helmet on and grabbed the laptop-sized cube. She pushed the door open and exited the people hauler. She stood in the Martian moonscape, looking around. "I don't see a hole, Becka."

"Patience."

The bubbles reappeared on the ground about twenty feet in front of Abigail. A large hole, ten feet wide, rendered a small dirt path spiraled down to the bottom.

"I could've just read a manual instead of actually climbing down this hole for a soil sample," Abigail muttered as she started to walk down the path into the hole.

She reached the bottom, twenty feet down, and pressed the box's touchscreen, and a menu appeared. There were many options. One said "open hatch." She pressed it, and the top slid open quickly. Abigail placed the box down in the soft dirt and used her hands to scoop some dirt into the box. She pressed the screen again, and it glowed with a large button that said "close and test."

This is so simple. A toddler could do it! Abigail thought as the opening closed. She smiled to herself, feeling accomplished. As she waited for the box to finish its cycle, an alert appeared on her heads-up display in bright red letters.

"INCOMING TERRASTORM. SEEK SHELTER."

"Oh shit," she said, rapidly ascending via the path. She poked her head out of the hole and saw a massive dust cloud about two hundred feet from her.

Seeing there was no way she would reach the people hauler in time, she ducked back in the hole. The dust cloud hit with a ferocious growl. She let out a little scream, surprised by the storm's power.

Within a few seconds, Abigail heard metal creaking. Her curiosity got the better of her, and she peeked out.

The wind nearly ripped her helmet from her suit. Instinctively, she used her hands to steady it. She scanned for the source of the metallic creaking. She found the source as the people hauler lifted off the ground before it was thrown in her direction. Abigail's eyes went wide as she quickly dove to the path on the other side of the hole and looked up. She watched the behemoth slowly sail over the hole.

The people hauler landed a few feet beyond with a thunderous crash that was all but drowned out by the raging storm.

"TAMR, what are my options?"

"You can send a distress signal to HQ and wait, rough it like Mr. Stetson, or if we can contact the shelter over a commlink, you could ask him for aid."

He went out in this? He's crazier than he looks, Abigail thought to herself as she contemplated what to do.

After weighing her options, Abigail asked TAMR to send a distress signal. Two LED light strips rose from her helmet and immediately began pulsed blue. Concurrently, in the upper-left-hand corner of Abigail's helmet, a blue text read, "DISTRESS SIGNAL TRANSMITTING."

"Is there a way those can produce a steady light for me to see?"

"Yes," TAMR responded as the lights illuminated the hole.

She breathed a sigh of relief as she leaned against the side of the hole. Abigail looked up and saw the dust flying over the top of the hole with the ferocity of an angry hornet's nest. She sat there for thirty minutes while the storm continued to rage around her.

"TAMR, why has no one come to rescue me?"

"I am not sure. Usually they are here by now."

Abigail debated what she should do. She was trapped with no way out. She didn't want to ask Julius, but she was out of options. "TAMR, can we try Julius?"

"I will try to reach his shelter."

After a few minutes, TAMR spoke. "I cannot reach the shelter using the suit's transmitter, but I think I can connect by using the transmitter on the people hauler. If it was not damaged."

"Well then, try it."

After another few minutes, TAMR spoke again. "I have a connection to the people hauler's transmitter."

"Then make the call!" Abigail said harshly.

"Sorry. I am doing that now." As the call was being made, Abigail glanced at a blinking red line that caught her eye at the bottom of her heads-up display.

Back in his shelter, Julius laid on his bed, nodding in and out of sleep. He was trying his best to stay awake to make sure Abigail made it back safely. Julius was snapped awake by the sound of TAMR in his shelter's speakers.

"Mr. Stetson, Miss King would like to speak to you."

"Well, put her through, TAMR."

"Of course, sir."

There was a click as the call cut over to Abigail's audio. Julius heard the sound of shallow breathing and wind howling in the background.

"Abigail? Are you there?"

"Julius, I can't get to safety."

Abigail was screaming into her microphone. She had become more panicked after she read the blinking red line. Her oxygen was down to 25 percent.

"Julius, my oxygen is starting to run low."

"Okay, Abigail, you need to calm down. Get in the people haul—"

"I can't get in the people hauler. It flipped over, and I am trapped in a hole."

Julius realized the gravity of this situation. She was in a higher category storm with no shelter.

"Julius? Are you still there?"

"Yes, I'm here. Give me your position, and I'll try to rescue you."

"You heard him TAMR, give him my position," Abigail ordered the robotic assistant.

"Yes, ma'am," TAMR replied as he transmitted the coordinates to Julius's shelter. Julius looked up as a small flat TV that activated and displayed where Abigail was on the MPS.

"I'll be there soon, Abigail," Julius said, dashing into the air lock. The air lock was shaking from the violent storm while Julius put on his suit. Once it was on, he heard TAMR's voice.

"Sir, it is unwise to venture out in a category four terrastorm."

"I don't care, TAMR, she'll die if I don't help her. I have the speeder, now activate lights." The lights on his suit popped out and turned on. He opened the door only to be met with tons of dirt and dust. The debris flew into the air lock while he forced his way out.

Once outside, Julius forced the door to close and lock. He then started to walk toward the collapsed air lock. The storm was so powerful that if he jumped off the ground, he would have never landed again.

Julius fought his way to the bike and struggled to pull it out from the broken air lock. He was able to move it out of the lock before the wind almost took it. He pulled with all his might to keep it grounded. Quickly mounting the bike, he began driving against the wind to Abigail's position. As he drove, he found himself dodging huge rocks that flew past him.

This is suicide. Maybe I should've listened to TAMR, he thought as a rock hit the front of the bike, almost sending him crashing to the ground. He was just able to hold control of the bike as he continued on toward Abigail.

The trip seemed to take forever. Julius wondered if she would still be alive when he got there. He glanced at the MPS, which told him he should be right on top of her. He squinted, and through the flying sand, Julius could barely see the overturned people hauler. Next to it, he saw a large hole.

Julius activated his commlink. "Abigail, where are you?"

"I'm in the hole," Abigail said, quickly poking her head out to look for Julius. She was holding her hands on the helmet, making sure it wasn't ripped off. Julius saw her and immediately maneuvered the bike to park next to her.

"Get on!"

Abigail hoisted herself out of the hole and into the storm. She was not prepared for the power of the wind, which blew her into the bike frame. She groaned as she hit the bike.

"You okay?"

Abigail did not reply; she just moaned in pain. He grabbed the back of her space suit and lifted her onto the back of the bike. "That's gonna leave a mark."

The storm raged, pelting them with little rocks and dust. Abigail wrapped her arms around Julius's torso and held on as he began to drive back.

Abigail looked at her oxygen meter and saw it was at 5 percent. "Julius, hurry!" Abigail's voice sounded weak as she struggled to get quality air. Julius drove as fast as he could, using the MPS to navigate to the shelters.

"TAMR, can you turn on the shelter lights?"

"Yes, sir," the robotic voice replied as a small blip of light in the distance flickered on.

"Hold on, Abigail!" Julius yelled, trying to keep her conscious and alert. Abigail did not reply. She had become dizzy as her oxygen levels dropped. Little black spots began to appear in her vision. He arrived at the shelter complex and stopped the bike.

Abigail fell off the back of the bike and slammed to the ground. Julius jumped off the bike and went to her. He bent down and picked up her limp body. He hoisted her over his shoulder and carried her to her shelter's air lock, shutting the door behind him. Before the air lock was completely pressurized, Julius held his breath, put Abigail down, and ripped off his helmet. He then went a step further and opened the door to the shelter. There was a gust of wind as the oxygen rushed to fill the air lock. The rapid decompression alarm sounded as the yellow lights blinked in the room.

"You cannot open the shelter door when pressurization is in progress." Abigail's TAMR flew over to Julius's face.

"Fuck off!" Julius yelled before he aggressively shoved TAMR. Julius quickly knelt next to Abigail's body and used a knife to rip open the space suit.

"Abigail, wake up!"

Her face was lifeless and colorless. He gave up yelling at her and initiated CPR.

Julius laced his hands together and began compressing Abigail's chest, counting to thirty, taking care he did not use too much pressure and injure her further. He then positioned his face over Abigail's and pressed his lips to hers. He breathed into her mouth, watching her chest rise and fall.

As Julius was about to give his second rescue breath, Abigail coughed and breathed deeply. He pulled back as her eyes opened and she realized what he did.

She slapped him across his face.

"What was that for?" Julius asked, holding his cheek.

"Sorry, force of habit," Abigail said, smiling as she looked up at him from the air lock floor.

"You're welcome for, I don't know, literally saving your life. For the second time today."

"Thank you, Julius. Sorry for hitting you." Julius could feel the sincerity in her voice.

She looked at him as she sat up. "Won't you come in?"

Julius felt his heart race a little. "I couldn't."

"You could, I wouldn't mind. I have to thank you for saving me again." She was standing now and backed into her shelter.

"How about a kiss as my reward?"

"Don't worry, I wasn't going to give you more than that." Abigail stood at the threshold, waiting for him to approach. He walked up to her and put his hand under her chin, pointing it slightly upward.

"Hey, I won't wait forever. I almost died. I'd like to go to bed." Julius leaned in and kissed her. It was over quickly, and she pulled away.

"There's your reward. Now, let me get my beauty sleep."

Julius took a step back before she closed the air lock door. He felt like he was lifted into the air. He placed his dust-covered helmet on his head before walking to his shelter. The storm had stopped by this point. Julius assumed since he and Abigail were at their shelters, there was no need to keep that part of the simulation running.

He lay down in his bed and thought of the day he just had. He was happy he met Abigail. He definitely wanted to get to know her better, and he fell asleep thinking about her.

FOURTEEN

Out of the Rendering Room

During the night, Julius had a strange, abstract dream. Through the haze, he could tell that Abigail was present, and they were standing in the middle of the Martian plains. There was a hole beside them, similar to the one he had just rescued her from. She shoved some climbing gear in his hands, and they rappelled down the hole.

As they descended, a bright light engulfed them. He felt instinctively that there was something past the light. Before his eyes could adjust to the brightness, she turned to him.

"Time to get up." Julius looked at her then woke up, startled.

He heard a metallic clang as he slammed his head into TAMR's body.

"Ow! What the hell?" Julius rubbed his head, which was throbbing in pain.

"Sir, it is time to get up."

"Why are you so close to me?" Julius put his arm up and pushed the robot away.

"You were breathing heavily and talking in your sleep. I was scanning your vitals to make sure you were okay."

"I'm fine!"

"I see, sir, I am sorry for the intrusion of your personal space. Your food will be in the mess hall today."

"Thank you, TAMR." Julius rose to leave his shelter. Once outside, Julius turned to his left and saw a new building. It looked to be a permanent structure built out of concrete and had many windows, like an office building.

Julius walked to the building and entered a scaled-up version of his air lock that looked like it could fit thirty people. On the far wall were five additional doors with the red and green lights indicating if it was safe to enter or not. He entered one of the five doors and found himself in a smaller air lock that could fit a few people. He changed out of the suit and entered the next room, which he expected to be a hallway. Instead, it opened up to a locker room.

"You'll have your own locker on Mars inside a specific air lock changing room for your drill team. These are unisex changing rooms." Martin's voice reverberated throughout the room. Julius placed his suit in a locker before exiting.

He found himself in a hallway that had a floating sign pointing him toward the mess hall. Abigail was already eating her breakfast of eggs, ham, and pancakes.

"Julius, good morning!" She flashed him a warm smile.

"Good morning, Abigail. Uh, you look very nice this morning."

"Thank you. I would look better if I didn't almost die last night. Thanks again for saving me."

"It was nothing really. I, uh, I mean, anyone would do the same."

"I still appreciate it. Food's over there, you can serve yourself." Abigail pointed an opening in the wall. He got his food and sat across from her.

"Abigail, I know we're terraforming Mars, but why? Isn't it better to keep it natural in case there is life there?"

"Earth is suffering from the effects of climate change. Our grandparents tried to curb it when they became the majority in the North American Union Legislation, but it was too late. Now the American Union has mandated that AMSPACE start to make Mars suitable for humans to move some of the population here. We've searched for life on Mars long enough. It's time to save ourselves. Plus, Martians don't exist."

"I'm not saying Marians exist, but what if say, bacteria exists?"

"The safety of humanity is more important."

"Is that what made you want to become a planetologist?"

"Basically. It also pays well." She looked at him as she ate the last of her pancakes.

"Money isn't everything. Doing what you love is important."

"True, but money helps."

"Abigail, about last night," Julius started to say before Martin's voice came over the loudspeakers in the building.

"Miss King, you're to go and explore the terraforming facility further. Becka will guide you. We won't try to kill you this time. Julius, you're going to receive mining training from me."

The two trainees exchanged glances and began to walk back toward the locker rooms. "So, Abigail. About last night I…" Julius stammered.

"No need to bring it up. You got a kiss. Maybe you'll get more at a later time. Let's just get through training."

Julius was a little surprised at her response. He expected she would have had more feelings about their kiss than she let on. They went back to their locker rooms.

They both exited the building at the same time. In front of them was a single people hauler and a hover bike. Instinctively, Julius started to walk to the hover bike.

"No, Julius, that's Abigail's. You get the people hauler." Martin spoke sternly.

"Seriously?" Julius could not believe it; he wanted to ride the bike again. Abigail walked right by him and mounted the bike. She turned around and winked at Julius before she hit the accelerator, leaving Julius in the dust.

"Bitch," Julius muttered to himself as he walked to the people hauler and drove off creeping along at a slower pace than the bike. "Where am I going, Martin?"

"Head toward the mountains, you'll stop when you see a tunnel boring machine."

"Sweet, and I get to operate it?"

"Yes, why else would you be going to it?"

"Maybe because I would need to do maintenance checks on it, I don't know."

"I see, good point. Now, where was I? You'll learn how to operate the machine. Regardless of the skills, you learn here. It's unlikely you'll operate the machine as an entry-level miner." Julius neared the mountains as Martin talked.

"That's okay. I'm just happy to learn the skill." Julius tried to hide his disappointment.

Now in the foothills of the Martian mountains, a large metal cylinder materialized behind the white bubbles. It was lying on the ground glinting in the late morning sun. As Julius approached the cylinder, he realized its sheer size. It was mammoth, dwarfing the people hauler at twenty feet tall and at least one hundred feet long.

His mouth agape, Julius stopped the people hauler on the machine's port side. He exited the hauler and inspected the outside of the cylindrical monstrosity. The side of the machine had the name given to the borer, Red Planet Worm. He walked to the front and gazed upon the diamond-tipped drill head.

"This machine looks complex." Julius wasn't sure where he would start.

"Kid, it's a lot easier than you think. Grab the control tablet on the passenger seat of the people hauler."

Julius returned to the vehicle and grabbed the tablet, turning it on by waving his hand over the screen. There was only one application present on the device called Dig a Tunnel.

"Dig a Tunnel?"

"Don't laugh at the name, kid. I know it sounds like a song from a B-list Disney movie."

Julius clicked on the app, and a user interface opened. It had a bunch of text box parameters and three large buttons across the bottom. The buttons were labeled "Connect," "Dig," and "Emergency Stop."

"This seems pretty self-explanatory."

"I would hope so. All you have to do is fill in the parameters. AMSPACE is pretty efficient when it comes to determining where the mineral deposits are. You have to just put in the latitude, longitude, and elevation of the mineral deposit given to you by HQ, and the AI in the tunnel borer will take control."

"I see. So what about the other text boxes?"

"Those will be filled in when it is completed, like how long it took the dig to complete and speed of the borer."

"Got it, so just those are just statistics for reports?"

"Precisely. We keep very meticulous records, it's a part of our contract with the American Union government."

"I understand. Do you have some inputs for me?"

"Give me a moment." While Julius waited for a reply, he pressed the "Connect" button. The background of the app turned green, signaling Julius was connected to the Red Planet Worm.

"Got 'em, 4.59 degrees south, 137.44 degrees east, elevation negative one hundred meters."

Julius inputted the values and pressed the "Dig" button. The borer roared to life with a long and deep metallic grunt. The drill began to rotate clockwise. The cylindrical body coiled up like a cobra, lifting its front toward the sky, then arching toward the ground. The machine hastily lowered to the ground and started to chew the Martian ground away, creating a large hole. The sound was deafening, like standing in the middle of a factory floor with no ear protection. As the machine dug deeper, it stabilized the tunnel behind it, preventing cave-ins.

Julius walked toward the massive hole the machine created. Before he could reach it, the bubbles appeared, and the hole was removed. It was like the massive digger had never dug a hole in the first place.

"Martin! Why can't I go down there?" Julius was clearly upset. He looked down at the fresh dirt where the hole once was.

"You have other lessons to learn, Julius. Plus when you are on Mars, you aren't permitted to enter a hole. Only the precision miners are allowed."

Before Julius could ask another question, the bubbles appeared in front of him. When they cleared, Julius saw a vehicle that looked like a people hauler. The big difference was a large drill bit on the back. The bit looked similar to the drill section on the borer.

The drill bit was mounted to crane that allowed it to be lowered to the ground. "You're going to use that to drill a hole. You must dig thirty feet so a soil sample can be taken by a terraforming specialist like Abigail."

"Okay," Julius replied before he sat down in the driver's seat. TAMR showed him how to work the hauler with the helmet just as they'd done the day before with the hover bike. Julius switched into drilling mode and started the drill. The drill was electrically powered off the same power cell that made the drill hauler run. Operating the controls used for driving, he lowered the drill to the ground. Soon the sound of crushing rock was heard as the drill head hit the Martian surface.

Julius extended the drill until the depth indicator on the dashboard read thirty feet. He disengaged the drill and raised it before he exited to observe at his handiwork.

"Good job, Julius. Remember how to use that machine. It is also used to add relief tunnels for the borer in case we lose it." Martin went on to explain a few more simple gadgets that Julius might encounter. He learned about how to use the handheld digger and a force field generator to save him in the event of a cave in. After a few hours, Martin told Julius to return to camp.

Julius got in the people hauler and drove toward camp. He was excited that he seemed to be doing well. On the way back, Martin said, "When you return to camp and meet up with Abigail, you two will exit the simulator."

Julius was confused; he thought he would be there for much longer than just a few days. "Martin, I don't understand. I've only been in training for a couple of days."

"We've been directed by Camilla to accelerate the training, so you will be getting a crash classroom course with Becka and I outside the simulator. You launch tonight." Those words swirled in Julius's mind. He could barely contain his excitement. Tonight, he would begin his journey to Mars.

Abigail was already waiting in the center of camp next to her hover bike. As Julius pulled up to her, she waved at him and smiled. He exited his vehicle and strolled over to her.

"What did they have you do?"

"Oh, trivial things, like learning how to operate a terraforming building. I could make a category five terrastorm if I wanted to." Abigail lowered her voice to sound sinister.

"Okay, let's calm it down, Abi-*gale*." Julius felt a little uncomfortable but took a chance on making a joke. Abigail rolled her eyes at him. "All I know is, I wouldn't want to cross you." Julius laughed a bit nervously.

"Yeah, you don't want to do that. I can be quite vengeful." She winked at him.

Suddenly, the bubbles appeared in front of the two. When they had finished popping, two large metal doors remained.

"Walk through the door," Martin said to Julius. Becka told Abigail to do the same. The two grabbed the cold handles and opened their designated doors. All Julius could see was blackness. He felt anxious, looking into the door. He glanced to his right and saw Abigail was already gone, so he walked through the threshold.

After passing through the dark door, Julius found himself in an air lock. It was much larger than the one he used a few days prior. Now outside the Rendering Room, he was completely naked since the computers could not generate clothes around him. He walked the short distance in the steel-plated room to a door with a small port window.

He gazed through it and saw a form of a woman he thought was Abigail changing into an outfit. He could not make out who this person was because the window was made of frosted glass. He waited for her to exit the next room to her right before he entered.

Once inside, he saw she had entered the current room from another air lock. He looked around the small room that had a layout similar to a department store changing room. A strange-looking suit, like one a NASCAR pit crew member would wear, hung on the wall. The suit was white with red stripes that ran from the neck over the shoulders and down to the wrists. Across the waist was a black belt that permitted the tightening and loosening of the fabric. The chest had the AMSPACE logo over his heart. When he flipped it over to see the back, he saw his last name in bright red letters.

Julius quickly put the jumpsuit on over the undergarments also laid out on a bench. He looked around the small room. Now facing where he had come from, Julius saw the room had four doors. The two metal ones he and Abigail exited were in front of him, and the other two were to his left and right. Julius decided to follow where Abigail went and took the door on his left. Julius opened the door and found himself in a room he did not think belonged in a research facility. It was a grand office, with thirty-foot ceilings painted blue with beautiful wood crown molding weaving throughout.

The lower half of the walls were made of fine wood paneling from the redwood forests. A large white-marble fireplace was to Julius's right and seemed to be the centerpiece of the room. Two brown-leather couches and a coffee table sat in front of the extravagant fireplace. A large oriental rug covered the hardwood flooring.

Julius felt as though he was dropped into an upper-class living room. To his left was a mahogany desk that was hand carved and looked like the *Resolute* desk in the White House.

Abigail stood in front of the desk, looking at Martin and Becka, who were standing on either side of the desk's chair. In the chair was Camilla with her fingers interwoven resting on the desktop. Seeing Camilla made Julius sweat a little.

"Mr. Stetson, won't you join us?" Camilla asked in a cold monotone. She gestured with her hand for Julius to stand next to Abigail. As Julius approached and stood next to Abigail, he noticed the intricate carving on the desk.

Each section of the desk was divided into panels that depicted a significant event from space exploration history. Julius scanned in awe at the craftsmanship; he saw a panel of Ben Lewis planting the US flag on Mars. The next one to the right was of the first AMSPACE shuttle launch, and the center one was the AMSPACE logo.

"Mr. Stetson, am I boring you already?" Camilla's cold voice sent shivers down Julius's spine as he looked up at the woman.

"Yes, si—I mean, no, si—I mean, no, ma'am," he said.

Abigail cracked a smile and tried to hold back a giggle that ended up slipping out anyway.

Camilla glared at Abigail, who stopped smiling and stood at attention. "Sorry, ma'am," she said quietly enough to show respect but loudly enough for Camilla to hear her.

"Now, if we are done with these silly games, Mr. Stetson. And childish behavior, Miss King. I've decided that you two will be on the shuttle leaving for Mars tonight!" She paused for a second.

"As I said on the phone, Miss González, Julius and Abigail are nowhere near ready to go to Mars. I have many more trainings for Julius to complete before I give my stamp of approval. Becka has more work for Abigail as well." Martin's voice held a lot of concern, and that made Julius a little nervous.

"Nonsense, Martin. They can have real on-the-job training. We need more people up there now. There was an incident at a terraforming facility, so we need more bodies," Camilla said.

"But, ma'am, we haven't scheduled a rocket to take them to Mars."

"They'll take the shuttle line I just said. We had a backup arrive this morning. It's currently transporting some special cargo from Vancouver." Camilla started at Martin coolly. Martin sensed that she did not care what he had to say.

"I understand, Miss González. We'll get them prepped."

"Do you two have any questions?" Camilla asked, turning her head to Julius and Abigail.

"What's the special cargo?" Julius asked, looking around awkwardly.

"It's what you're going to Mars to mine, Mr. Stetson," Camilla said with a hint of sarcasm, instantly making Julius regret asking. He also wondered what she was hiding since he did not know what he was mining for. Camilla stood up and gestured to the door.

"I need to prepare for the arrival of the cargo. I'll see you four on the tarmac at 2100." Camilla watched the group exit the massive office.

As soon as they walked out, the automatic door closed. Camilla reached under the desk and pressed a button. A large glass screen slid out from the center of the desk and turned on like an old vacuum-tube television from a century prior.

Once the glass plate was on, Camilla saw a beaming chairman sitting behind his desk in Chicago.

"You've done well, Camilla. The company and I thank you for your devotion to its continued success."

"Thank you, Mr. Chairman. I take that means you saw the footage from the experiment and read my report?" Camilla felt a sense of pride well up inside her at his praise.

"I did see the experiment, and I have to say I'm surprised at your commitment. You could have made one of the grunts do it, but you took it upon yourself. That is commitment! Did it hurt? Have you felt any adverse effects from the experiment?" The chairman seemed genuinely interested in hearing her firsthand experience.

"It did hurt, I felt a burning sensation all over my body both inside and out as my body accepted the change. It took me a little time to gain control of my body again. Other than that, I haven't felt any adverse effects. I came here to New Mexico to be monitored by our top scientists. The assets are on route in case we need them."

"Good, Camilla. Your commitment is unwavering. You have had quite the accomplishment for someone who rose up through the ranks so quickly. I'm very proud of what you've done and continue to do."

Camilla could not believe what she just heard. The chairman had never said that to any of his employees. "Th-th-thank you, sir." She felt as though her insides were relaxing and falling into each other.

"Now go prepare for the shipment. I expect daily updates on your status. What you have done will make us a lot of money and change human evolution, so don't be surprised if I come by to see the experiment in action."

"I'd be honored, sir." The chairman nodded and terminated his feed.

Camilla sat in her large chair and felt relief wash over her body. She was so happy the chairman had been pleased about the reckless experiment she performed on herself. She worried her actions would have gotten her fired or worse. So far, it seemed to be paying off. She blinked once, and a video feed was opened up in her glasses.

"Yes, Miss González?" a woman asked.

"Prepare for my arrival in the lab. I want everything to be ready to continue the experiments when the cargo arrives from Vancouver."

"Yes, ma'am," the woman replied before Camilla ended the feed with another blink. She stood up and walked toward her fireplace and looked into the fire and ruminated.

The dancing flames began to form shapes in her mind. She saw her neighborhood in Buenos Aires, where she had lived with her sister and her niece. She watched as the United Air Force flew overhead. She could hear the air raid sirens blaring. Her sister grabbed her daughter and ran for the house while Camilla stared up at the bombers. She snapped out of it and started to bolt for the house before a bomb fell through the roof and exploded, destroying the house. The shock wave knocked Camilla back, slamming her into the ground. Flames bellowed out of the destroyed structure. Camilla ran toward the house as she began to weep angry tears. That day, she vowed to destroy the union and joined the resistance forces in Brazil.

Back in the office, tears were flowing down her face as she continued to stare into the fireplace.

"Never again will I be so helpless." She wiped the tears from her face. "I'll become the most powerful person in this company!"

Everything was going according to the plan she built after her family died in the Amero Wars. She was in the right position to take over AMSPACE. There was one burning question, and she could not move forward until she knew the answer. Who is the chairman?

FIFTEEN

The Launch

The door slammed behind the group, making them all jump forward a little. The shock quickly wore off, and Julius turned to look at Martin. "That was entertaining."

"Watch it, kid, don't piss off Camilla. She can be a real bitch if you get on her bad side," Martin warned.

"Oh really? I just don't feel like she's very trustworthy."

"It doesn't matter how you feel, she's the boss."

Julius went silent as the group of four walked down a crowded hallway full of office workers, robots, and guards. Eventually, Martin opened a door, and the quartet slipped into a small room.

The room was a classroom with a computerized wall at the front. A few chairs were arranged in a semicircle in the center of the room. Julius and Abigail took the two seats in the middle while Martin and Becka stood at the front.

"All right, you two, we need to give you a crash course on what is about to happen," Martin said with frustration in his voice. The situation was not ideal since he could not follow protocol.

"I have this Martin, you can sit for a moment," Becka said. Martin took a seat at the end of the semicircle. Becka put on an obviously fake smile.

"Okay, listen up. This isn't normal, but we're going to do our best to deal with the situation. Since you two will be traveling on an advanced shuttle, your trip will only take a week compared to the month it would take regular rocket-based spacecraft. During that week, you both will be put into a deep sleep. You'll be woken up on final approach to Mars. Once there, Dave will make sure you reach designated teams." Becka continued to lecture them on how the shuttle worked and what the emergency procedures were. She also used the computer wall to show them scenarios of what to do in a specific emergency. Julius and Abigail paid attention as they were lectured; Julius found himself thinking about how it would be better to learn this in the Rendering Room. "Now it's customary for you to get a phone call home before you leave for Mars."

Martin stood up and handed Julius a phone. "Better make the call home, kid."

Becka gave Abigail one too, and the trainers withdrew to the other side of the small room.

Julius looked at the phone and dialed his mom's number. He listened to the phone ring and ring and then ring some more. Just as Julius thought it was going to go to her voicemail, he heard his mom pick up.

"Hello, this is Marie." She had answered like he was any other person on the planet.

"Mom, it's Julius."

"Oh my goodness, Julius. I'm so happy to hear from you!"

"It's great to talk to you, Mom, is everyone at home? Can you put me on speaker?" Julius was excited to talk to his siblings and his father.

"Well, Alicia is out on a date."

"She is? They're lucky I wasn't there. I would've taught them a lesson."

"Relax, Julius, your father took care of the standard alpha-male intimidation."

"What about Dad or Antonio? Are they home?"

"Antonio's out with his friends. They went to Detroit for the evening. He should be on his way home soon." Julius picked up that Marie was suspicious of Antonio's whereabouts.

"Your dad is sitting next to me, let me put him on speaker." This excited Julius. He was finally able to talk to his dad.

"Hey, bud, how's New Mexico?" Hearing his dad's voice made Julius happier.

"Hey, Dad, good to hear from you. New Mexico is good. Just been training a lot."

"It's great to hear from you too, son. So to what do we owe this honor of getting a call from an astronaut-to-be?"

"I wanted to tell everyone I'm getting on a shuttle to Mars in a few hours." Julius waited to hear his parent's reaction to the news.

"That's great, Bud! Enjoy the ride."

"Be careful, sweetie, you mean the world to us. I don't know what this family would do without you," Marie said. Julius could hear her trying to hold tears back.

"I'll be careful, Mom, I promise. Thanks, Dad, I'll do my best to enjoy it."

He looked across the room and saw Martin pointing to his wrist as if he was wearing an old Apple.

"Mom, Dad, I have to get ready to launch. I love and miss you both. Can you please tell Alicia, Antonio, John, and Misty what's going on? I want to keep them up to date since my communication is limited." Julius was reluctant to end the phone call.

"We understand, son. Your mom and I are so proud of you. We love you so much. Be safe."

"Thanks, Dad. Love you both, bye." Julius looked at Martin before he walked over and handed him the sleek phone.

"We need to get you two prepared for launch," Martin said before he opened the door to the hallway. There were significantly less people in the hallway than before. The four stepped into the hallway and made their way down to a door on the end.

Julius thought it might lead outside. Martin swung the door open, and Julius was surprised to see a small indoor garage. A few floating golf carts were in the room. The carts had a flat back for

151

cargo and only had room for two passengers. There were no steering wheels, so Julius assumed an AI controlled them. Across the room was a ramp that descended slightly into a lit tunnel.

"Why're we in here?" Abigail asked.

"We're here because this the easiest way to the launch site. Rockets are prone to accidental combustion. We cannot risk the research center being destroyed. Therefore, the launch site is a few miles away," Becka replied.

She and Martin climbed into two different carts. Julius climbed into the seat next to Martin and Abigail sat next to Becka. Once Abigail and Julius were seated, the carts began to move. Maneuvering to the tunnel, the carts went down the ramp. When they reached the bottom, they traveled down the dimly lit tunnel. Julius looked around and thought it looked similar to a subway in Chicago.

"Nervous, kid?" Martin asked Julius as the golf cart floated down the tunnel.

"I'd be lying if I said I wasn't," Julius replied.

"That's a good thing. Nerves are a sign that you care."

"I guess so, but that doesn't mean that I'm not worried about leaving my planet."

"It's worth the views."

"I'm sure it is, Martin, but what's the ride up like?"

"It's quick, and you'll be lucky to remember it. That drug they use to knock you out usually takes away some memory of the launch. Few people remember it."

"Well, that's a shame. I hope I'm one of the few who remembers. I'm sure it's beautiful."

"It's one of the coolest things you'll see."

As the conversation went stale, Julius's mind wandered to the meeting with Camilla. He felt a strong sense of distrust toward her. During their last meeting, he got a strange feeling from her, as though something had changed from when they'd met in Pontiac till. Her demeanor was different. Her face was redder than last time too. He wondered if her strange demeanor was just the time he had spent in the Rendering Room messing with his head or if it had to do with this mystery cargo.

"Martin, what will I be mining for on Mars?"

"I can't tell you that, Julius. You have to be a member of the precision mining team to be privy to that information. Also, I don't know the answer either."

Stonewalled again, Julius went back to his own thoughts. He was trying to deduce what he could possibly be mining. He couldn't believe Martin didn't know either. He assumed that was a lie.

Julius was pulled out of his thoughts when the vehicle moved up another ramp and into a large hangar. It was immense; Julius estimated it could fit three Boeing 7007s inside it. The cart drove along the side of the hangar and parked itself in the back corner. The four got out and walked along the right wall before they came to a door.

"You two go in there and change into the space suits. It is 2030, and Camilla requires her transports be punctual," Becka said.

Julius allowed Abigail to enter first, showing some chivalry before he followed her into the room. Once inside Julius saw the room was tiny and allowed no privacy from the other occupant. "Well, this is awkward," Julius said, breaking the silence.

"You think? No peeking." There was no flirtation in her voice.

"You change first." Julius turned around and stared at the wall while Abigail changed into her space suit. *Not even at the trusting phase yet*, Julius thought to himself.

"I'm done," she said.

"So can I change now?"

"Of course, thanks for being a gentleman."

"I want the same courtesy that you wanted me to give you."

"Oh right, sorry," Abigail's voice had a slight disappointment in it.

Julius quickly changed into his suit. He didn't notice Abigail stole a few glances at him. Once he was ready, he turned to look at her, and their eyes met. Julius looked into her eyes and debated what to do. Before he reached a decision of what to do, she said, "Well, let's go."

"Yeah, we don't want to be late."

Julius exited, and she followed him out of the door. Once back in the hangar, Julius and Abigail met up with Martin and Becka.

"Let's get moving. Camilla wouldn't be happy if we held up her schedule," Martin explained with an urgent tone of voice. He power-walked, with the rest of the group, to the end of the hangar, where the large hangar door stood open.

Outside, the sun had set, and the stars were just beginning to appear in the darkening sky. Julius looked up and was amazed at the sheer volume of stars he saw. The Greater Detroit area had so much light pollution; the stars were hidden from his sight. He noticed a few twinkling lights that were moving too quickly to be a distant satellite or a shooting star.

As lights approached the landing strip, a shape began to form between them. Julius knew what it was. It was a Lewis-class shuttle, the very same he had helped build in Pontiac. He felt a wave of excitement flood his body. His ride to Mars was on final approach.

The shuttle gracefully landed on the runway and deployed its parachute. Julius was so immersed in watching the shuttle he did not notice a car pull up to his right. The door was opened by the driver, and Camilla emerged.

She slowly moved her way over to the group until she stood beside Julius. He looked over and saw Camilla; her sudden appearance frightened him a little. Luckily for him, she did not see him jump to his left. If she had spotted him, he would have received an earful about how he should respect her.

The shuttle taxied over to the group. Once it was stopped, the rear hatch began to descend. Julius watched in awe as the back gate revealed the ominous looking people in red suits and blackened helmets. They brought the same hovering metal crates from British Columbia, but the screens were blackened.

The red-suited group walked past the quintet in complete silence with the exception of the hum of the antigravity generators in the crates. Julius saw the top of one of the crates was oozing a reddish-orange slime.

What the shit do they have in those crates? Julius wondered to himself as the crates entered the tunnel. The presence of the substance puzzled Julius, as it didn't look like a normal by-product of mining.

"I must go with the shipment. Good luck on the launch." Camilla's voice had unmistakable excitement in it.

"You better get going then, ma'am. We have this covered," Martin said.

"Thank you, Martin." Camilla walked away from the group heading toward the tunnel.

"Let's get you two on your ship," Martin said before he and Becka lead the two travelers to the ship. Julius and Abigail were brought aboard via the open rear hatch. A lot of other cargo was present in the ship. There were food supplies, computer equipment, toy drill haulers, and people haulers too. The presence of the miniatures confused Julius. The interior of the craft looked like the inside of a military transport aircraft.

At the end of the cargo hold was a ladder that led up to the second level. They climbed the ladder to another area. There were two rows of single seats lined on each side of the ship. The seats were positioned to the front, near the door to the cockpit. The seats look like they belonged in a first-class space cruise. They could recline, which was useful for the hibernation. Next to each seat were small circular windows.

"Here's the deal. You'll be strapped in here for the duration of the weeklong trip. You, along with the pilots, will be automatically administered a sedative that slows down your heart rate and basically puts your bodies into a hibernation. Your seats will recline to prevent hibernation stiffness," Becka said as Julius and Abigail took their seats.

"Once you're out of the atmosphere, the AI will give you and the crew the sedative. At that point, the AI will take over flying the craft. There will be multiple passes around Earth to ramp up the speed and keep the g-forces your body experiences low. Your suit temperature will be lowered to freeze you and prevent the need for food and water. Once you're an hour from landing on Mars and the AI has begun the rotation around Mars to gradually slow the ship down, your suit temperature will rise, and you will be given an antidote to the sedative. At that point, you will awaken," Martin explained.

Martin and Becka checked to see if the travelers were ready to fly. They grabbed the helmets for their designated person and placed them on their heads. Julius shook with excitement as he looked around. He did his best to take mental pictures of everything around him. He did not want to let the sedative make him forget any detail. He didn't hear Martin tell him good luck. Julius just nodded at Martin absently before Martin and Becka exited the craft.

Julius looked over at Abigail, who seemed completely calm. He, on the other hand, was ecstatic and could not sit still. Julius heard the rear hatch close.

"Shuttle four to AMSPACE control request permission to leave New Mexico Station." Julius heard the pilot speak.

Julius didn't hear a response from AMSPACE control before the ship lurched forward. It taxied away from the hanger out to the end of the runway, where it stopped. During the pause, Julius felt a pit form in his stomach.

This was it, the moment he had been waiting for all his life. He could hear the muffled voices of the pilots talking to AMSPACE control in the cockpit. As he listened, he picked out the words he had been waiting to hear for years.

"Shuttle four, you're cleared for launch."

"Roger, control. Pulling away."

Before he could mentally prepare, Julius's head was thrown back in the seat as the pilot floored it.

The shuttle rocketed down the runway like a Japanese bullet train. Julius felt his adrenaline spike as he craned his neck to look out the small window next to him.

Everything outside was just a blur. The ship broke the sound barrier just after it left the ground, where it angled toward the sky as it climbed. This was not like any airplane Julius had ever been on. The sideways shaking was unbelievable, so intense Julius could not see Abigail clearly. She was nothing more than a blurry blob as the shuttle continued to rocket upward.

The vibration gave him wave after wave of goose bumps as his body tried to vent the adrenaline rush. *Please don't ever let this end. This must be how Neil Armstrong felt when he flew to the moon*, Julius thought as he tried to imagine what it was like to fly in a Saturn V. He turned back to the window and saw the ground was far away.

Julius managed to pry his eyes away from the shrinking ground to watch the shuttle reach the thermosphere. He saw the curvature of the earth and the glow the planet produced against the darkness of space.

There were small dots twinkling above the earth that Julius guessed to be satellites. He even caught a glimpse at the massive AMSPACE station that regulated the space traffic above Earth. He kept watching the beauty outside his window with childlike wonder. Julius had always dreamed of this moment; now he was living it. He wanted to pinch himself; he couldn't believe it was real.

Suddenly, Julius felt a small pinprick in his cubital fossa that caused him to wince uncomfortably. He looked over at Abigail once more to see how she was doing. She was already being lowered to a reclining position.

That pinprick had to be the sedative Martin and Becka were talking about, Julius thought as he turned back to the small window. The ship continued to vibrate as it began to circle Earth to increase its speed safely. Julius watched the planet he called home spin. As he stared, darkness clouded his vision as his eyes closed involuntarily. A minute later, he was asleep.

SIXTEEN

Arrival

Julius shook violently as he woke in a cold sweat. He was restrained by the seatbelt of the chair. "Relax, Sleeping Beauty, we're here. See for yourself," Abigail said, pointing out Julius's window.

He looked out and saw something he only dreamed of—Mars. The planet was massive and looked more amazing in person than any picture he had seen.

The ship had completed its slow downturns to safely bring the ship down from its high velocity.

Far off, Julius saw the AMSPACE Mars Station. It was a hive of activity; rockets and shuttles were coming and going. Due to its position relative to the asteroid belt, the station was used as a staging area for the asteroid mining crews. Julius's shuttle approached and passed by the station. The shuttle began its descent, and he watched Mars grow closer.

The shuttle glided through the thin Martian atmosphere, creating a fireball as it descended. After they had slowed, down the fireball disappeared, and Julius looked out the window. He smiled as the red-tinted ground got closer and closer.

His eyes were drawn to a building that stood next to a landing strip. The ship banked and lined up with the runway. As it landed, the cabin jolted before a rapid deceleration that made Julius and

Abigail lean forward. The shuttle taxied to the hangar next to the building.

As it approached, he recognized some hyper-rail tracks that terminated at the hangar. Inside was a train comprised of one passenger car and a storage car. It looked very similar to a bullet train where the power came from each individual car. The train was streamlined with a shiny silver exterior.

Once the shuttle had entered the hangar, Julius saw many people in space suits waiting. The door to the hangar was closed before the rear cargo hold was opened. The oxygen had already been removed. Many people began to unload the supplies in the cargo hold, while two guards holding assault-rifle-shaped electronic weapons came into the passenger area. They ordered Julius and Abigail to follow them. The duo quickly unbuckled their straps before following them out the rear of the shuttle.

The hangar was buzzing with people loading the supplies into the waiting hyper-rail car. As he walked toward the hyper-rail through the hangar, he caught a glimpse of one of the strange, hovering cargo containers he saw back in New Mexico. To Julius, it made sense why it was there since this seemed like a distribution center. He just found it strange it was unguarded; perhaps it was empty.

Julius and Abigail walked up a platform and onto the lead passenger car where they sat. The interior looked like a metro car with lots of standing room.

"You two are not to say anything about what you just saw," one of the guards said.

"But why? All we saw were some crates full of food and stuff. Maybe a toy people hauler or two," Abigail said.

"Again, you speak nothing of what you saw. Regular people such as yourselves don't come through here. We can't risk rogues raiding our supply chain. Camilla felt she could trust you with the location of the cargo loading dock. Don't make her regret it," said the other guard.

Julius really didn't care about the location of the cargo building, but he took a mental note of where it was, as did Abigail. The guards took their seats, and Julius and Abigail removed their helmets. Now that they were not dodging people, he was finally able to get a look at the two guards. They were wearing ruggedized Martian camo space suits. Their faces were generic and cleanly shaven, and their hair was well kept. They looked to be ex-military.

The hyper-rail began its smooth acceleration. It pulled away from the interior of the hangar through an enormous door. It had opened to allow the train passage through the wall of the building.

Julius continued to look out the window and saw the train was approaching a metal perimeter wall. The train passed through the wall via another passage that opened to let it pass. He saw numerous AI-controlled plasma weapons lining the wall. A handful of people, dressed similarly to the guards on the train, were roaming on top of the wall, checking the turrets.

Are they really worried about rogue settlements and terrorists that much? Doesn't seem like the small groups up here are able to pose a significant enough threat for that kind of firepower. They are just a few religious groups and people who want a new life. I guess they could be a real threat if they banded together. The rules of Earth don't really apply here it seems, Julius thought.

He tried to focus back on the fact that he was on Mars. This might not have been how he thought his first few moments on Mars would be spent, but he was going to enjoy them. He looked around at the landscape as it rushed by. He felt happy; this was really Mars, unlike the simulation. He was actually here.

As he looked around, his eyes were drawn to a building in the distance. The structure looked familiar, like the mess hall Martin had manifested inside the Rendering Room.

It was metal and had lots of windows on the first few floors, but this building was slightly different than it was in the simulation. It had extra floors and a massive parabolic dish communications antenna on the roof.

"Any idea what that antenna is for?" Julius whispered to Abigail.

"I would guess it's to enable communications with the AMSPACE Mars Station, orbiting the planet," she theorized.

"Makes sense, I just wonder why Martin didn't render that in the simulation. I thought he wanted it to be as realistic as possible."

"He probably just forgot. It's not like the lack of an antenna affected your training. Are you enjoying yourself? You've been silent since we got off the shuttle."

"I'm good, just taking it all in."

"Me too. Quite the spectacle, isn't it? The internet doesn't do it justice."

The train traveled for about twenty minutes before another metal wall appeared on the horizon. Julius felt the hyper-rail begin to slow down before the train slid past another barrier. This one was less guarded than the last, but still had weapons dotting it.

The train pulled off the mainline and entered a wing attached to the building with the communications tower. It was a massive station that had multiple garage doors that sealed off the entrances to the main building. The air pressurized inside the station before the guards ordered Julius and Abigail to disembark.

They complied with the guards, who guided them out into the station. It was a white room with a tan floor from what Julius could see. The platform was filling with personal preparing to board the hyper-rail. Julius looked back through the crowd to see the storage car being removed.

As they reached the far wall, he saw additional passenger cars being attached. It was early morning, and the train was preparing for the large crowd of people heading off to work the mines. The guards led them to an elevator where they aggressively gestured for the duo to enter.

The doors stood open as an alarm began to sound, and Julius saw a blue flashing light. The oxygen had to be removed from the room prior to the train's departure since the side doors needed to be opened. People were moving quickly to get off the platform. The doors to the elevator closed before he could see what else happened.

The floor number counted up to six, where the elevator stopped, and the doors slid open. The guards nudged Julius and Abigail forward with the butts of their rifles. They wandered into a hallway sparsely populated by other people. Julius and Abigail kept walking until they reached a grand metal door with a holographic sign on it. The sign read, "Dave Hughes, Head of Martian Operations."

The guards knocked on the door and waited for a response. A few seconds later, a gruff and commanding voice uttered one word: "Enter."

Julius felt a chill go up his spine. The last time he talked to Dave, the man had been a jerk. Julius braced himself for another unpleasant experience with his childhood hero.

One of the guards opened the door, and Julius and Abigail entered the room. Julius scanned the space and saw it was not the traditional office he came to expect from AMSPACE. There was wood flooring, a drafting table for a desk, a few books on bookshelves, and many paintings of Mars.

Behind the drafting table was Dave with a cigar in his mouth and feet propped up. Julius took note that Dave looked very unprofessional. There was a silence in the air as the two breathed in the thick smoke that hung in the room.

"Welcome to Mars FNGs." Dave finally spoke after looking them both up and down.

"Uh, thank you, sir," Julius said timidly.

Abigail looked over at Julius then back to Dave. "Beg your pardon sir, I can't speak for Julius, but I wasn't expecting to be roughhoused or intimidated by your thugs. Then you have the audacity to call me an FNG. I might be new, but I worked hard to get here. So I don't think I am a fucking new guy."

"Damn, I don't think anyone has stood up to me like that on their first day, Miss King," Dave said with pure shock in his voice. He put his feet down and turned to Julius. "Come on, Stetson. I was bein' a jerk! You should stand up for yourself."

"If you want me to stand up for myself, I will…I didn't appreciate you blowing me off the first time we met. You were my role model," Julius said.

"I'm sorry about that, kid. I'm a busy man. Here's a life lesson for you. Never meet your idols, they will always disappoint you."

Dave turned his leather swivel chair away from the two. Julius was about to say something else but felt Abigail grab his hand. He turned to her, and she gave him a look that told him to let it go. Julius was surprised that she kept holding his hand.

"Sir, why are we here?" Abigail asked.

"I wanted to size you two up. See what Camilla produced. I'm not sure if you both know. She's supposed to let me evaluate every employee. But since you're here, I have some assignments for you. Miss King, you're to report to the terraforming unit immediately. Mr. Stetson is to report to his drilling team."

Julius felt a little of his anger melt away, replaced by nervous excitement.

"I intentionally held Dig Team Mike back from assignment so you could meet with them today, so enjoy drinks on the house. Now, living arrangements. You two were training partners and seem to get along well." Dave gestured to their handholding.

Immediately, Abigail released Julius's hand and looked away, making Dave chuckle.

"You two will be living together as shelter mates. The soldiers will escort you to where you need to be. Good luck out there." The door to his office opened on cue.

The two men walked back in and motioned for Julius and Abigail to follow them. They got up and left the office. Julius's anger was now gone, and he felt only excitement and anxiety. He was excited to be with Abigail more often and intimidated by that prospect as well. Plus, he was about to meet his dig team. He looked at Abigail, who was avoiding his gaze.

When they reached the end of the hallway, one guard pushed Julius to the left and Abigail to the right. He watched her as she walked down the hallway entering an office. He went down a set of stairs.

The office Abigail entered had a glowing holographic nameplate that said, "Terraforming Specialist, Jasmine Tyson."

Julius went down the stairs to the main floor, where the mess hall was located. The corridors were empty, aside from a few custodians cleaning the floors from the morning rush.

Julius and his guard walked down the hallway of air lock locker rooms. As they walked, they passed a wide opening to what Julius theorized was the mess hall, since it looked like a cafeteria.

"Turn right," the guard ordered. Julius complied and saw a door with a sign over it that read, "Bar and Game Room."

Julius opened the door. *They actually have a bar here? Must brew their own beer because it's hard to transport it, I'm sure*, Julius thought.

He walked in and saw five people gathered around a small bar. There was a sixth person behind the bar preparing drinks. He was trying to observe them a bit before making his presence known, but the person behind the bar spotted him.

He was a big guy with tan skin, and a bushy black beard. That was all Julius could make out before the guy spoke with slurred speech and a southern accent.

"New guy's here."

Everyone sitting at the bar turned and looked at him, and an awkward silence followed. Julius stood there, unsure of what he should do.

"Well, come on over and have a drink," the short woman on the end said. Julius walked over and took a seat next to the woman.

"'Ello, Julius, I'm Irene Fokina, leader of Dig Team Mike," the woman said in a light Ukrainian accent. She was very muscular and had a nose ring. Her black hair was trimmed to a pixie cut.

"Let me introduce you to the rest of the team." Irene turned to look down the bar.

"Before you do intros, Irene, what'll you have new guy?" the bearded man behind the bar asked.

"Give me whatever's good on tap, you look like a man who knows."

"Rock Light it is!" the man declared before he began pouring the beer.

"Logan, usually you introduce yourself when you meet some-one new," Irene said to Logan before looking back at Julius. "That's Logan Clarke, our resident redneck and beer connoisseur."

"Ya know I prefer Tex." He turned around and put the beer down in front of Julius spilling a little on the counter. Tex then grabbed some whiskey and poured himself a shot.

"Tex is from Texas, if it wasn't obvious. You think you can take it easy on the alcohol intake, Tex?" Irene asked.

"Hell no! Shit's free. There are two good types of booze. The first is free. The second is cold. I'm getting both so you can be sure I'm taking full advantage." Tex took his shot.

Julius took a sip of the light lager as he evaluated Tex. Quite the character, rough around the edges but seemed like a decent fellow at his core.

"The big boy next to you is Bobby Mauer," Irene said as Julius turned to his left. Bobby was probably 250 pounds. His hair was blond and unkempt. On his face was a large grin, which made Julius think he wasn't all there.

"Nice to meetcha, Julius," Bobby said as he extended his hand.

Julius grabbed his hand to shake it, before he felt a shock go up his arm. Julius immediately pulled his hand away.

"Ow, what the heck was that?" Julius shook out his hand, trying to get the pain out of it.

"Oldest trick in the book, Julius, you need to get on your game," Bobby said, showing a very crudely put together circular button in the center of his hand.

"How's that the oldest trick in the book? I've never seen anyone do that."

"The pranksters of today will hack your glasses or something. I'm a man of class and prefer to use only vintage pranks."

"You mean you're too stupid to pull off modern pranks, so you rely on old tricks to get your laughs?" Tex interjected. Everyone else at the bar laughed.

"Shut up, Tex, or I'll give you toothpaste Oreos again," Bobby said with a smirk.

"You'll find your fat head in a toilet if you try to screw with me again, dingus!"

"All right, that's enough, you two. Pay him no mind, Julius. There's a reason his nickname is the Digging Dingus. If you stop giving him a reaction, he'll move on to bother Kitten or someone else," Irene said, pointing to a scrawny five-foot-nine ginger.

"His name's Kitten?" Julius asked, confused.

"We don't acknowledge his real name because he is annoying like a kitten," Irene said as the rest of the group laughed.

"My name's James Morris, Irene." James tried to act calm, but his tone sounded downright whiney.

"Oh, shut it, Kitten! If you could hold your own out in the wilderness, we would change your nickname," said a large black man sitting next to James. He sounded like he had a northern accent.

"Julius, this is Jaivan Carr, he's from Winnipeg. He doesn't have a nickname," Irene said.

"I prefer to keep it that way. Nicknames are so juvenile, which is why those two have them. We let Tex slide because he's from down south and doesn't have an edumication."

Tex was busy pouring another shot for himself to hear what Jaivan said.

There was a small Asian woman on the other side of Jaivan. She had black hair, glasses, and a petite body. "Kon'nichiwa, Sakanaka Sadakodesu," she said, smiling at Julius.

"What?" Julius asked.

"Your universal translator isn't working again," Irene said. Julius watched the woman put her hand into her mouth and press something.

"Can you understand me now?" the Asian woman asked in English.

"Yes, now can you repeat what you said before?" Irene requested.

"Of course, hello, I am Sadako Sakanaka."

"Better known as Saké!" Tex yelled out.

Jaivan reached over the bar and punched the drunk Texan. "Shut it, Tex; no need to be a jackass."

"Screw you, man," Tex choked out, trying not to vomit after the punch to the gut.

"Well, it's nice to meet you all," Julius said, looking at all of them.

"So where're ya from Julius?" Jaivan asked.

"I'm from Detroit. Well, Pontiac, to be exact."

"Screw that team up north," Bobby said.

"I'm not a Michigan fan, more of a State fan," Julius replied.

"Still, it's late morning in Columbus, and Michigan still sucks."

"Where are you from? Columbus?"

"Nah, I'm from Cleveland."

"How're those Browns doing on their seventy-nine-year Super Bowl drought?"

"At least we have a win, unlike your Lions. Who goes almost two hundred years without a Super Bowl win?"

"Enough sports," Irene said, looking at both of them.

"Sorry, Irene," Julius said.

"How'd you get here?" James asked.

"He flew here on a spacecraft," Tex answered sarcastically.

"That's not what I meant, and you know it!"

"I understand what you meant. I won my factory's lottery," Julius replied.

"That's how Bobby got here too. It's the only way he could've made it. Dumb ass can't even do math right," James said.

"Shut your pothole, Kitten. I could've made it without that lottery."

"No way you could, you're too stupid!"

Bobby lunged for James, who backed away. Jaivan grabbed Bobby and pulled him back into his seat.

"Enough! One more time and both of you will be flying home! Do you understand?" Irene said.

"Yes, Irene," both James and Bobby said.

"Good, now, James, why don't you tell Julius how you got your job?"

"My father helped me get an interview," James said softly.

"Kitten, you got it through nepotism," Tex said.

"No, I used my connections."

All the fighting made Julius finish his beer quickly. "Tex, can I get another? Pretty good beer you recommended." Julius tried to distract himself. It seemed like his digging team was a merry band of misfits.

"You liked it? No one ever does. They say it tastes too much like Busch Light."

"I love Busch Light. That's America's beer."

"Damn right it is. I'll keep the beers flowing." Tex poured and served Julius another drink.

"How did you get here, Irene? You look like you've seen some things," Julius asked the woman. He was keying in on the scars on her arms that her tattoos were meant to cover.

"I came here after receiving a promotion from miner to team leader."

"That's great, so you've been with Dig Team Mike awhile, then?"

"Not exactly, did you ever hear of Alpha-Bravo-Twenty-Three?"

"Wasn't that an asteroid that collapsed because of overmining for gold?"

"The very same. I was on that blasted rock when that idiot took out a central support column. I was in the mine when the alert for immediate evacuation came over the radio. I ran as hard as I could and barely made it into an escape pod before I watched the whole thing break apart. A lot of my friends were on that, including my brother. I never saw them again. Now I'm here," she said, taking a shot of vodka Tex had poured for her.

"Shit," was all Julius could think to say.

"Yeah, it sucked a lot and still does."

"We should change the subject. Irene, what's tomorrow's dig?" Sadako asked.

"Tomorrow we'll be working with Dig Team Golf, that's all I know. We'll get further instructions at the drop point. We're hyper-railing tomorrow."

"Damn it, I wanted a bike," Tex said.

"Get over it, you redneck, you'll get to use one again soon," Jaivan said.

The group kept drinking, as did Julius until they were all intoxicated. Conversations continued, but to Julius, it was all a blur. Eventually Julius heard a knock at the bar door some hours later. A robot with the body shape of a woman entered the bar.

"Dig Team Mike, you need to report to your shelters for curfew, or the security forces will be summoned."

"Okay, chill out, robo-bitch," Irene said, standing up, stumbling toward the door to the bar.

Tex walked out from behind the bar. "This ain't fair. I'm not ready to go back to my shelter." Tex threw his glass of beer on the ground, causing it to shatter into a million pieces.

Almost immediately, Jaivan grabbed the big Texan and shoved him against the wall. "Dial it back, big guy. We don't want you to end up in the drunk tank again, do we?"

"No! I don't wanna go back there!"

"Good. Now let me help you out of here." Jaivan put Tex's arm over his shoulder and carried him out. Julius followed Jaivan and Tex.

Saké and Bobby hastily followed Julius out, leaving James at the bar. The robot turned to James before she spoke, "James Morris! Clean up that broken glassware."

"Hell no, I didn't do it!"

"Too bad Kitten, better step to it," Tex slurred.

Julius looked back and saw James stooping down to clean up the glass; he looked upset. Julius stopped in his tracks and turned around. He walked back in and knelt down next to James.

"Can I give you a hand, James?"

"Seriously?" James asked, shocked that Julius came back.

"Yeah, why not? Tex shafted you. You know, you should try to stand up for yourself more." Julius helped pick up the shards of glass.

"I try, but they ignore me."

"I can tell. It takes time. You aren't as bad as Bobby. He's worse."

"That guy's an idiot. I don't know how anyone tolerates him."

"Maybe because they have to, he seems very juvenile. A little strange for him to be here, isn't it?"

"Yeah, but they give him all the stupid and easy assignments, so that's a plus."

"That is a plus because we don't have to do them. And then he'll be out of the way. So what does your dad do, James?"

"He's the head communications and data storage officer on the planet. Since the space station is so limited in storage, they have all the company's data archives here in this building. My dad helps keep it secure. There's only one terminal to access it all unless you want to work through all the security the other computers have."

"Interesting, sounds like he knows a lot."

"Yeah, he has one of the highest company clearances. He sees all the data in the archives come in, so he has to know what's going on."

"Gotcha, makes sense."

Seems like his dad knows what is really in those crates I saw in New Mexico, Julius thought. Maybe there could be a chance to learn what they were.

"Thanks again for your help, Julius," James said as they finished up.

"No problem. You aren't as bad as they make you seem. You're cool in my book."

"Thanks, Julius."

The two walked out of the bar and down to their team's air lock locker room. Once inside, Julius found a locker just for him with a few space suits. He and James put them on and walked outside onto the Martian dirt.

Once outside, Julius saw a plethora of shelters with varying numbers of individual pods on them. In the far distance, Julius could make out the barrier wall that encased the entire outpost.

Julius saw a few drone forklifts moving shelters around.

"I'll see you tomorrow, Julius," James said before he walked away.

"Bye," Julius replied as he realized he was lost. "Well, maybe I'll get lucky and guess the correct shelter." Julius then started off in a random direction.

Julius walked around aimlessly for thirty minutes. He roamed the rows of shelters in a drunken haze, trying to find any clue to where his shelter would be. Just when he was about to give up, Julius heard a familiar feminine voice.

"Looks like my training partner got himself lost." He whirled around to see Abigail standing behind him with her hands on her hips.

"Abigail? What are you doing here?" Julius asked.

"Well, you never showed up to the shelter, so I came looking for you. Did your new friends not show you where your shelter was?" She closed the distance between him and her.

"Are we in the same shelter?"

"Yeah, we're shelter mates. Remember our meeting with Dave?"

"No?"

"You're obviously too drunk to remember. Remember we are in the same shelter, but in separate rooms."

"Yeah, uh…sure." Julius nervously laughed as Abigail grabbed his hand.

She dragged him down a row of shelters to one with just two bubbles off to the side like Julius's original one from training.

Abigail opened the main air lock and brought Julius into it. They removed their spacesuits. Abigail had to help Julius out of his since the alcohol was really affecting him. They then entered the living room section of the shelter.

"I'm just going to sleep here," he said as he lay down on the couch.

"I mean, it isn't that far to the bed," Abigail said before she looked down at him. He had passed out, already snoring.

"Whatever," she said, a little disappointed he didn't stay up to talk with her. She turned and walked to her section of the shelter, where she went to sleep.

SEVENTEEN

First Real Day of Work

Abigail shook Julius awake. "Morning, Stu!" Abigail said, laughing.

"Who's Stu?"

"Did you never see the remake of that movie *The Hangover?*"

"No, why would I watch a comedy about getting blacked out?" Julius was rubbing his head, not seeing the irony of his statement.

"I don't know, because it's funny?"

"Okay, Abigail. Uh, thanks for helping me last night."

"Yeah, it's whatever. I think it's time for breakfast. You don't want to be late for your first day on the job," Abigail said before she walked back to her section of the shelter.

Julius groaned and rolled off the couch. His head was pounding, and the bright light was not helping. Julius got to his feet and felt very dizzy. He stumbled to his section of the shelter. There he saw a change of clothes folded on his bed along with a tablet that had a few email notifications. He scrolled through the notifications and saw there was a bunch from his mom.

This made him excited. He couldn't wait to look at the emails. There was one in particular that caught his eye, from Gerald. Julius quickly opened it and began to read.

Julius,

I wanted to reach out and see how Mars is treating you. Camilla told me you were sent to Mars early because you were a critical need. I heard the chairman personally approved it. Congratulations on making it there. Your friends are doing well, still producing the best spacefaring ships the world has ever seen. If you feel like writing me back and informing me about what it's like to be on Mars, I would appreciate it. I have always wanted to go, but I'm far too old, and my body is too broken for that to be a reality. Hope to hear from you soon.

Sincerely,
Gerald McGinnus

Julius smiled to himself, reading this email. It was nice to know someone outside his family and friends was rooting for him. Julius hastily wrote a reply.

Mr. McGinnus,

It was very nice hearing from you. I made it to Mars safely, and so far, it has been a whirlwind of a time. It was different than I expected. I am actually late for my first day, but I wanted to reply, so you knew I saw your email. I will reply later with a summary of my first day.

Thanks,
Julius

Julius sent the email before he went back to the main room. He checked the air lock and saw it was safe to enter. He opened the door, walked in, and bumped into Abigail, who was changing into her suit.

"Ow!" Abigail stood up and glared at him.

"I'm sorry. I thought you left."

"Well, pay attention next time."

"I will. Honestly, I'm glad you're here. I don't know if I could find my way through the maze of shelters."

"Okay, I'll help you, but just this once."

Julius got into his suit, and the two walked toward the central building.

"Did you get any emails, Julius?"

"I did, but I haven't had a chance to look at them all. I only looked at one from the president of my old factory."

"He sent you an email?"

"Yeah? What's wrong with that?"

"Just seems peculiar that you would get an e-mail from someone so high up. Do you have a personal relationship with this person?"

"Well, no. I guess it is a little peculiar, but we had a good conversation before I shipped off. He seemed like a nice man, so I don't see anything strange about it."

"Okay, Julius. I was just saying."

They had reached the central building where they separated and entered their respective locker rooms. There was no one in Julius's locker room, but he guessed they were eating already.

Meanwhile, Abigail was changing in her locker room. There was another woman whom she met the previous day, Laura Martinez. Abigail saw her and decided to start a conversation.

"Excuse me, you're Laura, right?" Laura looked at Abigail.

"I'm Abigail. We met yesterday."

The Latina woman across the room looked at Abigail and gave a slight smile. "Uh, yeah. Hi. Nice to see you again."

"Same to you. Would you want to get breakfast before we need to head out to the lab?"

"Really? You'd want to hang out with me?"

"Why not? You seem like a nice woman."

"That's very kind of you," Laura said as the two walked out together.

Julius had been waiting for a good ten minutes before he finally saw Abigail emerge from her locker room.

"Well, it's about time," Julius said. Laura followed Abigail out, which surprised him.

"Julius, this is Laura. We'll be working together." Julius raised his hand to shake. Laura took it and shook it.

"Nice to meet you, Laura."

"Nice to meet you too, Julius."

"Anyone hungry?"

"Yeah, let's get going," Abigail said as they walked to the mess hall.

It was buzzing with a few hundred people. Julius saw his dig mates sitting at a table close to the door they walked in.

"Abigail, I'm going to go sit with my team, if you don't mind."

"Not at all, I'll see you after work." Julius watched as Abigail and Laura walked to the food line. Julius slowly walked over to his team.

"Morning, Julius," Irene said as she ate her scrambled eggs.

"Better get some grub," Tex said pointing to the line.

"We have twenty minutes till the train leaves," Saké said. She was looking at Julius from behind a tech manual for a new drill.

"Okay, thanks." Julius turned around and walked to the opening. He returned a few minutes later with some eggs and bacon on his plate. It smelled so good and he was mighty hungry after not really eating much yesterday.

The only seat open was next to Bobby so it would be a tight fit. Bobby had a smug grin on his face, which made Julius feel nervous.

"What's so funny?"

"Nothing."

Julius sat down on the small stool attached to the table. When his rear hit the seat a loud farting sound emulated from the seat.

Bobby smashed his fist against the table and burst out laughing.

"I got you, man!"

Julius looked at his teammates and saw they were all straight-faced. Except for Tex, who was still eating his country-fried steak, not even acknowledging what happened. Julius stood back up and inspected his seat. On his seat was a pink plastic bag.

"What the heck is this?" Julius lifted it up to inspect it closer. Across the center were the words "whoopee cushion."

"It's a whoopee cushion. Haven't you ever seen one?" Bobby asked, trying to regain his composure.

"No, is it some old toy?"

"You could say that. It's an antique, and no one uses it anymore, so it's perfect for a prank master like myself."

"Prank master? Look at everyone else. They aren't even laughing! James, how many times has he pulled this prank?"

"I would say this is the tenth time this month."

"Sounds about right," Tex said, his mouth full of food.

"A prank master would get new material. You're too unoriginal to think of new pranks." Julius threw it at Bobby, who caught the toy and pocketed it.

"Fine, I'll show you," Bobby muttered as Julius sat back down and started eating his food.

"Bobby, you will do no such thing! Let Julius eat in peace. We can't be late again because of one of your dumb pranks," Jaivan said to Bobby sternly.

"Thank you, Jaivan. Bobby, we're getting sick of your pranks. Don't make the new guy request a transfer," Irene said.

"Fine, you guys are no fun!"

Julius focused on eating his food. As soon as he finished up, the team stood up and walked to the exit.

James walked with Julius. "He loves that stupid pink bag," James said.

"Yeah, I can tell. Why is he like this?"

"You get used to it, I guess. I think he was bullied when he was a kid, and this is his coping mechanism. He tries to get attention, no matter what it is. He was bothering me until you came, so thanks."

"You're welcome, but I'm not thrilled to be the butt of his jokes."

"Again, you get used to it. It seems Irene is standing up for you. Not something she does for me."

The team reached the locker room. Bobby stopped before the door and waited. When Julius was about to enter, Bobby spoke up, "I'm sorry, Julius. How about I extend the olive branch?" Bobby held out his hand. Julius looked at his face then to his hand. Wrapped around his palm, Julius saw the fabric of the shock buzzer.

"I'm not falling for that again, Bobby. Even when Irene tells you to stop, you can't help yourself!"

Julius pushed past Bobby and entered the locker room. He changed into his space suit, as did the rest of the team. When everyone was ready, they went back out the door they entered.

They walked down the hallway until they reached a series of garage doors. A substantial crowd stood around them. A long strip of red lights lined the top of each garage door.

They stood there for a while until Julius heard an alarm. It was the same alarm as the one he heard yesterday on the elevator. He realized he was standing by the station for the hyper-rail.

"Okay, Julius, you need to get on the train as fast as possible. Try to stay with the team," Irene told him.

All Julius could do was nod as the red lights switched to green. The garage doors opened, and the crowd of people walked into the train station. A train with five cars stood ready to depart on the platform. The multitude of people boarded the front few cars.

Julius and his team entered the last car. He looked around and saw there were no seats in it. He assumed it was a cargo car. There were three handrails that ran down the length of the car. The design was meant to accommodate any extra mining equipment. Everyone in the car grabbed onto a rail and held on.

A few moments later, the alarm sounded again. People ran around, trying to get on the train or went back to the doors. Once the platform was cleared and sealed, the train lurched forward and exiting the station.

Outside the station, the train began to gather speed heading for the outer wall. It passed through and went out to the Martian desert. Julius turned to look out the window as the train slid along the extensive Martian landscape.

He awed at the Martian scenery. He wished he could stop and take pictures because it was stunning. The train traveled for a long time before it slowed to a stop at a small makeshift platform. It looked like it was a train car that had folded out. The train's speaker came to life, and a robotic humanoid voice spoke.

"This is Site Alpha. Teams Alpha, Bravo, Golf, and Mike are to exit all others stay on for the next stop. This is Site Alpha for Teams Alpha, Bravo, Golf, and Mike."

There was shifting in the cars as a total of twenty-eight people, including Julius prepared to exit. An alert was given from the same voice.

"All personnel, please secure your helmets. The doors are opening in thirty seconds. All personnel please secure your helmets. The doors are opening in thirty seconds."

Martian air was filtered in, and regular oxygen was removed to equalize the train with the outside environment. The doors opened, and the members of Mike, Golf, Alpha, and Bravo disembarked. When all had exited the train, the doors slid closed and the train pulled away, speeding to the next drop point. Julius looked out at the red moonscape and identified two people haulers. They were covered with dust and sat next to the platform. Julius turned to James. "How did those get out here?"

"There are two ways. One is they use large drone transporters that pick up and move equipment. The second way is using minimizing technology to transport the equipment in the hyper-rail. This is the more common way. They deploy the vehicles every day so we can get our jobs done."

The other diggers were already walking to the people haulers, Dig Teams Golf and Mike went to one and Alpha and Bravo went to the other.

Julius observed Irene entering the driver's side of the cab with someone else. He could not identify who the passenger was, so he assumed it was a member of Dig Team Golf.

Julius walked with James to the people hauler, where the rest of his team was getting strapped into the side seats. He saw there were only two seats left, and they were on the end. James got into his easily and began to talk to Sadako about something. Meanwhile, Julius was struggling to get his harness on. Eventually, he buckled himself in.

"Hey, Chatty Kitty, help the new guy strap in," Tex barked.

"Fine, Tex," James answered roughly. James looked at the harness across Julius's chest.

"He is all strapped in correctly."

"Then he didn't press the ready button on his harness," Tex said from down the row.

Julius looked down at his harness and pressed the button quickly before James could. "Done," Julius declared.

"Away we go," Irene said from the cab as the people hauler began to drive forward.

James turned back to Julius. "Sorry about that. The button is just to tell the cab you're ready. Did they not teach you that in training?"

"Must've slipped Martin's mind."

"It happens. So tell me about yourself, Julius." He had already told the team where he was from and how he came to Mars yesterday. He wasn't sure what James wanted to talk about.

"My shelter mate and I trained together."

"That's not uncommon. I'm in a shelter of six, and we all trained in the simulator in New Mexico together."

"Very interesting. So were you trained by Martin?"

"Yeah, Martin Fisher. He didn't like me. Said I ran my mouth too much."

"That's a shame, we seemed to get along."

"We didn't get to talk much yesterday. I appreciate the chance to talk, Julius."

"The feeling's mutual, James."

Julius turned away from James to look out at the Martian landscape, which was beautiful. The mountains were off in the distance; it looked like southern Utah before they drilled it for oil in the early twenties.

"Beautiful, isn't it?" James asked Julius.

"Yeah, it sure is, ever get tired of it?"

"Nah, as much crap as I'm given, the views make it worth it."

Julius watched as the Martian ground became rocky and hilly, as they got closer to the mountains. The people hauler soon stopped, and everyone dismounted. Julius walked with his digging mates to the other side; in front of them was a large tunnel-boring machine named Dark Gem.

Team Golf was already starting to prep the large machine. It looked like it was previously digging into the side of a small hill. Team Mike joined team Golf in preparing for the machine to resume its work.

179

"What's wrong with it?" Julius asked Jaivan, seeing it had a lot of dust on it. Additionally, there were quite a few scratches and burn marks on the side.

"She got stuck partway down, and we had to get her out over the last few weeks. Our job now is to try to repair her. Team Golf is a mechanical crew," Jaivan explained.

"So what is our purpose here?" Julius asked.

"Our purpose, Stetson, is to assist Dig Team Golf. Once the Gem is ready, we resume the task of completing the dig," Irene said, walking up to him.

"I see. How long do you think this will take?"

"Days, so get ready to be doing a lotta sittin'," Tex said sarcastically.

The day went by slow, Julius sat around the people hauler with the majority of his team and got to know them better. Sometimes he was asked by Saké to fetch a certain tool and other boring tasks. They camped on-site that night in makeshift shelters.

The next few days were full of waking up and repeating the same type of tasks. After a few days of repair, the machine finally breathed its first breath. Both of the dig teams rejoiced when the beast started up.

Julius was particularly excited because he no longer had to be the team tool man. He could finally do what he came here to do, dig. Julius walked around the back of the machine, marveling at the idling behemoth. As he walked back to the front, Julius saw Irene. She was holding the tablet that controlled the borer.

"Stetson, do you know how to work this?"

"Yes, I do. I learned in training."

"Good, take it and put these parameters." Irene looked at her HUD and read off a latitude, longitude, and altitude.

"Everyone, clear the borer, it's time to dig!" Irene ordered all members of both teams.

Both teams backed away from the machine to a safe distance. Julius stood among them and waited for Irene to give the green light.

"Julius, start the Gem." Julius pressed the Dig button, and the Dark Gem began to move forward. It reached the previously started hole and entered. After a few minutes, the teams could hear it churn up the rock as it moved down the hole.

"Now we wait, like always," James complained, kicking a small rock.

"Quit your complaining Kitten, and have some fun!" Bobby pulled a small aerosol can out of his equipment pouch and sprayed the front of James's helmet with silly string. No one laughed at Kyle's prank and James's misfortune. He tried to get the silly string off his face but smeared it.

Irene walked over to James and cleaned his helmet with her sleeve. "That's enough jokes for the day! Everyone is tired of your pranks, Bobby."

"But Irene, it's a classic! I made it myself; you can't even buy this stuff anymore."

"I said enough, Bobby! Bobby, get on the people hauler. Julius, hand me the tablet," Julius complied, handing Irene the tablet before he took his seat.

"Why do we even have people here when it could just be a drone?" Julius wondered aloud.

"Because if something goes wrong like before, we need to fix it," Saké said through her translating device. Julius realized it was a stupid question.

Julius saw Tex, and Jaivan had moved away from the group with drills that looked like jackhammers. He meandered his over to them. "Why are you guys over here?"

"Well, we're making probing tunnels in case there's another deposit nearby. Command likes us starting them, only going down about fifteen feet. The scan drones will come later to go farther. It also gives us miners a use because the machine could do big digging all by itself," Jaivan answered.

Tex just kept drilling, not paying attention to Julius, who went back and sat down on a rock and stared at the large hole. Time went on, and Julius felt very bored.

I got paid to come up here and do this? The factory was more fun, Julius thought to himself.

Eventually, the borer stopped moving before it backed itself out of the tunnel shutting down when it was out.

"Did the damn thing break again?" James asked.

"No, there is no error on the tablet," Irene replied.

Julius jumped up from his position and started to walk down to the machine. He wanted to see what resided at the end of the tunnel.

Before Julius could move further, rocket engines were heard just beyond the hill. Julius thought they sounded like they were rapidly approaching. He turned his head and saw three flying machines that resembled helicopters. Julius watched them crest the horizon and rapidly approach.

The craft had a streamlined helicopter body with dual circular rocket pods on the sides. They flew over Julius, and the two teams before they circled to land in front of the hole. Julius looked closer and saw all three crafts had sizable doors on the sides and a hatch on the bottom.

The doors opened, and Julius could see soldiers in spacesuits sitting on the edges. They were all carrying electric guns like the guards from a few days prior. The helicopters landed, and the soldiers poured out running down the hole. The same guys in the red suits Julius saw in New Mexico followed them. The red-space-suit guys had the containers with them.

As Julius stared at the scene in front of him, he felt two people grab him. "What the? Let me go!" He couldn't see who grabbed him, but they pulled him back to the people hauler. Where he was forced into his seat, Julius saw it was Tex and Jaivan.

"We'll explain later, but we need to go. Our work here is done," Jaivan said, strapping himself in.

"Good to go, Irene," Tex said, glaring at Julius.

It was a silent ride back, and Julius tried to analyze what just happened. They drove all the way back to the main building, which took the better part of the day. James attempted to talk to Julius a few times, but Julius ignored him. He was trying to wrap his head around why there were so many troops.

When they got back, the vehicle was taken to a garage, but Julius was too deep in thought to really pay attention. He and Team Mike went to the mess hall to eat a late dinner.

"Okay, what was that?" Julius asked.

"They didn't tell you, did they?" Irene asked flatly.

"Tell me what?"

"Central command doesn't let us see what we're mining. Company policy. It's so we don't steal any intellectual property and bull crap like that," Tex grumbled.

"I know that, but who were the suit guys and the military guys? It seems shady." Julius felt an uneasiness in the pit of his stomach.

"That's a precision mining team. This is the way it is Stetson, get used to it," Irene said, taking a bite of her veggie burger.

What are they trying to hide? Julius thought as the others chatted about other things and ate their food. James sat with Julius as the rest began to leave. Julius was still deep in his thoughts; trying to figure out what mineral was so valuable on Mars, they would invoke intellectual property rights.

"Julius, you know, it's not that big of a deal. It's just a bunch of dumb rocks."

"What if it's not, James? What if there is something more?"

"If there was something more, my dad would know about it. Let it go, man. I'm going to bed, you should too."

James got up and left Julius alone in the mess hall. He sat there for a little longer. He was about to leave when he felt someone tap him on his shoulder. He turned around to see Abigail.

"How've things been, roomie? I haven't seen you in days. How was the mining?"

"Oh, it was good."

"Just good? You've got something bothering you. I can see it in your face."

"Yeah, something's bothering me."

"Well, come on, out with it."

"I don't want to say it here. Someone could be listening." Julius looked around to see if anyone was watching.

"Uh, I guess it is the mess hall. You okay? You're acting strange."

"I'm fine, I don't trust some of the people here like I trust you." Julius stood up as did Abigail.

"That's sweet, but I'm still a little weirded out." The two went down the hall into Julius's team locker room. Julius saw it was void of people and felt more comfortable.

"Okay, Julius, out with it. What's wrong?"

"My dig team and I spent the last few days repairing a tunneling machine. Today we got it working, and then we mined and completed our job. We weren't allowed to extract the resources. To make sure we didn't, a ton of soldiers rushed into the hole. Not only that, but those guys we saw in New Mexico were there. The ones with the red suits."

"Okay, I see what you're saying. Now do me a favor and think of it from the company's perspective. They want to keep their resources a secret, or at least keep it a secret from us. I'm not sure if you know this, but the AU government is preparing to open up Mars to more than just AMSPACE mining operations. They want to make a larger off-world colony here and are going to create contracts that other companies will win. AMSPACE probably wants to keep what they have found here a secret in case other companies come. They don't want them to know about the resources. By the way, those red suit guys are everywhere. I saw some on the hyper-rail yesterday. They're just the precision mining team."

Julius sat there in silence, thinking about what Abigail just said. In his mind, she was logically correct. The company would want to protect what they do, but there was something that still did not make sense. If these caverns selected by the scanning crews were full of traditional precious metals like they claimed, then miners would need to get them out. Why would they need soldiers with guns if there were a bunch of rocks?

"Julius!" Abigail yelled a little, bringing him out of his deep thoughts. "Do you understand what I mean?"

"Yeah, I get it. I'm still suspicious."

"You need to get over yourself. You are here to mine and enjoy being on Mars. How about I bring you back to reality?" She leaned in and kissed him on the lips. Julius let her kiss him, and he kissed her back. She backed off.

"Better?"

"Much. Maybe I could get another?"

"Nice try, maybe later. I'm meeting up with Laura for a glass of wine. Try to relax, Julius, and let that kiss sink in a little." She stood up; her blond hair flipped around as she headed back into the main building.

Julius got on his space suit and went back to his shelter. Gone were his thoughts about the day. Now he was thinking about his shelter mate and how beautiful she was. When he sat down on his bed, he began to think about the strange figures guiding boxes and how they were there today. Julius felt a pit growing in his stomach. He wanted to get his mind off mining, so he opened the tablet. He read a few emails from his parents wanting to know how he is and what he was doing.

Julius replied to his parents:

Mom and Dad,

I made it to Mars safely a few days ago, sorry for my lack of reply. They have had me in the field working with a machine that needed repair. Let me tell you, though, it's been hard dealing with all the sitting around. I thought this would be more hands-on.

I've made a few friends with my dig team when I first arrived. They are rough around the edges, and it might take a while to become one of them. James is one on the team, and we get along well. I also met Abigail, my shelter mate, in training. She and I are good friends to say the least.

You all should've been getting the checks from AMSPACE. I hope that's the case. I plan to send you some pictures of Mars very soon. It's so beautiful here, more amazing than I could have imagined. How are Ant and Alicia? I also hope you both are doing great.

Talk to you soon,
Julius

185

He sent the message to them and continued to read his other messages. There were two others that were not from his parents. One was from Gerald, and the other was from John. Julius opened the one from John first.

> *Julius,*
>
> *What's going on? Misty and I haven't heard from you. We know you are kicking some Martian ass. We missed you at Vinnie's funeral. It was a great service. Even Nancy was there. We wanted to check in on you and know that we are thinking of you.*
> *With regards,*
> *John*

That was a hard one for Julius to read. He had forgotten about Vinnie and his funeral. Now he felt guilty for not going. Julius replied to John, telling him what he was doing and how things were going. One he had replied, he opened the last email from Gerald.

He read through it, all it said he was happy things were going so well for him, and he waited for a reply to him. Gerald even went as far to say that Julius could tell him anything, and nothing would be held against him. He felt that was a strange statement, but he didn't think more about it.

Julius replied to him, telling him about what it was like to be on Mars and how he was doing. He left out his feelings about the soldiers entering the mine. He hoped he would get the chance to talk to Gerald about it at some point, but for now, he did not want to tell anyone else but Abigail. He felt tired after all the emails and went to bed.

A few hours later, Julius woke up in a cold sweat and was very disoriented. It felt like he had just come down with a cold that threw off his equilibrium. He was in a dreamlike haze when he heard movement from outside his shelter. His eyes snapped to the wall of his shelter, where he saw a tall humanoid figure's shadow. It was about seven feet tall and looked like it had long arms and a round head that connected to its neck seamlessly.

"What?" Julius felt a chill run up his spine. He sat in his bed, not moving for a good five minutes. Julius opened and closed his eyes multiple times, but the figure was still just standing there.

"I'm not dreaming. This has to be real." Julius said to himself as his heartbeat in his throat.

After the paralyzing fear subsided, Julius moved slowly to his personal air lock and put on a suit. As he was in the air lock, he lost the ability to see the figure.

He exited the shelter into the cold Martian night. Julius walked around his shelter to see if he could find the source of the shadow. After checking around the exterior of both his and Abigail's shelters, Julius found nothing. It was like the figure had just disappeared into thin air. After a few minutes, he gave up and returned to his shelter. He was exhausted.

"Probably was Bobby messing with me again, or I imagined it." He got back into bed and fell asleep.

EIGHTEEN

A Member of the Team

Over the next few weeks, Julius continued working with the team, mainly with boring machines, which caused him to be away from Abigail a lot. It was hard, but they texted often, which helped. Julius felt like they were getting closer. He would tell her about his day and what he was doing, and she would tell him about what it was like in the terraforming unit.

As much as Julius worked with the team, he didn't quite feel like he belonged. Bobby continued to play stupid jokes on him, which got on his nerves. Julius had no idea how to break through to Tex and at least establish a cordial relationship. Julius extended an olive branch a few times, but Tex always seemed to dismiss him entirely. James was great though, always was willing to talk about anything and everything.

Julius had continued his correspondence with his parents, John and Gerald. His parents were getting his paychecks, and the money was being put away into a trust for him. Some of the money was being used to make changes to the house in Pontiac. His siblings were doing well and were continuing to go to school. Julius felt a little depressed as being on Mars was not what he imagined it would be. He thought this life was going to be far more exciting than his life in Pontiac. He had grand expectations it would have been like what

Ben Lewis or Neil Armstrong experienced. Nevertheless, Julius was making a better life for the ones he loved.

Julius woke up early back in his shelter. He had not had another rude awakening in the weeks since the mysterious figure visited him. In his mind, this all but confirmed it was Bobby playing a prank on him. He got himself ready for his day before going to the main building for breakfast. He entered and got some food before sitting down at a table.

He was so early the mess hall was sparsely populated. He finished up his food before he saw Tex, Jaivan, and Irene walk in, followed closely by Bobby, James, and Saké.

"Well, look who's already up and ready to go. You slackers could learn a thing or two from Stetson," Irene said, laughing as she walked by him. The rest followed her to get their food and quickly returned to Julius.

Julius watched his digging mates chow down on their food. He looked over at Irene. "What's today's job?"

"It is a simple effort. We're going to dig holes for disposal."

"Well, that just sounds thrilling," James said, rolling his eyes.

"Oh, shut it Kitten, we always have to listen to your whining. I am getting tired of it. In my country, we would have already cast you out of the family," Saké said as everyone else at the table got quiet.

They were stunned that Sake, who was usually quite reserved, had come out of her shell in such grandiose fashion.

Tex cleared his throat before speaking. "Saké, do you realize your translator was on?"

"Of course, I do. Someone had to say it."

"Well, I—" James started to say before Jaivan cut him off.

"Enough, let's all just eat our meals, then go to our vehicles."

"I agree with Jaivan. Knock it off. The last thing we need is for this team to not be united," Irene said, finishing up her food. She stood up, signaling that it was time to go. The rest of the team followed her out of the mess hall.

Julius walked over to James. The two of them had grown closer over the last month. "Hey, man, I agree this won't be much fun, but we should keep our mouths shut about it," Julius said, slapping James's shoulder.

"Thanks, Julius. I don't know why you're so kind to me." James and Julius turned to follow the team.

"I don't like seeing people get picked on, so I always try to be a friend. Plus, you're a pretty cool guy."

"Thank you for that. I'm glad we're friends."

They went to the locker room and changed into their suits. After they were changed, the crew walked a different direction from the train station.

"Where are we going?" Julius asked Tex.

"To the garage," he replied to Julius dismissively, as if Julius should have known this.

"Not like I'd know. All we have done is go to the station."

"Fair, but I don't care."

Ass, Julius thought to himself. The team walked to a massive garage that looked as vast as an AMSPACE shuttle bay.

There was an abundance of vehicles, including people haulers, hover bikes, and drill haulers all lined up in neat rows. In addition to the vehicles he was familiar with, Julius saw other vehicles. One was a strange-looking floating doughnut-shaped drone. Irene was talking to a man in a mechanic's uniform behind a kiosk. Julius watched them talk for a while before the man pointed to an area in the hangar.

Julius looked in the direction he was pointing. There were two drill haulers prepped and ready to go along with three hover bikes. The team walked down the stairs to the hangar floor before they walked over to the vehicles. Irene jumped into the driver's seat of one of the drill haulers, and Tex got in the other. James sat down in the passenger side of Irene's vehicle, and Saké went to ride with Tex. That left Julius, Bobby, and Jaivan to take the hover bikes. Julius was thrilled he got to ride the bike instead of the haulers.

"Everyone ready?" Irene asked as the bikers mounted their vehicles. The three responded in the affirmative.

"Okay, move up to the air lock," Irene ordered as the drill haulers began to move toward the first see-through fortified door. With the keys already in their bikes, Julius, Bobby, and Jaivan gently turned their accelerators and followed the drill haulers. As they approached, the first set of doors slid open. Julius noted the door had a sleek and efficient design. The drill haulers paused to allow the bikes to go first before they formed up behind them.

Once all the vehicles were inside the air lock, the doors closed.

"Proceed to the coordinates on your MPS," Irene ordered. On the other side of the second heavy see-through door was a metal ramp that led up. The vehicles were bathed in red light before the door in front inched open. Julius and the two other bikers hit their accelerators as soon as they could. They tore out of the air lock, drove up the ramp, and into the Martian moonscape.

The hangar's exit was outside the security perimeter that surrounded the facility for ease of access. The three bikers looked at each other and had a silent realization that they were in a race to reach the dig site. Without hesitation, Julius took off with an early lead.

Within seconds, Bobby flew past Julius. "How can someone that fat go that fast?" Julius wondered to himself. As he was thinking, Jaivan blew past him as well.

Not wanting to crash, Julius was left in the dust by the more experienced drivers. He kept following his MPS but did not catch up to the other two. A while later, he stopped at the coordinates on the MPS. Jaivan and Bobby were already there with smug looks on their faces.

"You seem a little slow, Julius. You shouldn't let me beat you. I bet a snail would've been faster than you," Bobby said, laughing.

"Yeah, yeah, whatever, Bobby." Over the last month, Julius had been avoiding Bobby and his childish antics as much as possible.

"We need to get the probes out to check for optimal drilling points," Jaivan said, taking out a single winged solar-powered drone. He threw it up in the air, and the drone automatically engaged its small antigravity generator to fly high into the air.

It scanned the ground and found two optimal spots for the disposal of the hazardous waste. The results were uploaded to the computers in the team's suits. The drone returned to Jaivan's hand just as Julius could see the drill haulers approaching in the distance. Drill haulers were more agile and faster than people haulers, but they still were slow. The machines stopped at the drilling locations identified on the MPS.

Irene's angry voice came over the commlinks. "You three are morons. You're lucky I don't report you to Dave. Don't go racing again."

She put on her helmet and got out with James. "Sorry, but hey, we already completed the scan," Jaivan said.

"I saw. At least you can do something right. Get the drills ready."

Julius walked over to Tex's drill hauler to monitor the drilling of the holes from the ground. Jaivan and Saké operated the drills from the driver's seats. James and Bobby were sent off to drill smaller probing holes thirty meters away. Irene was watching over them so they wouldn't fight.

Julius watched Saké lower the drill before it started to eat away at the ground. Julius kept his eyes on the drill when he caught something out of the corner of his eye. Julius looked over at the drill hauler Tex was monitoring and saw a steel cable used to steady the drill was hanging too close to the drill bit. Julius felt like he watched it snag in slow motion. He instinctively ran over and shoved the muscular out of the way.

Before Julius could dive to safety, he felt a stabbing pain in his right leg. He hit the ground hard, burying his face into the dirt. In addition to the pain, Julius felt he was having trouble breathing. He saw blinking text on his heads-up display. It was his oxygen level; it was dropping rapidly. His suit was compromised and leaking air.

Tex picked himself up and ran over to Julius. Using all his strength, Tex threw Julius over his shoulder.

"Get him in the hauler," Irene shouted as Tex threw Julius into the passenger seat next to Jaivan, who luckily still had his suit on. Saké had exited her vehicle and jumped into the cab. She straddled Julius and immediately began to apply pressure to Julius's leg. Jaivan retracted the drill and started driving like a mad man.

"Hold on, Julius," Jaivan said as he hit a bump. Saké lifted off Julius, losing the pressure on his right leg. It gushed blood, creating a small pool on the floor.

"Damn it, Jaivan, hold it steady!" Saké said as she reapplied pressure to the wound. Jaivan didn't reply as he tried to keep focused on getting back as fast as he could.

Jaivan drove back to base and through the air lock. Meanwhile, Julius was drifting in and out of consciousness.

"Julius, stay with us," Jaivan said as Saké kept shaking him to keep him conscious. Jaivan drove through the hangar, almost hitting a people hauler before parking the vehicle.

"Get me a medic now! He's bleeding out!" Jaivan bellowed into his commlink. The hangar was in chaos. People were running around, trying to get a handle on the situation. Through the chaos, a person was able to activate a robotic stretcher that unhitched itself from the wall and hovered over to the passenger-side door. Jaivan and Saké brought out Julius, who had passed out, still bleeding profusely. They laid him on the stretcher, which flew off to the medical bay.

Julius was rushed into an operating room where doctors were ready for him. They immediately injected him with the same green liquid that was injected into Abigail when she broke her leg in the simulation. They had to conduct an emergency surgery to reset the broken bones and put Julius's leg into a cast.

The cable broke his tibia, fibula, patella, and femur in multiple places. It also left a massive gash in his leg. Once they had the leg cast set, the doctors took Julius out of the operating room and gave him a blood transfusion since he had lost so much. They sent him to a small recovery room where he would be monitored.

While asleep, Julius had a dream, but it was more than just a dream. It felt real as if it was a deep subconscious memory or vision. Julius was back in the car with Martin on his way to the New Mexican Research Facility, except Julius could see himself asleep next to Martin.

"This had to be after Martin knocked me out," Julius said as he watched.

There was something peculiar. Nothing was moving. It was like the dream was on pause. "Why am I here?" he wondered.

He looked around, trying to find an answer. As he searched, the dream seemed to hit Play, and things began to move. Julius turned focused on Martin. His trainer reached for the right arm of the passed-out Julius. He pulled out a syringe and flipped Julius's hand over to expose his forearm.

Martin lined up the syringe and stuck it into Julius's arm before pushing down the plunger.

"What the hell? Is that why my forearm was so sore when I woke up?" Julius wondered as he sat baffled at what he had just witnessed. He began to reach for his own forearm before he woke up in a hospital bed, dazed and confused.

Julius looked around to see a ton of people in his room. "Vegas, you had us worried there," Jaivan said.

"Vegas?" Julius asked, confused. His leg was throbbing.

"Yeah, that's your new team nickname, because you're lucky," Irene said.

"At least it wasn't Dumbass," Julius joked with a half smile. Everyone in the room laughed.

"It could've been gimpy or peg leg. No one liked my ideas," Bobby said.

"That's because they're dumb," James replied.

"They aren't dumb, they're gold. You just can't understand my comedic genius!"

"Enough!" Irene almost yelled, which caused the two to go silent.

"Tex, do you have something to say to Julius?" Saké asked, looking up at the tall man.

"Yeah, uh, thanks for, you know, saving me," Tex gruffly mumbled, clearly embarrassed to show gratitude toward Julius.

"You're welcome," Julius responded.

"Okay, we have to get back to our shelters. Unlike you, we have work in the morning," Irene said before the team walked out of the room. As the team left, James gave Julius a thumbs up.

"Way to play the hero," he said before he left. Julius returned the thumbs up. Two other people remained in the room. One was a doctor; she was of Indian descent and had her black hair pulled back behind her ears. Her green eyes were emphasized by her light-blue surgical mask. The other person was Abigail. Julius felt his heart flutter a bit. She gave him a nervous smile.

He tried to sit up to get a better look at Abigail.

"Mr. Stetson, please don't move." Julius ignored the doctor and kept trying to sit up before he felt even more shooting pain in his leg. He retreated back into his bed.

"What happened?" he asked, looking at the doctor.

"Well, all four of the bones in your leg were shattered. We're trying to fix it, but your bones are proving difficult to repair. I think you'll be on your feet in a few SOLs. Just rest, then you can be on your way. Also, I have these orders from Mr. Hughes." The doctor handed him a small tablet, which said,

Julius Stetson:
Temporary reassignment to assist Miss Abigail King
Assignment: drilling terraforming test holes. Orders
are effective immediately, no exceptions.
—David Hughes

"What?" Julius asked, disappointed and surprised.

"Oh, you don't want to work with me, Julius? I see how it is," Abigail said teasingly as she stood up from her chair.

"No, I want to work with you. I just like my current job. I don't mind working with you. I mean it."

"I know, I was just messing with you." Abigail smiled and winked at Julius.

"Oh, good. It's so hard for me to get when you are joking or when you're serious." Julius said.

"Yeah, I get that a lot. Keeps you on your toes. Look, I would love to stay, but they don't allow visitors overnight. I have to go since I need to work tomorrow too." She leaned over him.

"Am I about to get one of those Abigail kisses?"

"Yes, you are." She gave him a kiss on the cheek, then pulled back.

"That wasn't what I was expecting."

"Good, I want to surprise you. Get better, I'll see you tomorrow." She started to walk out the door.

"Okay, see you tomorrow. I won't go anywhere."

Abigail turned around and blew him a kiss and winked before she walked out the door, leaving Julius with the doctor.

"She's a good one. Been here since you got out of surgery. You're lucky."

"We aren't dating."

"You should be. She definitely likes you, Julius. We'll be monitoring you through the night. If you need anything, press that button, and the attending nurse will be alerted."

"Okay, thank you, Doctor."

"You're welcome, Julius. Sleep well." The doctor said before she left.

Julius was surprised how long Abigail had been there. She really did care about him. Now that he was alone, he finally had a chance to look around the room.

It was small but quite nice for its size. Abigail had been sitting in a corner chair. There was a small doctor's desk in another corner with a few computerized papers on.

Next to his bed was a nanobot IV pole with a small table attached to it. The table had scalpels, and other medical tools laid out neatly. His mind was wandering; he thought about how to make a move on Abigail when he remembered his dream.

Julius grabbed his right forearm and felt around the area where he watched Martin insert the syringe. He felt nothing on his first attempt to find the object. He probed a little further and found a small lump. His heart rate increased, having found the object.

"What the hell is this?"

Julius was both scared and confused. He had to know what was under his skin. His hand shook as he reached out for a scalpel sitting on the small table. He gripped it in his left fist and brought it to his eyes to inspect it.

The blade was very small but looked keen. Julius slowly lowered it to the center of his right forearm. The blade's cold touch sent goose bumps crawling around his arm. He had to be careful; one wrong move and he could cut too deep and injure himself.

Julius took a deep breath and pressed the surgical instrument into his skin, causing drops of blood to spill out and onto the clean pale blue sheets on his bed. Julius winced in pain and felt sick after seeing his own blood pour out.

Julius dragged the knife down his forearms about an inch before he stopped and pulled the blade back. He realized he was holding his breath and released the air.

He hastily placed the bloody scalpel back down on the table and grabbed some tweezers with his trembling left hand. The wound was bleeding profusely. He needed to move fast before he lost more blood. He gently guided the tweezers into the small opening in his forearm, searching for a sign of some foreign object. Julius looked into the wound and saw a small glint of metal. He gripped the metallic sliver with the tweezers and pulled it out with ease.

Once he had the object out of his body, he placed it in his right hand. He then took a cloth and put pressure on the incision. As he was trying to clot his self-inflicted wound, he felt additional pain in the arm. Julius removed the cloth and saw the gash sealing up by itself.

He was astonished but quickly realized he had millions of nanobots in his body trying to heal his broken bones. He guessed that some must have repaired the damage leaving no evidence of the wound. Julius looked at the object. It was covered with blood, but he could make out a small blinking blue light on it.

"What is this?"

He realized he could not afford to lose the object. He had to safely store the sliver, so he could show Abigail. Julius looked around for anything in reach. Fortunately, there were small alcohol wipes in packages. Julius tore one open with his teeth. He did not want to put down the mysterious item and risk losing it in the bedsheets.

He was able to remove the wipe and deposit the strange object into the empty package. He used the alcohol wipe to clean both the tweezers and scalpel. He also cleaned off his skin so the doctor would not know he removed whatever that thing was in his arm.

To explain the bloody bedsheets, he would lie and say he had a nosebleed. Julius put the object in the pocket of his hospital gown and closed his eyes, relieved to not have the object in his arm. He was now wary of everyone who worked for AMSPACE.

Over the next few days, Julius's leg continued to improve until he was able to walk on it again. Abigail texted and said she was unable to see him because she was sent to a terraforming facility on the other side of the planet. Julius understood but was disappointed. He spent the time in the hospital room watching TV and relaxing.

He was discharged from the medical wing after the doctors removed the cast and performed a scan to confirm the bones had healed. Julius changed out of his hospital gown and subtly put the alcohol package in his shorts pocket.

After changing, Julius went straight for the mess hall; he needed food that didn't taste like it was from a fifty-year-old refrigerator. On his way to the mess hall, Julius ran into Abigail.

"Look who's walking again. Took you long enough. If you remember, I was moving around hours after breaking mine. Sorry I haven't been around. I was just on my way up to see you."

"It's okay. I did miss you, though." Julius gave her a hug. They both walked together to eat dinner.

"Where were you?"

"I was out on a far terraforming outpost with Laura."

"What were you doing out there?"

"We were trying a new technique that might speed up the 'Earthification' process. In theory it will make Mars have an atmosphere like Earth in one hundred years instead of two hundred fifty."

"That's amazing! You're doing what you wanted to do."

"Yeah, I am. Starting tomorrow, you get to help me."

"I know, I'm ready, boss."

"Oh, shut up, Julius."

After they finished their dinner, Julius and Abigail returned to their shelter, but before they parted and went to bed, Julius grabbed Abigail's right forearm. "Miss me that much, you won't let me go to bed." She had a hopeful tone in her voice. He kissed her on the cheek.

"You missed."

That was all Julius needed before he planted a kiss on her lips. He kept holding her arm and massaged it up while he kissed her. Suddenly, Julius felt the same lump that he'd felt in his own arm. He broke the kiss.

"Something wrong?"

"Yes, but it wasn't the kiss."

"Well then, what is it?"

Julius reached into his pocket and pulled out the alcohol wipe pack.

"Are you telling me I'm dirty?"

"No, no, that's not it. It's what is inside." He poured the contents out into his hand. The little metal object tumbled out of the packet and rested on Julius's palm.

"Uh, what's that?"

"I was hoping you could tell me."

"What makes you think I would know?" Abigail moved her face closer to Julius's hand and inspected the object.

"I've seen this tech before. It is a tracker that can also detect and record vital body data. My father was working on something similar a few years ago when he worked at Shield Biomedical. Where'd you get it?"

"It was in my right forearm," Julius said.

"Why did you remove it if you put it there?"

"I didn't have it put there, I cut it out a few days ago."

"You cut open your arm?" Abigail asked, shocked.

"I had to get it out, and I had nanobots already in my system."

"Whatever. So what was the point? What's the tracker for?"

"I have no clue, but I think you have one in your arm too. I felt it while we were kissing." Julius pointed at the part of her arm; he felt the tracker.

"You really know how to kill the mood, Julius."

"I'm sorry, I didn't want it to end, but I think this is important. I think AMSPACE is monitoring us for some reason."

"Okay, conspiracy theorist Stetson, you're looking way too far into this." Abigail rolled her eyes.

"I'm serious."

"I know you are. Can we get this thing out of me?"

"Okay, let's try to figure this out." Julius looked around the living room for materials to take out Abigail's tracker. Julius found a sharp pocketknife, some string from a sewing kit, along with a needle. After seeing Julius return with such unsanitary objects, Abigail began to have second thoughts.

"I can't do this." She backed away from Julius.

"You want the tracker in your body?"

"No, I don't, but I also don't want you cutting me open in an unclean environment." She shielded her arm from him with her body.

Julius put his hands up in mock surrender. "Okay, calm down. Let's just find another way to get it out." He put the knife down on the coffee table and backed away.

Abigail walked back over to him, but she continued to guard her arm.

"Do you have another idea? Because I have squat!"

"I have a hunch, if that counts." Abigail walked to the air lock to get a suit.

"What are you doing?"

She didn't answer him as she came back in with her suit.

"What do you need that for?" She ignored him and laid the suit out, stomach up.

"Knife," Abigail said, holding her hand out. Julius handed her the knife, which she used to open the suit, compromising it.

"Abigail!"

"Relax. I know what I'm doing." She took some wires from the suit's computer and put them on either side of where the chip was under her skin.

As soon as she touched the two wires to her skin, there was a pop as an arc of electricity came out of the wires. Abigail screamed as her forearm took the shock.

"Why did you do that?"

"To short out the chip. You were going to cut me open with something unsanitary."

"I understand but still that shock could've hurt you."

"You did what you had to do, and I did what I had to. Now we both won't be affected by those chips."

"I still think they're more significant than we think."

"It's not a big deal. Let's get to bed, Julius."

"Fine."

The two headed back to their respective shelters. Julius lay down on his bed and got lost in deep thoughts. Why did Martin put a tracker in him? Who was tracking him? Was it Camilla? The more questions he asked, the more he realized there were no answers. Julius tossed and turned for the longest time before he gave up.

Julius pulled out his tablet and began typing an email addressed to John. Inside the email, he mentioned the trackers and how he had no idea who or what it was. Julius also sent him a picture to see if he could do research. He sent it encrypted so it wouldn't get caught in a filter as he was using an AMSPACE server.

NINETEEN

❧

An Accidental Discovery

There was a knock on the executive quarters in the New Mexico Research Facility. Camilla was asleep in the California king four-poster bed. Another sharp knock roused Camilla from her slumber. It had been a long day for her. Her continued involvement on the British Columbia experiment had been exhausting.

The door opened, and Camilla shot up in bed. "What could you possibly want at this hour?"

"Apologies, Miss González. The chairman is currently on hold. He said to not keep him waiting," a young woman said nervously.

"The chairman's on hold at this hour, Helen?"

"Yes, ma'am."

"Mierda, put him through at once."

"Right away."

A TAMR robot flew into the room and produced a lens. It projected a hologram of the chairman at the foot of her bed. Camilla quickly threw off her eye mask before addressing the figure.

"Mr. Chairman, to what do I owe the pleasure, sir?"

"Camilla, we have a situation at the Martian base. We intercepted an encrypted message from Julius Stetson. He's a miner on the planet."

"Yes, sir, I know of him. We sent him there a few weeks ago."

"He seems to have found a bug tracker that looks very familiar to the ones we produce for the United Forces."

"The ones they use for home surveillance, sir?"

"Yes, the very same. How did this bug tracker end up active in a miner in our facility?"

The chairman paused, waiting for Camilla to respond. "Sir, I have no idea how this happened. I'll start a full investigation immediately."

"Find out who did this. We cannot afford any bumps in the road." Camilla became more nervous as she listened to him talk.

"Sir, I'll get to work right away."

"You'd better, Camilla. We can't have anyone discovering what we're doing up there. If word got out about the test subjects, jail would be the least of your worries."

"Sir? Wouldn't it be *our* worries?"

The chairman paused thoughtfully. "Yes, our worries. My mistake. We're in this together. Fix this, Camilla, I'm counting on you."

The chairman reached somewhere off to the side before the TAMR bot stopped producing the hologram.

In the chairman's executive office, Burt sat waiting for the transmission to end.

"You know it's kind of ironic, Arnold. The same devices we use to track the location of each member of the Red Hand is now being used against us on Mars."

"Burt, shut the fuck up. Figure out how extensive this is and prepare to remove them from all my employees."

"I can do that, but it will take time."

"I don't care. Get it done, now. We don't know who is bugging the Martian base, and we cannot afford to let things get out. What if they've bugged a precision mining crew member?"

"Right, sir. That wouldn't be good. I'll start to fix it right away." Burt stood up from the couch and ran out of the chairman's office.

Camilla sat in her bed. The way the chairman spoke made it seem as though he would abandon her. This upset Camilla and shook the woman to her core. She knew something was not quite right about him, but she didn't think he would sacrifice her to save his skin. Her anxiety slowly turned to anger. She began to shake.

"Helen!"

There were quick footsteps outside the door before it opened. "What can I do for you, Miss González?"

"Get my directors on a conference call. We have work to do." Camilla was out of bed in a robe going toward the bathroom.

"Yes, ma'am. What should I tell them?"

"Tell them we have a problem."

Helen closed the door, as Camilla got ready for this impromptu meeting.

Fifteen minutes later, Camilla was down in the executive office seated behind the desk. Martin was in the room with her, and Dave was on the computer. "I'm going to get straight to the point, gentlemen. Someone has bugged the Martian base."

"Impossible," Dave immediately responded.

"The chairman has intercepted a communication from the base that indicated a bug was placed in a miner. I need you two to get to the bottom of this immediately," Camilla said.

"There's no need for an investigation, ma'am. It was an experimental bug only meant to go into Julius Stetson. I believed there was no risk to the corporation thanks to the research and development clause legal puts in all contracts our miner's sign. I'm sorry for causing such a scare, but I figured it could be a valuable tool if successful. Obviously, it was a failure, and I will scrap the program," Martin explained.

Camilla looked at Martin. "You did this without consulting me?"

"Yes, ma'am, I'm sorry. It won't happen again."

"No, it won't. You're to write me a report on this incident, and I will send it to the chairman. Get out of my sight." Martin nodded and left the room.

Dave was still on the line, "I don't trust Martin, Dave. We cannot let him get in my way. Find a way to remove him."

"My pleasure, Camilla," Dave replied with a smirk before ending his transmission.

Back on Mars, Julius was sleeping soundly when he heard Abigail's voice in his head. "Hey, are you getting up?" Julius ignored the voice and continued to sleep.

"Hey!" He was startled awake, falling out of bed and hitting the ground hard. His body throbbed with disapproval. Julius looked up and saw Abigail standing over him.

"Morning, Sunshine." Abigail looked down on him with her hands on her hips.

"What's wrong with you?"

"What? We have work to do! Now get up." She reached her hand out to him. He took it and she helped him to his feet. "Here, how about I give you something to make you less grumpy?" Abigail leaned in and kissed him.

"You know how to make my morning better, Abigail."

"I know." Abigail turned around and walked out of Julius's room. "Get dressed. I want some food before we go out to take soil samples."

"Okay, give me a second." Julius grabbed his clothes and changed.

Julius walked into the common area where she was waiting for him. Their eyes locked for a minute. "You know I like you a lot, Abigail."

"What's not to love?" She winked at him and turned. "I'm going to eat now. Are you coming?"

Julius smiled and followed her into the air lock. They both quickly put on their suits and started walking to the main building. "You know, you're quite the tease."

"But you like it."

"You aren't wrong."

When they reached the main building, they went through their respective locker rooms. Once changed, Julius exited where he saw Abigail waiting for him on a bench talking to Laura.

"Took you long enough," Abigail said.

"Hey, I just started walking again yesterday, cut me some slack. Good to see you again, Laura."

"Likewise. I hear you're working with Abigail today. Be careful. She can be really hard to work with."

"Seriously?" Abigail looked at Laura with concern.

"No, Abigail, I'm kidding. You're awesome to work with." The three walked into the mess hall where they got some breakfast. As they walked out of the line, Julius saw Dig Team Mike sitting at a table.

"Abigail, I'm going to sit with my team for a bit."

"Okay, I'll join you. Do you mind, Laura?"

"Not at all. See you tonight for wine night?"

"Wouldn't miss it."

The two shelter mates walked to Dig Team Mike and sat down at their table. "Vegas, great to see you walking again," Jaivan said.

"Don't mess up on your temporary assignment," James said with a joking tone of voice.

"Shut it, Kitten! We're going to miss you, Julius, but I've already asked Dave for you to get assigned back to me. We can't afford to lose a great miner like you. No offense Abigail," Irene said.

"None taken," Abigail said. Julius found it strange how they were all interacting as though they were friends, but he remembered they were all in his hospital room together. This might have given them time to get to know each other.

"We have to catch the train now. We can't miss it," Saké said as most of the group stood up.

"Yeah, we have a large deposit to dig up. We have the good old Gem back," James said.

Tex was quiet, but Julius noticed he had been eyeing Abigail. As he stood up, he looked over at her. "Hey, miss, if you ever want to experience Texas, just let me know."

Abigail gave him a look, before answering in a mock Southern accent. "I hear Texas ain't that impressive downstate, if you know what I mean."

The rest of the diggers on Team Mike looked at her and burst into laughter. Tex turned white and sulked away. The rest of the team followed him out, still snickering, except for James.

"Want to get a drink at the bar tonight, Julius?"

"Sure thing, pal. I'll meet you there after Abigail lets me go." Julius turned and winked at her.

"Careful. I might never let him go."

"Sounds great, either way, see you then." James dashed off to catch up with Dig Team Mike.

Julius turned to look at Abigail. "Okay, your comment to Tex was clever."

"Thanks. I hate when men try to swoon women like that. It's just unattractive, like they're living in the last century. There were so many of them in California. The only difference was, they were mostly surfer dudes instead of rednecks."

The two ate their food as the mess hall cleared out. Abigail looked up at a digital clock. "Is that the time? We need to get going."

"Where do we need to go?"

"We need to get a drill hauler from the garage." Before they went to the hangar, they got their suits from their locker rooms. The duo met back up and went to the garage. Abigail walked up to the attendant standing behind the kiosk.

"Hi, Abigail King, terraforming unit. I need a drill hauler for my digger to make test holes."

"Take DH162," the guard said, pointing to the drill hauler section on the other side of the hangar. Julius and Abigail strolled across the garage, passing moving vehicles, including people haulers, and speeder bikes.

When they reached the drill hauler area, they walked along the rows, checking the top of the cab for the correct number. Finally, they found their designated hauler.

Julius entered via the driver's side, and Abigail entered using the passenger side. "Ready to go?" Julius asked.

"As ready as I'll ever be. Remember the last time we drove together? I ended up in a terrastorm." The robots that roamed the hangar directed Julius around the rows of vehicles toward the exit.

"I'm glad we haven't had one of those yet. I'm sure it's thanks to your amazing terraforming team."

"Yeah, Martin and Becka sure made it seem like we were going to have a lot more than we really did."

Julius moved the DH162 into the air lock. He looked to his left and saw another drill hauler, DH159. Laura was inside the passenger seat with some other driver. Abigail saw her and waved, which Laura returned.

Julius focused on the air lock going through its process to release them. He waited for the second door to open. When it did, he drove up the ramp and into the Martian plains.

"We have quite a few holes to dig today. I've programmed them into my MPS, so it should be easy. Just follow my directions."

"Wouldn't it just be easier to give me the coordinates?"

"You wanted to drive, and I have the locations. You're just going to have to listen to my direction."

Julius groaned as Abigail guided him to each location. Once at a location, he drilled the hole. Abigail would set up climbing equipment to lower herself into the hole, taking the Soil Analyzer 3000 with her.

Once the sample was collected, she would use the auto retractor on the winch to raise herself. They would then drive to the next point on the MPS.

The sun was getting low in the sky after a long day of drilling test holes. They reached the last point on Abigail's MPS. "Last one, then we can go home."

"Thank goodness. And we have to do this all over again tomorrow?"

"Yeah, I know it's boring, but maybe they'll give us a different assignment."

"I hope so. I can't take much more of this."

Abigail got out and began to investigate where exactly they needed to drill. Julius sat in the drill hauler and stared blankly over the Martian plain when he saw a large rock nearby. "I wonder if the hauler could crush that rock," he said.

Impulsively, Julius drove the hauler over to the rock.

"Julius, what are you doing?" He ignored Abigail's question and started up the drill. He lowered it into the rock, causing red chunks to fly up as the rock shattered into a million pieces.

"That's awesome!" he yelled.

"No, it is not awesome. That isn't where we're supposed to drill."

"It's fine. I'll still get your sample. Watch this." He lowered the drill further. His intention was to go down the specified thirty feet. The drill lowered about ten feet before a hissing sound emitting from the hole.

"Abigail, duck!"

Suddenly, there was a change of pressure, and a white mist that looked like steam was released from the hole and passed around the drill. The drill stopped cutting anything and freely spun as if it had broken through something.

Julius raised the drill and got out of the cab. He ran over to Abigail, finding her face down in the dirt.

"What was that?" She got back to her feet.

"Beats me, but it seems too strange to not check out." Julius walked toward the hole.

"Are you insane?"

He ignored her as he reached the edge of the hole. Before he looked down, he inspected the drill bit. There was brown, rusted metal twisted in it.

"That shouldn't be there. Abigail, you need to see this." She walked up behind him.

"What the actual fuck is that?" The metal was slightly rusted and covered with Martian dirt. "That's not natural, Julius."

"I know it's not natural, but what is it?"

"I don't know."

They were both stunned, but Julius decided to take action.

"Lights on."

Julius's suit produced the LED strips. He looked down into the hole he had created. "No way!" Julius's eyes widened.

Abigail looked in and gasped. "Oh my god! What is it?"

At the bottom of the ten-foot hole was a brown metal shell that had been ripped open and pushed in by the drill. The two stared into a black void. Julius's light wasn't powerful enough to reveal what was past the thick metal casing.

"I don't know what this is, but I'm going to find out." Julius turned around and began to almost run to the drill hauler. She watched him gather up the climbing gear she had used to enter the other holes.

"Please don't go down there. We should call this in."

"Something isn't right here. I need to see what is down there. What if this is what I've been mining for? I need to see what's down there. If you want to come, you can. We've got two winches." He pointed at the secondary winch on the rear of the hauler.

"Fine. If we die in there, I'm haunting you for eternity."

She walked over to the drill hauler and prepared her climbing gear, while Julius did the same. Once they were both tied off, he walked to the edge of the hole and looked back at Abigail.

"Look, um...I like you a lot. If we come back from this, want to be official?"

"Seriously? Now you're asking me? How about you ask me after we live through this?"

At a loss for words, he took a deep breath before he jumped off the side and descended into the abyss.

Julius's heart rate was accelerating, and he could feel sweat all over his body. He swung the lights on his helmet around wildly, trying to get a grip on where he was descending. As he went further down, he remembered the dream he had that was very similar to this situation. This time he wasn't going to wake up.

When he got close enough, his light revealed the contents of the room. There were some odd-looking hunks of metal that looked like alien spacecraft. He guessed it was a hangar bay. He counted three of the strange crafts that were covered in thick layers of Martian dust. They were skinny tubes in the middle, with two sets of folded metal what Julius assumed were wings. One set resided in the front of the craft, and one in the back.

Julius's feet hit the ground fifty feet in front of one of the spaceship contraptions. He unhooked himself, leaving the harness dangling. He was about to walk up to the craft when Abigail touched down behind him.

"What are those?" She pointed at the large crafts.

"You think I know?"

"No, but can't you venture a guess?"

She unclipped from her harness, letting it dangle as well.

"Maybe they're some sort of advanced AMSPACE aircraft?" Even Julius didn't believe his guess.

The tubes were too abnormal to be anything conventional. The dust on them also didn't support his theory because that indicated they had been there for a long time.

He continued to inspect them. The machines were partially off the ground on stilts. Stairs led to the bottoms of the aerodynamically shaped tubes. A small hatch resided on the bottom for a person to slip in, but it looked to be a very tight squeeze. The two looked at the folded wings closer.

"Those must be wings that are able to fan out like a bird's," Abigail said.

"I guess that makes sense." Julius walked around to the rear of the ship. There he noticed small engines covered with a sort of dust cap. They looked similar to AM Drive engines.

Abigail had wandered away from the ship as Julius inspected the aft section of the spacecraft.

"Julius, over here!" He whirled around and saw Abigail was on the other side of the large room but realized she was not there.

"Abigail, we have to stick together. We don't know what this place is or what's in it." He hastily walked over to her.

"I know, but something caught my eye. I needed to check it out," she said, standing by a pile of rods. Julius had assumed they were guns, but there were no triggers. They seemed to be long metallic sticks with open ends. Julius picked one up and pointed the opened end toward a wall.

"Hey, remember what you said about being careful?"

"Relax. I don't think they do anything." He still tried to make the object do something. He shook it and hit the ground with the rod, but nothing happened.

Defeated, Julius gently placed it back down on the pile of other tubes. "We should get out of here. I don't like this."

"I think that's a good idea. This place is giving me the creeps."

They started to walk back to their retracting lines when they heard a bone-chilling noise. It sounded like a moan from a ghost, mixed with the gargle of a drowning person.

Both of them jumped and turned toward the area the strange noise emitted from. Abigail instinctively grabbed Julius's hand. Their combined lights showed a small door on the other side of the room.

"What the hell was that?"

"I'm, uh, I'm not sure." His voice was shaky. He was frightened out of his mind.

"I think we should leave." She started to pull away, but Julius held firm.

"No, I think we should check it out. I had a dream back in the simulation about this place."

"You what?"

"I had a dream that you and I went exploring on Mars. While we were exploring, we went into a cave, but a bright light prevented me from seeing what was below, and then I woke up. That's why we need to investigate this noise. I think it was a sign."

"Listen, I like you, but you sound crazy. Let's get out of here and pretend this didn't happen. Okay?" She tried to pull him back to the ropes again, but he held firm.

"Look, I know it's strange, and I can't explain it. Please. We have to check this out."

She looked at him. "I can go myself, and you can leave if you want."

"I'm not leaving you. I'll go."

Julius gripped her hand, and the two began to quietly move toward the door.

When they reached it, Julius whispered to his suit to activate the knives. The long blades protruded from Julius's wrists.

"Abigail, open the door." He spoke in a low whisper, so as not to alert whatever was behind the door. She nodded in reply and gripped the small handle.

She pulled it open, creating a loud metallic creaking sound, which probably altered whatever what's in there. As she did, Julius rushed into the small dark hallway that was illuminated by his helmet's lights. The lights showed him something that made him abruptly end his adrenaline-fueled charge.

Sprawled in the middle of the metallic hallway was a red-orange humanoid figure gasping for air. "Holy shit!"

"What is it, Julius?" Abigail poked her head around the corner.

"Abigail, are you seeing what…"

"Yeah, I see it." Julius could hear the fear in her voice.

Julius retracted his knives, seeing the creature was no threat. He cautiously approached the strange-looking figure, inspecting it but also stayed on his toes in case it became a threat.

"Stay away from that thing!"

"If it was going to hurt us, it would have attacked us by now." Julius knelt by the figure and got a closer look at it.

It had well-defined facial features with a visible body and appendages that looked almost human. The creature had arms that extended down to its knees, culminating in tentacles like an octopus. The main torso had a thick build but had no clear ridges.

Julius looked down to where its feet should have been, but there weren't any. The legs seemed to just widen at the bottom. They had a flat base that looked like a tree trunk with roots.

Julius's eyes were brought back up the alien's face, where he saw two large black eyes. As Julius looked into them, he saw what looked like bright white stars twinkling.

As Julius observed the figure, Abigail approached, standing behind Julius. They both simply stared at the tall creature. Without warning, the white stars in the eyes began to swirl like a whirlpool. As they swirled, a picture began to form; it was the plains of Mars.

"How the… What is this?" Julius wondered aloud.

"This memory," the figure struggled to speak.

"Who and what are you?" Julius asked, astonished the creature knew English.

"Was Martian leader, when aliens first appeared," the Martian said.

"Aliens? You mean us?" Abigail asked. The Martian nodded. Suddenly a sonic boom emanated from the Martian's mouth. Julius and Abigail looked into the eyes and saw the NASA lander from the first mission to Mars descending.

Fascinating, it looks even more realistic than the archive footage, Julius thought to himself; his eyes glued to Martians.

Abigail was stunned. It seemed the Martian had the ability to show sights and sounds from his memories. The two watched the eyes as the lander came to a stop on the Martian moonscape. In the foreground, other Martians could be seen running before vanishing into the landscape.

"They disappeared!"

"My species can change shape, unless exposed to very cold temperatures, which is why we don't live on the poles." The Martian groaned after speaking. Julius looked away from the eyes and saw the Martian's lower body had lost its definition. It was now a blob shape.

"What's happening to you?"

"Dying, losing brain power, can't hold shape." His eyes switched to another memory.

Abigail and Julius were drawn back into the creature's eyes. This memory showed the Martian approaching the NASA camp with a few other Martians. After scaring the humans to death, they spoke to Ben Lewis and presented the astronauts with a gift. It was a battery, which Julius found peculiar. In return, Ben Lewis presented the Martian leader with a dictionary.

"So NASA covered up the existence of life on Mars? That explains the blackout in the footage." Julius was stunned that this was kept secret. The Martian's eyes swirled again before the next memory flashed up. "Many sundowns after the second lander came."

"He must mean after the AMSPACE lander." Julius said to Abigail. They watched as a drill smashed through a similar bunker to the one, they were in now.

After the drill crashed through, ropes came down, and people in space suits rappelled into the room with stun guns. There was shrieking as the humans began to round up the panicking Martians. The memory stopped there, and the Martian's eyes reverted black starry night.

"So Martians are real?" The Martian ignored Julius's question.

"Hack computer for answers," the Martian said before he exhaled. His body stopped holding itself together and turned to dust right in front of Julius's and Abigail's eyes. It was like a bunch of Martian soil was deposited where the Martian once was. Julius and Abigail stared at each other in shock.

"We need to get out of here," Abigail said.

"Yeah, we do. I knew there was something fishy about them sending soldiers into the mines, but I never expected this!" He realized that he had aided in the busting of the Martian bunkers.

"He died from our incursion. We killed him, Abigail!"

"What do you mean? He's a Martian, he should be able to breathe Martian air."

"The terraforming is killing them. We spent a while in the bunker before we discovered him."

"Yes, it seems to be killing them, but, Julius, you need to focus. We cannot say anything about this to anyone." Abigail was reattaching her repelling rope.

"I know, but this is fucked up." He reached for his own rope. They both activated a button on the remotes that lifted them out of the cave.

Once out of the bunker, they looked around. It was dark, and they were alone. "We need to call this in. If we wait any longer, they'll get suspicious."

"If we do, they'll find those ships and that technology."

"They already have a wealth of knowledge if they really have been busting bunkers for all these years. We have to save ourselves if we're going to make this right."

"Fine, make the call." Abigail sent a four-word signal to headquarters. "Discovered something. Send backup."

Julius quickly put the climbing gear back in the drill hauler's toolbox. There had to be no proof of them entering the hole. Thirty minutes later, Julius and Abigail looked into the distance and saw the lights of three hovercopters approaching their location. On the ground, they could also see the lights of at least hover bikes.

TWENTY

Data Breach

The trio of hovercopters encircled the hole; their search lights caused Julius and Abigail to shield their eyes with their hands. They held their position about fifty feet off the ground. The bottom of the hull opened, and soldiers rappelled down and immediately began to enter the hole. One man walked up to the duo and started to question them.

"Did you two go in the hole?"

"No," Julius and Abigail answered in unison.

"You're sure about this? You're aware you drilled in an unsanctioned location?"

"Yes, sir. It was my fault, sir. I didn't listen to my planetologist."

"I see. Mr. Hughes has requested your presence in his office immediately." The man motioned for two soldiers to come over to him.

"These men will escort you back to base." Julius and Abigail looked at the two military men who signaled for them to follow them. They complied, returning to the drill hauler, and prepared it to depart. The soldiers lingered for a few seconds before they returned to and mounted their bikes.

"Drive, Julius." Abigail's voice was tense. Julius simply nodded to her; he could sense her fear. He drove the drill hauler away from the chaotic scene toward the base.

He wondered if the soldiers and scientists were in awe at what they had discovered down there or if this was par for the course. The strange crafts alone probably could allow AMSPACE to keep their competitive edge when Mars opens to other companies.

Julius was so deep in thought; he didn't realize Abigail was trying to get his attention.

"Julius!" she yelled. The sharpness of her voice jarred him from his thoughts.

"What?"

"You need to slow down. We're almost back." She pointed at the rapidly approaching ramp to the hangar.

"Oh, thanks. Sorry, I was just thinking."

"I can tell. Relax, we can't let them know we are aware of their secret."

They entered the main hangar and parked DH162 in its designated spot before they exited the vehicle. The two soldiers from before met them.

"Come with us please," one of them said in a tone that made the please seem worthless.

Julius and Abigail walked with the two soldiers. They exited the garage and walked to an elevator that took them to the sixth floor.

Once there, they were brought to Dave's office. One of the soldiers knocked on the door, and then waited until they were told to enter.

The door opened, and the soldiers gestured for the duo to enter Dave's office. Once they were inside, the door shut, leaving the soldiers outside.

Dave's office was filled with thick cigar smoke. Julius and Abigail could barely see Dave's desk. They made their way through the room and found two seats in front of the desk.

"You two have assisted in a great discovery, but you violated statute 801-LT, which outlines that you have to dig where you are told, no exceptions." Dave's face emerged through the thick smoke.

Seeing Dave's face appear suddenly caused Julius to move back in his seat instinctively. Julius composed himself quickly and spoke. "I'm sorry, Mr. Hughes. What was discovered?"

"Sorry isn't going to cut it, Stetson. You found a great wealth of the material you are mining for. Even so, your recklessness has forced me to mandate classroom training for both you and Miss King." Before they could argue, Dave smashed out his cigar. "Get the fuck out of my office. You're lucky I didn't fire you."

Julius and Abigail quickly stood up and walked out of the office. Once outside, Abigail turned to Julius. "I'm late for girl's wine night. I need to go."

"Are you going to the bar?"

"Yeah, where else could I get wine?"

"I'm going to come with you. James is supposed to meet me there as well."

Julius and Abigail walked down to the bar where Laura was waiting. "What took you two so long? I thought you were going to ditch me, Abigail."

"I wouldn't do that to you. We just had an incident that needed to be resolved."

Julius looked around the bar and saw that James was nowhere in sight. "Hey, Abigail, James isn't here. I'm going to see if I can still get some food, and then I'm going back to the shelter. See you later?"

"Yeah, I'll see ya later."

Julius went to the mess hall to eat a late dinner. He continued to let his head swirl with thoughts. He had just found out Martians existed and couldn't tell anyone. After slowly picking at his meal, which he didn't finish, Julius returned to his shelter. He sat down on his bed, and his mind kept replaying what he just witnessed.

After an hour or two of sitting there, he heard Abigail enter the shelter, but he did not speak to her. He stayed lost in his thoughts of the events of earlier in the day. Eventually, sleep took hold of him.

The next morning, Julius woke up long before Abigail. He went to the living room portion of the shelter and sat down. Julius was still fixated on what had transpired the day before. He saw the images of the soldiers capturing Martians. Seeing those scenes play out in his head made him feel guilty for enabling the torture of the Martians. It was then he realized he had to do something to stop AMSPACE.

He thought of many ways he could try to pull it off. But he realized he couldn't do it alone. Who else would be willing to help him?

Julius listed many people off in his head before he came to the one person he knew would help. "Abigail," he said out loud.

"What?"

The woman's voice startled him for a moment. "Oh, you're awake."

"Yeah, we have our training course."

"I know, I know. But can you really go to a training course right now, given what we saw yesterday?"

"I can. It's not my business. Why are you being so dramatic?"

"We can't just let them do this to the Martians."

"You think we can help those things? We're just two people." To his surprise, Abigail was getting defensive.

Julius composed himself and spoke. "It only took a few people to take out the North American Union prime minister. One person started the First World War. Everything in this universe changes with a single spark. I remember the old saying, if not you, then who? It's time for us to stand up for what is right."

Abigail looked at Julius. The conflict was evident in her hazel eyes. She wanted to help, but she was unsure what she could do. If she acted, this could torpedo her career.

"Do you even have a plan, Julius?"

"Kind of, it sounds a little crazy. I think we need more information than what the Martian gave us. James told me about a data archive located in the main building a few weeks ago. If there's any information on the Martians, it would be there. I suggest we break into the archives and take as much incriminating evidence as we can. Then we'll sneak it onto a shuttle disguised as a package to my friend John. Once we get leave, we return to Earth and expose them for the corrupt cooperation they are!"

"First, I love the enthusiasm. Just one issue here. Who's going to hack the archives, and how will you determine its location?"

Julius's expression changed to one of depression, like a balloon that lost all its air.

"I was kind of hoping you'd be able to hack it. As for the location, James knows where it is."

"I mean, I can try, but there is no guarantee I could get past all their security. How will you convince James to tell you?" Abigail sounded very skeptical.

"I could just ask him. We're friends, after all."

"Just ask him? There is no way he'll give up that information." Abigail looked at the clock in the common room. She realized it was getting close to the time their training class was supposed to start.

"I'll get the information out of him before the week is out."

"Okay, great. You do that, and maybe I'll help. For right now, we need to get going to class."

"Fine."

They left the living room and entered the air lock to go to class. They spent a dull day in a class, reviewing company procedures and policies.

After their class, Julius left Abigail to find James and talk to him. After searching most of the main floor of the central building, Julius found him at the bar. He looked disheveled and dirty. He had a drink in his hand and many glasses around him.

"James, what's going on?" Julius took a seat next to him.

"I got canned yesterday, that's why I didn't come here to hang last night. I'm sorry. I'm a bad friend." James was slurring his words and was clearly intoxicated.

"You got fired? How? Why?"

"Bobby was making fun of me again. He did that stupid silly string gag. Once I got it cleaned off, I remembered the advice you gave me. The one about how I should stand up for myself. So I tried to speak to him cordially. Instead of listening, he put more silly string on my helmet and told me to lighten up. So I punched him in the gut. He hit me back, and we kept trading blows till Tex and Jaivan separated us."

"That's not exactly what I intended for you to do. But that got you fired?"

"Well, Irene told Dave, and he fired me on the spot. I'm on a shuttle back to Earth tomorrow. Bobby's getting transferred to an asteroid mining operation. What am I going to tell my mom?" James was getting emotional and almost fell out of his seat.

"Your mom won't care; she'll be happy to have you home. It sucks, man, but you hated it here. Think of it this way, now you get to go back and find a better job."

"Yeah, I hated the job, but I didn't want to be fired."

"Being fired sucks, but it's okay. This is a new start for you."

"I guess you're right. I'm man enough to blaze my own path!"

Julius thought about the Martians and his plan. Julius realized this would be his only shot if he was going to get the information from James. In addition, it would be easier to get the details on the data archive out of James since he was so intoxicated.

"Yeah, you could find a better job than your dad's. What was his job again? Assisting with data security?"

"Yeah, he collects all the data in the Martian space library for the on-planet executives to access when they need it."

"I see. And these archives. They're stored where?" Julius felt guilty exploiting his friend like this, but it was for the greater good.

"They're secret, but you're my friend. I'm sure I can trust you. Plus, I'm leaving anyway, they won't suspect me. Just don't tell on me." James spoke in a slurred whisper as he slapped Julius's shoulder.

"I promise to not tell."

"Good deal. So the archives are located on the third floor. They're behind a door marked 'Janitor.' To the right of the door is keypad. The combination is constantly changing, so you have no chance of getting in without the key."

Julius was worried his plan was shot. His eyes filled with dread.

"Fear not, though. My dad designed the system. I believe he put a back door in, so he alone could always access the system. He did this for our home computer when I was a kid. Type in '43054,' and it should work. He uses that for everything. It was his zip code when he was a kid."

"James, I think you told me a bit too much. How about I take you to your shelter?"

"No, I'm fine. I just want another drink." James turned away from Julius and helped himself to a beer. Julius stood up.

"All right, my friend, I'll be seeing you around. Don't forget to write." James just waved his hand and didn't even look at Julius. Julius walked to the mess hall and had a good dinner before he went back to his shelter. He closed the door and saw Abigail was sitting on the couch.

"Well? How was the rest of your day?"

"It was good. I now know where the archives are, but our way in could be interesting." He sat down next to Abigail.

"James gave me a theory on how to get into the data room, but that's all it is."

"A theory? You're basing the success of this entire plan on a theory?" She sounded irritated.

"Look, I think it's more than just a theory, but he couldn't tell me as he was really drunk."

"You're not helping your case. He was drunk? How do you know his information was accurate?"

"I know it's not the most reliable source, but it's all we've got. The Martians are counting on us."

"You're asking me to risk my entire career and life on a drunk guy's statement and a conspiracy theory from a dead Martian."

"Listen to what you just said. A conspiracy theory from a Martian. A Martian, Abigail! The proof is in the data archives. I know it."

"It's a lot to think about. I need some alone time." Abigail stood up and walked to her room.

Damn it, Julius thought as he sat there on the couch. Even he was starting to question the logic in his plan. He got up from his seat and went to his part of the shelter and went to bed.

The next morning, Julius walked out to find Abigail sitting on the couch. She looked deep in thought and conflicted. "Morning, Abigail." He stood behind her, worried what she was about to say.

"Morning."

"Are you okay?"

"I want to help, but I don't want to get involved unless we have a solid plan of attack."

"We have a real chance here. James is gone, shipped back to Earth. We have no other options right now. We need more information and proof. This is how we're going to get it."

"I don't disagree, but we need a way to get out if it fails. I want a plan B."

"I have a plan B. We're going to break in, and if it fails, you run and I take the fall. If it works, we go forward, with mailing the information to my friend John."

"No, we both run. We're a team."

Julius sat there for a moment, letting her words sink in. He smiled and looked at her. "Deal."

"Okay, I'll help Julius. When are we going?"

"I think now is a good time."

"Now?"

"Yeah, it's still early in the morning. Most people are still asleep, so we won't have to worry about the main building being crowded." Abigail was apprehensive. It seemed too soon to attempt this.

He walked to the air lock and looked back. Abigail was still sitting on the couch. "Are you coming?"

She sighed and stood up. "Yeah." Her voice sounded defeated. She walked over to Julius and got in the air lock. They walked to the main building where they went straight for the elevator. "This is stupid, you know?" Abigail kept her voice low in a small whisper.

"I know. I don't know where the door is, but it's labeled 'Janitor.' You go right, and I'll go left. If you find the door come get me, and I'll do the same."

"Sounds good to me. Let's get this over with."

The elevator's doors opened. Julius and Abigail stepped out and went their separate ways. As he walked down the hallway, Julius scanned all the doors. Most were simply marked with a number. Eventually, he found a room with a sign on it that said "Janitor." Julius turned and went to get Abigail.

He found her down the hall, looking at the doors on the other side. "I found it," he whispered.

"Take me to it." He led her to the door.

Once there, the two scanned the door for any abnormalities. It was a regular door with a handle. Off to the side was a holographic keypad with the digits zero to nine glowing bright on the display.

"Well, get on it. We don't have all day."

"I'm sorry, I'm nervous." He typed in "43054," and the little light on the top of the keypad turned green and the door unlocked.

"Holy shit, it worked." Abigail had a surprised look on her face.

"I'm as shocked as you are." Julius pushed the door open. Behind the door was a very small room with a computerized wall and a desk. A door was on the other side; it had a different keypad and retinal scanner.

"Looks like this is it. Can you hack that?"

"We'll see. Let me work my magic." She sat down at the small desk and opened the computer wall's command prompt. She began typing furiously and started to backdoor the firewalls.

Julius sat, watching her fight with the computer for twenty agonizing minutes. He eyed the door as well, fully expecting it to be kicked down by the security forces.

Abigail ended her typing with a silent "Fuck yeah." As she gained access to the archives, Julius rushed over to see a large folder open with multiple subfolders. She began to open the subfolders that contained different video files.

"Click on that one." Julius pointed at one titled "Hive 34 Breach."

The video player opened. It displayed a soldier's point of view as he or she breached a bunker. Abigail quickly closed it before it played, which disappointed Julius. She left that subfolder and opened one named "Camps."

It had a lot of pictures. She opened one of them and saw something that looked like a concentration camp. There were Martians standing behind a glass case with guards all around.

"What the actual fuck?" Julius said, astonished.

"Julius, we don't have much time left. I think they know there has been a breach."

"Okay, take this and get as much on as you can." Julius handed her an eight-petabyte USBD stick.

"Do I want to know where you got this?" Abigail plugged it in and began to copy files to the memory stick.

"You probably don't." As the files downloaded, Abigail browsed through the files. She saw hundreds of MP4 files labeled "Test Subject 191," "Hive 45 Breach," and "Dark Gem Incident," to name a few. One caught her eye, and she clicked on it. The file was labeled "British Columbia Test Subject 240 Integration Test." The video player opened, and what the duo saw next shocked them.

On the large computer wall, they saw a lab with a few people in it dressed in lab coats. There were also guards standing by the boxes that Julius saw when he boarded the shuttle in New Mexico. The camera swung around. They both saw Camilla.

"Open crate 240 and bring out the test subject. I'm ready to start the tests," Camilla said as the box labeled "240" was opened to reveal something covered up. The people moved the test subject onto the table, still covered by a sheet.

"Call in the doctors and surgeons. I have deadlines to meet," Camilla said. Julius and Abigail watched as more people entered the room.

The sheet was pulled back to reveal a semi-frozen Martian.

"For the record, the test being performed with Test Subject 240 will be to help these beings breathe Earth's air. This will prevent premature death via suffocation." Camilla prepared a syringe.

"Oh my gosh, she's going to experiment on them!" Abigail held her hand over her mouth as they watched, unable to look away. Camilla narrated to the camera.

"As you can see, the subject is frozen. This is due to their gelatinous body composition. When frozen to a certain temperature, about –150 degrees Fahrenheit, their cells stop moving. This prevents them from having the ability to morph and move."

Camilla moved so she was standing over the motionless Martian. "The Martian has melted enough to allow this test to commence. This is integration test number one, human DNA bonded with Martian DNA."

She took the syringe and jabbed it into the now semifrozen
Martian. A blood-curdling screech emanated from the creature as the
liquid that looked like blood drained into the Martian. It began to
shake and change colors at random, stopping on a lighter red color
that looked similar to a sunburn on a tan body. The Martian took
a deep breath of unfiltered air and didn't seem to have any negative
reaction.

"We will continue to monitor the results of this test subject,
then determine if the test was a success. Put it back in the crate. The
chairman will be very pleased."

"The chairman is involved with this?"

"I couldn't tell you, Julius, shut up," Abigail said.

They kept watching as the people returned the Martian to the
box. "Madam, it's ill advised to continue with the second test," one
of the men in the room said.

"I don't care. We have to complete this test to appease the chairman," Camilla said as she grabbed another syringe from a different
person then plunged it into her arm.

"Integration test number two, Martian DNA bonded with
human DNA." Camilla strained before she collapsed on the ground,
shaking violently. The medical staff and scientists rushed in and tried
to lift her up onto a table. As they lifted, her skin stretched as though
it was putty.

People recoiled as Camilla screamed in pain. No one knew what
to do; the room was in complete chaos. During the commotion, the
cameras were shut off, ending the video.

After the video ended, Julius and Abigail stared at the black
screen.

"What the fuck was that?" Julius asked.

"I-I-I think she made it so they could breathe air, then it looked
like she made herself part Martian. Did you see how she turned into
goo?"

"How is that even possible?"

"It's possible obviously because she did it. I guess the Martian
DNA is adaptable to human DNA. Camilla seems to possess some
of the Martians' power."

"There's another video below that, the one called 'Hybrid Integration Tests.' Click on it." Julius pointed at a file.

Abigail opened it up, and it started to play.

At first the screen was dark. "Idiot, you're blocking the camera," Camilla's voice could be heard.

"Sorry, Miss González." The person moved, and the camera focused on Camilla sitting in a traditional dentist's chair.

"Okay, Miss González, today we're going to test your ability to change the shape of your body. We want to see if you possess the same extent of powers the other test subjects have." A man in a protective bio suit said.

Camilla's arm stretched out and grabbed the man around the neck. "I'm not a test subject. I'm the first of a new line of superhumans."

"Apologies, ma'am, I meant no disrespect, please let me go." There was fear in his voice. Camilla released the man who coughed, trying to catch his breath.

Another man stepped up. "Ma'am, can you attempt to change your hand into something else?"

Camilla's facial expression changed to one of extreme concentration. Her body began to shake as her hand began to ripple like waves in the ocean.

"What's happening to her?" Julius asked.

"Concentrate, Miss González. Think of what you want it to become. Stretching your body is one thing, but changing it completely is another," the man in the bio suit coached.

"I know, you fool!" Camilla's hand then turned into a blade like it was made out of programmable metal. It extended out and sliced through the man's bio suit and through his neck.

Everyone else in the room jumped back in panic as blood gushed out of the man's mortal wound. Camilla's arm changed back to normal before she smiled.

"Guess we can call that a successful test. What's next?" The camera shut off after that, leaving the screen blank.

Julius looked at Abigail. They were both stunned. Camilla had killed a man and didn't bat an eye.

"Did she?" Julius asked.

"Yes, she just killed that poor man without hesitation."

"Note to self, don't confront her. Abigail, we've been in here long enough. Are all the files we want on that memory stick, including that one?"

"Yes. You're right, Julius, we need to go!" She disconnected the USB, and they both ran out of the room.

As they quickly ran out, they didn't realize an exit code was required. The room's security system began to count down from sixty. As they quickly ran down the hall, away from the data archives, Abigail and Julius thought they were home free. That was until an alarm began to sound. A female voice droned "Data breach" on repeat as red lights flashed.

"Time to initiate plan B! We need to head back to Earth!" Julius and Abigail ran down the stairs.

"You didn't tell me escape to Earth was plan B."

"Because if I told you what it was, you wouldn't have gone along with it."

"Of course I wouldn't have gone with it. How will we get back to Earth?"

"The Martian spacecrafts, we found yesterday."

Now on the main floor, the two ran toward the locker rooms. Two floors up, armed guards were swept around the third floor near the data archive. Dave was standing among them red with rage. "Find the people responsible for this and bring them back here immediately, dead or alive."

TWENTY-ONE

Plan B

Julius and Abigail walked quickly down the hallway and slipped into Dig Team Mike's locker room. Julius hastily put on his suit while Abigail stole the suit James left behind. It was a little snug, but it would work. They grabbed the helmets and left the locker room. The duo walked casually toward the garage so as not to raise any suspicion.

Once in the garage, Abigail walked up to the garage manager and cleared her throat to get his attention. "We need two hover bikes to take additional samples in the holes we dug yesterday."

"Let me see if there's a request from the terraforming unit for you, Miss King." The man looked down at the kiosk.

Julius scanned the immediate area for a means of escape. He knew there was no way Abigail had any change to get them a ride using this approach. Julius saw another garage manager handing some operator keys to another group.

The man looked up from his kiosk. "Miss King, I have no request for vehicles for you or your friend. In fact, you seem to be skipping a mandatory training class." The man signaled for the guards to come over.

Julius sprang into action. He bolted toward the group he just witnessed receiving the digital keys. Julius's blitz was enough to confuse and prevent a guard he nearly knocked over from apprehending him.

He forcibly removed a key from one of the people, then bounded down the stairs and ran through the main hanger. As he ran, he turned the USB-like key around in his hand and saw it was labeled "HB010," meaning "hover bike 010."

He turned his head around and saw Abigail running after him, waving her arms and yelling for him to run faster. Behind her, Julius saw three guards, including the garage manager chasing them.

Julius ran toward the hover bike section with Abigail right behind him. "Find HB010," Julius told Abigail as they ran through the rows of hover bikes, searching desperately for the one that matched the key.

The two separated, each frantically attempting to locate HB010. Luck seemed to be on their side because Abigail started frantically waving at Julius; she had found it. He ran to her, throwing on his helmet. She was already sitting on the bike with her helmet on. The bike sensed the key, and Abigail activated the bike. Julius put his hands around her waist, and they took off.

Abigail drove straight at the pursuing men who instinctively dove for cover. She moved the bike around the garage and drove up to the air lock. Julius looked at the touch pad to the side of the gate. It was red and said "System Locked."

"Julius, do something!" Abigail yelled from the bike as Julius desperately looked around for a way out. The guards were running toward them. They were trapped.

Julius dismounted the bike and ran over to the touch display. Below the display was a button labeled "Manual Override." Julius punched it, causing the red lockout screen to go away. There was a digital button on the screen that said "Open," and Julius pressed it.

The door opened slightly, and Abigail moved the bike into the air lock ahead of Julius, who was running back. A bullet flew inches in front of Julius and smashed into the glass air lock, causing a spiderweb of broken glass to appear.

He looked up and saw Dave Hughes holding a .44 Magnum pistol that glistened in the fluorescent light. Julius slipped into the air lock as the door closed. He jumped onto the back of the bike just as the second door opened. Abigail punched the accelerator, and the bike tore away from the facility.

They drove toward the last hole they dug yesterday. Julius held on to Abigail for dear life as she pushed the bike to its limits. He managed to look back and saw the guards were giving chase.

"Drive faster, they're behind us!"

"I see 'em!"

They were flying across the Martian plains at top speed. Soon they reached the hole and were slightly relieved they had made it without being caught. Julius's relief evaporated when he realized there was no way to get into the hole safely.

"What do we do now, Abigail? There's no way down!"

Abigail turned the bike. "Hold on!" Julius instinctively tightened his grip around her.

She started driving toward the hole.

"Are you insane?" Julius cried out, his body tensing up as they fell down the hole. Just before they hit the ground, Abigail turned the alternator, and the bike repelled against the ground and came to a soft landing next to one of the ships.

"Don't ever do that again."

"I'm saving our asses. A simple thank you would suffice."

The two quickly scrambled under one of the ships and looked for a way to open the skinny hatch.

After searching for a moment or two, Julius and Abigail heard vehicles above them accompanied by the hum of hovercopters. Then they heard a voice over comms, "They went down the hole!"

"We have them now. It will be unfortunate for them to be in a mine collapse," Dave's sinister voice said high above them.

"Of course, sir, I'll take care of it," one of the guards said as he grabbed a plasma launcher.

"No, you moron! I meant that's what we'll put on the autopsy reports. We can't run the risk of damaging the assets." Dave signaled for the men to prepare to enter the cave.

"We need to get in there now," Julius said as he desperately tried to pry the hatch open. Meanwhile, Abigail took the more logical route and searched for a mechanism to open the trap door.

Julius could hear the soldiers high above him, preparing to enter the cave. In a desperate attempt to escape, he punched the trap door with all his might. To both their surprise, the ship's hatch unfastened.

He felt like he broke his hand and was shaking it off. "You did it, Julius," Abigail said as she peered into the hatch. Dim lights illuminated the narrow way up.

"Go on. I'll be right behind you," Julius said to Abigail.

She squeezed her way into the ship. Julius quickly followed as he heard the guards descend into the cavern. He looked back and saw the hatch close. The guards and Dave landed next to the hover bike and began to sweep the room, unsure where their targets were.

Julius climbed the short distance to an open area that ran the length of the ship. The area had an off-white interior with two seats toward the front that looked out a window that was so covered in dust, he couldn't see out. There was a large panel that had a multitude of buttons and lights.

Abigail was already sitting in a chair, trying to figure out how to make the ship do anything. Julius walked up behind her and whispered.

"Hey, I don't think they know where we are."

"We know exactly where you are, Stetson," Dave's menacing voice came over the commlink.

"Shit, can you get this thing moving, Abigail?"

"Good luck with that, Stetson. Our top scientists have been trying to get those clunkers moving for years. I do have to thank you though, the last time we found them was 2081." Julius began to sweat. Abigail had a look of intense focus as she continued to try to get the ship moving.

"Did you fools forget you're using our comms to chat? How could you two be so dumb to think you could escape me? I know this planet, I conquered it and its pathetic inhabitants." Dave started to hit the side of the ship with the butt of his handgun. The metallic clangs rang through the ship, making Julius and Abigail jump at every strike.

As Dave struck the side of the ship, he began to whistle like a madman. He was whistling two long tones that oscillated down and up.

"I bet you watched the Test Subject 191 film. That was the start of it all when we realized we could use these creatures for profit. That one experiment got Camilla her current position and put me here on Mars. We needed someone who knew what we were really doing here to watch over the operation. You know, I love listening to the creatures scream, just like how I am going to enjoy listening to your screams when I launch you into deep space. What a waste. You were so talented, Miss King."

Abigail felt a chill go down her spine and adrenaline rush into her body. After he finished speaking, Dave continued his sinister whistle. The other soldiers in the cave joined in. The chorus of whistles was pure nightmare fuel.

Julius shook Abigail's shoulder. "Have you figured it out yet?"

"No, shut up! Let me think." She smashed her hands against the controls. "We're dead, Julius. There's no way out. These stupid-brain beings are going to be—"

"These stupid-brain beings are going to be what?"

"Shut up! They're going to be our salvation. Their brains hold their bodies together. That must mean their ships have to be powered by their brains. I can't see any other. This ship has to be powered by brainwaves."

Abigail stood up and looked around the room; her sudden movements surprised Julius. She looked all over the interior of the ship. Outside the creepy whistling continued as more guards began to beat on the side of the ship.

"Julius, help me find anything that can scan brain waves." Abigail frantically looked around the ship as the beatings got louder and louder.

"Let us in, Julius. Make it easier on yourself. Think of it this way, we'll have to pay your family handsomely for your death. They won't even miss you!"

Dave laughed maniacally as Abigail stumbled across a small door with a handle on it. The door handle had a rectangular shape and something that looked like a keyhole.

Martians probably stick their shape-shifted arms into it in order to open the door. Abigail thought as she inspected at her hands, trying to think of a way to get in.

"Little piggies, come out and play!" Dave's high, shrill voice mocked them.

"Why has he not broken in yet?" Abigail was focused on how to get the door open and didn't answer Julius.

"Because, Piggy One, I don't want to damage company property. If you and Piggy Two come out, I'll make your deaths painless."

"F-fuck you, Dave," Julius stuttered as he realized his childhood hero was trying to kill him.

"Suit, terminate connections to AMSPACE Martian Network," Abigail ordered her suit. "Right away, Miss King." Abigail's suit complied.

"Sounds like it's just you and me, Piggy One. So what's it going to be?" Dave asked Julius, whose eyes were glued to Abigail. She pointed to the little antenna on their suit and pulled her hand across her neck. Julius understood what she meant.

"Go fuck yourself, Dave. Suit, disconnect from all AMSPACE networks." The two were all alone now; all they could hear was the banging on the side of the ship from the people outside.

"Activate knives!" Abigail said to her suit. The knives extended from her wrists like giant needles. Abigail took her right hand and thrust the knife into the lock and twisted. The door opened to reveal a silver helmet. The metal seemed to be moldable by the user.

To Julius, it looked like a crown with loads of wires protruding from it that led to a central computer. There were sensors all over the helmet that blinked and glistened in the low-lit room.

How have they never discovered this? Julius wondered to himself.

Abigail reached in and grabbed it. *There's no way I can put it on with my helmet on.* Abigail thought to herself before she began to mentally prepare herself for what she had to do.

Outside, Dave was fuming. "We have two other ships. On my mark, we blow down the door and we get them out of there."

The guards began to run to the bottom of the ship, taking up tactical positions to breach the door.

"Set charges on my mark, five, four, three..."

Abigail looked at Julius and mouthed three simple words: "I got this." She took a deep breath before she ripped off her helmet and cast it aside. She put the strange Martian device over her head. It molded itself around her and began to hum and blink. As Julius watched her, he wanted to scream for her to stop, but she had a look of complete determination in her eyes.

As soon as she put the Martian helmet on, Abigail thought of two things with all her might. She wanted the air changed to the consistency of Earth and the ship to activate. Out of nowhere, Julius heard a loud crack, like thunder, followed by a loud metallic hum, like an AM Drive engine, but deeper and way louder.

Outside, Dave's countdown was interrupted by a loud thunderclap. The men under the ship were knocked to the ground by the shock wave from the ship's start-up.

"Get that fucking door open now!" Dave bellowed as the whole ship began to vibrate from the pulsating engines. Some guards began to run to the hatch, where their comrades were knocked down.

Abigail channeled all her thoughts into the image of the ship taking off. Julius tried to steady himself. As the ship began to move, he failed in his attempt and was knocked off his feet. A metal buckle came out of the wall and secured Abigail to the room she was in.

Outside, the ship began to lift off the ground, its landing stilts retracted. The folded-up wings slightly extended outward, making four wings that were shaped a hawk descending to strike. The wings connected at the aft and front of the ship. *Activate weapons. Make a way out*, Abigail thought as she felt her lungs burning. They were begging for her to take a breath.

Two small cylinders popped out of the port and starboard side of the craft by the cockpit.

"Run for cover!" a guard yelled before the tubes discharged lime-green circle-shaped plasma blasts at the metal frame of the bunker. The guards and Dave ran to seek shelter from the falling debris as the ship punched a hole in the roof large enough to fly out. A hovercopter fell into the hole and crashed to the ground.

Fly to Earth, Abigail thought as the rear engines charged.

"Stay down!" Dave yelled as he threw a tracker that stuck to the bottom of the ship. Just then, the ship blasted out of the bunker, kicking dust and debris everywhere.

The ship flew away from the red planet at a speed no human had ever experienced. Julius was pushed to the back of the ship as it accelerated. As the ship spun around the planet to safely gain speed, Julius began crawling toward Abigail to check on her. He glanced out the window briefly and saw the ship was now out in space. He saw the orbital space station getting closer and closer.

Julius kept crawling until he was perpendicular to Abigail's chamber. She was passed out, still being held up by the metal brace.

Julius forced himself to stand before he moved to her. He began to look for anything he could use to get her some air. He was opening cabinets with his knife like a can opener when he heard her start to cough and vomit behind him. Julius ran back up to her, surprised to see her alive. He looked at her shocked as the ship left the Martian atmosphere and blasted past the orbital station, rocking it.

"How are you alive right now?"

"The ship works through concentrated brain signals. I guess the Martians have similar brains to humans, just more advanced. I ordered the ship to make oxygen, and it seemed to listen." Abigail was struggling to speak. The metal brace released her, and Julius caught her, hugging her tightly.

"Don't think I would leave you so easily, Julius. I'm not quitting this early in the game. So what's your plan?"

"Here's my theory. We fly to Roswell and try to find some allies to help us. Then we break into the research facility."

"Okay, so I have a few reservations with this plan. First, why are we going back to Roswell? Second, who would help two fugitives on the run?"

"We need to go to Roswell to save the Martians Camilla is experimenting on." Abigail let those words sink in. She felt bad for them, but risking her life for them didn't seem logical. "Do you not want to help them Abigail?"

"It's not that I don't wanna help them. Julius, think logically. That place is a fortress. There's no way we will be able to penetrate it."

"Look, we will figure this out. Someone will help us. You have to trust me."

"So, say I suspend my disbelief of us making it to Roswell, who is going to help us? I bet AMSPACE has already contacted the government. As I said a second ago, there's no way anyone would help two fugitives on the run."

"I'll figure this out, just land us in Roswell. They'll expect us to go home. They will never expect us to go into the lion's den." Abigail huffed and complied, or so Julius thought.

Back on Mars, Dave flew on a second hovercopter back to the main base.

"When we get back, I want everyone to fill out an incident report. And please keep them clean. Say nothing about threatening to kill the fugitives. You know the drill. We've done this before."

The interior of the hovercopter was silent. The security forces had never let someone escape. There were also lives lost during the escape. When the ship blasted off, it knocked the other two ships around, crushing two men. Another man's helmet flew off from the blowback, and he suffocated.

This made the flight back sobering for the survivors. The men and women in the hovercraft were covered in red dust and looked like they had been through hell. They arrived back on the roof of the main building and entered through an elevator on the top.

As they went down to the sixth floor, the elevator pressurized to have breathable air. Dave got off the elevator and walked to his office.

He was fuming at the situation and the coming chewing out he was going to get from Camilla. Once inside his office, Dave took off his space suit and left it in a heap on the floor. His assistant would deal with it later.

He grabbed a Cuban cigar out of the box on his desk and sat in his chair. He lit the cigar, took a puff, and reached down to his lower-left-hand desk drawer.

"What a fucking day."

He pulled a bottle of Scotch out from the drawer along with a small glass. He poured himself a splash and took a sip, mentally relaxing himself for the call he was about to make. After his taste, Dave used his computer to call Camilla.

It didn't even ring once before Camilla's voice hissed, "What is it, Dave? I'm very busy, too busy to deal with your Mierda."

"Calm yourself, Camilla. You're going to want to hear this. It's going to come back on you too." Dave took another sip of his Scotch.

"What did you do?" Camilla's voice changed from a flat voice to a deep guttural voice.

"There was a data breach. The breachers got the secret experiment files. The perpetrators were Julius Stetson and Abigail King. We pursued them, but they escaped."

"What exactly did they look at? And what did they get away with?" Camilla sounded enraged.

"They looked at the archived files of the beginning years of the Martian project. They also took the archived pictures of the camps. Finally, they viewed and copied the videos of your experiment in British Columbia. It's also possible they looked at Test Subject 191. Their means of escape was one of the Martian spacecrafts we discovered yesterday."

"What?" Camilla roared. "If any of those files get in the hands of the government, our company will go under. That means I won't become chairwoman. The chairman is going to fire both of us or worse." Camilla sounded more worried than angry.

"He won't fire us. We're too valuable."

"You want to bet? Look what happened to that guy, Targen. He was head of asteroid mining operations until the collapse of Alpha-Bravo-Twenty-Three. No one has seen him since. You keep this under control on Mars. We do not need any more of those worker drones finding out what is really going on there. If you see this on the news, you should just end it because the chairman will come for you first."

"End it? Like off myself? Camilla, he's firing me, not trying to kill me. You need to relax."

"Get off your soapbox and trust me. The man is not who we think he is. There's something off about the chairman." Camilla cut off the transmission. Camilla's words hung in Dave's mind.

"This fucking sucks." He took another puff of his cigar.

Dave stood up and left his office, still smoking. He was going to lock down the data room and increase security measures.

"That idiot Morris is going to get his ass transferred for not building a more secure system." Dave got in the elevator and took it down to the third floor. Dave went to the data center, where two armed guards stood watch.

Dave walked in and spoke to the head of security, a black man with a Haitian accent. "Samuel, I want you to secure this building. All nonessential personal are not permitted past the second floor."

"Yes, Mr. Hughes."

"Thank you. And keep this whole thing under wraps. We can't have it getting out." Dave left the man and went to his quarters.

In New Mexico, Camilla was fuming. "Tests are over for now!" The man assisting her was shaken by her outburst. He was testing to check the stability of her molecular structure.

He quickly backed away as she used her skin to pop every probe out of her body. They flew across the room as people dove for cover. She stood up and walked out of the white lab room and went to a small room attached to the main lab.

As she prepared, she looked around the room. There were a few vending machines along the wall and a table in the center of the room. She walked over to the table and sat down, then took out a tablet and called the chairman.

Within seconds, he appeared on Camilla's tablet screen behind a desk. Things were different, though. He wasn't behind the same desk from his office in Chicago. This made Camilla nervous because she could have interrupted him.

"Miss González, to what do I owe this unpleasant interruption?" His voice was flat.

"Hello, sir. We have a problem."

"What's the problem?"

"It seems that two employees on Mars, Julius Stetson and Abigail King, hacked the data archives and escaped with damning evidence of the company's actions there."

"What are you going to do to correct the problem?"

"I plan to inform the American Union government of two rogue employees who stole an experimental AMSPACE ship. They will apprehend the suspects and return our data. We then will pay for their bail. Miss King will return to Mars so she can show our scientists how she made the Martian ship fly. I say Miss King because I don't think Mr. Stetson is smart enough to make a Martian craft fly. I will make Mr. Stetson disappear."

"For your sake, Miss González, I hope you fix this situation, or you and Dave Hughes will find yourselves out of a job, permanently."

Camilla nervously swallowed before replying, "I'll fix it, sir. We won't let this get out."

"I'm coming to New Mexico in a few days to see the progress you've made on your experiment. This problem better be resolved by then. You know what will happen if it's not."

The man turned off his screen, leaving Camilla in silence.

Camilla slammed her hands down on the metal table and screamed loudly. The metal table dented under the force of her fists. She stood up and walked out of the breakroom.

"Someone get me in front of a camera. I have to inform the public we have some fugitives on their way to Earth." She looked across the lab, past all the medical equipment at a glass wall that contained a handful of frozen Martians.

"You all will remain here with me until we finish the experiments. I want to see what I can do to make your genetic code a product. I could make superhumans with body composition like me. Then, once I get my promotion, I won't need you anymore!"

Camilla turned away from them and ascended some stairs to the second floor, where there was a catwalk that surrounded the outer edge of the square laboratory.

As she walked to the center of the catwalk and stood in front of an elevator, a woman dressed like a secretary ran over to her. The elevator doors dinged and opened. The women stepped into the elevator as Camilla looked back at the Martians and smiled.

There's no way I can lose now. I'm a superhuman. I'm going to succeed where others like me have failed, all thanks to these Martians, she thought as pressed the up button. The woman looked at Camilla and smiled.

"Helen, we have to warn the country about these fugitives. I need you to get me on the air with all the major news outlets. Even the ABCF Streaming Service." Camilla wanted to make sure Julius and Abigail did not get their story out.

TWENTY-TWO

Fugitives on the Run

Julius and Abigail's ship broke through the upper atmosphere of Earth after doing multiple revolutions to slow down. The course was set for Roswell, New Mexico.

Land near Assaria, Kansas, USA, AU, Abigail thought as the ship changed course.

"Why's the ship turning?" Julius asked as the ship drastically changed direction.

"I'm landing the ship in Kansas. Then I'll order it to self-destruct."

"I don't know what geography class you took in your master's degree, but Kansas is really far from New Mexico, Abigail."

"I know. Trust me, if we land in Kansas, they won't realize we're going to New Mexico. My aunt has a farm in Assaria. She'll loan us money to take the train to Santa Fe. From there, we can get to Roswell via a regional rail, bus, or something like that. We'll figure it out when we get there."

"Okay, but this isn't very smart. We're running a huge risk. The government could know we're coming."

"We have to run that risk." The ship began to slow down and touched down in the middle of a cornfield full of dead brown cornstalks that seemed to stretch for miles.

Julius slid down the hatch and into the high noon sunlight. Abigail came out right after him. "This is exactly how I imagined Kansas would look like," Julius said.

"Yeah? Well, if you like this, I should take you to see Nebraska. We better go. The ship's going to explode in about three minutes."

Abigail pushed past Julius and rushed into the corn. Julius ran after her, trying to put some distance between himself and the ticking time bomb. They were deep into the dead cornfield when there was a massive explosion behind them as the Martian spacecraft disintegrated into millions of pieces. Julius and Abigail were thrown to the ground as the shock wave rolled over them and went on to shatter windows ten miles away.

"Where'd it go?" United Forces Colonel Mixon watched a blip disappear from the radar on a Vulture-class hovercopter.

"Colonel, we believe the fugitive's ship has exploded," the pilot said, relaying a message from central command at McConnell Air Force Base in Wichita.

"Then they have to be dead," the colonel said as the ship approached the rising smoke in the distance. The colonel's hovercopter was in a V formation with two other hovercopters. On the ground were a few armored personnel carriers with extra troops meant to apprehend the fugitives.

"When we get to the site, I want you all to secure the scene and search for the fugitives." The colonel spoke into the radio that transmitted to the other hovercopters and the ground vehicles.

Julius was the first to stir and stand. His ears rang from the deafening explosion. He reached down and pulled Abigail to her feet and yelled, "We need to get to your aunt's!" Her ears were also ringing she could barely heard Julius.

She pointed her finger in the direction she believed her aunt's house to be, and Julius assisted her in walking toward that direction. The two exited the corn stocks and realized they were on a dirt road.

"Go that way," Abigail said weakly as she pointed down the road. Julius moved with Abigail as the sound of the flying fire drones descended on the site of the explosion. It had become a small brush fire that spread rapidly through the dried-out corn.

A few minutes after the fire drones arrived, the United Forces landed and took over the scene. Soldiers exited their hovercopters and began to secure the area. "Find the bodies," Colonel Mixon barked.

Above them, the drones fanned out to fight the brush flames as fire engines began to arrive. The soldiers kept the firefighters back as they searched the wreckage and surrounding area for the fugitives. The colonel remained in the hovercopter, which took off and flew circles around the wreckage.

After a few orbits around the area, Mixon asked the troops on the ground for a report.

"Sir, we haven't found any human remains. Either the ship was unmanned, they burned up in the explosion, or they made it out," a female soldier said.

"Understood. Send out the mini drones to scan five klicks around the crash site. Get the forensics team out here I want to know if they really died in the crash. And, Major, don't let those AMSPACE fuckers near the ship. It's United Forces property."

After a few miles of ducking in and out of the corn to avoid the United Forces mini drones, Julius and Abigail saw a farmhouse in the distance.

"That's it," Abigail said, now able to walk on her own. She and Julius picked up their pace until they were running to the house. It was a dust-covered off-white two-story farmhouse with a wrap-around front porch. The paint was peeling, and the exposed wood seemed to be suffering from dry rot.

They knocked frantically on the door before a short, plump woman answered. "Abigail? What are you doing here? You look terrible." The woman stood behind a screen door. Abigail's face was covered in dirt and dried blood from the explosion.

"Auntie, can we please come in?"

"Oh, of course, dear, come in and bring your friend." She pushed the screen door open. They sat down in the living room. Julius looked around briefly and saw the walls were covered with computerized wallpaper that was set to a flowery print. Every few seconds, it pixelated, showing the wallpaper's age. In a corner was an old vacuum tube television tuned to a live AUN broadcast.

"Want to explain to me how you got here from Mars?"

"We escaped Mars, Aunt Amy.

"Don't tell me you two are the fugitives."

"We aren't fugitives," Julius blurted out.

Abigail glared at him briefly. "What Julius is trying to say is that we have a good reason for why we did what we did. AMSPACE is doing terrible things up there. We discovered their cover-up, and they decided we knew too much. They were going were going to kill us! So we ran."

"That's terrible. So much for whistleblower protections. We need to get you two to safety. They'll figure out why you landed in Kansas soon."

Julius tuned out what the two women were saying as he looked at the TV. He read the headline on the bottom of the screen: "Rogue AMSPACE Employees in Kansas."

"What they're saying is crap. They don't even want to hear our side of the story. The mega media has already taken the AMSPACE's side!" Julius yelled at the TV.

"Calm down, Julius, we'll get our story out. We need to stay levelheaded." Abigail turned back to her aunt. "Aunt Amy, can we get cleaned up before we get on a bus?"

"You can get cleaned up, but there's no way I'm letting you get on a bus or train. They'll be looking at each one as it leaves the station in town. There's a fully charged General Ford F150 in the back. Go upstairs and take some of Mckenzie's clothes. Julius, take some of my husband's clothes."

Where's Uncle Rich?" Abigail asked.

"He at a farming conference in Omaha. Your cousin Mckenzie is at school in Wichita."

"Thank you, Aunt Amy." Abigail kissed her aunt on the cheek. She ran upstairs to her cousin's room, washed off the dirt and blood, and changed into a clean outfit.

Julius went with Amy. "You take care of my niece; she's a good girl and doesn't need trouble. I'm pretty sure she did all this for you because it's out of her character to stick her neck out."

"I won't let anything happen to her." Julius felt intimidated by Amy and a little guilty for putting Abigail in this situation. Amy handed him a pair of sun-bleached overalls, a red-and-blue flannel, and a pair of beat-up work boots with holey socks.

"I can tell by the way she looks at you that she likes you, so don't hurt her heart either."

"Yes, ma'am."

Amy left, Julius cleaned himself up and changed into the clothes before he returned to the living room.

Abigail was hugging her aunt. "Thank you again, Aunt Amy."

"You're welcome. Now go!" She waved the two out the door. Julius and Abigail ran across the yard to the pickup, and Abigail got in the driver's seat.

"We need to get moving before we get cut off by the police." Abigail put the truck in drive. The truck's tires threw up grass and dirt as they tore out of her aunt's farm.

Julius was having trouble containing his nerves. They had come all the way from Mars and still could be easily apprehended. He took some deep breaths to keep calm. Abigail remained focused as she drove on the side roads to get to the Skyway. She entered the lower level of the Skyway heading south toward Roswell. Once they had settled into their lane, Abigail engaged the auto driver.

"I need a nap." She relaxed herself and fell asleep. After thirteen hours and a few pit stops, Julius and Abigail drove into the city limits of Roswell, New Mexico. Abigail turned off the auto driver and resumed driving.

Abigail drove through downtown Roswell heading south. "I felt more cheerful last time I was here," Julius said, looking around at the dimly lit city.

"Yeah? Well, we felt better about the future last time we were here."

"Abigail, why are we leaving the city?"

"Because it seems safer, we're going to Carlsbad. It keeps us out of town and away from any patrols."

Eventually, Abigail pulled the truck into a run-down Holiday Inn right off the highway.

"Check the glove compartment. My aunt keeps a credit chip or two in there along with cash." After opening the glove compartment, Julius found a Visa, a MasterChip, and a pile of cash.

"We'll use the cash, but bring the credit chips too. You never know when you need crypto."

They exited the truck, walked up to the main doors, and entered the building. Julius looked around the lobby. He saw the wallpaper was peeling off the walls, and he could smell a faint musty smell. Abigail had a look of disgust on her face, but they had few other options.

Behind the desk was a pimple-faced teen with greasy brown hair. He gave them a crooked toothed smile.

"We need one room, please." Abigail put on her prettiest smile for the desk attendant.

"Sure thing." The teen sniffled as he typed on the computer. "I need a credit chip or cash. How long will you be staying?"

Abigail pulled out two hundred dollars in fifties. "Will this cover two days?"

"Yes, miss, that will actually cover three, is that okay?"

"Yes, that's perfect."

"Okay, let me get your keys." The attendant began to search for some room keys. Julius watched him as he pulled out the old-fashioned plastic keycards. He scanned them before handing two faded keys to Abigail.

"Please enjoy your stay. My name is Thomas if you need any assistance."

"Thank you, Thomas."

Abigail turned around and walked toward their first-floor room, which was down a hallway, behind the lobby. Julius following her as they made their way through the rundown hotel.

"Abigail, you're okay with this hotel?"

"Uh, yeah? We aren't exactly going to go to the Hilton." They made it to the room and opened the door.

Julius was expecting the worst but was pleasantly surprised to see the rooms were updated.

Julius looked into the bathroom and saw it had a small single vanity, toilet, and a shower tub. Abigail went into the main part of the hotel room. Julius entered a few seconds after to see her already lying on the single king-size bed.

"Guess he assumed we're together."

"Well, technically we are together, Julius."

"I guess so. But do you want me to—"

"Julius, I'm tired. You're tired, get in the bed, and stop over-thinking it!"

"Okay, make some room." Abigail moved to one side of the bed, and Julius lay down. "Turn on the TV to American Union News," Julius said to the hotel's virtual assistant.

"Why do you want to watch the news? Just take a nap." Abigail groaned from her side of the bed.

"I want to know what they know." The TV turned on and tuned into the AUN broadcast. They were still reporting about them.

"The fugitives, whose identities have not been revealed, allegedly stole an experimental AMSPACE spacecraft. They flew it to Earth and crashed in a rural Kansas cornfield. A brush fire that resulted from the crash has been contained. The United Forces have neither confirmed nor denied if the fugitives perished in the explosion. Camilla González, head of AMSPACE Mars Division, had this to say."

The TV cut to a clip that showed Camilla standing outside the New Mexico Research Facility. "We at AMSPACE are cooperating with American Union investigators looking into this incident. We believe the two fugitives, whose names I will not reveal, are armed and dangerous. They murdered three members of the Martian Base's security team during their escape. I hope we can bring this incident to a peaceful conclusion."

Julius was red with rage as the female news anchor came back on to continue to speculate about what happened.

Julius turned off the TV. "That's total bull. What will my parents think if they end up releasing our names?"

"Relax, Julius, only the cops have our names, no one else knows. They won't know about it until we reveal what's behind the veil.

We'll get this to the media, then everyone will think hail as heroes, not criminals." Abigail scooted over on the bed and snuggled up to him.

"Please nap, we need our strength." Abigail yawned.

"You know no one will believe us until we get hard evidence. We need a Martian for an interview. People will just say our side of the story is fake news."

"I know, but it's okay. We'll get into the facility and save the Martians Camilla has in captivity. That's enough proof. Now relax."

"How?" Julius had no clue what their plan was. His mind wandered to the facility's security. If the wall and robots were not enough to stop them, there was the saber wall. "Abigail, we need to talk about this more."

"Julius, it's like four in the morning, and we've been up most of the night. How about we sleep? When we get up, we can determine what we will do." She turned away from him.

"Fine." Julius lay next to her on the inside of the bed near the phone. He pulled her closer, and they drifted off to sleep together.

A few hours passed as they slept. Julius had no dreams that mattered, mostly a dark void. He was suddenly jolted awake by the sound of electronic ringing. His heart was racing as he realized the ringing was coming from the hotel phone. His throat went dry as he picked up the receiver and put it to his ear.

"H-hello?" His voice shook as he spoke.

"Kid, did I scare you?" Martin's voice came over the phone. Julius said nothing to his trainer. He didn't know if he should be relieved or frightened.

Julius looked over at Abigail, who was still asleep. He didn't want any harm to come to her. If Martin had found them, he had to protect her.

"Martin, it was all me. Please don't hurt Abigail. I'll surrender. Please spare her."

"Stetson, I'm on your side. I know the truth, but we can't talk on the phone. Camilla and the chairman could be listening. Meet me at the International UFO Museum and Research Center in downtown

Roswell at 1300. I'll be near the Incident Exhibit." Martin didn't even wait for Julius to respond before he hung up.

"Who was that?" Julius looked over at Abigail, who was groggily putting on her glasses. He didn't reply to her because he was trying to comprehend what Martin said.

"Julius! Who was on the phone?" Abigail sounded a little scared.

"It was Martin. He told me to meet him at some UFO Museum at one o'clock. He claims to be on our side and that he knows the truth." Julius paused briefly before speaking again, "I don't feel comfortable with this. It could be a trap. I mean, how did he know where we were?"

"I don't how he knows we're here. Maybe he knows people? This could easily be a trap, but it's in a public place, meaning he can't hurt us."

"Should we do this? If we do, we need a plan."

"I agree we can't go into this blind." They both began to think about what to do.

After a few minutes, Julius's face lit up. "I have something!"

"Okay, hit me because I've got nothing."

"I'll go to this meeting with Martin and you'll hide in plain sight nearby. You'll use your glasses to upload the files to the internet if things go south.

"Hold on. You think I'll just sit on the sidelines?"

"That's not it at all. I want you to be safe because I care about you."

"That's so cheesy and sweet." Abigail kissed him on the cheek.

"Plus, we need to get the word out, and you know what to do. If things go well, we can adlib the rest of the plan."

"Well, minus the fact that I want to help you, I think it's a good plan. Just give me the files so I can wirelessly upload them to my glasses." Abigail held out her hand to receive the memory stick.

He handed her the memory stick and looked at the clock. "It's noon. Do we want to get going?"

"Yeah, let's take the truck. Plus, we need to scout a good place for me to hide. I also need a view of the museum."

"Okay then, let's get going." Julius grabbed a room key and headed to the door. "Two seconds." Abigail grabbed a hair tie.

"What are you doing?"

"I am putting my hair up. It's greasy, and I can get away with a ponytail. Plus I don't want it in my face if we are running for our lives."

Julius waited at the door as she put her hair up. "Okay, I'm ready." She walked past him.

They drove north into Roswell down Main Street toward downtown. The road into town was not very crowded, which made Julius a little worried.

"It seems odd, there aren't a lot of people out."

As they got closer to town, more cars and people appeared. "No need to worry." They drove to the Second Street light; the International UFO Museum and Research Center was in front of them and to their right.

Abigail made a right turn to drive up Second Street. On the corner across from the International UFO Museum and Research Center was a sub sandwich restaurant called SUBspace Sandwich Shop.

"That's the perfect place for me to camp out." Abigail pulled the truck into the parking lot.

"This is where you want to hide out?" Julius was concerned it was too close.

"Yes! You got a problem with that?" She parked the truck.

"Uh, no, looks like a great spot."

"That's what I thought, glad you agree with me. Why don't you go in the museum? Better to be early than late." Abigail exited the truck and went into the sandwich shop. Julius got out of the truck as well and started walking to the museum. He looked back at her as she ordered a sandwich at the counter.

He was worried this could be the last time he saw her. She looked back out the window and saw him looking at her. She quickly blew him a kiss and signaled for him to hurry along. That made him feel better as he walked across Second Street.

As he walked, Julius decided that if Martin didn't shoot him on sight, then he would tell Abigail his true feelings and ask her to be exclusive. He walked up to and entered the museum, paying admission as he walked in.

The digital clock in the museum read "12:45." Julius had some time to look around before he had to meet Martin. It was the typical museum for alien enthusiasts, full of conspiracy theory exhibits. Julius chuckled, looking at the statues of little green men.

"That's not what they look like at all." It was nice to get a laugh, but Julius's body was shaking; he was afraid of what was about to happen.

"Hey, kid," a familiar voice said, which caused him to spin around. It was Martin; Becka was standing next to him.

Julius looked at him, unsure what to say.

"Since I asked you to meet me, it seems only fair that I explain myself."

Julius did not let Martin get another word out. His nervous energy made him launch into a slew of questions and accusations. "Why did you want to meet? You two work for Camilla, and it's pretty obvious she and the rest of AMSPACE want Abigail and I dead."

"As I said before, Julius, we're on your side."

"Doesn't feel like you are. You probably just want the files we stole so you can be promoted or some shit."

"I don't want to take the files back. Check this out. It might help you believe my side, if I could get it out." Martin flipped a coin double the size of a quarter to Julius who caught it.

"What's this?"

"Just look at it."

Julius brought the gold coin to his eyes so he could closely inspect it. The coin had a NASA symbol on one side, and on the other side were letters rounding the coin that said Mars Mission Control. The center was an image of an SLS Orion rocket on a launchpad.

"Where did you get this?"

"It was my grandfather's. He was a member of Mission Control during NASA's mission to Mars. He was the first man to receive word about the existence of intelligent life on Mars from Ben Lewis. NASA swore him to secrecy. The United States government was never informed to avoid any chance of a public meltdown. My grandfather then started a group called the Protectors of Mars. They work to protect the Martian secret."

"Well, your little group seems to have been doing a bang-up job."

"Look, kid, it's been difficult since AMSPACE keeps their files and information on the Martians a secret. Only a select few people have seen the full reports. The only reason I know they exist is because my grandfather told me. We didn't even know AMSPACE had discovered them. I had a feeling you and Abigail stumbled on something when you cut out my trackers." Martin took the coin back.

"Your trackers? I thought they were Camilla's. Why did you track us?"

"It was nothing personal. AMSPACE knew nothing about the trackers till you sent that email to your friend John. Don't worry, he's safe. We collected him and his wife before AMSPACE detained them. After you sent that email, Camilla blew a gasket, and I had to cover my ass. Our group purchased the trackers and have been implanting them into each person we train."

"AMSPACE tried to capture my friends? Why? Implanting trackers seems really unethical."

"And genocide isn't?" Martin asked.

"What happened to your friends isn't important right now, Julius. What is important is that we move forward," Becka interjected.

"Genocide doesn't give you an excuse to stoop to Camilla's level Martin," Julius said in an aggressive tone.

"Desperate times call for desperate measures, Julius."

Julius paused. "So how do the trackers work?"

"The trackers listen to vibrations from the skin that are translated into words. This way, our group can keep track of the entire Martian base. We finally turned on the system when you two launched. We found out they knew about the Martians instantly because a security officer we trained here is on Dave's staff.

We knew about you and Abigail because one of the guards you killed on Mars was bugged. We knew everything because we listened the whole time. Once we heard Dave planned to kill you, we knew we had to find you. It was quite easy to track you down I had a feeling you were going to come back here searching for answers. All I had to do was ask hotels around Roswell if you two showed up."

"I figured we were being sneakier than that." Julius had calmed down.

"Okay, Martin, what's your plan?" Julius felt some relief. He and Abigail might make it out of this alive.

"We plan to expose the whole house of cards AMSPACE has built over the last eleven years," Becka said.

"Yes, we plan on using the information you stole to get the word out to the world about the atrocities AMSPACE is committing," Martin said.

"Look, this is all great and everything, but you both still work for Camilla, who is running this whole show. Not to mention she's insane. You would agree with me if you saw the shit she has done. How do I know you won't stab me in the back to save your own skin?"

"We've laid our hands down. It's up to you if you trust us or not."

"Let me speak to Abigail, and we'll decide what we want to do."

"Let's sweeten the pot. Becka and I will get you into the facility. We know there is a secret lab there. The only hang-up is you'll have to find where the lab is. In addition, you'll need to steal Camilla's badge. Her badge has unlimited access to all the doors in the facility." Julius's eyes lit up as he realized he would have the chance to save the Martians.

"You'll help us find the lab?"

"No, we can't blow our cover. We have to maintain our positions, or we become targets ourselves."

"I understand, Abigail and I appreciate the help." Julius was disappointed but still happy he might get a chance to rescue the Martians.

"You have an hour to decide and meet us back here. At that time, Becka and I will return to the research facility. If you choose to join us, we'll smuggle you and Abigail in. If you choose to continue on your own, we wish you the best of luck. You also might need this." Martin handed Julius a couple thousand dollars in cash.

"What's this for?"

"Just in case you choose to cut your losses and travel to the EU. I don't want to leave you high and dry." Martin nodded before he and Becka walked away.

Julius slowly made his way out of the museum. He was constantly looking over his shoulder to make sure he was not being followed. He exited the building into the cool midfall air; the sun warmed him a little as he walked back down the street to SUBspace.

He entered through the front door. There was a sandwich counter in the back like an old Subway. Booths and tables had been placed in the fore space of the store. He searched for Abigail and found her sitting in a small booth browsing the internet on her glasses.

He walked over, relieved to see her. He thought about what he promised himself while he was walking to the museum, *I'll ask her later, now isn't a good time*, he thought to himself. When she saw him, Abigail smiled.

"You're alive. Guess they're on our side."

"Very funny. Can I get you something to eat? It's on Martin." He joined her in the booth and pulled out some cash.

"I already ate, but you're more than welcome to eat. Why would Martin give you that money?"

"He said it's money if we want to run instead of helping them."

"Help them? They actually care about the Martians?"

"Yeah! Let me explain quickly. Martin and Becka are members of a secret society tasked with protecting the inhabitants of Mars."

"Well, they've done a banner job."

"That's what I said, but the point is that they are willing to help us expose AMSPACE and Camilla. To do that, they want to help us get into the facility. Once inside, they told me there's a secret lab where the Martians are being held. The only issue is that they don't know where it is."

"How will that help us? We need to know where to go if we are going to free the Martians."

"Correct, but I think I have a hunch on where it could be. Remember that desk in Camilla's office. She got really protective when I stared at the panels too long."

"You're overthinking things. You weren't listening to her. That doesn't mean she thought you were going to find her secret lab."

"Maybe, but come on, we have to save the Martians, and her office is the best bet we have. Martin and Becka said they would wait until 1415 for us."

"I'll admit, I'm concerned about how they plan to get us into the facility. That being said, your instincts have been spot on, so I'll trust you."

"Great, thank you. I don't think I could do this without you."

"Of course you couldn't." She winked at him as she stood up.

"Where're you going?"

"We're getting you a sandwich. After that, I need a backup pair of glasses. I want more memory, so I can record our heist."

"That's supersmart. Then people can't dispute it." Julius stood up and followed Abigail to the counter, making sure to hide the cash in his pocket along with the memory stick. He bought a turkey club sandwich and walked out of the store, munching on it.

He and Abigail walked down Main Street away from SUBspace and the museum. Julius looked around the small town as they walked down the street. It was a quaint little town with lots of simple store fronts. He felt a pair of eyes on him, causing him to glance toward Abigail, where their eyes met.

"What?" His mouth was full of sandwich.

"Just enjoying the view of this kid in front of me." Abigail blushed a little as her cheeks turned a rosy red. Julius felt light on his feet.

"You're only eight years older than me."

"Yeah, that's eight more years of experience, kid." She winked at him again.

They kept their eyes fixed on each other and walked in relative silence until Abigail broke her gaze.

She crossed in front of him and went into a store. The store she entered was a small rundown storefront. An old RadioShack sticker was in the window. It was peeling and sun-bleached to the point it was almost unrecognizable.

Julius saw Abigail had noticed a pair of glasses behind the display window. He threw the rest of his sandwich away before he approached the door. He saw Abigail was already paying for the pair with her aunt's credit chip.

Julius quickly approached her, not wanting to alarm anyone. He whispered in her ear, "We have the cash for a reason. What if the United Forces have a trace on that credit chip?"

"That only happens in the movies." Abigail signed the printed receipt. They both thanked the cashier behind the counter and left the store. As they walked back up the street, Abigail removed her old pair of glasses and deposited them into her pocket. She then unboxed the new pair and placed them on the bridge of her nose.

"How do I look?"

"You look just like Athena."

"Knowledgeable and cute." She set up the glasses to record but did not start recording. She would use these glasses to record their actions in the research facility. When the time was right, the glasses would be used to upload the recording to the internet. They walked back down the street toward the museum where they were to meet Martin and Becka.

TWENTY-THREE

The Experimentation Lab

One hundred and sixty-nine miles from Roswell, in Albuquerque, New Mexico, a phone rang in the office of the New Mexico Air National Guard. A young woman in a desert camo uniform answered the phone.

"New Mexico Air National Guard, 150th Special Operations Wing, Corporal Hernandez speaking."

"This is Commander Baker of the United Forces. I need to speak to Major General Horton right away," a gruff, youthful male's voice said on the other end of the line.

"Yes, sir, right away," the woman replied as she transferred him to the Major General's extension.

The phone rang in the room left of Corporal Hernandez's office. Behind a metal desk sat Major General Horton. The man groaned as the electronic ringing of his phone chimed. He was in the middle of eating his lunch. He picked up the phone after a few rings.

"This is Major General Horton."

"This is Commander Baker of the United Forces."

"Yes, Commander, what can the New Mexico Air National Guard do for you?"

"United Forces Intelligence has received a hit from a credit chip owned by the aunt of one of the Martian escapees."

"Okay, what do two idiots who crashed a ship into the ground in Kansas have to do with me?"

"The hit came from Roswell. The New Mexico Air National Guard is the closest asset. We need to dispatch a response team immediately to Main Street in Roswell. The credit chip was last used in an electronics store there."

"I'm getting a response team in the air now. I'll contact the local PD to set up roadblocks to prevent their escape." Major General Horton hung up.

"Hernandez, get me Major Ferguson!" Horton bellowed from his closed office.

"Yes, sir," Corporal Hernandez replied as she connected Major General Horton's digital phone out to the hangar.

A woman with messy blond hair in a mechanic jumpsuit picked up the phone in the hangar. "Hovercopter hangar, this is Private Nelson."

"Private, this is Major General Horton. I need to speak to Major Ferguson immediately."

"Right away, sir."

The line was silent for a few minutes before a younger man picked up the phone. "Major Ferguson."

"Mac, I need you to take a strike team and two Vultures to Roswell. The United Forces has tracked down those two fugitives and need a rapid response team."

"Right away, sir, I'll see to it personally. We'll turn and burn. Should be there in forty minutes."

He hung up the phone. Within ten minutes, two Vulture-class hovercopters were on the tarmac with forty-four souls onboard. The crafts lifted off and turned southeast.

Back in Roswell, the police had received a call from Major General Horton to spread out and create roadblocks. The police cruisers deployed along the major roads, leading out of the city. Major General Horton had ordered the officers to wait for the arrival of the Air National Guard strike team. Once the hovercopters had shown up, the police were to reduce the number of roadblocks and crash down on the city. They would form a net around the far side of town, near the electronics shop and city hall, and assist in a grid-by-grid search.

Julius and Abigail walked back across town to a parking lot next to the International UFO Museum and Research Center. In the middle of the parking lot, Martin and Becka stood next to a vehicle. It was a gold 2003 Suburban, with a lift hatch in the rear.

Julius stared at the old Chevrolet gas guzzler. It was one of the nicest trucks he had ever seen. It was in very good condition, considering it was almost a century old. As Julius and Abigail approached Martin, they began to hear the sound of approaching aircraft.

"Coming up on Roswell, sir," the pilot of the lead Vulture said to Major Ferguson. Major Ferguson turned first to look at the jump indicator, which had turned red. Then he faced the troops in cabin. "Get ready!"

The seats were against the wall, facing each other. There was a rail with reels for repelling in front of their seats. The ground was a giant hatch. All the men and women in the cabin turned to face him. Once he had the attention of all the people in the cabin, he spoke again.

"Stand up, hook up, and check equipment!"

Everyone in the cabin stood up almost simultaneously and hooked their harnesses up to their respective reel. They then checked themselves to make sure they had all their tactical gear in place. Major Ferguson did the same.

Julius looked to where he heard the rocket engines and saw two fast approaching Vultures. They blasted over his head, causing papers to fly around them and kick up dust.

"Kid, we've got to go!" Martin and Becka waved desperately for Julius and Abigail to hurry up. Julius ran toward the Suburban while looking at the Vultures, captivated by how gracefully they flew down Main Street. The Vultures stopped and hovered sixty feet above the store where he and Abigail had purchased the glasses.

Inside the Vulture, the drop indicator light turned green and the floor dropped out beneath the airmen. They gracefully descended to the ground and began to spread out to search for the two fugitives.

Julius and Abigail reached the Suburban and ran to the back. Martin had opened the trunk to reveal a large black box bolted inside. It was recessed into the bottom of the trunk. It did not look comfortable. Abigail scrunched her nose.

"No way I'm riding in that."

"If you want to talk to those soldiers, you're more than welcome to." Becka gestured to the commotion down the street.

Abigail looked down the street and saw the troops descending from the hovercopters. "Point made." Abigail quickly climbed into the box.

"How will this protect us?" Julius asked.

"The box blocks all of the scanners and tricks them to thinking the back is empty. It also hides your heat signatures so the guard bots won't detect you. Now get in." Martin shoved Julius in.

The box was very sophisticated, with its own air tank and lights. It was tall enough for Julius and Abigail to sit crisscrossed somewhat comfortably. Julius wondered how many people Martin had previously smuggled into the facility using this method.

"Let's hope we can slip past the United Forces. It's going to be a short trip if not." Martin closed the trunk sealing the box. A single light allowed Julius to see Abigail's silhouette.

"That didn't make me feel better."

"I'm sure we'll make it. We have to," Julius said.

They heard the doors close right before the old internal combustion engine turned over. That was the first time Julius had heard a gas-powered engine in a car. Even though it gave him chills, he was not really able to enjoy the moment. Then the vehicle began to move toward the parking lot exit.

As the vehicle pulled out of the parking lot, the commotion down the street expanded. The Air National Guard strike team had found nothing in their initial sweep of the area and was now spreading out.

Martin maneuvered the vehicle around the cars parked in the middle of Main Street. Their passengers were watching the spectacle in the center of town. Martin then drove north out of the city. He gripped so tight his knuckles went white. He had smuggled people countless times, but this time was different. He had never needed to work around the United Forces.

"Martin, what if…" Becka began to ask before she was cut off.

"We can't think about that, Becka. This is going to work. It has to."

They got out on the county highway. As they drove, Martin saw red and blue flashing lights approaching heading south. He gripped the wheel and pulled to the side of the road.

Inside the box, both Julius and Abigail heard the approaching sirens. Abigail snuggled up to him, and he wrapped his arms around her. They listened closely as the sirens got louder and louder.

Martin watched as the police cruisers rushed past their stopped vehicle. They were on their way to assist the Air National Guard with the search.

Once all the cruisers had passed, Martin resumed his driving toward the AMSPACE facility. Julius and Abigail relaxed as the sirens faded away.

Just before Martin turned onto the road to go to AMSPACE's facility, they ran into a traffic jam. Martin scanned ahead to see were two New Mexico Highway Patrol cars blocking the road. Julius felt the car stop and looked down at Abigail. He was still holding her. She looked completely relaxed.

Abigail removed her new pair of glasses and put her old pair on. She began to work through something; her eyes moved rapidly.

"What are you doing?" he whispered as he felt the vehicle inch forward.

"I'm prepping the glasses to upload all of the data we took to the internet if a kill switch isn't deactivated."

"Not a bad idea." Julius closed his eyes and took a deep breath.

"Not a fan of tight spaces? Or stressful situations?"

"Not a fan of either. I think we're at a roadblock."

"Martin said this is safe. You need to relax." Abigail grabbed Julius's hand.

Julius felt his body relax, having her close.

The truck had reached the front of the line and they could hear Martin talking to someone. "Where you headin'?" a man asked.

"We're employees of AMSPACE. We wanted to get out of the facility for lunch."

"Interesting. We don't see many of you outside those walls."

"Yeah, they rarely let us out nowadays. The new contract coming up is going to kill us."

Julius and Abigail held their breath. It was silent in the box except for the vibrations of the idling engine. What they couldn't see or hear was a second officer walking around scanning the vehicle for any signs of people. After doing a lap around the vehicle, the other officer gave a thumbs up.

"You have a good day, sir," the officer said to Martian backing up.

"You too," Martin replied before driving the Suburban away from the roadblock.

Abigail let go of Julius's hand. "See? Nothing to worry about."

"You're right." Julius closed his eyes and continued to try and stay calm.

They sat in silence for a little until she turned to look at him.

"When I was waiting in SUBspace, I realized I truly cared for you. If we make it out of this, would you want to date exclusively?"

Julius opened his eyes in shock. He answered in the affirmative and leaned in to kiss her.

They were interrupted by the rough application of the vehicle's brakes. The two slid forward and hit the front of the box. All they could hear was their own breathing. They listened harder and heard distant stomping. "That's the sound of the robots. We're at the first gate," Julius said in a hushed tone.

"I know. Shut up," Abigail whispered in reply.

They could barely make out the sound of footsteps approaching the vehicle.

"Papers of the occupants," the muffled voice of the scar-faced soldier from the first gate said. Abigail and Julius held their breath. At this point, they knew the car was being scanned. They might have made it past the police, but AMSPACE had better tech. Julius was sweating and held Abigail's hand tightly.

Inside the guard shack, both the scanners on the robots and the ones in the wall were scanning the vehicle. The computer displayed the Suburban, along with its two occupants, Martin and Becka. Julius felt like the scan was taking longer than before. Abigail squeezed his hand to let him know she was still with him. After what felt like an eternity, the car began to move forward. "Where are the metal gates?" Julius whispered to Abigail, not hearing the creaking.

"Maybe we can't hear them?"

"But we could hear the robots walking."

"I don't know, but what I do know is that you need to relax. We'll get through this."

Julius held her close as the vehicle drove down the main dirt road. He did not want this moment to end. "I don't want to lose you, Abigail."

"I'm not going anywhere."

He felt the sincerity in her voice just before he felt the car slow down as it approached the second checkpoint, the Saber Wall. Once again, they went silent.

"Mr. Fisher, very unlike you to leave the facility for such a short amount of time," Megan said to Martin.

"Becka and I went out for some lunch at a diner at Fifth and Main, Megan. We got tired of the food here and wanted to get out, you know?"

"You recommend it? The new guy has a car and has offered to get us food."

"Oh yeah, good burgers."

"Sounds good, Mr. Fisher. Let me scan these quick."

Julius couldn't hear anything besides their breathing, the idling Suburban, and the electronic humming of the Saber Wall.

Julius closed his eyes and took a few deep breaths as they waited for the feeling of the car moving forward.

Outside, Megan returned to the vehicle. "Thank you, Mr. Fisher. You may pass."

The hum of the Saber Wall disappeared as the vehicle moved forward and over the speed bump. Relief washed over Julius; they had made it in.

The Suburban made a few sporadic turns before it went down a steep incline causing the two to be pushed up against one end of the box. Once it leveled out, the vehicle drove a few seconds more before stopping.

Abigail had put her old glasses into her pocket and was now wearing her new ones. Not wanting to reveal Martin's and Becka's identities, she had not set the glasses to record. The doors to the front of the truck opened then closed with an audible slam. Seconds later, the truck and box were opened. Julius and Abigail shielded their eyes as brightness flooded the box.

"See? Piece of cake," Martin chuckled to himself.

They climbed out of the box, slightly disoriented from their long stint inside. The room they found themselves in was an underground concrete parking structure. A handful of old fossil fuel vehicles were strewn randomly around the garage. An old 2015 blue Mustang caught Julius's eye, and he stared at it.

"I meant to ask about your vehicle. Where'd you get it?" Julius asked.

"My grandfather had it as his first car and eventually gave it to my father after saving it from the North American Union's conversion to electric vehicles. Eventually, my father passed it down to me. I added the smuggler's box. The engine noise is another element used to distract the scanners. They aren't calibrated for the noise of an internal combustion engine."

"Where exactly are we?" Abigail asked, looking around the garage.

"We're below the main building. This was an old parking garage made for the people to commute. Now that most of the staff live in the facility, there's no need for commuting lots, so this remains mostly abandoned," Becka responded.

"That explains the lack of people and cars," Abigail commented.

"All right, let's get down to brass tacks. From this point forward, you're on your own. We cannot interfere once we leave this garage.

But we can give you the tools to succeed in your mission," Martin said.

"How are you going to do that?" Julius asked, now worried about the possibility of the mission being a success.

"So here's the deal. You two are going to go to the same office where we met after you exited the Rendering Room. Once there, you need to find Camilla's badge. It's the only way you can access to the lab. I told you before I don't know where the lab is, so that's up to you to figure out. If you can't access the lab, you both have to get out."

"How do you know the badge will be there?" Abigail asked.

"She never carries it around with her. She needs it to use her computer, so she leaves it there."

"That's all you can give us a slim chance the badge is there?"

"Yeah, that's all I have. You and Abigail are smart enough to figure out where the lab is. So are you two in or out? Careful how you answer, both answers have different consequences."

That statement made Julius wonder if Martin would turn him in if he said no.

"We're in," Abigail said, speaking for both of them.

"Excellent. You'll be needing these." Becka handed Julius and Abigail two badges with their faces on them and fake names. Additionally, they received two fully functioning plasma pistols and a change of clothes to match the other workers.

"Holy cow," Julius said, inspecting the gun. The gun was shaped like a 1911. The plasma canister was in the stock where bullets used to be stored. As he was looking, Julius accidentally pointed it at Martin, who instinctively pushed it away from him.

"Watch it! I don't want my head blown off. No more gun for you." Martin snatched the gun out of Julius's hands. Abigail laughed as she clipped her own weapon to her waist.

"Don't worry, Martin, my dad taught me how to handle a gun."

"If all goes to plan, we should meet back in this garage. Becka and I will have a transport ready to get you and the Martians out," Martin explained, putting the gun back on his hip.

"Martin, we need to go. She's waiting in your office. You know she hates waiting." Becka looked nervous and pale.

"Right, thank you. Excuse us. We have a meeting with Camilla. Good luck, you two." Martin and Becka left the garage.

Julius and Abigail were left in the massive underground structure alone. "Let's get going. Time is of the essence. Get changed."

Abigail went to the other side of the truck and changed out of her cousin's clothes and into the uniform. Julius did the same, leaving his clothes under the Suburban.

Abigail came back around and grabbed his hand, pulling him to the door. She started the recording using her glasses. They passed through the same doors Martin and Becka used to enter the facility.

Just past the doors was a brown metal grate stairwell. Julius looked up it and saw it only went up one floor. They ascended, finding another door that Abigail slowly opened. The door was rusty from lack of use, which caused it to creak a little.

She peeked out and saw a long, empty hallway. "Okay, Julius, there's a hallway. Which way should we go? I think we should go right."

"I don't think so. Left seems more reasonable."

"You're just saying that. You have no idea."

"Fine, we'll go right."

Abigail opened the door again and nonchalantly walked into the next room, followed by Julius. This seemed to be the same central hallway where they got their crash course before they launched to Mars. There was something different about this area, though. Above them, they could hear footfalls that sounded like crowds of people were walking around.

"This looks familiar," Julius whispered to Abigail.

"Yeah. I think we're a floor below the main hallway where Camilla's office is."

They walked past a row of doors. They were a metallic blue color and had LED nameplates next to them. Julius read the nameplates as they walked by. One said Wormhole Lab. Another a few doors down said Shrink Ray Storage. That particular storage door had an additional sign that said Do Not Enter.

"Is that how—" Julius started to ask.

"Yeah, I think that's how they reduce costs to fly things to Mars," Abigail said as she led him down to a door that said "Stairs to Levels B-5." She pushed the door open and entered.

They climbed the stairs to the next floor, the first floor. They were right—there were crowds of people moving through the hallway. They slipped into the crowd hoping to blend in with them. Julius was following Abigail because he really did not remember the location of the office.

Finally, after passing many doors and people, Abigail saw the door that said Executive Office.

"This is it." She leaned against the door to listen for movement. People looked at her, but no one said anything. Hearing nothing, Abigail opened the door slowly to reveal the office that looked like it came out of the Biltmore Estate.

Not wasting any time, Julius walked to the desk and started to open drawers looking for some sort of badge, wherever it was. At the same time, Abigail looked around the living room area of the office. There was nothing of value in the drawers, just papers and other office supplies.

As he was looking in the drawers, he saw something peculiar engraved into one of them. It was a carving of a Martian. Julius pressed his finger to it, and the carving acted like a button. They heard a clicking sound as a small badge reader popped out of the coffee table across the room. Its sudden appearance caused Abigail to jump.

"What did you do?"

"I don't know, but we need to find that badge to see what I did."

"It's a good thing I found Camilla's badge, then." Abigail waved the badge in the air.

"I don't understand how she leaves something so important lying around."

"Maybe she isn't as smart as everyone makes her out to be."

"So now that we have the badge, let's use it on that reader." Julius waited for Abigail to do the honors. She took the badge in her hand and waved it over the black badge reader with a red light on the top of it.

They watched as the light turned green, but nothing happened. "I thought that was supposed to do something?"

"So did I. What gives?"

Suddenly, there was a low rumble emulating from the fireplace. Julius and Abigail looked at it with puzzled looks. The fire went out, and the fireplace began to lift up until it was hidden away in the ceiling. Behind the lifted fireplace was a large steel freight elevator door with a button that only went down.

"No way." Abigail walked up to the door. "Come on, Julius." She pressed her finger on the Down button, and the elevator silently opened.

Julius and Abigail entered the elevator. "What if there are people down there?"

"We'll play it off or something."

The interior of the elevator looked very generic. There were only four buttons on the right-hand side of the doors. He saw the top one was labeled OFFICE, the second one said HANGAR, the third said LAB TOP, and the bottom-most said LAB BOTTOM. "I guess this is the way to the lab."

"I mean, it says lab on two of the buttons, Julius." Abigail rolled her eyes before she pressed the button labeled LAB TOP. The doors closed, giving a metallic clang as they connected. The elevator began to descend rapidly.

They had no idea what would be waiting for them in the lab below, and that made Julius nervous. After a few minutes of silent thinking, the elevator began to slow down.

"Are you ready?"

"As ready as I can be."

Contrary to what he said, Julius was not ready. He was scared they would get off and be met with the barrels of plasma rifles. Abigail was focused and had her hand hovering over her plasma pistol. She wasn't going to go quietly.

The elevator stopped, and a loud ding emanated from it, possibly alerting anyone in the lab. The doors opened to reveal darkness on the other side. The only light in the room was the light emitting from the elevator.

Abigail was the first one to step out. Her foot connected with a metallic mesh floor. She took another step before the lights were activated by her motion. The light revealed a massive white room.

There was a black catwalk that wrapped around the room, halfway up the wall where the elevator had dropped them off.

On the opposite wall were two doors with a large section of wall between them. Immediately in front of them were metal mesh stairs. They stretched down to the main floor below. Randomly placed medical stations were on the white floor below the catwalk. Each station had a computer for note-taking.

Inside each station was an examination table large enough to fit Martian on it. Pale turquoise curtains surrounded each section, isolating them from each other. There were cameras of different sizes placed around the medical stations.

They descended the stairs to the main floor. They looked around briefly before they walked to a station. Julius felt sick to his stomach as he came face-to-face with AMSPACE's vessels of torture.

"Oh my god." Abigail covered her mouth. There were buzz saws and scalpels on the tables. Most of them were still dirty with red dust from use on a Martian.

Meanwhile, Julius was inspecting the examination table. He lifted one of the table's restraining straps. There was copper wire running over and through the fabric. Julius traced the copper wiring to a DC power source. Upon inspecting the power source, his eyes went wide.

"They use this to shock them. Electricity must be very painful for them." Julius turned to Abigail. "You're getting all of this, right?"

"Yeah, I'm recording." She was as white as the floor of the lab.

"Come here." Julius outstretched his arms and embraced her. "It's okay." He held her there for a while.

She looked up at him. "This is just so awful! We have to find the Martians. We can't let them be tortured anymore."

"They have to be close. We'll get them out, I promise."

They fanned out to keep searching for the Martians. Julius wandered through the medical stations till he was at the back wall. It was just a white wall with a touch display in the center. He stared at it for a little before he moved on. He passed Abigail as she approached it.

"There's nothing there."

"Okay, let me take a look."

Julius went back into the field of medical station. Meanwhile, Abigail found the touch display and clicked it. It lit up and presented a temperature value of –250 degrees Fahrenheit.

"What the…" The appearance of this display puzzled her. She remembered what the old Martian said about his people not living on the poles because it was so cold.

"Wherever this room is must be where the Martians are." She felt invigorated as she started to look through the touch display's menus.

Eventually, she found an option for glass opaqueness. "That's peculiar, it's set to one hundred percent." Abigail changed the setting to zero. She was shocked when the wall in front of her became clear.

"Julius!" Abigail could see that behind the glass were thirteen Martians, and they weren't moving.

Julius heard the concern in her voice. "What is it?" He stared, stunned at what was behind the wall. They both stared at the thirteen frozen bodies. These Martians looked different than the Martian back on Mars.

Their skin pigment was paler than the one on Mars. They were frozen in haunting poses of fear and terror. Some were banging on the glass, and others were holding each other. Their glossed-over, star-filled eyes made the scene even eerier.

"We need to get them out of there!" Julius said desperately. He looked around for options on how to break the wall. His eyes fell on Abigail's hip and the pistol attached to it. He pulled it from the holster and aimed it at the glass.

"Julius, don't!"

Not thinking, he discharged the gun on the glass. There was a loud zap as the light blue plasma bolt flew toward the glass. Instead of shattering the glass, the beam bounced off and flew toward them. Instinctively, they both hit the ground. The beam smashed into the wall behind them, making a dark mark on the clean white wall.

"How many classic action movies have you watched, you idiot? It's plasma-proof, like most military-grade glass is." She yanked the gun from his hand and slapped his face. "Don't do that ever again, or you and I are done."

"I honestly thought that would work," Julius said, rubbing his sore cheek.

Abigail rolled her eyes. She kissed him on the cheek, where her red-hand print was. "Sorry for yelling at you. Let me work on getting them out. How about you find another way for us to get out of here. I doubt with this many Martians we'll get back to Martin and Becka." Abigail went back to the display screen and resumed investigating the settings.

"Good call. I'll check out those doors."

Julius walked to the left side of the glass, passing through one of the small metal doors he saw earlier. After passing through the threshold, he found himself on a loading dock. Beyond the dock was a small cement garage, like the one Martin had parked his Suburban. On the far end of the garage was a ramp, which Julius presumed led out of the facility.

Parked to his right, in the center of the loading dock, were a few North American Union troop-carrying trucks from the Amero Wars. They were light cargo trucks with armor on the bottom to prevent a bomb blast. Julius walked up to one the trucks and began to inspect it.

The cab was standard with the barebones controls. He realized they were fingerprint scanner starters. He started to stress about not being able to get out, but he remembered the Martians could adapt their body to anything.

"Good. These are what we need."

He went around to the back where the soldiers would sit. Inside Julius saw a plethora of wooden crates. The tops of crates were misaligned, allowing Julius to look inside. He saw various weapons he couldn't identify, but they seemed to be a mix of high and low tech weaponry.

Julius wondered what they were for, but he didn't dwell on that thought long. These weapons were a godsend. He, Abigail, and the Martians could use them to blast their way out of the gates.

Julius didn't see the large crimson hand stamped on the side of the boxes. He left the truck and returned to the laboratory. He was surprised to see Abigail still messing with the display.

"Any luck?"

"No, this stupid thing is being a pain, but I won't be deterred." She pressed harder on the controls as she talked.

After a few seconds Abigail let out a soft "Aha!"

"You got it?"

"Yup, let's warm it up." Julius watched as the screen showed the temperature rising.

"How exactly will we get them out since they can't breathe Earth air?"

"I haven't thought that far ahead. Maybe they have some thoughts? One thing at a time."

Julius was getting more and more anxious. He could tell because his stomach was in knots. They had been down there for a long time. He didn't want to risk getting caught here. A tapping on the glass in front of him interrupted his thoughts.

He looked up to see a pale red Martian drumming on the glass with its octopus tentacle-like arm. They stepped back, surprised at how fast the Martian thawed. The arm quickly changed into a pale red human appendage as the Martian seemed to be mimicking them.

Julius looked up into its star-filled eyes. They swirled briefly before they displayed the glass box's door opening. The Martian then pointed its human hand toward a rectangular outline in the wall.

"I think it wants us to open the door."

"What? Do you remember what happened to the Martian back on Mars? He turned to dust after being exposed to the terraformed air."

"If it's telling us to do it, then I think we should listen."

"Fine, gosh. We're going to kill them." Abigail pressed some buttons on the screen. A door opened to their right. Abigail fully expected the Martians to seize and turn to dust, but after a few seconds, nothing happened.

"How? They should be turning to dust."

Julius walked through the door and into the cube. She watched him from the control panel. Julius looked back at her. "It's regular air."

"But how are they breathing Earth air?"

The Martian who pointed at the door approached Julius, walking on its strange-looking legs. "I'm not sure. Maybe this one will show me."

The Martian changed its arm back into the tentacle and bent down to Julius, who looked into the starry eyes. They swirled again before the laboratory from the video he and Abigail watched came into view.

This was from the Martian's point of view. Camilla was standing over the Martian with a syringe. It showed her jamming it into the Martian. They heard screams as the memory faded, and stars reappeared in the Martian's eyes.

"What does that mean?" Julius asked as the Martian just stood there.

"What did you see?"

"It showed me Camilla jamming a syringe into it."

"Remember she said it was fusing human DNA with Martian DNA? It must have been a success and changed their molecular structure."

The Martian held out its arm. "What does it want now?"

"I think it wants to shake my hand." Julius extended his hand too and gripped the Martian's tentacle. It wasn't slimy but felt more like silly putty.

"Ah!" Julius pulled his hand away. In the center of his palm was a small bleeding dot; the Martian had pricked his hand.

"What happened?"

"It poked me, and now I'm bleeding. What was that for?" The Martian stood motionless.

"Maybe it's a cultural thing? Just smile at it and be respectful." Julius looked down at his hand and saw the bleeding had stopped.

"Come on, we should go now. We found the Martians. We have the evidence we need to clear our names. Now it's time to get out of here. Did you find anything to get us out?"

"Yeah, there's a few old troop transports in a garage behind that door on the left. One even has some weapons in case we have to get aggressive. The only issue is that it's a fingerprint start, but I think our Martian friends can help."

"Awesome, but I hope we don't need those weapons."

Julius exited the glass case, as did the thirteen Martians. The group of fifteen began to walk toward the door. As they walked, the Martians changed their shape to look more human. Their only differences were that on average they were taller than most humans. Their pale red skin remained.

"Abigail, we did it and all without—" Julius was interrupted as the ding from the elevator echoing through the room.

TWENTY-FOUR

The Great Escape

Julius, Abigail, and the Martians froze in place. The group stared at the elevator door like deer caught in the headlights of an oncoming semi. From Julius's perspective, it seemed like the doors were opening in slow motion.

Julius could make out five figures. Camilla was in the center of the group with two security guards on each side. The guards were in light tactical armor holding stun guns. "Round up the aliens. Leave Stetson and King to me." The security forces raised their weapons to fire but hesitated until Camilla gave the word.

Camilla's body language was disturbingly calm. She seemed to know she would find them trying to escape. The group was still too shocked to move.

Camilla walked along the catwalk, assessing the situation. "So you two thought you could just walk into my lab and take my test subjects. You didn't think I had cameras all over the place for security? These idiotas didn't inform me about your presence until you released the test subjects. Those thirteen things are AMSPACE intellectual property."

"Bitch, they're living beings, not assets."

"Watch your tongue, Miss King! They're my key to becoming chairwoman, and I'll be damned if I let you and a pinche minero take them from me."

Camilla suddenly leaped over the railing and fell. She hit the hard surface like a lump of clay thrown on the ground. Julius and Abigail winced, seeing her body flattened out like a pancake. It didn't last—Camilla reshaped her body quickly and became herself again.

She looked back up at the security forces. "Well, round them up!" The four security officers began to shoot from their positions along the catwalk.

The guns shot metal teardrops with electrified tips at the Martians. They impaled the putty-like skin of three Martians and electrified them, causing them to convulse, tense, then pass out. The others dove for cover as Julius flipped over a medical table and pulled Abigail behind it.

"Get to the truck. I'll hold Camilla off while you and the Martians escape."

Camilla started slowly walked across the lab toward Abigail and Julius. She was laughing loudly, picking up and throwing medical equipment across the room.

"I can't leave you," Abigail said as Julius grabbed the gun out of her holster.

"Go, Abigail." Julius paused. "I love you." He kissed her on the lips. Abigail kissed him back briefly.

He stood up, shooting the plasma gun at Camilla. The plasma bolts passed through Camilla's body harmlessly.

"Oh, shit!" Julius looked around for something else to fight Camilla. He dove behind a medical station's curtains. He spotted a cabinet and opened the doors. Inside he saw a stun baton and grabbed it.

Abigail looked back at the Martians and saw they were afraid. Ten of them were in scattered hiding places while three others were lying paralyzed in the open. Abigail couldn't hold her tough girl attitude anymore. She began to hyperventilate as she sat behind the overturned medical table. Julius inspected the baton. There was a place to grip it, a dial for the strength of the voltage, and two pointed sticks at the end. Julius turned it up to the highest voltage and exited the curtain. No sooner had he emerged from the curtain, his ears were ringing. His head throbbed, and he was falling forward.

Julius whirled around to see Camilla. Her hands had transformed into the heads of a hammer. Julius stumbled to the side, crashing into a rolling metal medical table. He raised his left hand to the back of his head, where he felt a small crack in his skull that pulsated warm blood.

Hearing the cringing thud and crash of metal, Abigail snapped out of her panic attack and poked her head up from behind the overturned table. She saw Julius struggling to keep his balance. Blood was running down the back of his uniform, leaving streaks of bright red stains.

"Julius!" Abigail started to run to help him. Midstride, Abigail was suddenly embraced by a putty-like substance and pulled back in the opposite direction. "No! Let me go!" Her voice held a frustrated anxiety. She looked at her waist and saw the pale putty arm of a Martian. She looked back and saw it was the same Martian with whom Julius had interacted behind the glass.

She fought the whole way, tearing at the Martian's arm. She was crying tears of frustration as she got further away from Julius. The Martian pulled her back behind some of the metal boxes where the others were taking cover from the guards.

Julius had regained his balance after the blow to the head, but he was still seeing stars. He swung his fists wildly, trying to find Camilla. Just as he found her, he felt his left leg buckle, bringing him to a lunging position. She had delivered a swift kick to his shin, causing him to lose his balance.

"Fight back!" Abigail's strained scream came from the other side of the room as she fought to get free from the Martian. Invigorated by her support, Julius attempted to stand up but was immediately shoved down by Camilla. He was now flat on his back, his head wound leaking more blood onto the floor.

Abigail gasped and tried again to escape the Martian's grip, but it held firm and shook its head. "You fucker, let me go! I have to save him!" Enraged tears streamed down her face.

Camilla stood over Julius, her limbs turning back to that of a normal person. "Did you think you had a chance to steal company property from me? You and Miss King are the epitome of stupid. How did you think this was going to end, Stetson? With you riding off into the sunset with the girl in your arms?"

Julius looked over and realized he had dropped the baton. It lay to his right. He reached for it and grabbed it, but not before Camilla delivered a hard punch to his face.

"Pay attention!" The room was once again spinning from Julius's perspective, and Camilla continued. "No way you would ever escape, especially with my ticket to becoming chairwoman. How dare you try to ruin my career! You will pay for that with your life! I didn't join this company to fail. I failed back in Brazil, and I won't fail now because of you!" Camilla started to deliver punch after punch to Julius's face.

The security forces stopped firing and watched in shock as she beat Julius. After a few punches, Camilla noticed the lack of progress in the capture of the Martians and briefly stopped brutalizing Julius. She stood up and looked back at the security guards. Julius, who was bloody and barely holding onto conscience, fell back to the floor.

"I don't pay you morons to stand around with your thumbs up your culos. Do your maldito job and get them!"

The guards put down their guns and grabbed batons similar to the one Julius held in his hand. They then began to make their way toward the stairs to round up the escaped Martians.

While Camilla was distracted, Julius activated the baton, creating an electric hum. Hearing the hum, Camilla's head shot back to look at Julius.

"Fuck you, Camilla," Julius slurred calmly. He jammed the stick into Camilla's gut and pressed the shock button at full power. Camilla screamed, her body shaking. Waves rippled through her body as the elastic cells tried to adapt to the high voltage shock.

With a few arcs of electricity, her body seemed to deteriorate and lose its shape. Everyone, including the guards, watched as she let out one final scream before her body exploded outward from where the baton was lodged. The flesh and red putty that once was the head of the AMSPACE Martian campaign now covered the floor and experiment stations around Julius.

The explosive end of Camilla caused the Martian, holding Abigail back to release her. Without hesitation, Abigail ran over to Julius and knelt beside him. "Julius, I am so sorry!" She leaned in and hugged him.

"It's okay, I'm glad you are safe."

"Julius, I love you!"

"I love you too," Julius said weakly.

There were tears in Abigail's eyes as she held Julius in her arms. "You're a stupid kid sometimes."

"Yeah, I guess so, but you still love me."

"What's not to love?" Tears streamed down her face while she tried to clot his head wound.

"You have to get them out, Abigail. I'll be right behind you."

"I'm not leaving you."

"I'm coming. I'm more than capable of getting up on my own."

"So damn stubborn. Why can't you let me help you?"

"Because I guess I'm just crazy."

The guards above Julius and Abigail were stunned and did not know what they were to do now. They fell back to the elevator and prepared to make a run for it.

Abigail ran back and led the nonparalyzed Martians through the side door. They also dragged the ones who had been hit with the electric darts out to the garage. The one who held Abigail back remained behind and watched the guards to make sure they didn't hurt Julius.

Julius stood up. He was covered in his own blood and some of Camilla's putty flesh. He held the towel. Abigail tried to clot his wound with against his head. He began to slowly limp his way across the room toward the Martian and the exit. He heard something that made his heart drop. The elevator doors opened.

A man in a gray suit stepped out with a few other guards in heavy armor. The lightly armored guards standing at the door looked at him and stood at attention.

The chairman stared back at them. "What are you idiots doing?"

"Sorry, sir. We didn't know what to do after the boy killed Camilla, so we thought we would retreat."

"Killed Camilla? At least the boy didn't make me get my hands dirty. I'll have to thank him." The chairman waved his hand at one of the guards.

"Get out of my sight, traitors."

The light-armored guards moved past the chairman and onto the elevator. The chairman looked down at the destroyed lab and shook his head. "What a waste of a good lab, Camilla really mucked this up."

He turned back to the remaining guards before speaking again. "You'll stop those assets from escaping. I want them dead or alive. No one will know about this. Oh, keep Miss King alive, she has some knowledge I need."

"Yes, Mr. Chairman," they said before they ran down the metal stairway toward the side door.

"Time to clean up the only other loose end."

A small plasma pistol was attached to his hip. The chairman removed the pistol and raised it in his right hand.

He took aim and fired across the room. Julius felt tremendous pain in his back, just below his heart, and then heard the shot. He didn't even cry out as he fell forward and struck the floor with a loud thud, rolling slightly to his side. The Martian who was looking over Julius fled.

In the garage, Abigail heard a shot come from the lab as she waited in the vehicle. The other Martians had entered the back of the cargo truck. They also had laid the three paralyzed Martians in the back. The Martian who remained behind got in the passenger seat next to Abigail, she looked over at it.

"Julius?" The Martian looked at her briefly before its star-filled eyes began to swirl. "No, I don't want to see it." Abigail knew something bad had happened to him.

"Can you please start this thing? It has fingerprint start, and I'm probably not programmed into it. The Martian took its thumb and pushed it against the finger scanner below the steering wheel. It changed and molded itself until the electrical display turned on, and the battery indicated full. Her heart ached as she put the vehicle in drive and drove toward the ramp.

As the truck began to pick up speed, the door to the lab opened as though it had been forcefully kicked. The four guards exited and began to fire on the truck. Plasma bolts flew all around the truck.

Following orders, the guards were not trying to keep the Martians alive anymore. They had to prevent Abigail from exposing AMSPACE's extraterrestrial secret.

Abigail guided the accelerating vehicle to the ramp that led up and out. There was shouting and cursing behind them as the guards tried to start the other cargo truck, but their fingerprints were not in the vehicle's computer.

Abigail drove up the concrete tunnel lit by orange lights. She watched the lights go by for a minute or two. Her mind was numb. She didn't want to think about anything but escape. If she had, she would have broken down over, leaving Julius behind.

The truck emerged into the setting New Mexican sun. The tunnel exit resided beyond the inner plasma wall, which meant all Abigail and the Martians had to pass the metal outer wall.

Abigail was sweating bullets as she drove the clunker. Behind the nervous exterior, adrenaline pumped through her veins. She thought about how they would get past the large wall. The Martian sitting next to her turned to her, and its eyes swirled to show the back of the truck.

The view was from the perspective of one of the Martians in the back. "That's trippy, do you all communicate with each other through telepathy and pictures?"

The Martian gently moved its head in the affirmative. She looked back at the road then back at the Martian. In its eyes, Abigail saw the large wooden crates with weapons in them. She recognized them—they were plasma grenades and plasma launchers. There were a few old-style smart bullet assault rifles. The eyes turned back to the starry night.

"I have a plan, but you need to tell the others." It nodded in acknowledgment.

"We need to use those weapons to fight. They'll know we're coming, and this is our only shot to escape the facility. There will be attack robots, so we have to take those out first. Then neutralize the human guards. Kill only if necessary."

The Martian was relaying Abigail's voice telepathically as she spoke. In the rear of the truck, the nonparalyzed Martians began to grab the weapons. They integrated the various weapons into their arms by forming their moldable limbs around the base and triggers of the weapons. Soon they looked like strange humanoid cyborgs.

Abigail continued to drive as the wall peaked over the horizon with its dark-gray color. The sun had set and dusk approached, hindering her from seeing the wall. Luckily, the checkpoint was illuminated with searchlights. They acted as a beacon for her to steer the truck.

While racing toward the wall, the dead man switch on her old glasses timed out. The glasses connected to the internet and began to send all the information to every news agency in the American Union. The documents had been released.

Her current glasses began to upload to a private cloud just in case they were destroyed or she was killed. If the worst happened, the cloud was programmed to send an email with the video to the same news agencies.

About three miles out, Abigail was finally able to distinguish the force called to prevent their escape. Three attack bots were armed and ready to fire. Flanking them were at least fifty guards in exosuits.

"They pulled out all the stops." Abigail scanned the checkpoint more and realized the gate was wide open. She did not know it, but the gate had been receiving its yearly maintenance and was locked in the open position.

She felt a wave of excitement and relief wash over her. "Hell yeah!"

A metallic robotic voice cut through the desert. "Halt, or you will be vaporized!"

"Up yours!" Abigail responded quietly. She waited a few more seconds before she yelled, with a voice backed by pure adrenaline, "Fire!"

The Martians leaned out of the truck, aimed, and fired their plasma launchers at the robots.

The truck they were in had no countermeasures. The bots would easily obliterate it. The plasma rockets flew at the attack bots at breakneck speed, way too fast for them to react.

The first robot was hit directly in the head. There was a large fireball, sparks flew, and a smoke bellowed from the gaping hole that remained. The metal body of the robot crumpled to the ground in a heap.

Abigail focused on driving as two rockets smashed into the second bot's in plasma cannons. The impact caused an explosion that decimated the top half of the bot. All that was left were the robot's smoldering legs still standing upright.

The third received a single rocket, but its target was a little off compared to the first three. This rocket slammed into the bot's left leg, causing it to fall over like Humpty Dumpty. The third bot was not disabled from the rocket attack, but its plasma cannons were inoperable. To compensate, the grate under the eye opened up, revealing a bank of three rockets.

Abigail was too busy trying to get to the gate to notice the imminent danger they were in. The disabled robot used its active tracking system to lock onto the truck, and it fired all three rockets at the same time. They flew on target toward the fleeing truck. The light from the rockets igniting caught Abigail's attention. It made her almost jump out of her seat.

"Oh shit, this is how it ends!" Abigail closed her eyes and prayed to God to make it quick as her life flashed through her. While her eyes were closed, the Martian in the passenger seat turned itself into putty and shot out of Abigail's driver's side window.

The Martian expanded itself to catch the rockets in a gooey net. The rockets exploded inside the Martian's body. This sent the Martian's flesh all over the New Mexican desert sand.

The shock wave rocked the truck, causing Abigail to open her eyes. She realized the Martian that sat next to her was no longer there. She saw the mess all over her windshield. She realized it had sacrificed itself.

In the line of guards preparing to keep the truck in, the man with the three jagged scars spoke. "Don't let those Martians escape. They're a threat to humanity. They're what gave me these scars. Open fire!"

Light-blue plasma beams shot out of their guns flying toward the cargo truck. Abigail again closed her eyes.

The light-blue beams hit the truck before they shot off in random directions. "Switch to bullets. It has a reflector array!" the scar-faced man yelled.

The bullets began to hit the truck, but they bounced off the armor. "Shit!" The scar-faced man looked out as the truck kept coming. His men were standing in front of the gate. "Dive for cover!"

The guards moved to the side as the truck blasted past them and out of the gate. The guards recovered and kept shooting at the rear of the truck. To prevent a pursuit, the Martians used the assault rifles to shoot at the guards and cause them to dive for cover again. Abigail pushed hard on the gas pedal to put as much distance between her and the facility. Abigail had no plan and no help. She and the Martians had one goal: survive.

After being shot, Julius continued to drag himself toward the garage. The guards jumped over him, trying to reach the truck before it left. Julius stopped his progress when he heard the truck begin to accelerate. He was trapped with no chance of escape. He felt his heart sink.

There was blood all over the floor around Julius. He struggled to breath. The only feeling he had left in his body was where the Martian had stabbed him in the hand. The chairman slowly walked over to him. His boots stomped down the mesh stairs, then crossed the lab. The man stood over Julius, his teeth glinting in the room's bright light with a big smile across his face.

Julius squinted, attempting to stay focused on the man.

"I knew you had spirit Julius, but I never expected this."

"Wh-who are you? How do you know me?"

"You haven't figured it out, my boy? Good, that means I'm fooling everyone."

With his left arm, the chairman slipped his fingers in the bottom of his neck and peeled back a thin piece of skin. He moved his fingers around and began to lift. He peeled back his face, which pixilated and became see-through before the chairman held the augmented reality facial mask he had just removed in his hand. Under the mask was the real face of the chairman—Gerald McGinnus.

"Much better," Gerald said as he fished his glasses out of his jacket.

"G-G-Gerald, w-why?" Julius coughed up blood as he looked up at the man.

"Gerald? No, that's a fake name. Real name's Arnold. Why what? Why did I shoot you, or why did I lie to you about who I am? Or why did I seem so nice to you?"

Julius was too weak to reply.

"Gerald is nothing but a physiological experiment my therapist and lawyer concocted to try to get me to be less bitter. Obviously, it doesn't work, but I humor him. I shot you because I can't have you telling anyone about my operation. If you got away, it would ruin my plans for taking over the American Union. You really think my end game was Mars? That was Camilla's dream. I want absolute power in the Western Hemisphere. The way to do that is by taking over the American Union. Soon I'll run for Prime Minister and consolidate my power."

"W-w-why a-are y-you telling me this?"

"Because it's such a relief to get this off my chest, and you're such a good listener, Julius. Plus, I can tell you and not have to worry about you blabbing to anyone about who I am or what my plans are."

"W-why's that?"

"Because you aren't making it out of this room."

"Y-you w-won't g-get away with this!"

"On the contrary, my boy. I already have and have been for years. I've even already tried this once. I underestimated the power of the North American Union when I killed my old commanding officer, Nunez. You'll die here, and my men will catch the Martians and Miss King. Then I will continue to exploit Mars for everything it has. Using the money to fund my campaign and using fear to keep people in line. No one will stop me!" Gerald smirked and chuckled to himself as he turned around and began walking away.

"Goodbye, Julius. I'll see you at your funeral."

Gerald ascended the stairs placing his mask back on concealing his identity. Julius still couldn't move. He thought of his family and how they would never know what really happened to him. Julius began to weep as he felt the darkness closing in. Julius thought of Abigail and how he wished he could hold her close or hear her voice one more time. He kept crying, but he didn't feel cold. He felt warm and then he was gone.

The chairman returned to the executive office and sat down at the desk, feeling accomplished. He had eliminated Julius and Camilla was no longer a threat to his power. Now he patiently waited for a status update from the guards on the inevitable capture of the Martians and Abigail. He pressed a button on an intercom.

"Helen, please send for Martin Fisher."

"Yes, Mr. Chairman."

Martin was in his office sitting behind his desk. He ran his hands through his short hair and had a nervous look on his face. Becka was sitting on the couch overlooking the Rendering Room.

"Do you think they got captured, Becka?"

"I don't know. When they didn't meet us in the garage, that's what I thought happened. I heard a call over the security network that a truck escaped with valuable cargo."

"Maybe that means Julius and Abigail got away with our Martian friends." Martin had a small amount of hope in his voice. Suddenly, Martin's phone began to ring.

Martin answered it right away. "This is Fisher." There was a pause. "I'll be right there." Martin hung up the phone with a drained look on his face.

"Who was it?"

"Camilla's secretary, Helen. The chairman has requested I come to the executive office."

"Be careful."

"If I don't come back, you need to inform the group to find that truck."

"Of course. Good luck."

Martin left his office and walked to the executive office and knocked on the door.

"Enter," the chairman's voice reverberated from within. Martin opened the door and walked in, standing in front of the desk. The chairman stood up and walked over to Martin extending his hand. The chairman cracked a warm smile.

"Martin, congratulations on the promotion!" The chairman shook Martin's hand.

"Promotion, sir?"

"Yes, Camilla is no longer able to perform her duties, so I need a replacement. Dave Hughes is not a suitable replacement for Camilla. Especially after his mishandling of the escaped employees. Additionally, I think he will be taking a leave of absence."

"Thank you, sir, it's an honor. May I ask why Camilla is unable to perform her duties?"

The chairman paused. "I regret to inform you that Camilla has passed. She was killed by Julius Stetson."

"Dead? How?"

"It doesn't matter. We have to look to the future. There's a mess down there. The boy's dead. We shot him as he tried to escape the lab with the test subjects. Abigail left him there to die." It took all Martin's strength not to lunge at him. Martin knew the man was lying, no way Abigail would have left Julius behind.

"Stetson's dead, sir?"

"Yes, Martin, he's dead. He's lying in a pool of his own blood in the lab."

Before Martin could respond, there was a knock at the door. The chairman glared at the door. "Enter."

Becka walked into the room, "Mr. Chairman, I have news on the fugitive Abigail." Becka tried to sound monotone but let some gloominess into her voice.

"The way you are speaking, I suspect it's not good news." The chairman looked down at Becka.

"No, sir, they escaped."

"That's unfortunate." The chairman walked slowly back to his desk with his fingers folded behind his back. "Is there anything else?"

"Actually, yes, sir." Becka sounded very nervous.

"Please enlighten Martin and I."

"The media has obtained raw footage of the Martians and the experiments Camilla and the company performed on them."

"I was afraid this might happen. I was prepared for the data to be released." The chairman's continued calm demeanor surprised both Martin and Becka. Martin half expected the chairman to shoot himself in the head when he heard about the whole scheme being exposed.

"We'll have to see how to mitigate our exposure. I didn't expect them to actually escape with test subjects. This is going to cause some issues, but no matter. I have to return to Chicago to address the investors and the members of the board."

It was as though the data release was good news to him. "Martin, can you please take care of the mess in the lab? Make Camilla and Julius disappear. Pay off the families or make up some accidental death excuse. I do not care how you do it, but leave me out of it."

Martin's and Becka's faces were white as they realized Julius was lying on the ground below their feet.

"Look, I know it's hard losing people we were close to, but we have to move on for the good of the company. So can you do it, or do I need to find someone else?"

"We can do it, sir. We're just still shocked at Camilla's passing. We'll take care of it," Martin said, trying to recover.

"Completely understandable, thank you for your work, you two. Its greatly appreciated." The chairman stood up, walked across the room, and exited.

Martin and Becka stood in silence, trying to absorb what just happened.

After a few minutes, they slowly walked to the elevator, went down to the lab, and surveyed the damage. What was once clean and pristine was now covered with the remains of Camilla's body, which had turned to dust.

"Holy shit!" Becka said as she put her hand over her mouth.

Martin and Becka walked down the stairs to the main floor. They walked through the overturned equipment looking for Julius's body. They came across a wide pool of congealing blood located next to a drain. Just next to it was the body of Julius Stetson.

Becka gasped.

"Fuck," was all that Martin could say.

"What are we going to do? We can't just leave him here."

"We won't, but we have to make up some fake death for him, cover this whole mess up."

"We have to tell his family the truth, Martin."

"No, that will put them in danger. We need to treat this like any other dead trainee. We put him in the morgue and cremate him. The only difference is that we will delay returning the remains, so his family thinks he died on Mars."

"But, Martin—"

"No, Becka, we have to do this. If we don't, our cover is blown. Now please dispatch the cleanup group so we can deal with this mess."

Becka went over to one of the medical stations and sent a message to the cleanup crew.

Five minutes later, the elevator doors opened, and five people came out with large robotic vacuums. The cleaning and bleaching began immediately.

A second wave of people accompanied by a hover stretcher came out of the elevator and went to Julius's lifeless body. Two people lifted his body, which had already begun to turn cold, onto the stretcher. Once on the stretcher, one of the medical curtains was draped over the body.

Martin and Becka followed the body to the garage like a makeshift funeral procession.

Julius's body was loaded into the back of one of the cargo trucks and driven up the ramp and across the desert. The truck stopped at a small windowless brick building with a smokestack that was just outside the saber wall.

Above the door was a small old sign that said Morgue. The procession stopped in a single room. The floor was white tile, and the far wall was filled with large lockers with magnetic locks.

The cleanup crew opened a locker and pulled out the drawer. They placed Julius's body on the cold stainless-steel slab before they retracted the drawer and then slammed the door.

"Goodbye, kid," Martin said under his breath as everyone began to leave.

"Sir, when shall we burn the body?" a woman asked.

"I'll come back tomorrow to see the cremation. He's not going anywhere."

"Yes, sir. Understood, sir."

There was a spare maintenance truck there, and the cleanup crew took it, leaving Becka and Martin outside the morgue.

"I'm going to hate telling his family about this," Martin said, turning to Becka.

"I'll come with you. We can do it together."

"Thanks, Becka, you've always been there for me." The two got into the truck and drove back to the facility. Martine looked up and watched the morgue get smaller in the rearview mirror as they drove away.

About the Author

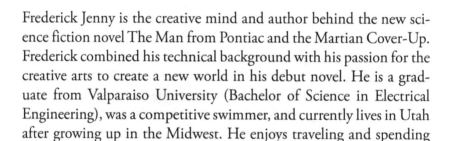

Frederick Jenny is the creative mind and author behind the new science fiction novel The Man from Pontiac and the Martian Cover-Up. Frederick combined his technical background with his passion for the creative arts to create a new world in his debut novel. He is a graduate from Valparaiso University (Bachelor of Science in Electrical Engineering), was a competitive swimmer, and currently lives in Utah after growing up in the Midwest. He enjoys traveling and spending time with his family at their cabin in Northern Wisconsin.

CPSIA information can be obtained
at www.ICGtesting.com
Printed in the USA
LVHW112308051021
699620LV00003B/84/J